Indigo

Legacy

Courtney Pierce

Windtree Press
Hillsboro, OR
http://windtreepress.com

Copyright © 2018 Courtney Pierce

This book may not be reproduced in whole or in part, by any means, in any form without explicit written permission.

Windtree Press
Hillsboro, OR
http://windreepress.com

Cover Illustration:

Rosalind McFarland

Images Used by Permission

ISBN-10: 1-947983-79-2
ISBN-13: 978-1-947983-79-3

Dedication

To my husband, Jeff, and my stepdaughter, Micah. My arms are too short to make it around both of you for a single hug, but I'm working on it.

"Age does not protect you from love. But love, to some extent, protects you from age."

~ *Jeanne Moreau, French actress, b. 1929*

Acknowledgements

The toughest challenge for a writer is to go through a major life change while creating a book. It requires a street team to emerge on the other side with a whole heart. Over the course of writing this book, I became single after 37 years of marriage, then I met an amazing man and married him, and I also became a first-time mom to a twelve-year-old stepdaughter. I lost my seventeen-year-old calico cat, Rosey, and gained Princeton, a brainiac, noisy fluff ball. This book became more than therapy; it held a roadmap to a new life.

Courage to emotionally bleed came from my two sisters, Debbie and Christina. Like bookends, they held me upright and inspired me with wacky wisdom.

Not many authors thank their bank, but everyone at Umpqua Bank planted me squarely on my feet through my transitions. They even promoted my books in their lobby.

A million thanks go to Rosalind McFarland for nailing my cover. Writers can't be objective, and Ros made it so easy.

My editor, Kristin Thiel, buffs and polishes without changing my intent or unwarping my sense of humor. After editing six of my books, she recognized every bit of me beneath the dialogue.

Carole Florian, my über-editor and dear friend, insists with her whole heart. She's the grammar police who pulls me over with sirens and lights for violations of detail. A word can make her laugh out loud or choke with tears, which makes me feel more important than I am.

Best-selling author Karen Karbo is a fantastic coach. Her suggestions and raised eyebrows made it a better story.

Thank you to Loma Smith, my photographer. She captured a new me to present to the world, both as an author and as a fresh bride.

I love Windtree Press—*a lot*. I'm part of something special.

And then there's my Mom. This trilogy wouldn't be possible without her, a unique and strong woman with a heart of Play-Doh. Her voice soars above the dialogue to whisper in my ear. *I love you, Mom.*

Chapter 1
The Auction

Olivia Novak felt the chandelier's heat before she glanced up at the sparkling crystals dangling above the gathering crowd at New York's Swanson Auction House. She pictured the beveled prisms letting go. If they did, the shards would slice through the book collector buzz and shellacked hairdos in the room to stop the looming sale of the most pristine assemblage of classic fiction Olivia had ever seen. That collection belonged to the handsomest man in the room, the one sitting next to her. Woody had no trouble dispensing of his mother's books after her death, but to Olivia, the books held Woody's impoverished childhood history in their pages and were the seeds of her and Woody's relationship. When his hand slipped over her knee and squeezed, it served as a reminder that his mother, Della, had been quite a handful in her attempt to keep them apart.

Over the past five months, Woodrow Rainey had become much more than a lawyer and her mother's cousin's son. After a rocky start of sparring over his mother's attempt to sue Olivia and her sisters, infatuation turned him into Olivia's closest friend, and her new love. Or was it lover? What do people call a budding relationship after a marriage of thirty-two years and five more as a widow? Woody's intimacy bike still had training wheels. At sixty-two, he'd been solidly on a path of lifelong bachelorhood until Olivia had barged into his New Hampshire law office with her two sisters in tow. Competition over who grabbed the title of "Large-and-in-Charge" in the relationship had morphed into an unmistakable electric attraction. When the boxing gloves finally came off over Della's death from a stroke, so, too, did Woody's and Olivia's clothes.

"Quite the crowd for a Thursday night," Woody said as he took her hand. "Bodes well for whipping up some serious competition."

In what had become a new habit—everything was new—Woody twisted Olivia's old wedding band around and around. She pulled her hand away. The gesture served as a constant reminder that he wanted it off her finger. Losing Adam to a hit-and-run accident made letting go of anything hard if not impossible, most of all her wedding ring. Olivia had tried a few times to remove it with olive oil, then soap and hand cream, but gave up when her finger turned blue. Arthritis had arrived early. Her knuckle had taken the shape of an old-growth burl. Only a raging forest fire, or a proposal, could signal renewal.

"I'm not sure that Della would've wanted you to sell these books, Woody," Olivia said. "She left them to you. They're part of your childhood."

"Need I remind you, Liv, that you started this whole process when you first looked at the books after she died?"

"But how can you be so calm? Do you only care about what they're worth?"

Woody was right, of course. She had made a big deal about the collection's value after Della died two months ago. How fitting for her death to have happened around Halloween. His mother had been a witch of the highest order, but the woman was considered part of Olivia's relative lineup too. Olivia's mother, Ellen Dushane, and Woody's mother, Della Rainey, were second cousins. Ellen's mega-selling book, *Indigo to Black*, had fictionalized a very real crime purportedly committed by Della: the murder of Woody's father. Olivia's mother had unwittingly set off a firestorm by writing that book. Decades later, Olivia had found the manuscript in her mother's safe and published it. The book fused Olivia and Woody together when Woody attempted to sue Olivia and her sisters for a cut of the royalties on behalf of his mother, Della. Sometimes Olivia, herself, couldn't keep the twists and turns of hate-turned-love straight when she figured in the mobsters who had kidnapped them.

To add to the combustion at that time, Woody had been plopped in the middle of an estrogen-depleted war zone and come out of it in love with Olivia. As she thought about it, the situation was quite the Shakespearian farce—only deadly serious.

As a best-selling author and rabid book collector in her own right, Olivia felt Woody's parting with his mother's collection like a stab to her insides. His gain of a substantial inheritance from this sale would become Woody's loss of a chance to hold them, baby them, read them all again. The lot of over three hundred rare editions were about to be sold. Olivia and Woody had flown three thousand miles from Portland, Oregon to witness the sale in person.

Slipping her hand from beneath Woody's, Olivia proceeded to flip through the program. Lot 3 made her stomach clench. An uncomfortable dampness formed in the armpits of her crimson silk blouse. A flush rose in her cheeks and crept beneath her scalp of thick brown hair, no doubt deflating the poof. The photos of the book covers were like meat to be thrown to lions with low blood sugar. Woody would regret this night. She would regret this night too. *Once they're gone . . . they're gone.*

Looking for a distraction from that which she could not change, Olivia glanced into her open red-leather satchel on the floor. She nudged it closer with the toe of one of her new crimson pumps. Inside, the thick manuscript of her latest book—a mobster's memoir—gave her a sort of permission to be sneaky in general life. She plucked out the compact mirror and a tube of her favorite lipstick: *Make My Day* red. The color matched her blouse perfectly. No matter what happened to those books, she couldn't let go of Woody. At her ripe age of fifty-eight, a second shot at love was rare. Her gaze pivoted between the mirror and Woody as the color deepened on her lips. The late, great B. B. King was wrong. The thrill wasn't gone.

Woody's bright blue eyes danced with anticipation. He appeared to be sizing up the crowd. Women sparkled with expensive jewelry, their polished nails clutching numbered paddles. Men made quick adjustments to their silk ties, pretending not to be assessing the competition as they took their seats. Woody smoothed his own freshly cut hair, trying hard not to look nervous but Olivia knew that he was already counting the winning bid.

"I'll be right back," Olivia said. "I'm going to pee now, so I can forever hold my peace."

Woody chuckled. He delighted in her straddle between sophistication and irreverence. She'd break that Yankee sensibility yet. Olivia played to it for the reward of his warm smile, a reminder that they both deserved to be happy.

"Can't you hold it? We're the third lot."

Olivia stood with her satchel and smoothed her black skirt. She ran her tongue over her teeth and leaned close to his ear. "Not a chance. I love you."

Woody turned, his tanned face alight. "I love you too."

With quick steps on the polished hardwood floor, Olivia worked herself upstream to the carpeted lobby on a mission to register for her own paddle. An open credit line and an ability to raise her arm were the only advantages she had left to keep those books out of the wrong hands. The din of one-upmanship was muffled behind her when she reached the line snaking to the bidding registration table. She really did need to use the bathroom but acquiring a paddle before the action started had become a priority. Plus, a little chit-chat with someone in line might render some valuable information about the competition.

She squeezed her thighs and took her place behind a balding man in a long wool coat. His distinctive cologne, a brew of vetiver and cedar, tickled her nose like a holiday candle at Pottery Barn. The aroma prompted a tap on the man's shoulder.

"What's the poison you can't wait to drink tonight?" she said.

The man turned. His olive-brown eyes behind wire-rimmed glasses gazed at her. "Lot three. I came from Seattle to bid on them in person." His teeth were even, but upon Olivia's closer scrutiny the man's incisors appeared to sharpen.

Olivia whistled, more because of her distended bladder than from the gold-rimmed information but he didn't need to know that. "That lot's pretty expensive. You must be a mucky muck for Starbuck's. That eight-dollar cup of coffee makes for big profits."

The man hesitated, no doubt ruminating on whether her comment was a dig. His ego clearly won out, and he leaped at the opportunity to boast. "No. I was an early investor in Amazon. This collection would give me an instant library. What's *your* poison of choice?"

Dammit. Mr. Wannabe had no appreciation for the fine art of hunting to build a collection. Olivia glanced at the catalog and made a random selection with her best high school French. "Lot 2. I want the *Les Maîtres de l'Affiche*. I'm a collector of turn-of-the century posters. A must. It's intact and in excellent condition."

"Good choice." He offered her his hand. "Barry Wannamaker."

Seriously? She squeezed his hand "Olivia Novak. I'm an author."

"I'm a doctor."

"What's your specialty?"

"Hematology. You could say I'm out for blood."

"I'm a faithful donor. Good luck."

Wannamaker offered up his payment details in exchange for a paddle. As she completed her own registration forms, Olivia's gaze followed Wannamaker to the auction room. The man swung number 408 like an Olympic Ping-Pong champion. By the time she logged her American Express card, Olivia's teeth itched. She slipped paddle 409 into her case. A good omen. Her favorite brand of spray household cleaner.

Like the lure of Oz, the women's restroom sign glowed at the other end of the lobby. A last-minute rush had several women streaming toward a line at the door. Olivia followed the gold swirly pattern in the carpeting to distract her focus from her bladder. In doing so, a plan formed that might not only knock Wannamaker's ego down a notch but prevent him on bidding on the books. An announcement boomed through the ceiling speakers: *Ladies and gentlemen. Welcome to Swanson's winter auction of rare and important books. Take your seats and we'll commence tonight's sale with the first Lot.*

Olivia wanted to take her seat, all right—in the restroom. If she did, she might miss her shot to drain Wannamaker's wallet before the book collection came up. She about-faced and sucked in short breaths on her way back to the auction room.

~ · ~ · ~

Woody turned to keep an eye on the entrance of the auction room. Where the heck had Olivia gone? She made even the simplest of tasks complicated. She overthought things with a second wash of her hands. When he caught her stepping back into the auction room, he breathed and fingered the small leather box in his pocket. Rehearsed words of a proposal floated around in his head like bees. The timing might be tricky, but he settled for the moment the hammer dropped on the book collection. It would be the drama that Olivia would appreciate. His gaze traveled with her shimmy down the row toward the open seat next to him.

"Place is jammed. I had to defend your seat," he whispered. "I shouldn't have checked my coat. I could've hung it over the back of the chair."

She leaned in. Olivia's citrus scent made him relax. "I was doing reconnaissance."

"For what?"

Olivia searched around the heads and bobbing paddles. Atop a library table covered in black velvet sat an original folio of Da Vinci sketches. The auctioneer buzzed:

"Six thousand . . . Add five hundred . . . Seven thousand . . ."

Olivia pointed to the balding man sitting on the end chair three rows ahead. "That man is going to bid on your mother's books. His name's Barry Wannamaker. Lives in Seattle."

"You found all that out in the bathroom?"

"I didn't piddle. I paddled instead." Olivia tapped her satchel with the pointy toe of her red shoe. The spikey heels drove Woody crazy. He wanted to whisk her out of the room and onto the deep-pile carpeting in coat check. His gaze inched from her ankle and dangled over the matching red satchel. The handle of a paddle sat next to her mobster manuscript like a smuggled-in weapon.

"What are you going to bid on?"

"The *Maitres*. The next Lot."

"You don't collect antique prints."

"I used to, though. An intact version of this book is pretty rare." Olivia nodded toward Wannamaker. "And I'll bet that guy will bid because I said I wanted them. Shhh . . . you'll see."

"I have no idea what you're talking about." Woody gave her his best attempt at a stink-eye. "We're not bidding on anything."

Again, the process didn't need to be this complicated. He and Olivia were supposed to sit back and enjoy the ride of watching the collection sell. Now, it somehow involved paddles, reconnaissance, and bidding strategy.

The auctioneer leaned toward the microphone, as if ready to take a bite. The room quieted. The gavel rose like an executioner's sword. "Do I hear nine thousand? Last and final bid. Eight thousand five hundred once. Eight thousand five hundred twice . . . " *Crack!* "Sold at eighty-five hundred to paddle number 276! Congratulations."

Woody gave a cursory clap as Olivia shifted in her seat. He thumbed the pages of the catalog to the second lot and gawked at the estimate for the *Maitres*: $35,000 to $40,000. He and Olivia had shared only general information about their respective financial accounts but tossing out that kind of money on something she didn't even collect seemed frivolous. Then again, he himself had spent over seventy grand for a charter flight to Portland to surprise her with a labradoodle, the amazing Beauregard. He wouldn't mind having the dog by his side right now. That crazy stunt had worked to win Olivia over, but spending the money had been an advance against the sale of his mother's books.

A set of five large portfolios was positioned on stands. The auctioneer announced, "Our second Lot is a rare, complete set of *Les Maitres de l'Affiche*. Translated as 'Masters of the Poster,' the portfolios contain two hundred fifty-six examples of the finest turn-of-the-century advertising posters ever printed by ninety-two renowned artists of the Belle Époque, including Cheret, Steinlen, and Toulouse-Lautrec. It is rare to find a complete set intact. Each lithographic plate is valuable on its own. We will start the bidding at twenty thousand with increments of one thousand."

Woody spotted the balding gentleman three rows ahead turning in his seat. The man flashed a smile when his gaze found Olivia. The guy obviously knew more about Olivia's plans than Woody did. Olivia set the paddle on her lap and acknowledged him by sticking up her thumb. Woody glanced at the number on Olivia's paddle: 409. Her cleaning obsession now included artwork.

"We have twenty-five thousand . . . Twenty-six thousand . . . Twenty-seven thousand . . . Twenty-eight thousand . . . "

Olivia didn't make a move as paddles popped up like ducks in a shooting gallery. Then the bald nerd raised his.

"Thirty-four thousand!"

With pursed lips, Olivia jabbed the air with her paddle. "Thirty-five thousand!"

"Paddle four-oh-nine, lady in red, we have thirty-five thousand! We've topped the estimate." The room quieted. "Do I hear thirty-six thousand?"

Woody grabbed her arm. "What the hell are you doing?"

"That's Wannamaker. I'm going to stick it to him."

"Olivia . . . don't you dare," Woody squeezed her elbow in his attempt to hold it down.

"A game of auction poker," she said. "If you're squeamish, look away." Olivia jammed her paddle above her head. "Thirty-eight thousand!"

Whispers squiggled the air.

"Forty thousand!" the bald man shouted back.

"To you, paddle four-oh-nine," the auctioneer said. "Your bid."

Olivia shook her head and set the paddle in her lap. Woody stifled a chuckle.

The auctioneer raised the gavel. "No? Forty thousand once. Forty thousand twice. All done? Last chance . . . Sold to the gentleman with paddle four-oh-eight. Congratulations."

The smug expression on Wannamaker's face held the results of Olivia's plan. Woody turned to Olivia, who brandished her own winner's smile. She flicked her clear-polished fingernail over her front tooth. "See? That's how you stick it."

"I'm glad you're not a trial lawyer," he said. "You made even my mouth go dry."

Olivia leaned in. "Do you think I have time to make a run for the bathroom?"

"Not a chance." Woody pointed to the stage and rubbed his hands together "You can't leave now. Here they come. The reason we're here."

Olivia crossed her legs and fanned herself with the paddle.

Chapter 2
The Bid

Olivia's gaze trailed the long library table being rolled to the stage, topped with ten of the most valuable books from Della's collection. Over three hundred first editions made up the Lot. These were prizes for any collector. A white-gloved assistant adjusted the line of delicate stands, which held *Dracula*, *To Kill a Mockingbird*, *Wizard of Oz*, *Twenty Thousand Leagues Under the Sea*, *The Maltese Falcon*, *The Canterbury Tales*, *The Great Gatsby*, *Pride and Prejudice*, *Rebecca*, and both original volumes of *Frankenstein*.

Della, Woody's mother, had garnered the works one book at a time, at pennies on the dollar, over a period of seventy years. For all her faults, Della knew how to hunt for prize literature. Olivia had held the original editions in her own hands, touched those covers, and breathed in the musty pulp scent of the paper: Dickens, F. Scott Fitzgerald, Agatha Christie, Louisa May Alcott, Hemingway, and Harper Lee. Della's refusal to turn on the heat in her tiny one-room schoolhouse had unwittingly preserved their pristine condition.

Only one book cover drew Olivia's focus: *Rebecca*. That book had been so important to Woody. Daphne de Maurier's haunting tale had inspired him to become a lawyer. What impressed Olivia most was that

Woody had been captivated by the subtlest of details: Maxim de Winter never uttering the name of his new wife, and his new wife conquering the ghost of his former wife, the one with a name—Rebecca—to save his life. The way Woody had talked about the story made Olivia fall in love with him. In a way, their roles were reversed. Olivia's ghost poked at Woody, and its name was Adam, though without the wickedness.

Sure, she could find another first edition copy of *Rebecca*, but not that copy. And that particular edition was the one that forged her relationship with Woody; the book had helped her to explain her inability to let go of Adam; it had allowed Woody to emerge from a childhood of pain and poverty to become a successful, caring man. And the novel held a murderous truth, much the way their respective mothers held their own murderous truth. Della had poisoned Woody's father. Olivia's own mother, Ellen Dushane, had been connected to the crime her cousin had committed, which inspired her to write the novel *Indigo to Black*. More than an intriguing cover and expert binding held *Rebecca*'s suspenseful pages together.

Chatter washed through the auction room. Woody grasped her fingers. Through the excitement, she sensed a bit of sadness, a thoughtfulness, in his touch. The gesture reminded Olivia of their shared history of pain. Her chest tightened as the auctioneer adjusted the microphone on the podium.

"With much anticipation, we present our next Lot. Three hundred of the most desirable first-edition fiction titles of the twentieth century awaits one lucky bidder. As you've no doubt previewed, every one of these books is a classic, ten of which are on this table. The fair estimate for the collection is between $550,000 and $675,000. We will start the bidding at $250,000 with increments of $25,000."

Woody blew out a breath and studied his lap. Olivia did the same to give her bladder some extra room.

Paddles rose with enthusiasm. The crowd's energy vibrated the air. Olivia could almost hear the electricity. She kept her gaze on Barry Wannamaker to see if he would start to bid. She could smell his antici-pation. He remained still, waiting like a spider for a juicy fly. Her plan to keep him at bay hadn't worked.

"Three hundred thousand . . . ," the auctioneer called. "$325,000 . . . $350,000 . . . $375,000 . . . $400,000 . . ."

"Think it might go over?" Woody said, his tone hushed.

She held her mouth to his ear to make him shiver. "We won't know until two bidders put up their dukes."

"Five hundred and twenty-five thousand . . . $550,000 . . . $575,000 . . . $600,000 . . . $625,000 . . ."

Woody rested his elbows on splayed knees and set his thinking forefingers to his lips.

"Now it could go over," she said.

"Six hundred fifty thousand . . ." The room quieted with a dare to scale the hill. "Don't let this opportunity slip by. Do I hear $675,000?" The auctioneer's gaze circled the room. With it, Olivia's head swam. No new paddles, or former ones, either. If she didn't get to that bathroom, she'd have a five-alarm embarrassment on her hands—rather, on her seat.

Wannamaker raised his paddle.

The auctioneer pointed. "Six hundred and seventy-five thousand! Number four-oh-eight. Thank you, sir."

In her panic, dialog from *Rebecca* screamed inside her head. Olivia wanted to shout out, *Maxim! This can't be true!* Instead, she tightened her grip on the paddle and straightened up her arm. "Seven hundred thousand!"

Woody turned with his mouth open, his eyes widened in shock.

Wannamaker reversed direction in his seat. His glare topped a devilish grin that zeroed in on her.

"To you, sir, the gentleman with paddle four-oh-eight," the auctioneer said.

Wannamaker shook his head and made a side-slice gesture with his hand.

Woody tried to wrestle the paddle from her. "Olivia . . . No . . ." She finally let go.

"Seven hundred thousand once. Seven hundred thousand twice .

. . Sold! Congratulations to the lovely lady in red with paddle four-oh-nine."

Applause erupted as Olivia turned to Woody, triumphant. "I did it. I got *Rebecca* back."

Woody stared at her, his eyes ablaze. "You did *not* just do that. Tell me this is a wicked joke."

The pit of her stomach dropped. "What? I did it because I love you."

The applause faded as the blood vessels squeezed in her temples. Olivia had seen that look on Woody's face only once before: when he'd burst through his mother's front door to find Della confessing to a decades-old murder to Olivia and her sisters.

~ · ~ · ~

Woody sat stunned as Olivia covered her mouth. She bolted from the auction room. The embarrassment of the relentless applause pulled him back to reality. Still gripping the paddle, Woody grabbed Olivia's red satchel and bumped knees to race after her.

From the other side of the empty lobby, Woody caught Olivia's red spike heels disappearing behind the door of the women's restroom. It swung closed. She couldn't run away from him in there. If he had to, he'd kick everyone out and lock them both in. A football field of gold-swirled carpeting lay between him and that door. To avoid a wave of disorientation, he slipped the paddle into her satchel and aimed for the target without looking down.

Woody gave the door a full-force shove with the sole of his tasseled loafer and stepped inside. "Olivia? Don't hide!"

"Woody? What are you doing in here?" Olivia said from behind the one closed stall door.

He marched to it and rapped twice. "Come out of there right now and talk to me."

A coiffed woman turned from the mirror with a lipstick tube frozen in front of her face. "The men's room is across the lobby," she said.

Woody took a calming breath. "I'm aware of that, ma'am. May I ask you to wait outside for a few minutes? I've got some emergency business."

The woman wrinkled her nose, made an exaggerated twist of the tube, and capped her lipstick. She dropped it into a black beaded purse and huffed past him.

"Don't let anyone in until I come out," he said over his shoulder as the door squealed shut.

He bent down to confirm Olivia's voice had two demon-red heels. "What were you thinking? Were you trying to prove something with that stunt?"

"I wasn't trying to prove anything. It was a mistake to sell those books. I saved them from going to someone who wouldn't appreciate their value."

"Like Wannamaker?"

"Can you give me some privacy? Talking to you through this door is downright weird. And I still have to go." She let loose a stream that would have shamed a racehorse.

"You crossed a line. This is what you get."

Olivia released an audible sigh. "I *had* to bid. That guy doesn't deserve your books. He's so smug and only wants them to show off his wealth."

"You can't afford this . . . can you?" She hadn't stopped peeing. He marveled at how much liquid a person could hold. The sound gave him the urge to go himself.

"No, but I have a credit line."

"You did have to go. Don't chip the porcelain, Liv."

"Told you. I was about to embarrass myself or pass out."

"I almost passed out when you raised that damn paddle." Woody started to pace in front of the door like a taunted tiger. "Let me get this straight. You're willing to spend seven hundred thousand, plus a buyer's premium of 20 percent, for a copy of *Rebecca*? That's eight hundred forty thousand dollars! You're *crazy*, you know that? Need I remind you of the additional 20 percent commission retained by the auction house from the seller, which happens to be me? And hopefully you?" He squinted as the words landed on the other side of the door.

A pregnant pause filled the tiled room with discomfort. She'd even stopped peeing, which had, until now, become a third entity in the room.

"That book was important to me . . . to us," Olivia said. "What do you mean that I would be on the hook for the seller's commission? You would have to pay that commission no matter who bought the books."

As though hanging from marionette strings that had been suddenly clipped, Woody's shoulders dropped. "Why didn't you tell me you wanted that book? I would've asked for *Rebecca* to be removed from the collection and just given it to you, like I did with the other four I brought out to Portland with me."

"Those books are your legacy."

"Those books are my inheritance."

He scuffed a loafer on the tile floor. "You don't get it, Liv. I don't want those books. They bring up things that I'd just as soon forget." With her satchel in hand, Woody started to pace in front of the door. "And I take issue with my . . . "—he struggled to find the right word—"—girlfriend . . . woman . . . lady friend—" He cringed.

"What am I to you, Woody? I've never been described quite that way."

And just like that, he'd succeeded in changing the subject to yet another topic he hadn't planned on discussing in a women's restroom. Another win for Woody this afternoon. A study of himself in the mirror served as a reminder that he wasn't getting any younger. His normally bright eyes took on a tired cast, especially when he was mad. He rubbed the back of his neck to loosen the tension.

"I don't want my entire inheritance funded by my . . . future wife." He stooped to check Olivia's shoes for a reaction. The pointy shoes had shifted to pigeon-toe. Not sexy, but certainly charming. Tissue gathered on the floor like a kitten dismantling a ball of yarn. Then she sniffed and sighed. Woody whirled his hand for a crank-up of tears.

"Did you just propose to me . . . in a *bathroom*?" Olivia said.

Woody rested his forehead against the stall door. "Wasn't my plan, but you hijacked my better idea." Her heels ignited a tap dance as she rearranged herself and flushed. The stall door suddenly unlatched and opened, causing Woody to pitch forward. Olivia planted a kiss on him that made his eyes bulge.

She pulled away, smudge under her dark lashes. "I'm so sorry, Woody, but I need to wash my hands before I finish that kiss."

He swung Olivia's satchel toward the sink. "You're not out of the doghouse, Liv. Not even close."

Trying his best to be annoyed, Woody started the count of Olivia's cleaning regimen: pump the soap dispenser six times, and then wring her hands for twenty seconds under a rush of water, mouthing the words of "Twinkle, Twinkle Little Star". Like a surgeon prepping for a heart transplant, Olivia held her hands under the electric eye of the dryer. He'd seen this neurotic routine of hers more than once. In truth, he loved her more for it.

"So how do we fix this?" The din garbled the last of Olivia's words.

"How do we *what*?" he shouted.

"Fix this!"

"You bet I will." Woody set her case on the counter and marched to the exit. He yanked on the handle and bumped into a middle-age woman coming through the door.

With a fist on her generous hip, the woman glared. "You're in the wrong bathroom."

"Oh, no, I'm not," he said. "It's the right one for the business I needed to take care of." Woody stuck his thumb over his shoulder. "But watch out for that lady in red. She should be using the one across the lobby."

A smile bloomed as the door squeaked shut behind him.

Chapter 3
Guilty as Charged

Olivia wished she could act more like a lady. Certain situations might sort themselves out if she could just cross her legs at the ankles and keep her mouth shut. Some things made no sense—like a half-ass marriage proposal in the women's restroom. She smacked the counter and rummaged in her case for her phone. There was only one solution for this mess. She needed a street team for a bonehead move this egregious.

That other woman was taking too long in the stall. Not good. Olivia moved to the bathroom door, with no clue as to where Woody had gone. She took a step into the alcove. With her shoulders pressed against the wall, she peeked around the corner and sniffed. Wannamaker was in the vicinity. On the other side of the lobby, he sat on a mustard-yellow couch with his arms crossed. Wannabe's stern expression focused on someone across from him in a high-back chair upholstered in cream and gold stripes. Olivia craned her neck to get a glimpse.

Woody! A creep of paranoia moved through her gut. Olivia watched Woody lean forward and rest his elbows on his knees, punctuating his conversation with hand movements. "Close your legs,

Mr. Negotiator," she said under her breath. Woody was probably convincing Mr. Wannabe that she'd escaped from a psychiatric hospital without a stash of meds.

Olivia checked her phone, and to her horror the battery indicated 16%, well on its way to zero. She looked left and right, and then speed-dialed her home phone in Portland, Oregon. Her older sister, Lauren, lived next door but was staying at the house to baby-sit Freesia, her Himalayan cat, and Beauregard, her new enormous labradoodle, who also happened to be a certified therapy dog. Freesia didn't think she needed therapy. Beauregard believed she did. Olivia hunched down when Lauren answered.

"It's me," she whispered.

"I can see that on the damn caller ID." Lauren's mood had been set on frazzle. "Come home and handle Beau, will ya? He won't leave Freesia alone, and she's turning his nose into a punching bag."

"I wish I had a punching bag. I don't know whether to laugh, cry, or sock Woody in the nose."

"Lover's spat? I'm not getting in the middle of that, kiddo."

Olivia recalibrated. "Okay . . . I've got a big problem, and I need to talk fast. My phone's almost out of juice."

"So am I. It's wine o'clock and Mama needs Merlot, so I gotta talk fast too. Hey, aren't you supposed to be at the auction right now?"

"I'm *at* the *auction*," Olivia said. The shrillness in her own voice gave her pause.

"What's the matter? Didn't Della's books sell?"

Olivia's shoulders dropped. "Can you bring Beauregard to New York? And Danny, Ryan, and Pogo too? I need all the reinforcements I can get."

"Are you crazy?"

Olivia winced. "That's the second time I've been asked that in the last hour. I blew it, Lauren. A complete and utter blowout."

"Oh, God. What did you do?"

"I bid on the books . . . and won."

Lauren gasped into the receiver. "How much?"

Olivia groaned. "Seven hundred . . . thousand, plus twenty percent."

"You don't have that kind of money to throw around." Lauren hesitated. "Do you?"

"Nooo . . . " The monetary reality sounded even worse when she said it aloud.

"Woody must've freaked."

"He's so pissed at me, and that's a mild word for it. But dammit, I'm pissed at him, too, for the way he reacted."

"Judge Judy would've ripped that paddle out of your hand and beat you over the head with it," Lauren said. "Where are you now?"

"Hiding by the restroom at 15 percent charge."

"You're right. This is an emergency. Plug in your phone. I'll talk to Danny and Ryan and call you back."

Lauren and Danny would help. Beauregard and Pogo would make it a therapy-dog sandwich. Ryan, Danny's husband and a Portland cop, needed to be in the mix too. He was more like a protective brother than a brother-in-law.

"You need to come here anyway, to meet with Karen about the Pogo book series. And Danny should go to Allenwood Prison to check on the therapy-dog program with Ben. There are other reasons for you to come back East."

Olivia's literary agent, Karen Finnerelli had become a ringleader for the Dushane family books: Olivia's romance books continued to make Karen a fortune, but getting the opportunity to publish her mother's book, *Indigo to Black*, shot her to one of the most powerful agents in the business.

Olivia had shifted her writing gears to memoir after her ex-neighbor and mobster-in-hiding, Ardy Griffin, told her his story. After Ardy's death, Danny had adopted his dog, Pogo, which had sparked a therapy-dog program for the aging goombahs incarcerated in Allenwood Prison. Not to be outdone, other mobsters had rattled the bars to have Olivia document their nefarious tales.

The mobster connection had become a family affair. Lauren's

artistic skills with drawings of Pogo ignited a children's series. To Karen that had become sweet book-marketing joy.

"Don't sugarcoat this, Liv," Lauren said. "You're in the doghouse, big time."

"Woody said that too. What's worse, I think he proposed to me tonight." Olivia fake-smiled as the woman came out of the restroom and brushed past her with pursed lips. "I think so, anyway. I can't quite tell."

"For a former romance writer, you know nothing about romance. Kicking a man in the fiscal nuts is kind of a mood killer."

Her sister was right. She'd bruised not one but two sets of family jewels tonight. Olivia glanced at the pointy toes of her pumps. "So, will you come?"

"Lemme call you back."

Olivia disconnected and ran her tongue over her teeth. She peeked around the corner. Woody was still talking. Now Wannamaker's hands were in wild gesticulation as Woody listened, his forefingers glued to his bottom lip. She was burnt toast, and her bank account held the scrapings of blackened bits to accentuate the point. An electrical outlet was worth a million bucks right now. None were in sight, unless she wanted to reveal herself in the lobby. She turned and dashed back into the restroom to wash her hands again, and then plug-in to set up camp in there.

Near the diaper changing station, the charger snaked like an umbilical cord supplying nourishment to her phone. Olivia stretched her tight jaw, just like her mother used to do, and eyed the dark screen. *C'mon, baby. Ring.* After fifteen minutes of wet paper towel and soap to clean the area, counting tiles, checking the soap level in the containers under the marble counter, and berating her image in the mirror, claustrophobia eclipsed rational thought.

"What were you thinking, you stupid, stupid, stupid, girl?" she said and smacked her hands on the counter. "Are you willing to blow up your relationship with Woody over this?"

The voice of the auctioneer trumpeted from the speakers in the lobby. *Sold! To the gentleman with paddle five-thirty-seven.*

Maybe she couldn't get a signal with all the stone surfaces. The battery icon indicated her phone had drained even further—down to 5 percent. Olivia yanked out the plug and dropped her phone into her satchel, its charger still connected. Her new destination became the terrace outside. Fresh air and thick glass would allow a safe vantage point from which to catch Lauren's return call, and to spy on Woody's expression.

Crossing the lobby to coat check without being seen would take some confidence.

Olivia squared her shoulders and walked with purpose, not daring to glance in Woody's direction. After over-tipping, she shrugged into her long, cream-colored wool coat and turned up the collar.

A blast of frigid air smacked Olivia in the face when she pushed open the heavy glass door. It banged behind her, catching the end of the charging cord that dragged on the floor. Woody turned and narrowed his eyes. He pressed his lips together. Olivia jerked the cord free and the door banged again. Panic churned in her stomach as she hunted for a dark corner, but the Christmas twinkle lights on the terrace lit up the place like a Broadway stage. One way out; one way in.

Beyond the plate glass window, Woody and Wannamaker started laughing. She pictured herself as the losing contestant on *So You Think You've Got Talent*. Were they making fun of her? Woody put something in the pocket of his suit jacket, stood, and shook Wannamaker's hand. They had traded business cards. Only men could draw blood from an adversary, then celebrate with a let's-do-lunch. Wannamaker turned to the window and acknowledged her with a you're-busted wave, and then headed toward the men's room.

Olivia's gaze tracked Woody's stroll across the lobby toward the coat check counter. He lingered there, chatting it up with the staff until he got his black cashmere overcoat. He took his time putting it on too. Then he looped his gray wool scarf around his neck. It matched the gray in his hair. *God, he was handsome.* His fit, six-foot-two frame and distinguished build released a flutter in her chest—love or fear, she couldn't tell—as he moved toward the glass doors.

Heat crept up Olivia's neck to meet the plummeting temperature of the air when Woody gripped the handle. He waited a beat, probably thinking of an admonishment before he pushed it open. Once outside, he guided the door shut to prevent it from slamming. Within five smug steps, he faced her. His expression resembled Beauregard's when daring Freesia to snatch his knobby rubber Garfield toy.

Without a word, Woody reached under his overcoat to the breast pocket of his navy-blue suit jacket. He held up a rectangle of paper with scrawled numbers. She squinted to read it: $810,000. The check was made out to her, Olivia Novak, in boxy capital letters that leaned to the left. Not Woody's handwriting. Her eyes darted to the account holder.

"I made a side deal with Wannamaker," Woody said. "Boy, did you piss him off. He would only agree to *his* last bid—not yours—plus the buyer's premium. The guy's good, but personally speaking, I think I was *bett-ah*." Woody tucked the check back into his breast pocket. "Until I receive my proceeds from the auction house for your bid, I'll hold this for safekeeping. When I make my deposit, you can make yours, and I'll chip in half of the extra thirty thousand you cost us both. You'll need to eat fifteen thousand. Consider it punitive damages." Vapor from his words dissipated in the cold air.

"But . . . that's not fair . . . " —*Shut up. Shut up. Shut up*—" . . . to you."

"See, Miss Money Bags? That's how I get to *stick it* to you for ruining a perfectly good half-ass marriage proposal in a women's bathroom." He spread his hands. The gold Yale class ring on his right hand glinted in the twinkle lights. Olivia stared at his long forefinger. "Now, if you think that's a raw deal, you go right into the men's room and stand at the urinal with Barry Wannamaker."

Olivia tried to curl her numbed toes. "That's low, Woody."

"You're the one who adjusted down the limbo bar. And I'm throwing in one other deal point that's nonnegotiable." A reach into the opposite pocket of his suit jacket produced a petite turquoise-leather box, embossed with the name *Tiffany & Co.* He reached for her hand and set her future in it. "Will you marry me? No prongs to snag on anything. And we still need to decide where we'll live. You can write from anywhere, but my practice is in New Hampshire."

Olivia blanked out those last words, preferring not to address the issue of living arrangements. No way would she leave her sisters three thousand miles away. With shaking fingers, Olivia cracked open the box to reveal a fiery show of a thick white gold band encircled with vertically channel-set baguette diamonds. Her breath streamed in a trail of puffs and dissipated. Hot tears cooled when she found it impossible to blink. Their spillover prompted a silent question to Adam punctuated by an under-eye swipe of her forefinger. Adam didn't answer. He never answered. Instead, a ring tone swirled the silence: the theme song from *The Jetsons*. Olivia glanced at her red satchel, and then raised her eyes to Woody.

"I gotta take this," she said. "My phone's almost dead."

His gaze locked on hers like a sniper scope. "Don't you dare answer that."

Chapter 4
The Ring

Technically, Woody's question gave her an out, not that she wanted one—but a writer's observation nonetheless. She could always say no. Olivia plucked the ring from the velvet wedge. This was the big-deal band, though, the forever one to withstand bleach, soap, and 409. She and Adam had exchanged only gold bands at their ceremony back in 1979. Olivia lifted her right hand. Wasn't that how it worked? Right finger until the ceremony? The ring stopped at her knuckle, refusing to scale its peak. If forced, then she'd be in double trouble.

"Yes, Woody. I'll marry you," she said, "but . . . it's too small."

"What's too small?" he said. "Me? Or the diamonds?"

The smart remark eased her tension. She hesitated. "The band, you goof. My knuckles are too big."

Woody searched the cloud cover and blew out a steam of breath. "Take off that old band and try your left."

Olivia shrugged. "That knuckle's even bigger."

Woody pointed to the paddle sticking out of her satchel. "Give me that damn weapon. If your sisters were here, I'd give them both my own brand of four-oh-nine. They picked it out."

Olivia's gaze volleyed from him to the diamond-encrusted band.

"Lauren and Danny knew about this?"

"I took them with me to Tiffany's in downtown Portland, two days after I got there. Lauren insisted you wore a size six. Danny dug in her heels for a size seven. I settled for six-and-a-half."

This debacle had her sisters' stamp all over it. Danny, the romantic, had wanted the ring to have a loose fit to prevent a complication. Lauren, the protective skeptic, had wanted to buy Olivia some time by creating a slight hitch. Olivia had an image of Woody plea bargaining to get the hell out of the store.

"Not a problem." She tucked the ring in the box and snapped it shut. "When I get back to Portland, I'll have it resized."

Woody blew into his fists. "Do you like it?"

Olivia took a step forward and ran her hands under his coat. "Mr. Woodrow Rainey, I love it, and I love you." Warm breath filtered through her hair when he kissed the top of her head. "Aren't we a pair."

Woody squeezed her waist. "Ain't we though. Go ahead and check your messages to see who called."

Somehow, the word *ain't* didn't have that humorous Southern hillbilly effect when quipped by a Yale grad with a New Hampshire accent. She loved him for the attempt.

Olivia broke away and slipped the ring box into her satchel. Next to her working manuscript for Nicky Palermo's mob memoir sat a hardbound copy of her own mother's murder mystery. She never went anywhere without a copy of *Indigo to Black*. The infamous novel kept her mother close. It also had started life's third act with her sisters, Lauren and Danny. She dug through her case and found her phone. She checked the screen: one missed call from Lauren's cell. The press of her finger released her sister's voice mail in her ear:

We're on the way to the airport, Liv. The whole damn posse. We're catching the red eye, and we'll land at Newark tomorrow morning at seven ten—me, Danny and Ryan, with Pogo and Beauregard. We have rooms at the Waldorf with you guys. Make sure you send a big car to pick us up at the airport.

Olivia disconnected and raised her eyes. "Well, be careful what you wish for," she said to Woody. She dropped her phone into her case and pulled out the bidding paddle. She handed it to him. "My sisters, Ryan, and the dogs will be here tomorrow morning."

Woody's eyes saucered. His grip tightened on the offending paddle. "Why?"

The absolute truth would guarantee her a permanent view from inside the doghouse. Instead, Olivia chose her own private blend of the truth, delivered in rapid-fire-BB-gun style. "We all have an appointment with my agent tomorrow. Karen called Lauren when she couldn't reach me. I have to deliver this draft of Palermo's manuscript, and we all need to discuss the movie deal for Mom's book. We'll need your legal expertise too. And then Lauren needs to discuss the Pogo children's book series. Maybe we can head down to Allenwood with Danny and Ryan, so I can meet with Palermo, and then you can meet him too, and Danny can check on the therapy-dog program with Warden Franklin." She inhaled. *Good. Sounded good.*

"Olivia . . . "

She wrinkled her nose. Lawyers. Especially irresistible ones. She broke. "I released the hounds when you got mad at me."

"Dammit, Liv." The paddle became a scythe. "No. Absolutely not. We need to drive up to New Hampshire tomorrow. I've been gone from my practice for four weeks. Call Lauren back." His brows furrowed. "And we *are* going to discuss where we'll end up living, right?"

"They're already on their way to the airport in Portland," she said. "Maybe we can all go up to New Hampshire together."

Woody groaned, but it came dangerously close to a whine. "That was *our* time, Liv. We were going to read Della's letters with a nice bottle of wine. And we still have to deal with Della's ashes."

"We will, but did you see the weather report? It's supposed to dump monster snow tomorrow by noon. And Indigo Lake is frozen. The ashes will skate around like Dorothy Hamill."

Woody inspected the tassels on his polished loafers. "Our rental car won't hold all those dogs for an airport pickup."

"Only two."

"Four with Lauren and Danny."

Olivia winced. "Five, with Ryan."

Woody's shoulders dropped. "The hotel has a van."

"Perfect. We can sleep in." She gripped the handles of her case and stepped toward Woody, close enough to feel his heat. "Because you'll be turning your lady-woman-girlfriend into a fiancée . . . Pretty Boy Man."

~ · ~ · ~

At eight o'clock the next morning, Olivia awoke to an empty space next to her. She smoothed her hand over the sheet on Woody's side—cool. The rowing machine in the hotel gym must have lured him to exercise. During the month he'd stayed with her in Portland, Woody had booted her in the glutes to use her gym membership, even on Sundays. Rough justice for criminally soft arms and tight back muscles. But each time they went together, Olivia had taken the opportunity to study him in action: determined, focused, and competitive.

The Waldorf's fluffy covers and soft sheets held her hostage. Fat snowflakes whipped past the window in a frame of heavy gold and maroon drapes. A tussle, a hustle, and a rustle of sheets had become the cornerstones of their relationship. Woody had thrown in a new ingredient, though—a proposal. She had fantasized about his making a commitment, secretly wished for it since Woody had surprised her with his arrival in Portland with Beauregard. Before she and Woody had flown to New York, she'd even talked to the imaginary ghost of her dead husband, Adam, about it in the laundry room while she'd cleaned the dryer vent of lint.

When she spotted her new ring on the bureau, Olivia eased from under the comforter and slipped Woody's T-shirt over her head. To prove a point, Woody had made a display. How could she miss it? The turquoise box sat open, waving her in like a beacon in a stormy harbor. Next to the ring sat a note on the hotel's stationery in Woody's calligraphic handwriting:

I'm down in the lobby waiting for your posse. You meant well, but trust in me next time. I love you.

Woody had underlined the word *me* in the note for a reason. He might as well have asked her to make a choice between him and her family. She shouldn't have made that rescue call. She did need to believe in him, to trust. Damn, she didn't know how to do this . . . but neither did he. Olivia glanced at the diamond band. She twisted her scratched gold one—loose at the base of her finger, but the knuckle was a semitruck blocking traffic. Soap. She needed soap and face cream—the heavy night-repair kind.

~ · ~ · ~

At eight fifteen on Friday morning, Woody sat in the expansive lobby of the Waldorf Hotel in his overcoat and tapped the arms of a leather bucket chair. A storm was blowing in, and the snow had started to fly outside. Concern crept into his fingertips. He tapped faster, willing the hotel's van to pull to the curb. Getting back to New Hampshire now would be impossible. He dialed the number on his phone.

"Margie?" he said. After one ring, his paralegal and life coach stood ready to offer wise words. "What's the weather look like up there?"

"Nice now," she said in her motherly voice, "but it'll turn wicked when that storm moves up. I'm closing the office after lunch." For over twenty years, Margie had proved her ability to read the weather while she kept the engine of Rainey, Bonner, and Braden LLC humming, and Woody's life humming.

"Good thinking," he said, giving consent to close early even though she hadn't asked.

"So . . . did you do it? Bonner and Braden took bets."

"Uh-huh." Woody traced the tight stitches along the seam of the leather upholstery. "The ring doesn't fit."

Margie groaned. "But she said yes, right?"

"Yes."

"And Della's books sold last night?"

"Yes . . ."

A pause in the receiver. "Sounds like someone dog-eared your pages."

"Not sure I like who they were sold to."

"Don't tell me. A dealer is going to split them up and make a killing."

"Not quite. Olivia bought them."

"Uh-oh. Hmmm." Woody could hear Margie processing the details like an old IBM mainframe. "Look at the motivation, Woody, not the result. You told me that once. She won't let go until whatever's in you—and her—about those books is resolved. You can't sell away the pain Della caused you. And Olivia can't buy back what she's lost, either."

"What do I do?"

"You love her?"

"More than anything."

"Then it's your move, Buck Rogers. But you still have a long way to go to understand women, and you've met your match with Olivia Novak."

"A lot to get past. More than I thought."

"Don't try to drive up here until after this storm blows through. I may stay at the office and use your guest room upstairs."

Woody's law office bustled on the ground floor of his 1840s Colonial in Wolfeboro. The second floor had been converted to his two-bedroom private apartment.

"Fresh sheets are in the hall closet," he said as he spotted the hotel van pulling to the curb. Woody let out a silent breath of relief, followed by an inhale of trepidation. "I gotta go. Stoke the fire, Margie, and stay safe."

Woody disconnected and stood. Luggage. Olivia's sisters would have a ton of luggage. He signaled the porter and called the hotel room. Olivia had instigated this storm's arrival. She needed fair warning.

"They're here. You ready?" he said when Olivia picked up.

"You let me oversleep." Olivia released an exaggerated audible yawn. He pictured her fully up, staring at the ring box he'd left open on the bureau.

"To put you at a disadvantage." He chuckled. "You owe me for last night."

"I got your note. I do trust in you, Woody."

"Then why am I in the lobby doing my best imitation of a greeting party?"

"I'll get in the shower," she said.

"Should I send them all up?"

"Not Ryan."

"Then I'll deal with Ryan and the dogs. I'm starving, and I'm sure he is too. That'll give you and your sisters plenty of time to carve me up."

"I'm showing off the ring."

"I want you to show off the ring to *me* in the shower—on your left finger."

Woody disconnected and slipped his phone back into his coat pocket. He enjoyed sparring with opposing counsel, and then bedding her as a plea bargain. A challenge to be conquered.

Outside, the van door slid open. Pogo and Beauregard sprang from the far rear seat in their yellow *Pogo Trust* service vests. Pogo, a jet-black standard poodle, held his rubber bullfrog in his mouth, his tail wagging like a scolding finger. Beauregard, a chocolate-colored labradoodle, searched for Olivia, his jaws clamped on his meowing rubber Garfield.

Woody buttoned his coat and moved to the revolving door, glad now for them all to be here. With thick booties on their paws, both dogs pranced toward him as he whirled to the sidewalk. Along with

Ryan's male perspective, Woody could use a few comforting licks too.

Ryan stepped from the front passenger seat and stood at the van's open back door, holding Woody's gaze as he reached for Danny's gloved hand. Even in jeans and a down jacket, Ryan carried himself like a cop. A much-needed testosterone injection calmed the erratic flow of estrogen that had arrived. Olivia's younger sister stepped from the car and planted two expensive, high-heeled black boots on the sidewalk dusted with snow.

"Pogo! Leave Woody alone," she said and beamed. "He'll turn you into a naughty boy. Where's Liv?" Pogo duck-walked back to Danny like he had wads of gum stuck to his paws. Beauregard nudged Woody's side to make his Garfield toy meow. Danny's dark eyes and long lashes, like Olivia's, made it impossible for Woody to be annoyed. She tucked her bobbed hair behind her ears like flyaway silk.

"She's up in the room." Woody stooped to give Olivia's labradoodle—their labradoodle—a vigorous rub. "Good boy, Beau." Turning in a circle, the dog's tail brushed Woody's face.

A heavy rubber-soled boot made an appearance. Then two black gloves slapped in succession to the sidewalk. Olivia's older sister, Lauren, the same age as Woody, took Ryan's hand in one of hers and with the other pulled herself out of the van with the help of the overhead safety handle. Her tufted down coat swished with puffy insulation. By afternoon, Lauren might be making snow angels in Central Park. Or she might be unable to right herself, like Ralphie's brother, Randy, in *A Christmas Story*. Woody stifled a smirk. He loved Lauren for telling it like it was—with a gun.

"Dammit, Woody," Lauren said. "New York in winter? We were all over the sky in that tin can. I'm going to kill Liv. Where is she?" She snatched up her gloves from the ground and stuffed them in her coat pockets.

"Woody says she's up in the room," Danny said. "I'll bet she's hiding in the bathroom."

Lauren dragged her oversize purse from the seat and stepped forward. She gave Woody a peck on the cheek and ruffled Beauregard's head.

"You look wonderful, Lauren," Woody said. "Have you lost weight?"

Lauren narrowed her dark eyes, an echo of Olivia's and Danny's. "A good line, potential bro. You just saw me a week ago. I'm in a big coat. How can you tell?"

"I can see it in your face."

"I found the secret."

"What?" Woody tried to wrestle the Garfield toy from Beau.

"More wine, less food."

"Good plan," Danny said and pulled her Louis Vuitton overnight case from the cart. "Your butt can be smaller than your liver." She patted Pogo's back. "Pogo and Beau need to get inside. It's freezing out here."

Lauren grimaced at her sister and turned. "What's the real story, Woody? Did *you* blow it? Or did she? You look guilty."

"We're both guilty as charged," Woody said. "Liv's guiltier. You didn't bring your gun, did you?"

Lauren nodded and patted her purse. "Ethel goes everywhere with me. Ryan's got his too."

Ryan shooed his arms. "All right . . . all right. Everybody inside. Lauren, why don't you go with Danny to check us in."

"Ryan and I'll get some breakfast and take the dogs," Woody said. "Liv's on the fourth floor. Room four-oh-nine."

"Of course she is," Lauren said.

Last night's specific room request had become another *stick it*. "What about Freesia?" Woody said. "Does she have a sitter?" Olivia's grumpy Himalayan cat demanded round-the-clock service. She hogged the bed too.

"Maria's at the house," Danny said. "I told her to count on a week."

"A week?" Woody's plan to take Olivia up to New Hampshire blurred with the morning's weather report. His gaze pleaded with Ryan.

In a response bigger than words, Ryan held up a duffel the size of gym bag. "Underpants, toothbrush, and a razor. What you see on me is what you get. And even my underpants can be washed in the sink with fancy shampoo. Our resident troublemaker in four-oh-nine described me in her book with pretty good accuracy. I guarantee she'll put this one in a book, too, someday."

Danny waved for the porter to follow with the luggage.

Pogo broke free and climbed on the cart, flailing his back legs to gain traction in his fleece booties. Beauregard pivoted his gaze to Woody.

He chuckled. Dogs might as well be kids. "Go ahead, General B. You can ride too."

Chapter 5
Guy Talk

"Mothers," Ryan said. "The root of all problems in a marriage." Woody's back stiffened in response to Ryan's comment over breakfast. The chunk of honeydew melon on his fork paused. "What do you mean?"

"*Your* Della and *her* Ellen." Ryan bobbed his own fork. "You and Olivia need to tackle those ghosts. If you let Olivia help you figure out what really happened between Della and Ellen, you'll have a wife for life. And she'll be a good one." Ryan went quiet and shook a sugar packet like a burned-down match. Woody sensed a hole being stared into his forehead. "There's an unsolved crime, Woody. I live with it too. I requested those police records up in Boston after Danny told me about Della's confession to you before she died. They don't want me digging. First, they said the docs were in storage. Then they said they couldn't find the case files. Not in the database, either. Something's not sitting right with me."

"Who's *they*?

"The DA's office in Boston. If your mother was telling the truth, then that case from 1947 is still open. Della wasn't caught. No statute of limitations on murder."

"Let's subpoena the police report. We have a legal right. I'm family." Woody had been avoiding that step so as not to puncture the bubble of his time with Olivia. Plus, the hurt of discovering that his mother had poisoned his father still stung.

"Don't think we'll need one. Took me almost two months of pushing, then I took another route." Ryan took a sip of his coffee and made a stinky face. He'd obviously opened one sugar packet too many. I charmed a clerk who didn't know anything but wanted to impress me with her sniffing skills. The scanned files are supposed to be emailed this afternoon. Let's see if she's blowing smoke up my butt."

"We're going to pursue finding my family?" Woody slipped in the *we* part. No way could he remain objective.

Della's deathbed confession about the identity of Woody's father had been a shocker. She'd lied to him for all those poverty-stricken years. At a personal level, to find out that his paternal family held the status of Boston blue blood had been both confusing and intimidating. He had done just fine on his own and had decided to leave that situation alone.

"Liv's got that writer brain; you're a smart lawyer, and I'm a scrappy cop. Lauren's got elbows, and Danny's got knees—nice knees. Plus, these two dogs can make anyone say just about anything. If this crew can't figure out what happened, then it's not solvable."

"But Della confessed. There's nothing to fix, Ryan. My mother's dead."

"Look . . . " Ryan took a bite of buttered sourdough. "Ellen Dushane's book, *Indigo to Black*, is holding us all hostage. Don't get me wrong—the money's been great—but that prickly ball got thrown to you when Della died. When we all find out what really happened between your mother and Ellen, the girls will stop obsessing." Ryan nodded his own agreement with himself. "Remember when Princess Diana did that tell-all interview with the BBC? She said, 'There were three of us in this marriage.' Well, you'll have four: you, Olivia, Adam, and a family in Boston that doesn't know you exist."

The tangled twists in the linked chain were adding up. "Don't discount the distance," Woody said. "Liv's in Portland. My practice is in Wolfeboro. And every time I bring it up, she changes the subject."

"Liv won't move to New Hampshire. Leave her sisters? Not happening. The lawyer for the Pogo Trust is retiring soon, though."

"Ted Beal. Liv's told me about him."

"All three girls are in denial about him not overseeing things, but you're the only lawyer who knows the family history and can make objective decisions for the family."

Woody noodled the revelation. "I need to introduce you to my buddy, Casey Carter. He was a helicopter pilot in the Gulf. That'll make it a team of three and three."

"Perfect. Fix him up with Lauren. He'll see fireworks over Baghdad again. If we wrap this up, then he can fly us up to Wolfeboro to get a goddamned doughnut at the Yum Yum Shop."

"You ever kayak? Casey and I are champs."

"Sailboat and a beer are more my style. I see enough action."

Woody craned for the server's attention and pointed at the table for the bill. "We should go up and check on the girls."

"Relax." Ryan tamped the air with his hand. "Have another cup of coffee. They're up there telling ghost stories . . . in the bathroom."

Chapter 6
Girl Talk

Puffs of steam curled against the ceiling of the bathroom. Like a tropical downpour, the shower spray washed over her from the rain-head fixture. "It's stuck halfway. I'm into bone," Olivia said, unable to twist her old wedding ring. She squeezed the travel-size Guerlain conditioner bottle over her gold band and finally pushed it back to the comfortable base of her finger. Blood oozed from a raw spot of missing skin.

"I'll call the fire department," Lauren shouted through the steam. "The jaws of life. That's what you need. I could use a fireman myself. Love firemen, maybe a military man."

"My knuckle's bleeding," Olivia pushed the shower lever to OFF and inspected her finger. "The edge cut into it."

A few seconds of silence ended with a sigh. Olivia stepped from the glass-walled shower and dabbed her knuckle with a towel. Bright red smudges dotted the cotton loops.

Lauren handed her a fluffy white hotel robe. "This has your logo—The Wal-'dork.'"

Olivia wrapped the robe around her and knotted the long belt.

"Your finger's going to swell," Danny said in singsong. "Hot water makes it worse. Stick your hand in the ice bucket."

Olivia toweled her dripping hair, watching Danny admire the diamond band in the turquoise box. Her younger sister sat on the bathroom's marble counter and swung her black boots like opposing pendulums. Even at forty-seven, Danny acted fourteen. Her deep-brown eyes and long lashes sucked everyone in, including dogs and mobsters.

"No, it won't," Danny said, changing her own advice. "Well . . . maybe. I'm taking all your Guerlain stuff. I've already packed mine away, so Ryan doesn't use the shampoo on his underpants. The body lotion's awesome."

Lauren leaned against the doorjamb with her arms crossed. At sixty-two, her older sister's brown eyes sagged with a cast of loneliness, a silent anger weighing heavy over the loss of her husband, Mark, and for their mother, to whom she'd failed to say goodbye.

Olivia wiped the mirror with the sleeve of her robe. Her gaze made a triple play, considering each of the three Dushane sisters in turn. Like Cinderella's menopausal castoffs, all three of them carried the same features as their mother had—dark eyes, an abundance of hair, and creamy skin—but each had inherited separate aspects of Ellen Dushane's personality in order of age: sneaky, bossy, and spoiled. After their mother's death, a fourth trait they all shared emerged as a life tenet: a belief that doing the wrong thing for the right reasons was a-okay. Maybe it was the other way around. Depended on the situation.

"How'd your boobs stay so perky, Liv?" Lauren said.

Sticking out her chest, Olivia posed with her hand on her hip. "No kids to suck the life out of them."

"I didn't have any kids either, but my boobs are talkin' to my shoes." Lauren stood straighter, but her arms remained crossed.

Danny rocked the ring box. "I had forgotten how beautiful this is, Liv. It's even more sparkly in these lights." She slipped Olivia's ring on her finger, stacking it above the band and substantial solitaire that had belonged to their mother. Ryan had proposed to Danny at Ellen's funeral. In divvying up their mother's possessions, Olivia and Lauren thought it appropriate for Ellen's wedding ring to go to Ryan, for a permanent place on Danny's finger.

Danny wiggled her hand against her chest and said: "It fits!. Daaahhhling, of course I'll marry you. Turn away, Lauren. Olivia's ring might blind you."

Lauren squinted. "Put a snuffer over it, Cinderella. With those baguettes set that way, it looks like the air filter on my Honda, but it's damn pretty. Woody spoiled you rotten, Liv."

"He certainly did," Olivia said. "I can't believe you both knew about the ring." She sucked on her raw knuckle. "That was way too big a secret to keep from me. This is all your fault, both of you."

"Whoa. Whoa. Whoa." Lauren held her hand in a stop motion. "You didn't even need a ring to see Woody marching down that road. You were practically married when he delivered Beauregard to your front door. What size is your gold band from Adam?"

Olivia shrugged. "Six?"

"See, Danny? A six should've fit. Woody was right. I was too, but—"

"Liv's knuckles got fat," Danny said. "She totally needs a size seven."

Olivia narrowed her eyes. "Arthritis."

Three rings were now stacked on Danny's left hand: her own wedding band, her mother's engagement ring, and now Olivia's new diamond band. She continued to admire them. "How come Adam never gave you an engagement ring, Liv? I always thought that was odd."

Olivia ran a wide-tooth comb through her shoulder-length brown hair. "Adam and I had nothing when we got married. We thought our wide gold bands were extravagant, and that they were twenty-four carat gold. We purposely got them a half-size smaller, so they'd never come off. Plus, I didn't want a ring that I had to clean after I cleaned. Diamonds look terrible caked with soap scum and hand cream."

"The secret is that you put diamonds in a glass of warm water with denture-cleaner tablets. Works like a charm."

Olivia paused the comb. "Seriously?"

"Now, Woody needs a ring," Lauren said. "Take yours to be resized and pick out one for him. Plain. No diamonds. He's more understated than that."

"Not all men wear one," Danny said. "You should ask him first."

The possibility of Woody's finger remaining empty had never crossed Olivia's mind. Wedding rings were sacred. After what she was going through to take her old one off, the suggestion ignited an image of a new tussle. "He'd better wear one."

Danny chuckled. "Woody would say *bett-ah*." She twisted off Olivia's new ring and tucked it back in the box. "Where's Adam's ring, Liv?"

The bathroom silenced with the echo of the question.

"Danny, don't," Lauren said and fingered Mark's ring on a gold chain around her neck.

Her younger sister's eyes started to glass at the admonishment. "I'm so sorry, Liv. I didn't mean—"

Olivia's throat tightened. "The doctors had to cut it off."

To cover the choke of tears, Olivia turned on the cold tap to full power. A splash to her face sent a snake of pink-tinged water from her finger down the drain. Bent over, with her head resting on the edge of the sink, she broke her shell and let it all out. The memory of that day couldn't be erased. A random nurse, faceless, had handed over a white drawstring bag containing Adam's clothes, wallet, keys, and the watch she'd given to him a month before the accident. Tucked in the bottom corner was a resealable snack bag that had held the two halves of Adam's ring. Only Lauren found the strength to go with Olivia for the handoff of Adam's effects. Danny had been consoling their mother about losing, yet another, son-in-law.

Finally, Olivia added, "The pieces . . . are in . . . my nightstand."

The build-up had been coming, and Olivia's words triggered the overflow. Danny set her hands over her face. Lauren stepped forward and rubbed Olivia's back to soothe her tears. Olivia pivoted and wrapped her arms around Lauren.

"This isn't getting you anywhere," Lauren said and reached to snatch two tissues from the box by the sink. She handed one each to Olivia and Danny and swiped her forefingers under her own eyes. "Fix your face. You, too, Danny. The guys can't see either of you this way."

Exchanging the soaked tissue for a hand towel, Olivia attempted to breathe. "Woody's never had a wedding ring. He has no clue how hard it is."

"Maybe he doesn't, but that old ring is like a car wreck on the highway. He can't take his eyes off the carnage."

"That's . . . a terrible image." Olivia sniffed and straightened.

"She's right, Liv," Danny said. "Better let Woody be the big dog. Let go of the books, because he's got his own stuff going on. You need to help him find his family."

To switch gears, Oliva changed the subject. "Why did Ryan agree to come on this trip?"

Lauren sighed. "Of all people, Ryan knows how hard this is for you. Hard for him too. He loved Adam."

"I know he did."

"But we love Woody too. He's a good man, Liv. And he loves you like crazy." The lid banged down on the commode. Lauren took a seat and wound a long length of toilet paper from the roll and swiped the wad over her eyes. "He needs to put this Della mess to bed, so Mom's book doesn't drive a wedge between the two of you. And the bonehead move you pulled with Della's books picked a damned crusty scab. No matter how ugly the truth is under that Band-Aid, rip it off. Woody needs to know. You need to know." She gulped to swallow. "We all need to know if Mom's book is true."

Olivia's cell phone twirled in a circle on the counter. Three pairs of red-rimmed eyes darted to it.

Danny leaned closer to peek at the caller ID on the screen. "Finnerelli Literary Agency."

Olivia tossed the hand towel on the counter and took a cleansing breath. "I left a message for Karen last night to make an appointment. I told a fib to Woody, before I came clean. We had planned to drive up to New Hampshire tomorrow to deal with Della's ashes . . . and the letters."

"Not today," Danny said. "A blizzard's due this afternoon."

"Answer that before it goes to voice mail," Lauren said with a wave of her hand.

Hesitant, Olivia nevertheless picked up the phone and fake-smiled. "Karen! Guess who's here in New York with me?"

"Palermo's manuscript?" Karen said. "You were supposed to send me the first fifty pages of the draft last week. I'm still waiting." Karen's abrupt New York delivery instantly disqualified her from the award of Miss Congeniality.

This second mob memoir had been a case of near extortion due to Palermo's jealousy and ego. The don wouldn't stand for her ex-neighbor to be the first to tell his story. R.D. Griffin—*Ardy* to her and her sisters—had become like family after they'd rescued him from a Murphy bed with a bad spring. He'd nearly died from the experience, but it had breathed new energy into Olivia's writing career. The story of his life and the account of his last days in the Witness Protection Program had been the first book in the mob memoir series. Palermo had attempted to hunt Ardy down with his minions, all from his prison cell, to make the hit. It hadn't worked, but a cat-and-mouse game with Olivia had forged a weird connection between the two of them. Palermo wanted his story to be published before Ardy's. But even though this draft was done, in a bigger sense it wasn't done yet with Palermo. Olivia could feel it in her bones.

"I can deliver the whole manuscript to you in person, typos and all. Lauren and Danny are here too. And you'll get to meet the real Pogo and Beauregard. They're exactly like Lauren's sketches for the children's series."

The imaginary bubble above Olivia's head contained an image of Wannamaker's hefty check. That American Express bill had *bett-ah* not beat the deposit of it into her bank account.

She needed the advance from Palermo's manuscript, too. But more important was that Palermo had *bett-ah* have been truthful in his interviews with her.

Lauren nodded and mouthed, *Damn straight, sista.*

"The dogs are here? In New York?" Karen's voice brightened. "Should I send Rick out for toys?"

"No. But I'm bringing one of my own. You can meet my *fiancé*." As Olivia uttered the word, she glanced at her sisters. "He has a suggestion for you about the movie deal for *Indigo to Black*."

"What, he's a Hollywood agent?"

"No. A lawyer. He's Della Rainey's son, Woodrow Rainey."

The phone went quiet for what seemed like an eternity. Woody's threat to sue the publisher of *Indigo to Black* on behalf of his mother had nearly given Olivia's agent a heart attack. Dueling dead mothers had ruined Karen's quota of lattes and lasagna. "Can you be here at noon?" Karen's voice had chilled to match the temperature outside.

"Done. See you then." Olivia ended the call and raised her eyes. "I gotta get dressed. We're all going to see Karen at noon."

"Witchiepoo?" Lauren said, her eyes widening.

"I'm waiting in Karen's lobby," Danny said. "No way will Ryan go."

"Oh, stop. She's just a tough woman in a tough business. You guys clean up." Olivia gave her knuckle a quick lick and held the blow dryer like a gun. "I need big hair and a new face. There's about to be a new dog in town. And his name is Woodrow Rainey."

Danny snatched up the ring box and slid from the counter. "Time to get goin'."

Lauren inspected herself in the mirror. "I'm as ready as I'm going to get."

Olivia switched on the dryer full blast and shouted, "Meet you guys downstairs in twenty minutes!"

Chapter 7

Sisters on a Mission

The Waldorf's lobby bustled with tourists as Olivia stepped from the elevator with Beauregard. She felt like a million bucks in her taupe gabardine suit, winter-white turtleneck, and cream-colored coat. She'd changed the dog's Pogo Trust yellow vest to his custom-fleece version with the same logo. Against his chocolate-colored curls, the vest and matching yellow booties turned Beauregard into a giant sunflower. Beau stopped on cue as Olivia set her satchel on the marble floor to retrieve her black leather gloves. She should have worn boots, but Woody loved her in heels. They'd be cabbing it to their next destination, anyway.

"Beau, let's go," she said. The dog mirrored her movements for the trek across the lobby. Her sisters stood with Pogo at one of the tall bronzed urns that flanked the staircase to the Park Avenue entrance. Pogo's black curls, yellow trust vest, and booties that matched Beau's made the stately poodle resemble a bumble bee. The sunflower-bee combo screamed a fashion statement that ignited a string of snickers from passers-by. Danny had dressed to the nines too. Lauren was dressed to the eights. Points were shaved for the oldest sister's choice of heavy rubber boots. They were practical, though, given the downward spiral of weather outside.

"Where's Woody?" Lauren said.

Olivia's gaze circled the lobby. "He should be here. He came down about half an hour ago. I was still getting dressed."

"Maybe he went to see Ryan in the business office," Danny said. "He's set up camp with his laptop and waiting for an email." She glanced at Lauren.

Olivia pulled back her glove and checked at her watch. Ten forty-five. "I have an idea. We've got enough time to go to Tiffany's to pick out a ring for Woody and drop off mine to be resized."

"I'll go find him," Danny said. "Wait here."

"No. Woody's got his phone." Olivia hit speed-dial. On the fourth ring, the call switched to voice mail. "Hi, honey. Not sure where you are, but Lauren, Danny, and I are taking the dogs for a walk. Meet us at Karen's office at noon. Forty-Sixth at Seventh. Third floor." She disconnected. "Huh . . . He's not answering."

Danny pulled out her phone. "I'll call Ryan." She walked in a circle as she talked.

"Remember the last time we were at this hotel, Liv?" Lauren said. "I thought I'd died and gone to heaven."

Olivia nodded. "Mom's book award. What a night."

"Yeah. Look at all that's happened in two years."

"I couldn't have made up a story like this."

Danny disconnected and clutched the handle of Pogo's service vest. "Let's go. Woody was in the business center with Ryan, then he left to run an errand. He told Ryan that he'd meet us at Karen's."

"Why didn't he call me?" Olivia said.

"Those two are up to something. I can smell it."

"Yeah. I can smell it too," Lauren said. "Just like the lotion you stole from my room. Liv and Woody's room too."

Danny took a whiff of her hands and tugged on her gloves. "Mmmm . . . Let's go to Tiffany's."

At the foot of the stairs at the Waldorf's side entrance, Danny held out her hand to halt the group. They all wobbled at the abruptness.

"Look at it outside. Isn't it beautiful?"

"I'm in heels," Olivia said.

The green, tree-lined parking strip on Park Avenue now sat under a blanket of white. The twinkle lights clung to the branches against the wind.

"Should we walk the nine blocks so Pogo and Beauregard can piddle?" Danny said. "I've got baggies if its poo. Or should we cab it?"

Lauren stomped her boots and swished her insulated arms in a marching motion. "Walk it. I'm game."

Pogo and Beauregard shifted in their booties.

"Cab," Danny and Olivia said in unison.

Danny handed Lauren the roll of bags. "Take the kids to the parking strip. We'll wait for you."

Lauren narrowed her eyes.

~ · ~ · ~

When a jewelry store has its name carved over the entrance in stone, it isn't going anywhere. Olivia hugged Beauregard next to her when she spotted the statue of a scantily clad man supporting an oversize Roman-numeral clock on the edifice of Tiffany's. She likened the art piece to Woody holding the weight of time on his shoulders while she got her act together. A giant Christmas wreath hung over the revolving doors, its blaze of lights melting the snow that attempted to stick to its bulbs. The scene would have been more beautiful if she didn't have to schlep around in it.

Olivia gripped the door handle before the taxi pulled to the curb. Lauren handed the driver a folded ten-dollar bill for the nine-block ride.

"Heads down. Here we go," Olivia said and swung open the door with a bounce. A wind gust whipped flurries through the car as the dogs jumped to the sidewalk. Pogo slid on his front paws like a snow plow, daring Beauregard to do the same. Beauregard took long strides to the entrance, appearing to pull taffy with his booties. To bring up the rear, Danny ejected from the front passenger seat and ran through the steamy exhaust to corral the dogs.

High heels required baby steps. Olivia held on to Lauren's arm to reach the revolving door. Freezing drips from the wreath hit the top of her head and trickled down her scalp. She whirled into a blast of heat. Danny wrestled both dogs through the side door.

Once inside, Pogo and Beauregard blinked to focus. The transition from flying snow to warm bright lights required recalibration of canine senses. Pogo sniffed.

"That's right, sweetheart," Danny said. "Smells like money."

Lauren's gaze swept up the curvy marble and glass staircase toward the back of the store. "Jeez. Am I allowed in here? Should I take off my boots?"

"No dallying," Olivia said. "We're on a mission. Men's wedding bands first. I'll lube up the salesman with a sale, so the resize will be free. We've got thirty minutes."

"Nothing's free in here."

Olivia smiled at a blond head, slick with hair gel, and the dark suit that accompanied it behind one of the counters. The young man was probably no more than twenty-five years old, but from the quality of the suit he made substantial commissions. Upon her approach, his blue eyes danced with a this-is-going-be-fun look.

"Men's wedding bands," she said.

The sales clerk glanced at Pogo's and Beauregard's vests with the words *Access Required* on the Pogo Trust logo badges. "My name is Adam. We'll go upstairs. I'll be happy to show you what we have." Like a pied piper, Tiffany's Adam led the procession.

Olivia closed her eyes at Lauren's whisper, "Christ. Why not Paul or John?"

Danny groaned at the foot of the stairs. "The kids' booties need to come off, so they don't slip."

Overheating in her insulated coat, Lauren huffed and puffed past Tiffany's Adam. "Shoulda waited to do this back in Portland."

The dogs stood still as Olivia and her sister popped off eight paw coverings at lightning speed and stuffed them in their coat pockets like newly hatched Easter chicks.

"Thick or thin?" Adam said, turning at the fourth step.

Olivia grabbed the steel railing as her heels clomped on the marble stairs. "Thick."

Lauren stood at the top to catch her breath and unzipped her overcoat. "Thin goes first," Lauren said and rolled her eyes.

Not out of breath at all, Adam buzzed himself in behind the counter. "Gold? Platinum? Silver?"

The hot lights under the glass surface of the display case practically burned Olivia's fingertips. Like a raccoon drawn to shiny objects, Beauregard pushed forward and left viscous nose prints along the vertical edge.

"Platinum," Olivia said. "And no gemstones. Clean and simple."

This was anything but clean and simple. Pogo stuck his head under her elbow, soliciting a head scratch. He sat and leaned against her leg when Danny slipped him his frog.

Ribbit. Ribbit.

The young whipper-snapper version of Adam lined five thick platinum bands on the counter in black velvet boxes. Turquoise boxes must be for the women's rings.

Lauren swished forward, inspected the assemblage, and pointed to the middle one like a lineup of potential perpetrators. "That one. It's the classiest. The edging reminds me of the Federal furniture in Woody's office. Trust me on this."

Danny pushed past Olivia's left shoulder to inspect the choice. "She's right. He's a Yankee. He's a modern, classy guy and appreciates antiques."

"Do I get a vote?" Olivia said. "He's going to be my husband. I have to live with this ring . . . for the rest of my life." She leaned forward but didn't touch it. A thin rope of tiny beaded decoration rimmed the top and bottom edges of the smooth brushed platinum. Lauren and Danny were right.

"A six-millimeter stovepipe," Adam said. "The double milgrain beading is exquisite."

"No need to look further. I love it, and I think so will Woody."

"Do you know the gentleman's size?" Tiffany's Adam glanced up with his chin down.

Olivia ticked her eyes at Lauren, who shrugged. She tocked to Danny, who also shrugged.

"Is he a large man?"

"How do you mean?" Olivia said.

Adam smirked. "His weight and length of his fingers."

"He has big feet and long fingers," Olivia said and slipped her foot out of her right shoe and wiggled circulation back in her toes. "He's quite fit. About one-eighty."

"Lucky you. Let's start with size eleven, which this one is. We can take it up or down, if necessary, but sizing down won't compromise the thickness." Adam plucked the band from the velvet and handed it to her with a devilish grin. "Bigger is better, so to speak."

The ring had more heft than she anticipated. The decoration was understated but unique and finely crafted, like Woody. Those stupid tears of hers couldn't make a reappearance, not here. She wished now that she had come alone, without a schedule, without pressure. This moment deserved wallowing and respect.

Adam glanced at her left finger. "Don't you want twenty-four-carat gold to match that one?"

Olivia followed his gaze to the angry spot of missing skin on her knuckle. Dried blood defined the tear with a ragged edge. "Uhhh . . . this one is coming off." She leaned her elbow on the counter and held up her ring finger like the marital version of flipping the bird. "My finger's thin on the bottom, but this band won't budge over that wicked knuckle. My fiancé bought a platinum one for me at Tiffany's in Portland. It needs to be resized."

"I see. Do you have your new ring with you? Let's see how they look together."

Olivia stooped to her briefcase and checked the pockets. Her stomach tightened as she lifted the satchel to the counter for closer inspection. "It's here. We were looking at it this morning." Heat crept up her neck.

Lauren held out her hands as Olivia dispensed the contents of her case. "It must've slipped to the bottom, Liv. Hurry. I'm heating up in here like a movie-theater hot dog."

Palermo's manuscript, her wallet, house keys, and makeup pouch made a pile on her sister's palms. Rummaging inside, Olivia found no ring box, only her and Woody's boarding pass receipts from the Portland flight and a travel container of hand sanitizer.

She turned to Danny. "No joking around. Give me the ring."

"I don't have it, Liv." Danny pushed her hair behind her ears. "I put the box back in your bag before we left your and Woody's room."

Her sister's words prompted Olivia to rake her fingers through her own hair, damp from melting snow and sweat. The hairspray had made her scalp sticky. "Okay. Don't panic. It must be back at the hotel."

"Maybe in the cab?" Lauren said, her tomato-red cheeks blanching to pink. "Did it fall out?"

"No. It couldn't have. I wedged my case between my feet. It didn't tip over."

"Back in the room," Danny said and nodded with confidence. "I'll bet it's on the bureau. You must've taken it out."

Olivia turned and gazed at blond Tiffany's Adam. He stood still, but his eyes shifted to draw an invisible triangle. The clerk was young enough to have been her son. "I believe we neglected to bring the ring with us." She glanced at her watch. They had fifteen minutes to get to Karen's office. "We'll take this band." Olivia handed over Woody's new band, trying not to linger on the irony.

"Very good," he said. "When you find yours, come in, and we'll be happy size it for you."

Without saying a word, Lauren held out the pile topped with her sister's wallet. Olivia unzipped it and slapped her loaded American Express card on the counter. She caught one last glimpse of the band before Adam snapped the case shut and moved to the register.

An uncomfortable silence settled around the sister trio as Olivia assembled the contents back into her satchel. Palermo's manuscript had begun to curl around the edges from the cold and heat. Customers whispered and nosed the counters, gawking at the glittering pieces in their natural habitat. A jewelry zoo. Olivia had never cared for zoos. They sacrificed freedom for display. At this moment, placing a high price on love somehow came off as cheap and tawdry.

Olivia flinched when Beauregard's tail thumped her leg. He yawned with a whine. Olivia stooped and held his muzzle. "I love you, General B. You're priceless."

"How much is it, Liv?" Danny asked.

Only her younger sister would dare to ask such an inappropriate question. "No idea. I don't want to know."

Lauren pursed her lips. "Less than three hundred first-edition books, for sure."

Ouch. Hair-gelled Adam set a cord-handled Tiffany's bag on the counter with her credit card, front and center. Olivia signed the receipt without daring to glance at the final amount, but she did calculate the number of days before the end of billing cycle. Ten. She needed to deposit that check from Woody.

Adam's expression brightened at her curvy signature. "I see quite a few celebrities in here, but are you the same Olivia Novak who wrote all those romances?"

She raised her eyes. "My pen name. The real one is *Dead Fiancé.*"

"Yep, she's the one," Danny said.

"My partner has read every one of your books," Adam said. "They're like *Fifty Shades of Yum.*"

The zipper on Lauren's coat got an exaggerated tug. "Well, there you have it, Liv. I smell a whole new marketing campaign for your backlist. Your real audience is packing equipment."

Adam smirked and threw her a sideways glance. "He'll be over-the-moon jealous when I tell him that I met you today."

"Give him a hug for me." Olivia dropped the receipt into the bag. She slid it from the counter as though it weighed a thousand pounds.

The bag's thick laminated paper crunched as she folded over the top and tucked the package into the bottom corner of her case.

Danny set her hand on Olivia's shoulder. "We'll find it back in the room. I'm sure we will."

Inching on her gloves, Lauren grimaced. "We'll never get a cab."

Olivia wobbled in her heels toward the top of the stairs. She reached for the handle on Beauregard's vest. The labradoodle slowed his steps and raised his appraising eyes.

"Woody's going to kill me," she said.

Behind her, Danny's voice absorbed into Olivia's long coat. "Maybe not kill you, but I wouldn't trade places with you for all the diamonds in this store."

Chapter 8
Sharp Elbows

At eleven thirty on Friday morning, the business center at the Waldorf Hotel bustled with guests checking flights and road conditions. Whispered words of profanity accompanied news of cancellations and traffic pileups. Ryan didn't have any of that nonsense on his laptop screen. He had two Internet windows open: one for his personal email account and one that linked to archived newspaper articles from the *Boston Globe* about Asher Woodard's death in 1947. Ryan copied them to his desktop. No new email had arrived with an attachment. Afternoon technically started at noon.

Before Woody left for his errand, Ryan promised to keep digging. He tapped the keyboard to look for more clues.

Asher Woodard, found dead at only twenty, came from a prominent Boston family and had been a first-year medical student at Boston University. Poisoned. No suspects were ever arrested for the crime. No further newspaper reports appeared, either, at least none that Ryan could find.

No email, yet, from his contact at the district attorney's office in Boston. Ryan checked the clock on his computer: 12:20 p.m. Woody was steeped in a meeting at the Finnerelli Literary Agency, working his smooth magic to negotiate on Olivia's behalf to write the screenplay for her mother's book, *Indigo to Black*. Good luck with that.

Now Ryan stared at the obituary, as brief as the Woodard's service, which had been for immediate family only. In lieu of flowers, a request for donations to the Little Buddies Memorial Trust. Survived by his father, William Woodard, a sister—a twin sister—Althea Woodard Pennington, and a brother-in-law, Simon Pennington.

A string of obituaries dotted Ryan's screen: Asher's mother, Alice Woodard, had died in 1935 from leukemia. Old Man William Woodard, died only six months after his son, Asher. Simon Pennington died in 1982 from anaphylactic shock.

Woody had only one family member who remained alive.

Ryan typed *Althea Woodard Pennington Boston* into the search engine and hit ENTER. His gaze pulled to the left. No new email had arrived. Then sunshine.

Ryan scooted the chair closer to the screen. A string of links about Althea scrolled before his eyes.

~ · ~ · ~

Olivia stabbed the cracked elevator button four times in succession. "Hurry, get in," she said and held the door. Melting snow dripped from her hair as Danny herded Beauregard and Pogo into the four-by-four claustrophobia-inducing box. Lauren squeezed in last, her wet down coat deflating as the Deco-patterned metal doors closed. The elevator started its long chug up three floors to the Finnerelli Literary Agency.

"I'm freezing," Danny said and smacked her gloved hands together.

Lauren's cheeks reddened. "Now I'm hot." She pulled back her hood and started laughing. "You look like you rode here on a snow plow, Liv."

Olivia stretched her face muscles, tight from battling a frigid wind. "How's my mascara?"

"Cleopatra after a hormonal meltdown."

"Ugh." She tried to fluff her wet, sticky hair, but hairspray had turned her locks to clumps of *al dente* spaghetti.

On cue, the dogs shook chunks of slush from their curls. Hands were no shield against the cold spray.

"Well, I'm sure I can't look any worse," Olivia said and brushed off her coat. "Now I smell like a dog kennel." She glanced down, aghast at the creep of salt that had soaked her tan pumps. "My shoes are ruined, and my toes might need amputation from frostbite." With her best imitation of the threatened raccoon, she narrowed her eyes at Lauren and Danny. "Not one word about the ring."

Pogo glanced at Beauregard and blinked. Beau shifted on his still-crunchy booties.

The elevator bounced to a stop, and the doors parted to a magazine shot of Karen Finnerelli's offices. The lobby had been designed to resemble the library of a modernized, yet tasteful, manor house. Floor-to-ceiling varnished-maple bookcases lined the walls, broken only by a row of three windows. In front of them sat a five-foot fresh Christmas tree, loaded down with white twinkle lights and candy-apple-red ornaments. The Douglas fir glowed against the backdrop of snow blowing horizontally past the panes of rippled glass.

The inviting arrangement of cushy love seats, flanked by matching chairs, was empty, no doubt from canceled appointments. No Woody, either.

Behind a curved reception desk, the agency's assistant, Rick Morick, grinned like a naughty Santa's elf. The knitted reindeer on his maroon sweater jingled when he stood to assess Olivia's disastrous visage.

"Mr. Woodrow Rainey must love you a lot, or he's blind," he said. "On second thought, Braille would make you look worse."

Olivia clenched her jaw. "Couldn't get a cab. We walked twelve blocks"—she pointed to the windows—"in *that*. Is Woody here, or did he leave?"

"You mean Mr. Gorgeous?" Rick's gaze pulled from Olivia to the hall. Shots of Karen's staccato laughter riveted from the offices. The source of the glee——? The lilt of Yankee in Woody's smooth voice. "Back there in the lion's den. Got here early. From what I can hear, he's the only man alive who's been able to transform her from Maleficent to Gigglepuss."

"How long has Woody been here?"

"Shy of an hour. We had a fascinating chat."

Without removing their coats, Lauren and Danny side-stepped toward the couches and shepherded the dogs with them. Olivia figured they wanted to avoid being hit by shrapnel.

"Buzz her," she said.

"Want to go to the ladies' room first?"

"No." Then she pictured herself with a Braille eye. "Yes."

"Wise choice." Rick's brows raised. They were several shades darker than his highlighted hair. He held up the restroom key with one hand and pressed Karen's extension with the other. "She's heeeere," he sang into the receiver.

In stereo, laughter emanated from the speaker and from the hall. "Oh, good. Send Olivia back first. Then I want to meet Lauren and the dogs."

Lauren pulled her sketchbook from her purse and plopped on the couch.

"We'll wait for you out here, Liv," Danny said and sat next to Lauren.

In exchange for the bathroom key, Olivia pulled a flash drive from her case. "Here, Rick. Can you please print off a fresh copy of Palermo's manuscript for Karen. The one I have now looks like me."

Rick peered over the desk to inspect her briefcase. The key dangled from a jumbo Homey the Clown pencil. "You mean a bit curled around the edges?"

"Yeah." Olivia wanted to snatch the pencil and bop him over the head with it. Instead, she smiled and did her best exit-stage-left down the hall.

No amount of spruce, fluff, or touch-up could cover the guilt Olivia saw on her face in the restroom mirror. She checked her briefcase one more time. No go. Only the crunched turquoise bag with Woody's new ring. She snatched a tissue, licked the corner, and ran it under her eyes to remove the black smudge. Of all the times to not have used waterproof mascara.

Every step down the hall to her agent's lair became a battle with her feet: left foot, dread; right foot, anger. *Top dog.* Woody must be enjoying this new position. Well, she was about to become top cat. Olivia slowed her steps to Karen's private corner office and peered around the doorway.

Woody sat in a high-back chair facing Karen at her desk. Karen ran her fingers through her new, smooth Brazilian blowout as Woody cooed legalese. Olivia's agent clearly had paid plenty to banish her kinky black curls. Woody looked relaxed until Olivia knocked on the door frame. He shot to his feet as though the cushion had zapped an electrical charge through his suit pants.

Of course, Woody looked perfect: his hair combed; his navy-blue suit pressed; his tasseled loafers dry and polished. A smile bloomed on his face; then he bit his bottom lip. Olivia couldn't tell whether his expression was a judgment about her appearance or a guilty reaction from being busted. Talking with her agent, without her being present, had crossed the line.

Karen laughed. "You poor thing," she said. "Where have you been?"

Olivia's gaze never wavered from Woody's. "I see you two have become friends."

In a few quick steps, Woody moved to stand behind her. He leaned close to her ear and whispered, "Take it easy. You're about to get everything you want." His warm breath lingered on her neck, weakening the cartilage in Olivia's knees. Woody slipped off her heavy, wet coat and hung it on a freestanding rack.

Karen spread her arms as she stepped from behind her desk. Dressed in her signature palette of all black, Karen wore a turtleneck sweater atop a gauzy pleated skirt over tights and knee-high boots with thick heels. "Give me a hug, you wet, raggedy doll, you."

Olivia widened her eyes at Woody for the Raggedy-Ann embrace, convinced an exorcism had taken place before her arrival. Karen's brooch snagged Olivia's sweater when she pulled away. The fiery Christmas wreath at Karen's collarbone sparkled with baguette diamond-like crystals, a snooty version of a wagon wheel. The reminder of her lost wedding ring squelched Olivia's anger over Woody's hijack of her literary agent—almost.

"Have a seat." Karen returned to her desk chair and adjusted her brooch, sticking out her chest. "Sorry, Liv. Woody and I were chatting about the potential movie deal for your mother's book. We think *you* should take the first shot at writing the screenplay for *Indigo to Black*."

Olivia took the open guest chair and set her briefcase at her feet. She attempted to fluff the ironwork of her hair.

Woody cracked a smile, sat, and leaned back in the chair. He crossed his legs. "I do think we should incorporate the language up front, to make that part of any potential deal. Nonnegotiable."

Olivia shifted. Her wool slacks had suddenly become itchy. "Yes . . . Woody and I discussed it. In fact, I first suggested it a month ago, but you might not have seen that email."

"Probably too much going on. Forget about it," Karen waved her hand and flicked her smooth hair over her shoulder. "It's a great idea. Wonderful for marketing and control of the story."

"Woody's suggestion, really. I think I'd enjoy the challenge." This top-cat act was harder than she thought.

"But I told Woody that your first priority is to finish the draft of Palermo's installment in the mob series before you do anything." Karen tapped her red pen on some poor soul's hard work, leaving meaningless marks. "Nonnegotiable."

Apparently, everything in Olivia's life had become nonnegotiable, and she hadn't even been in on the negotiating. Olivia hefted her case to her lap and pulled out the curled manuscript for Palermo's story, its cover page limp and stained from melted snow. She slapped all three hundred pages, secured in rubber bands, on Karen's desk.

"Rick's printing you a clean copy, but it's not final. I need to go one more round with Palermo," she said. "I've already started an outline on Tullio's and Rizzo's memoirs."

Woody scratched his lip. "Olivia suggested we go to Allenwood to see Palermo while we're here. Once the weather clears tomorrow, I think it's an excellent idea to speed the process along."

Olivia turned to Woody and cocked her head to the left. The decision to turn paddle four-oh-nine back in had been a bad idea.

"How'd you get this done so fast?" Karen said, wide-eyed, as she rolled the tight rubber bands from the manuscript. The twisted squiggles launched across the desk and pinged Karen's plastic latte cup.

"The flash drives, with hours of recorded interviews, were invaluable," she said. "Woody brought them to me when he came out to Portland. We listened to them together. You could say that he read between the lines, and I wrote them." Olivia sniffed to swallow her irritation and to muster up some credit. "That copy's mine, by the way."

"I like the teamwork approach." Karen started flipping pages with steely eyes.

"Teamwork," Woody said and nodded. "That's the ticket."

"Keep working on the mob series, Liv. Finish those other two goombahs before they die on you. I'll read this and make comments. Woody can work with me on some contract language, but a movie deal is at least a year away. *Fantasy Island* until we have a commitment from a studio. The option we sold is only the first step."

Olivia turned to Woody, openmouthed. He spread his hands in surrender.

A file, thick with Lauren's sketches, labeled *Pogo the Therapy Dog Series*, suddenly eclipsed Olivia's manuscript. Karen hit the intercom button on her phone. "Rick, you can send Lauren in here with those dogs." The button got a second press. "But bring me that fresh copy of Palermo's manuscript first. This one looks like somebody peed on it." Karen wrinkled her nose and slid the stack of rippled paper toward Olivia.

Like in a sixties sitcom, Rick appeared in Karen's doorway,

somewhat out of breath. A heavy clip secured Palermo's manuscript like the jaws of a crocodile. He set it on the desk and backed out of the office. Karen took the thick manuscript and dropped it to the floor with a *thunk*. An addition to the take-home pile.

"Don't we have more to discuss about the movie?" Olivia said. "Danny and Lauren need to be involved in any decisions too."

"Woody can fill you in. Don't worry—nothing will happen without you. Too soon for the rest. Get Lauren in here, otherwise I won't be able to drive home at all. The phone isn't ringing today, so Palermo and I can snuggle up in Connecticut this afternoon."

Woody stood and leaned over the desk with an outstretched hand. Karen's face softened to ooey-gooey when he squeezed her fingers. Olivia had an urge to inflict bodily harm.

"It was truly a pleasure meeting you, Karen," Woody said. "Now I know why Olivia speaks so highly of you. I'll draft some language for your review, which will also include approval rights for the director and lead casting."

Karen's hand lingered on Woody's. "Send it over at your convenience. I can't promise anything. I'm sure you understand." The crystals of her brooch sparkled, along with her eyes, as if Karen had been plugged into an electrical outlet.

To break the current, Olivia moved around the desk. She opened her arms for a hug but received only a back-pat. Karen leaned close to her ear and whispered, "He's a keeper. At your age, though, why don't you two just live together?"

Coffee breath.

Chapter 9
Sparks in the Bathroom . . . Again

Woody tossed his empty Starbucks cup in the trash bin by Karen's office door. He handed Olivia her coat and nudged her into the hall.

"Not one word," he said. Obviously, his help wasn't appreciated. He'd do anything for her, but she didn't understand how to negotiate to win. He got it, though. When it's personal, the emotion changes. This was an emergency, both for him and for her.

Olivia narrowed her eyes and set that jaw of hers on lock. She assumed their relationship was on the line, but he'd never let that happen. He pulled on her arm to rush her back to the lobby. When he spotted Lauren coming in the opposite direction with Pogo and Beauregard, he halted Olivia in front of the restroom. Lauren gripped her puffy coat for protection. The expression of defensiveness on Lauren's face reshuffled Woody's anger card to one of empathy. Still, his words were short when he turned back to Olivia.

"Don't move, Liv. I mean it."

"I'd rather be outside being pelted by sleet," Olivia said.

Woody stepped to Lauren and wrapped his arm around her shoulder. "There's nothing to be nervous about. Karen won't bite.

When an agent is excited about a project, she'll guide you to give her what she wants. Listen between the lines."

Olivia gawked at him, which he secretly enjoyed, and said, "How do you know about what a literary agent wants?"

Woody turned but kept his arm around Lauren. "All business dealings are the same. There's no magic. The only difference is language. Once you figure out who makes what, and how they make it, then the rest is easy. Follow the money."

"Don't patronize me, Woody," Lauren said. "I can handle that kinky-haired witch."

"Go get 'em tiger." He patted Lauren's back and then drilled his gaze into Olivia. "You, Miss Kitty, are coming with me."

"Where?" Olivia said. "Taking me to Yale to get another business lesson?"

Woody retrieved the restroom key from Rick, his blood boiling. He rushed back to unlock the door and pointed the ridiculous clown pencil for Olivia to join him inside. Unisex. They were both legal. The door hissed and latched behind them. Woody exaggerated the turn of the lock to OCCUPIED.

Woody set the pencil next to the sink and planted himself with his back to the mirror. He gripped the edge of the granite counter and studied Olivia's discomfort. "Where were you? You left me winging it in Karen's office for almost an hour."

"Forty minutes," she said.

"Forty-five." No way would he let her off the hook. "Were you late on purpose?"

Olivia shifted in her heels with her wool coat bunched in her arms. "I had to run an errand. We couldn't get a cab. If you hadn't noticed, there's a blizzard outside. I did call Rick to say we were running behind. Didn't he tell you?"

"Running behind is one thing, Liv, but that was way beyond reasonable. You should have sent me a text."

"Right. Trying not to slip in my heels and freeze to death, I'm going to stop and text? With gloves on?" Olivia leaned around him to look in the mirror. "I'm a mess. Twelve blocks in New York is over a mile."

Woody removed his tortoiseshell glasses and squinted, picturing Olivia, her sisters, and the dogs hunched against blowing snow. "A mile and a quarter." He glanced down and pointed to her tan stilettos, his second favorites behind the red ones. "Are *your* dogs okay?"

"Barking with frostbite. My toes have no circulation." Olivia straightened. "And where were *you*? We couldn't find you before we left the hotel. You disappeared."

Woody's mind flashed with a Google map image that expanded from a nine-to-twelve-block area from the Waldorf. He scratched his upper lip. "I had to run an errand too. Ryan and I were talking before that."

He had to hold back a smirk when Olivia leaned around Woody's other side, as if her mirrored self-image might get better. "You should've waited for me before starting that meeting," she said. "Karen's *my* agent, not yours."

"Do you honestly think Karen was going to let me sit in her lobby for that long? If you wanted to run the meeting, then you should've been here on time."

"I wasn't late on purpose. I told you."

"I'm here on your behalf, not mine. I'm trying to help you. If you'd prefer for me to send you a bill for my time, I'll draw one up." He studied Olivia's face. More than anger sat behind her dark eyes. "What else is going on?"

Olivia hesitated. She lowered her eyes to the right, an indication of recalling something and having an internal dialog about it. In an instant, the twelve-block location from Karen's address produced a fat, red exclamation point. It beamed at Fifty-seventh and Fifth Avenues. Woody's stomach dropped, and with the realization his anger dissolved. He'd been so focused on her ring that he'd not considered his own, or whether to even wear one.

"Nothing's going on . . . I've been doing this book business"—Olivia fluttered her hand—"by myself for a long time, thank you very much."

Woody rubbed his face and glanced up at her. "I know you have, Liv. No question about it."

"I wanted to negotiate to get that screenplay on my own, not have you hand it to me."

"You didn't need me to get a shot at it. But I like to negotiate."

"You were messing with me in there."

"Of course, I was. I like to get a rise out of you to keep it interesting. You know . . . drop soap in the grease and see what happens."

Olivia narrowed her eyes. "Mission accomplished, Counselor."

"You're a prosecuting attorney's dream. Too easy, Liv. Next time play with me in the sandbox."

"Tomcats use those for their business. *Miss Kitty* could get sick."

Woody chuckled and spread his hands in surrender. "I won't call you that ever again. But hey, that was fun with Karen. Got what we wanted, right? Good cop, bad cop?"

The pain on Olivia face eased to suppress a smirk. "Kinda was. Did you see the way Karen touched her face and flipped her hair when you talked? She never does that with me."

"I played to her weakness . . . and yours." He twisted his Yale class ring to accentuate the point. "There's one thing she's right about, though. We make a pretty good team."

Olivia glanced at the door and set her damp coat over her case. She kicked off her shoes and moved to stand in front of him.

He held out his arms. "C'mere."

"Tell me in advance what cop I should be," she said and wedged her legs between his knees. "More fun for me."

Woody pulled her to his chest. "Done." Her sweet ginger scent drew his lips to her neck. "At some point instinct will take over, and we won't have to discuss it. Read me." A rush of blood pulsed in his eardrums. "Fair warning—I'm a badass good cop."

Her roving hands made him swoon. "I'm a goodass bad cop . . . on the take—," she said.

Woody tightened his legs against hers. "When did you move to vice? I'm hauling you in."

"Arrest me . . . right here."

Tap. Tap. Tap.

"Woody? Olivia?"

Olivia pulled away with wide eyes. "Perfect timing."

"Sounds like Danny." He glanced at the counter and shook his head. "This granite's too hard, anyway."

Woody stepped to the door, turned the latch to AVAILABLE, and opened it to an odd expression on Olivia's sister's face. Danny's pleading dark eyes stared straight at him, drawing his concern for what it meant.

"Is everything all right?" Woody said. His libido evaporated.

"Ryan called a few minutes ago," Danny said. "He wants a family meeting as soon as we can get back to the hotel."

"Why?"

"He got that email he was waiting for."

Chapter 10

Careful What You Wish For

At two o'clock, Woody pulled an SUV to the entrance of the Waldorf Hotel. He'd turned in the rental sedan to switch it for an Expedition that seated seven. They needed a heavy vehicle with four-wheel drive to battle snow and ice in traffic. The storm was moving north. The first half of the three-hour trek to Pennsylvania would be bad, but then the brutal weather should ease off.

Ryan bolted from the revolving door and jumped into the passenger seat. He unzipped his jacket, and Woody spotted the lump of his gun in a shoulder holster under his sweatshirt.

"Where are the girls and the dogs?" Woody said.

"Still checking out, except for Olivia." Ryan stared at the entrance, fuzzy with blowing snow. "The registration desk is busy, so they won't lose any business because of us. Lauren and Danny have Pogo and Beau. The dogs are on full alert."

"I'm sure there's a line waiting for our rooms. Early checkout shouldn't be a problem. Liv's not with them?"

"She hadn't come down yet."

When Woody had finally urged Lauren from Karen Finnerelli's office and ordered a cab, he'd hustled Olivia, her sisters, and the dogs back to the hotel. The rushed family meeting in the lobby of the Waldorf had consisted of cryptic instructions more than information. He hadn't argued with Ryan's demand to pack up, check out, and move out for a trip to Allenwood Prison in Pennsylvania.

The statement about the dogs sounded odd. Woody took his shot for more. "Anything else you want to tell me while we're alone? You think the dogs know something we don't?"

"Definitely." Ryan never turned his gaze from the door. "Danny and Lauren have the dogs, right?"

"You already said that."

"I should go back in and check on Olivia."

Woody tugged on Ryan's sleeve. "Talk to me. It's just the two of us."

Ryan set his hands over the heat vent. "When your mother asked you to sue Olivia and her sisters over *Indigo to Black*, you opened a pretty big sink hole. This goes way beyond Ellen's book." He glanced toward the hotel's revolving door. "Your father had a twin sister named Althea."

"It was in the obituary you showed me this morning."

"But I found out more. Althea married Simon Pennington four months before her brother's—your father's—funeral in September 1947. My gut told me something was up when the police report ended a month *after* the funeral. No information after that. For all her faults, Ellen Dushane had instinct. She told me once that I should smell the fish before I cooked it, otherwise I'd pay for it all night. Ellen was a wise woman. What she told me applies to this situation. I'll bet somebody was paid off to drop the investigation. It stinks, just like Ellen said. I can smell it."

"Relax, Ryan." Woody turned up the temperature control on the dash.

"I won't relax until we're all in the car."

"What are you talking about?"

"Althea Woodard certainly didn't need to marry for money. She had plenty. But I'm not so sure it wasn't the other way around for

Simon Pennington. He was a lawyer, Woody, with mob ties." Ryan turned. "Deep ties. I did some more checking. You grandfather, William Woodard, died a month before Asher's funeral. Sudden death from a heart attack at fifty-seven."

"What about my grandmother?"

"William's wife, Alice, died from leukemia when Althea and Asher were only eight."

"And Simon Pennington?"

"Died of cardiac arrest in 1982."

"Any kids?"

"None."

"You're making me dig here, Ryan. You think Althea had something to do with my father's death, not my mother?"

"Della was never mentioned in that police report. But do you know who was interviewed and released?"

"Who?"

"Ellen Brooks. Ellen Dushane's maiden name was Brooks."

"I know," Woody said. A chill swept through his chest. "Be careful, Ryan. You're headed down a road we might both regret."

"Your mother's murder confession adds a piece to this that no one else might know about. And the girls' mother drops in another twist. I'll bet no one knew about that little nugget."

"Who found my father's body?"

"Ellen arrived at Asher's apartment when the police were already on the scene. They were acting on an anonymous tip."

"An anonymous tip?" Woody glanced at the windshield. Fat snowflakes melted on the warm glass on impact. "Ellen ran right into them. That's why they interviewed her."

"Maybe somebody set her up."

"All circumstantial. The police probably interviewed dozens of people who knew Asher."

Ryan turned to re-check the hotel entrance. "We'll talk more on the drive. We have three hours, and in this weather, maybe longer. The Ellen component will upset the girls, especially Danny."

Woody's mind whirled to sort out the rush of details. "You think Liv can get information out of Palermo, Rizzo, and Tullio?"

"Liv's in tight because of that mob series. They'll talk to her. Lauren draws pictures of their dogs. Danny arranged for all three of those cockroaches to have therapy dogs . . . These sisters can go where you and I couldn't hope to go on our own. But if something happens to any of them, I'll never forgive myself."

"Do you think *we're* under threat?"

"Possibly. There's something going on in Boston, and I think it's been going on for a long time. We won't be welcome." Ryan squinted and answered Woody's next question before he could ask it. "I know, I know, legal beagle, we need hard evidence."

Woody rubbed his face. Blood started to pound in his ears, but not in a good way, like when he was wrapped with Olivia. "Evidence of what? Enough to convict someone on a murder charge from 1947? My mother confessed and is now dead. I have the damn bottle she said she used to kill Asher with rat poison. Liv's mother's dead and can't corroborate the story. This *case* is dead. There's no one to convict. I only want to connect with a family I didn't know about. And my father had a twin sister who's still alive. Cut me some slack, Ryan."

"Then we need to find out what happened before you do—for *your* benefit. All the original detectives who worked the investigation are dead too. But somebody knows, or it wouldn't have taken so long to get that police report. Tucked away, nice and quiet. And since I forced the issue, I might've . . . piqued some interest."

"From the mob? Althea Pennington?" Woody searched Ryan's face, but his gaze kept landing on Ryan's facial scar. "She's my aunt."

"Althea's nearly ninety. And do you know how much she's worth?"

Woody could only offer a slow shake of his head.

Ryan paused for effect, then said. "A hundred thirty million."

"Jesus."

"At breakfast this morning, you asked me if I was here to protect Olivia. I am, because I need to know what she's marrying into, and so should you. But I want to know what I married into too. Not for the money, mind you, but for the truth."

"I respect that Ryan, but—"

"And when there's a seventy-year trail of deaths that involve that much money, then I guarantee the mob's still interested, which means they're interested in you and my sister-in-law—your future wife. You're the only heir Althea has, and she doesn't even know it. Then again—maybe she does." Ryan zipped his jacket and pulled on his thick gloves. He opened the car door. "Here come the girls. Don't tell them the money part or they'll want you to stop at Tiffany's."

Woody closed his eyes at the word. He'd need to make a call. "I don't see Olivia. Where is she?"

"I'll check."

A rush of blowing snow pelted Woody's face when he swung open the driver's door.

"No. I'll go up. You get Lauren, Danny, and the dogs in the car."

~ · ~ · ~

Bureau drawers slammed. Empty hangers swung in the closet. Thank God no one had seen her crawl around on the bathroom floor. Olivia couldn't think straight. Breathe. Panic solved nothing. Maybe she could ask Woody to stop at Tiffany's.

After Woody had left to pick up a larger car, she'd packed and unpacked her suitcase twice. A double- and triple check for the turquoise ring box yielded nothing.

Trying not to cry, Olivia sat on the corner of the bed and stared at her gold wedding band. Her finger would remind her every day that she'd been an idiot. Now, like that first edition of *Rebecca*, Woody's ring was the only one that mattered. The sentiment of the original. The one.

Olivia shrugged on her coat and took one last gaze around the room. Elegant and empty of her and Woody. It lacked their energy. She dragged her red satchel from the bed, heavy now with her laptop. After securing it over the handle of her suitcase, she moved to the door and tossed the key card on the antique desk with a *clack*. The knock on the door startled her out of a trance.

"Maid service," announced a woman's voice from the hall.

Olivia opened the door. "I'm leaving. We've already checked out. The room is available for you to clean. I put the used towels in the shower and wiped down the counter and mirror. The bed's untouched since you made it this morning, but the sheets need changing."

"I'll wait until you're ready." The woman had a kind, motherly face. She'd understand. She had a cart of spray bottles and a vacuum cleaner.

Olivia shifted in her ruined shoes, their once-pliable leather now stiff. "Did you happen to see a turquoise ring box when you cleaned the room?" She waited for a memory to brighten the woman's expression.

"No, ma'am. But if I do find anything, I turn it in to House-keeping, and then it goes to Lost and Found. The hotel contacts the guest."

"Thank you. Should I talk to Housekeeping?"

"Just tell the staff at the front desk." The wrinkles around the woman's eyes softened. "A pretty ring?"

Olivia's lip quivered. She swallowed the horse pill of emotion that burned her throat. "The most beautiful ring in the world."

The woman responded with a sympathetic press of her lips.

The wheels on her suitcase measured the distance past nine rooms to the elevator. Before she pressed the button, Olivia glanced into her satchel one more time. She pulled out the crunched bag containing Woody's wedding band. When she cracked open the velvet box, the bag fell to the floor.

She'd not had the time to really study his ring, all by herself, to be alone with what it meant to her, and what it would mean to Woody. Tiffany's Adam had been right. The tiny ropes of elegant beading along the edges were exquisite, the work of a master craftsman. She closed her eyes to see it with the tip of her finger. Smooth. Endless, like micro rosaries of whispers and sighs. Every bump became her and Woody's future journey, linking together their family histories to become something new. Neither she nor Woody were particularly religious, but right now those Holy Ghosts swirled around her in the empty hall.

"Did you take my ring, Adam?" she whispered. "Because if you did, it would be the meanest thing you've ever done, tantamount to torture. You don't want Woody to wear this ring, do you?"

Adam's indelible deep voice that never answered her back, but they morphed to the musical words of Woody's:

At some point, instinct will take over, and we won't even have to discuss it.

The sudden whir of a vacuum and a waft of bleach started a new phase of this pilgrimage, a sanitation of her core. Suck it in. *Toughen up and play in Woody's sandbox. Stop living life through prose.* She snapped the ring box shut, picked up the bag from the floor, and tucked the package back into her briefcase. There were no ghosts. She had screwed this up all by herself. The music needed to be faced—and a symphony waited for her in the car.

Olivia reached for the elevator button, but the arrival bell chimed before she could press it. When the doors parted, Woody's face registered surprise, then relief. He lunged for her.

"Where have you been?" he said and nearly lifted her off her feet. "Thank God. You had me frantic." Woody's breath became hers with the deep kiss.

She inhaled. "I . . . I had to make sure I didn't leave anything in the room."

Chapter 11
The Sting

On Friday afternoon, Althea Woodard Pennington set aside an hour in her favorite room of the Beacon Hill house: her study, a private space in what was once a very public house. Showy parties. Fund-raisers. Three o'clock teas. Secret meetings with cigar smoke and thugs.

Now, Althea sat at her Chippendale desk and scratched out checks: Animal Rescue League, Photos for Cures, Cradles to Crayons, and Artists for Humanity. The second stack heaped with regrets, accompanied by checks, that she wouldn't be able to attend the holiday fund-raisers at the Boston Opera, the Museum of Fine Arts, the Institute of Contemporary Arts, and the Children's Museum. Begging mail.

Quiet settled over the house. Too quiet. Since Ducky had passed away, her beloved springer spaniel, this third holiday season without him held loneliness. Staff didn't count. Parties had become tiresome years ago. Once the name Pennington had been etched on a brass plaque, the thrill was gone. Board members only invited her to attract new money to their cause. While flattering at one time, now she was no more than a dowager to round out the headcount for the caterers.

Althea raised her eyes, watery with thoughts, to the window. Outside, the sky darkened over the compact back garden, making the air appear dense and cold. Bare trees flailed in a kicked-up wind. The perennial bushes were no more than stiff claws reaching out for warmth. Snow flurries peppered the frigid air. It would get worse, so the weatherman said on the television.

The long, strident ring of the desk phone startled her. A call from the outside. Internal calls announced themselves with a short, bell-like chime. Althea set the silver pen on the leather blotter and waited for Posey to answer it. The Christmas tree next to the fireplace drew her gaze, the personal tree, the one only she could decorate. The glass-domed anniversary clock sat on the mantle, ticking and spinning like a meteorological instrument mapping the approaching storm.

The fresh forest scent of the tree had a cleansing effect. In a wash of white lights, silver-framed small photos dangled from red satin ribbons over the branches, all of her and Simon, from their wedding day in 1947 to the day he died in 1982. Dotted between them were petite Swarovski crystal ornaments—: bees. A private joke. Each year since Simon's death, she added one of the crystal insects to commemorate the occasion. This season's addition brought the count to thirty-three.

The house enjoyed three Christmas trees to honor her upcoming ninetieth birthday, a day meant to be shared. The ornaments on the Fraser fir in the living room were themselves works of art, most of which were thank-you gifts from museums. The Norway spruce in the foyer held silver bells and miniature musical instruments, decorated by her driver. Not much else for Freed to do. She didn't go out much these days.

"Mr. Corelli's on the phone, Mrs. Pennington."

Althea turned, her short respite cut even shorter. Posey's always-busy fingers gripped the polished-wood frame of the doorway. After so many years, her housekeeper kept a trim figure. Her black uniform hung without a wrinkle. When their eyes met, no more needed to be said. Althea nodded and gave a short wave of her spotted hand. Posey lingered for a concerned beat before retreating.

"Tony," Althea said, her tone flat when she picked up the receiver. She fingered her long rope of textured fresh-water pearls like a rosary of sorrows.

"Happy holidays, Althea. I got a Mister Sad Face when I sorted through the mail today. Our little buddies are waiting for their presents."

The sinister edge in Tony's voice never changed, and he was now in his eighties. Years of a cigar smoker's rasp. Tony still went into the office every day, seven days a week. Simon's former partner was a tick, one she thought had been scratched off when Simon had died, but Tony's head still sat lodged beneath her skin—to the tune of one hundred thousand per year, every year. While more fortunate people kicked off the holidays with lavish shopping, hers started with extortion.

"I haven't had time. I'm really quite busy." Althea rubbed the skin between her brows with her forefinger.

"Why do you make me call? Think I'll die before Christmas?"

"I'll raise a toast to your passing."

Tony's crass laugh quieted. "By Monday. On my desk Monday. No—wait—send Freed over before five today. The weather's gonna get bad."

While she preferred, at this moment, to slam the receiver, Tony had trumped the satisfaction. Maybe this would be the last time—the last birthday, the last Christmas—that required a personal visit. Althea set her polished finger on the cradle button and pressed Freed's extension. It would forward to his mobile. What he did in between her calls, she hadn't a clue.

"Bring the car around, Freed," she said when he answered. "I need to run an errand."

"Yes, Mrs. Pennington. I'll be right there."

Althea pulled out a fresh envelope from the desk drawer. The flap had been embossed with a scrolled *P*, sandwiched by a small *A* and *W*. As she did every year since 1982, she wrote out the name of the law firm that still bore her husband's name: Pennington & Corelli, LLC. A shame that people didn't send handwritten notes anymore. Though this was an unsavory one, Althea's old-world, flowing script inked the evidence that she was still alive—and still a force to be reckoned with.

Althea couldn't cease the slight shake of the pen as she made out the check to *Little Buddies*. Tony would never leave her alone.

"Here's your goddamned check, you miserable bastard," she whispered to herself, pressing harder. "You're nothing but a low-life hood."

~ · ~ · ~

By four o'clock on Friday afternoon, the heavy snow had eased to sleet as Ryan drove across the Pennsylvania border. Olivia ended a call with Ben Franklin, the warden of Allenwood Prison.

"Ben's putting us up," she said. "He's arranging for us to talk with Palermo, Tullio, and Rizzo when we get there."

"I've never spent the night in a prison," Lauren said. "Jail, yeah, but prison?"

"We're not going to be in a cell. He has another area."

"Like what?"

"The infirmary."

Woody grimaced. "Not sure I like that idea, Liv."

Ryan chuckled. "The dogs will."

"Are you kidding?" Danny said. "Mobster snuggle time."

Olivia nodded. "It'll give us more time with the boys."

"When were you in jail, Lauren?" Woody said. He didn't turn, but he kept his focus on the tablet.

"When I was fifteen. Dad called the cops to arrest me when I rode Danny's Big Wheel down the middle of a busy street. He thought it was a big joke, but it scared the crap out of me."

"Happens all the time," Ryan said. "Parents call to teach their kids a lesson. Works better in small towns where not much goes on."

Danny turned to Lauren. "I never got my Big Wheel back."

Olivia ignored the banter to focus on Woody, her view partially blocked by the passenger headrest. He'd used the three-hour trek to research the information Ryan had relayed about the police report. A coiled charging cord jiggled as Woody typed. Finally, she couldn't stand it.

"Find anything more?" she said and stroked Beauregard's long torso that stretched over her and Lauren's laps. Sound asleep. Pogo took up the whole third row of seats in the SUV, on his back with his paws curled, as if rigor mortis had set in. The dogs were exhausted from the tension and the weather.

Woody turned. "Simon Pennington's law firm is alive and well. You should see the string of thugs they defend. Most get off on technicalities."

"Either that or they have help," Ryan said.

Danny leaned forward and stuck her head between the front seats. "Look up their charities, Woody. Don't law firms list the ones they support to brag about their community relations?"

"I think you just saved me half an hour, Danny."

Ryan shook his head. "Outta the mouths of babes."

"I wish we had those letters between Asher and Della," Olivia said. "They could tell us more. Asher might've hinted at what was going on between them."

"Or at least be able to interpret the tone of their relationship," Lauren said. "We've only heard Della's side. And I wouldn't exactly call her reliable. Sorry, Woody."

Woody held up his hand. "Understood. And I think you're both right."

Olivia poked his shoulder. "Can you call Margie to overnight those letters from your office? They'll get here by ten tomorrow morning if you can catch her."

Woody threw her an assessing glance at the order. Nevertheless, he pulled out his phone.

To the lilt of Woody's voice, Olivia admired Beauregard on her lap. His paws twitched when his eyes fluttered, surely with dreams of snow, glittery rings, and his family. Palermo would be happy to revisit their bond through touch. Behind her, Pogo snored, still on his back with his legs splayed. "What did you do to these guys, Danny? They're comatose."

"While we were waiting for you and Woody to come down to the car, I loaded them up with an early dinner and gave them a good walk in the snow. Top 'em off, clean 'em out, and off they go to snoozeland. They love to ride."

Olivia went quiet, reliving her Waldorf moment before Woody found her at the elevator. Her sisters surely knew what she had been doing up in the room. Lauren glanced at her and raked the wavy brown fur on Beauregard's back.

Woody disconnected and reattached the charger to his phone. "The letters are coming to the prison by ten."

"Excellent," Olivia said and thumped Beauregard's ribs. "We'll set up in a conference room and pass them down the line. A lawyer, a cop, a writer, an artist, and a professional shopper. We'll each see something different."

"Hey," Danny said. "I'm the director of a charity."

Ryan glimpsed in the rearview mirror. "Professional shopper."

Chapter 12
Goin' To Prison

At five o'clock on Friday afternoon, Warden Ben Franklin administered hugs and handshakes at the security entrance of Allenwood Federal Prison. While Ben's imposing visage could intimidate even the worst offenders, his manner today was warm and welcoming. Olivia never wanted to get him angry, though, not at six-foot-five and in a suit that appeared bullet-proof. Ben's African-American features exuded strength, resilience, and quiet defiance of bureaucracy, his voice smooth with unchallenged authority. For the last hour of the drive, Olivia had taken notes of Woody's instructions for their discussion with *the boys*. Cut the niceties short and stay on point.

Olivia liked Ben and tested his willingness to bend the rules. Lauren liked Ben, too, and enjoyed challenging him with tit-for-tat. And Ben considered Danny a dear friend and colleague in their partnership to train and supply therapy dogs to those life-sentence inmates with disabilities. The deal for funding the program from the Pogo Charitable Trust had been sealed with a stamped paw print, on notepaper ripped from Lauren's sketchbook. Woody had only previously met Ben on the rooftop of the prison when he'd picked up

Beauregard in a helicopter. With a wide smile of even white teeth, Ben gave Woody's hand a warm shake. Ryan stepped forward and grasped the warden's bear paw of a hand. Hugs were administered all around, last being Danny, who became a Chatty Cathy doll in Ben's long arms. They had become quite close in their work together with the first publicized project of the Pogo Trust. Beauty shots of Ben with civic leaders lined both Danny's and Ben's offices.

"Palermo will be happy to hear your voice in person, Olivia," Ben said. "He complains about the audio on your video conferences. Here's a copy of Palermo's manuscript you emailed for me to print off."

Olivia tucked the clipped stack of paper into her satchel. "They're convenient, but nothing replaces talking in person."

Ben hitched up the knees of his suit pants and stooped. Pogo and Beauregard shimmied their hips to compete for Ben's embrace. "I missed these boys. Palermo wants see Beau." He raised his dark eyes to Olivia. "I arranged an early dinner for Palermo, Tullio, and Rizzo. They demanded veal parmigiana to talk." Ben chuckled, deep and low. "They're waiting for you. I had to put you in the big conference room, because they all insisted on bringing their dogs."

"How long do we get?" Olivia said.

"Now that they're full, they might fall asleep on you. I'd give it no more than half an hour but take all the time you need. They're not going anywhere."

"Did the dogs get dinner too?" Danny said. "I'd like a rundown of their diet. I don't trust those goombahs to not slip them people food."

Ben shook his head. "The handler makes sure. Let's go."

Lauren's snow boots squeaked to keep up. "Which dogs did you give the boys, Danny?"

Without stopping, Danny turned her head. "Palermo's got Willy, the golden retriever. Rizzo wanted Cheeks, the shar-pei. Tullio has Sparkles, the Jack Russell."

"What about Lionetti?"

"He passed away two weeks ago," Olivia said over her shoulder.

"I got his interviews, but I'm sorry to see him go. He was a colorful one. Big-hearted killer."

Ben didn't break stride. "Cancer."

Olivia grasped Woody's hand. A percussion band of loafer taps, heel clicks, boot squeaks, syncopated dog-toy squeals, and the tick of canine toenails accompanied Ben down a long corridor of shiny cement. Buzzes to pass through three wire-mesh doors interrupted the rhythm. Ben stopped at a conference room door. He nodded through the window for the guard to join them in the hall.

"Post yourself out here," he said. "No one goes in or out during this meeting."

The guard nodded and retreated to stand at the wall.

"What do you think, Ben?" Woody said. "I'm in favor of Ryan and me sitting behind the glass to listen. I doubt these guys will be as open with a cop and a lawyer in the room."

"I agree. I'll be in there with you. They trust Olivia, Lauren, and Danny. The dogs will keep the conversation flowing."

Ryan's gaze lingered on Danny and Lauren, and then settled on Olivia. "Are you three comfortable with that plan? Boys in the booth?"

"I'm game." Olivia glanced at Woody. The edges of his mouth upturned when she patted her satchel. "The three of them are used to my taking notes for the video interviews."

"They know me," Danny said, "and so do the dogs."

Lauren shifted, uncomfortable. She stepped to Woody. "I want to be in the listening room too. I'll sketch. Karen wants more drawings, and I like watching better than being watched."

"Fine." Woody held up three fingers to Olivia and Danny. "Remember, keep them talking, guide and redirect with questions, and don't offer any details of what we know."

"Got it, Counselor," Olivia said and flicked the end of her nose with her forefinger. "Meet you on the flip side with some prison food." She turned to her younger sister. "Good cop or bad cop? Pick one, Danny." Her glance at Woody produced a low chuckle.

Danny turned with her expressive brown eyes. "I'll be bad cop when I kick your foot, Liv." She reached into her purse and pulled out a small spray bottle of cologne. The air filled with a soft aroma of lilies and jasmine. "Palermo likes this scent. It'll butter him up."

Ryan shook his head and scratched his chin. "Stuff makes me crazy. Better get in there." He nodded to Pogo and Beauregard and held out both hands. "No toys."

"Not in the meeting, kids." Danny plucked the rubber Garfield from Beauregard's mouth and a worn, red-lipped bullfrog from Pogo's. She handed the slimy toys to Ryan with a *meow* and a *ribbit*. Two curly tails—one brown, one black—started to wag when Ben Franklin ushered the dogs inside first.

~ · ~ · ~

Olivia stepped into the conference room with bravado. She spread her arms and announced, "You're killin' me here. All three of you together for little 'ol us?"

"Olivia! Danny!" Tullio and Rizzo said in unison.

A hint of a smile shifted the crags on Palermo's face, but he didn't speak.

Pogo and Beauregard didn't react, waiting for their signal from Danny. She held out her hand, "Stay . . . "

"You bad boys being good?" Olivia pulled out a rolling chair. She reached into her briefcase and set a ruled pad and pen in front of her. With a rip of the paper, the page with her pre-meeting notes stood ready for additions.

Three octogenarians in orange jumpsuits, all of dubious fit and size, sat around the conference table, each with a dog. Danny had done a good job matching the mobsters with their companions. Sparkles, the Jack Russell, stood on Tullio's lap with his tail whipping in a blur. Tullio's compact, spherical form resembled an old Humpty Dumpty gone bad. The thick lenses of the mobster's black-frame glasses enlarged his watery brown eyes to twice their normal size. Sparkles released a quick yap that triggered Cheeks, the quiet shar-pei sitting next to Rizzo. Cheeks's muzzle puffed with a noiseless, gee-shucks response. Rizzo's spongy jowls on his long face appeared to pull down the bags under his wary eyes. His easygoing manner and humor disguised an intense ruthlessness. Both men were competitive, but Palermo still held court. Controlled. Calculating. Cunning. And loyal—to Olivia. His eyes, cloudy with cataracts, could see right through her like no one she'd ever known. The man could smell fear, and he took every advantage of the talent.

Palermo stroked Willy's ginger-colored floppy ears, listening. The golden retriever's eyes shifted, on alert.

Danny stepped to Palermo and whispered in his hairy ear. The don had lost his sight long ago, but his other senses were razor sharp. He respected Danny, not only for her floral scent but for her lack of fear.

With a snap of her fingers, Danny released Beauregard and Pogo to greet the other dogs. Beauregard trotted directly to Palermo and licked the don's long, bony fingers.

"General B is here," he said. "I missed him, Danny." Palermo stilled and inhaled. "You wore your signature perfume. You're trying too hard, my dear."

Danny didn't answer. With Ryan listening beyond a one-way mirror, Olivia figured her younger sister didn't want to encourage Palermo into an extended personal exchange.

"We get good snacks for gummin' stories to you, Olivia." Tullio said, and then let out a loud cackle. "So, how's mine comin' along, sweets?" The Jack Russell tiptoed a circle on Tullio's lap. The mobster winced. "Watch the jewelry, Sparkles."

"Don't push me." Olivia uncapped her pen. "I just delivered Palermo's draft to my agent this morning." She retrieved the water-stained, curled copy of the manuscript from her case and slid it across the table. "Can you read this to Palermo? I need feedback."

Tullio pulled the paper stack forward and set his face close to the first page. He grimaced. "Can't. Type's too small. Blow it up." He slid the manuscript to Rizzo.

"Forget about it." Rizzo shoved the papers across the table to Olivia as if it were a chunk of stinky cheese. She suspected that jealousy provoked their rejection to read about Palermo. Mob egos. She tucked the manuscript back into her briefcase.

Bored with the conversation, Palermo waved his skeletal hand. "We pay the guard to do that. He reads your chapters to us aloud." His clouded eyes stared at nothing. "You want something, Olivia. Questions sit in your mouth like a loaded gun."

Danny took a seat next to Olivia. Pogo followed and sat at her knees. Beauregard remained by Palermo's side with Willy. Five dogs held a gossipy conversation with a collective shift of their eyes.

The conference table became a drum for Olivia's fingertips. Her gaze shot to the one-way mirror. Woody had wanted her to open with something personal. "I'm engaged to be married. Should I do it? You know my history . . . All three of you do."

Tullio slapped the table and laughed. "Condolences to the unlucky fella. He's going to have full hands. Hope he doesn't drive a white Suburban."

Olivia tensed. *How did Tullio know that was the car that killed her husband?*

"Or have kids," Rizzo said. "I wouldn't call you a natural-born mother."

Rizzo delivered a second stab to her heart. Olivia took a cleansing breath to keep her composure.

"That's despicable, Tullio," she said. "I had a mother, so I know how to do it. I had a husband, too, so I know how to be a wife." To earn their trust, Olivia had been honest about her past with these men. The extraction of information for their stories required *quid pro quo*. The subject of Woody, though, had been discussed with only Palermo. For reasons she couldn't explain, his approval did mean something to her.

Rizzo turned his chair to the wall and said, "*Garçon!* Bring us champagne to toast the lucky lady!"

"What's the poor schmuck's name?" Tullio patted Sparkles's

haunches.

Palermo remained still, listening, only his fingers moving, raking through Beauregard's fur.

The sting from the "full hands" dig lingered. Still, Olivia said. "Woodrow Rainey."

At the mention of the name, invisible mob recall stretched around the table. Tullio and Rizzo exchanged glances, and then shrugged.

"Never heard of him," Rizzo said.

Palermo finally showed his yellowed teeth. "Not many men could have negotiated my Beauregard away from me, Olivia. Quite a show of feathers Mr. Rainey spread for you. I believe there's an exotic bird in South America that puts on a show like that to earn his mate."

Heat crept up her neck. "Didn't he, though. You two have talked, but Woody kept that conversation confidential. I respect that."

"Good talk . . . about you."

She didn't need Palermo's approval, but Olivia had to admit the statement meant the world to her. Their soul-bearing conversations for his memoir had earned him the right to an opinion. He was protecting her. Danny nudged Olivia's shoe, a reminder to stay on point—gather information by hook from crooks.

Danny leaned back and swiveled her seat, dangling her wrists from the arms of the chair in bad-kitten mobster style. "We're doing a little digging into his family, because we want to make sure Rainey is good enough for Olivia."

Olivia leaned forward and folded her hands, beaming inside that Woody was listening. "I have concerns. We need your help."

Palermo raised an eyebrow and trained his sightless gaze toward her voice. He didn't comment.

"What's he do for a living?" Tullio said.

Palermo raised his hand to stop Olivia from answering. "He's a lawyer."

"Who are his people?" Rizzo said. Cheeks turned his head from Rizzo to Olivia. The shar-pei's mug of short, wrinkled fuzz lagged a fraction of a beat behind his eyes.

Olivia inhaled, fighting the pull of the one-way glass. "From what we found out, Woody has one relative left alive. She's elderly and lives in Boston."

Rizzo turned. "Who works Boston now?"

"Tony. Tony Corelli," Tullio said.

"He's still alive?"

"Think so. Old as dirt— eighties, nineties. Nice racket, though. I'll give him that. Nice voice, too, back in the day. Did gigs at the Rocket Room in the Venus Club downtown. I went up there a few times in my prime days." Tullio started snapping his fingers in a slow rhythm and started to sing. "Volare . . . Oh . . . Oh . . . Couldn't tell him from Dean Martin. Hand to God." Tullio's voice came out like sandpaper coated with tapioca. "Tony gave up show biz to be a lawyer. Took care of all the business up there."

Olivia eyed him, hoping the mobster's rendition of "Volare" wouldn't be in her head too long. "What kind of business?"

"You know . . . business." Tullio's expression sobered.

"What was the name of his law firm?" Olivia scratched swirly doodles to fake taking notes.

"Pennington and Corelli," Rizzo said.

"And Pennington? What about him?"

Palermo tapped the table. "Will you be changing your name, Olivia?"

The art of redirect without answering the question had been mastered by the don. Time for a redirect of the redirect. "I haven't decided," she said. "Depends on your answer. Who is Pennington?"

The room quieted. Tullio let out a slow whistle and darted his gaze to Rizzo.

Rizzo shrugged. "Happens sometimes."

Beauregard and Pogo did a tandem pivot of their heads to Olivia. Her serve. "What happens?"

"Simon Pennington. Old lady Althea's husband. He ordered a hit on her twin brother but somebody else got there first. The stiff was a bloated mess. The guys chucked their cookies and left." Rizzo shook his head. "Story made the rounds for months. One you never want to hear around the Saturday night lasagna, I tell ya."

Palermo raised his finger with a slow bob. "Don't write that, Olivia. We don't know who did the job."

Tullio's chin gained a fat roll as he dipped his head. "Could compromise yourself."

"When was this?" Olivia's stomach tightened. She'd heard worse in her interviews with Ardy Griffin, but this was a description of Woody's father. And Woody was listening.

Tullio and Rizzo volleyed their gazes to Palermo. The old don savored the attention for a moment, and then said, "Nineteen forty-seven."

"Good year for Simon, though." Rizzo laughed. "Simon says, right Palermo?"

Palermo worked his jaw. Images appeared to flash behind his milky eyes. "The man was dishonorable. He deserved to die, but not soon enough. Took thirty-five years."

Olivia inhaled at the double standard. The room oozed with dishonor, but these guys had a caste system for killing, bribery, extortion, and torture. "How did Simon Pennington die?"

"Heart attack in 1982." By his expression, Olivia knew Palermo wasn't going to elaborate.

She turned to Rizzo. "What did you mean by 'Simon says'?"

"Simon *said* and his wife *did*." Rizzo nodded for emphasis. "He got to stick a hose in his wife's family's bank account when he married her, but she got him back good."

"How so?" Olivia couldn't keep up. Her pen had become a blur, not with doodles but with real notes. Danny nudged her foot beneath the table, a signal they'd reached pay dirt and bad cop territory.

Rizzo chuckled. "Old Man Woodard told him she'd been disinherited *after* they got married."

Tullio joined in with a guffaw. "'Althea *says*.'"

"Is that her name? Althea Pennington?" Danny said and tapped the table. Her gaze floated toward the one-way glass. Olivia pushed against Danny's black boot to stop her, sensing Woody, Lauren, and Ryan closing the distance, with Ben watching the show.

Tullio pushed up the end of his nose in an exaggeration. "Althea Woodard Pennington. Miss Snootity-snoot." He ruffled the Jack Russell's ears. Sparkles squinted and leaned into Tullio's fingers. "Charity takes bucks, right little buddy?"

Rizzo's magnified eyes filled the frames of his glasses. "I forgot about Little Buddies. Nice bonus program Tony had goin'." He elbowed Palermo's arm. "Wasn't the stiff Althea's twin?"

Palermo jerked away. His opaque eyes disappeared behind thin-skinned lids. "Is she Woody's people, Olivia?"

Five pairs of canine eyes shifted at once for her answer.

$$\sim \cdot \sim \cdot \sim$$

"Don't answer, Liv," Woody whispered. He set his forehead against the glass, willing her to hold back from Palermo.

Lauren set her hand on his arm. "Maybe they're not talking about Asher."

"I'm convinced of it." He squeezed Lauren's fingers. "My father was a dead man. Della didn't know."

Ryan stepped forward. "These guys have nothing to lose by telling the truth. They trust Olivia."

With his back to the cinder-block wall, Ben crossed his thick arms. "The mob can't get to them in here, Woody. They're perfectly safe, and they know it."

Lauren glared. "But *we're* not safe, Ben."

The speaker remained silent for what seemed like an eternity. Then Danny's voice erupted from it, not Olivia's. "Althea is Woody's aunt."

Ryan winced. Woody closed his eyes. Lauren groaned.

Ben blew out a breath. "There's room at the Why Me Inn, Woody. Get what you needed?"

"Right now, I don't know what I need," Woody said, his forehead still resting against the glass. "My aunt's too old to do time."

Ryan set his hand on Woody's shoulder. "Not Althea—He's talking about Tony Corelli. We need to see the autopsy reports for Simon and Asher."

"And meet your aunt, Woody," Lauren said, "but we should see what's in those letters between Della and Asher first."

Woody apparently needed a lot, but he wanted none of it. He lifted his head and drank in Lauren's concerned dark eyes. "They'll be here tomorrow morning."

"FedEx or UPS?" Ben said.

Woody turned. "FedEx. Two packages are coming. Can you give us this conference room tomorrow?"

"Whatever you need. I'll get those autopsy reports for you. A buddy of mine at the FBI can get them."

Ryan glanced at the one-way glass. "Hopefully not a Little Buddy, Ben."

Chapter 13
Family Revealed

At eight thirty on Saturday morning, charging cords snaked across the long table in the conference room, pumping juice into various devices. Olivia tapped on her laptop. Woody poked the screen on his tablet. Ryan swore at the virtual keys on his smartphone for being too small, Lauren ground colored pencils in a manual sharpener to make a point about her low opinion of high technology. Danny had risen at dawn to oversee the feeding of Pogo, Beauregard, Willy, Cheeks, and Sparkles. She'd literally gone to the dogs.

Olivia needed quiet for her retreat into a writing cave. Even a private cell would have been acceptable. The five of them had spent the night in the prison infirmary—thankfully with all empty beds. No curtains to offer privacy, and a line of thick glass windows let in too much halogen light from the hall. Their embedded wire created a shadowed grid over the walls. The spider-web effect reminded her of the similar moody wall projection in Alfred Hitchcock's *Suspicion*.

Taking turns in the bathroom commenced a ballet of preparations for a night of little sleep. Olivia had immediately become selfconscious. No tee-hees from her sisters at seeing Woody in his under-wear; no cracking of jokes when Ryan clicked off the safety and set his gun on the nightstand. In the bed next to her, Olivia had listened for Woody's breath to settle into unsettled dreams. She had attempted to read the posted signs: guidelines to avoid communicable diseases, reminders to inmates of their legal rights, and instructions to the medical personnel for the proper way to wash their hands. Everyone in this prison was on display, including her, Woody, Lauren, Danny, and Ryan. Pogo and Beauregard had earned a sleepover in the Pogo Trust Canine Care Room with the other dogs. It had been Ben's idea for the trust to fund the addition as part of the deal to supply dogs to disabled lifers.

Now, wired on coffee in an empty stomach, Olivia set aside her exhaustion to dig into the research of what they'd learned from Palermo, Tullio, and Rizzo.

"Anything?" Olivia said to the room.

"Only what Ryan already found," Woody said.

A tower of blueberry muffins sat on a paper plate untouched. The steel coffee pot, however, had been emptied an hour ago. Olivia reached for her thick paper cup of cold brew. No ceramics allowed, or anything that could be shattered to become a weapon. Ben managed the rules: which ones required adherence and which ones could be broken. Olivia scoffed at the contradiction of having to drink from paper this morning while Ben allowed Ryan to keep his gun after last evening's conversation with "the boys".

"What did you see last night, Lauren?" Woody didn't raise his eyes from his tablet's screen.

"I'm drawing Palermo's face. Did you guys notice how his hand slowed on Beauregard's head when you asked about Simon Pennington, Liv?"

Olivia craned her neck to inspect the image on Lauren's sketch pad. "No, but I think you nailed his expression. I watched his face, not his hand."

"I did," Ryan said. "Good eye, Lauren. Palermo knows more about Simon Pennington than he let on. He was pissed."

"I didn't sense any anger toward me," Olivia said. "We spar and psych each other out, but it's a game."

"No, Liv," Woody said. "He was protecting you—us. Tullio was the target. When you asked that question about Althea, Palermo knew I was listening."

"How could you tell?"

"Because you sounded like a lawyer," Ryan said and spread hands. "C'mon, Liv. You knew the answer to the question. At that moment, Palermo heard in your voice that you were coached." Ryan stepped to the conference room door and scanned the hallway through the window. "Where's Ben with those autopsy reports? Where's Danny?" He turned. "All I know is that if a guy goes down under suspicious circumstances, you gotta look at his competition. Who hated Simon? Althea? Palermo certainly does."

"Tony Corelli," Woody said. "When I worked at a big firm in Boston, the partners fought about everything— clients, billings, big cases—even competed to steal the secretaries who could keep their mouths shut when the wives called. It's a matter of keeping your friends close and your enemies closer."

Ryan paced. "Tony . . . Simon . . . Althea . . . Asher." The latch turned on the door. He stopped when it opened.

Danny stepped into the conference room, beaming. "Our little buddies are doing great. This program is working."

Lauren raised her eyes from the sketch pad and smacked the table. "Unbelievable, Danny! How do you do that?" She shook her finger at Olivia's laptop. "Liv, check out Boston charities. Dig more about Little Buddies. We need to see Althea and Simon together at some function. A picture."

"What did I say?" Danny set her purse on a conference chair.

"If Little Buddies is a charity, maybe they hosted events."

Olivia's fingers tapped faster. "Right. And so did the major arts groups—museums, the opera, symphony, and ballet."

Danny tucked her hair behind her ears. "I take full credit for whatever it was I said."

Ben charged into the conference room with a raised brow. "I got two out of three autopsy reports. No autopsy was done on Simon

Pennington, but I got the death certificate. Only Old Man William Woodard and his son, Asher, had autopsies."

"Give us all you got, Ben," Ryan said.

"And FedEx is here, but all packages need to be scanned and logged. Big haul for the holidays. Even I can't bypass that process."

"We wouldn't dare ask you to hurry—but hurry," Lauren said.

Like a blackjack dealer, Ben slid aside the muffin plate and lined up the documents on the conference table. "Merry Christmas," he said over his shoulder as he exited the conference room.

Olivia split her attention between the internet and Woody. He adjusted his glasses and leaned over the conference table. Ryan joined him with the same stance. They slid the documents like trades of oversize baseball cards. Olivia kept clicking links of archived charity functions, but kept her ears perked, listening for any gore. Her gaze made the rounds of her sisters. They didn't want the grisly details, either, but like drivers spotting roadkill ahead, the three of them were compelled to look.

"Hmmm . . . William Woodard died in August of 1947," Woody said. "Same year as my father, only one month apart. Fairly young. Only fifty-seven. Odd to think of him as my grandfather. I'm older than that now."

"Ryan leaned over Woody's shoulder. "Says cardiac arrest, acute myocardial infarction. Maybe something triggered it."

"Only look at the facts, Ryan. No conjecture yet."

"Then here's a fact—Chuck Yeager broke the sound barrier a month later."

Woody smirked. "Jackie Robinson joined the Dodgers."

Lauren worked a beige-colored pencil over the likeness of Palermo's hand. She raised her eyes. "Harry Truman created the CIA that year. Bye, bye *Howdy Doody*— hello Cold War."

"Good one, Lauren."

"Speaking of . . ." Olivia said. "In 1947, Anne Frank's diary was first published in the Netherlands as *Het Achterhuis* and was translated to *The Diary of a Young Girl*. Della had the first English edition in her collection, Woody." Olivia pursed her lips. "Shouldn't have sold it."

Woody narrowed his eyes. "Don't start, Liv."

Olivia held up her hands. "Can I deposit my check yet?"

"No wire from the auction house. You'll be the first to know when it comes in."

Danny rocked in the conference chair and peeled the pleated paper from a blueberry muffin. "In 1947, an alien spaceship landed in Roswell, New Mexico. We totally believe it. Ryan and I saw a whole documentary on SyFy about the cover up."

"Is this true, Ryan?" Woody said and peered over his glasses.

"Yeah. We watched it," Ryan said. "I've seen my fair share of cover-ups. Start with City Hall, my friend. Some bad decisions get made for good money." Ryan pulled Asher's autopsy report in front of him. "Whoa. Wait a minute. This says cause of death was suicide. What the hell?"

"Let me see that." Woody made a forty-five-degree turn of the document. "Somebody was paid off at the medical examiner's office. The only explanation."

"No conjecture, remember?" Ryan said. "September 4, 1947. Says that Asher died an hour before he was found."

Woody picked up the three-page report. Olivia stopped typing. Lauren stopped drawing. Danny swallowed and set the rest of the muffin on a napkin.

"Blood analysis is like Greek, but here goes," Woody said and cleared his throat. "Indicates high concentrations of 4-hydroxy-coumarin, 4-thiocheromenone, aluminum phosphides, brodifacoum, and diphacinone. I recognize zinc, calcium and vitamin D3. That's the cholecalciferol. The strychnine is obvious." He glanced at Ryan. "Those other chemicals ring any bells?"

"Rat poison," Ryan said. "Mostly anticoagulants. Thins the blood to where the rat bleeds to death internally. Can take a few days to work, up to two weeks, depending on how much is ingested."

"Inhumane," Danny said. "Should be outlawed."

"I've seen it first-hand. Pets and kids get into the stuff when it's stored in basements or garages. Poison Control gets flooded with calls in the summer."

Olivia shook her head. "Suicide? No one would be foolish enough to kill themselves that way. I'm completely with you on this, Woody. Della confessed to us that she put rat poison in the coffee pot after Asher bedded her, then kicked her out—cruelly, I might add. In that hour between Della leaving and the cops showing up, hit men went into his apartment."

"And so did Mom," Lauren said and pointed, "according to that police report."

"They let her go," Danny said. "Mom didn't know anything."

Olivia flipped through her yellow notepad. "I go back to what Tullio said—from his graphic comparison to Saturday night lasagna. It sounded like days, but that couldn't be true. The report says there was an hour between Asher's death and when he was found. Can all those chemicals cause death in only an hour?"

"I don't know," Woody said, "but the list certainly confirms he was poisoned, and it jibes with what my mother told us. But I want to focus on the other circumstances in play."

Olivia reached into her satchel and pulled out the hardback edition of *Indigo to Black*. She pushed it to the center of the table. "Mom knew what Della did. It's all in there, blow by blow, in the fictional character of Becky Haines." Catching Woody's eye, she added, "*Rebecca* Haines."

Woody ran his fingers through his hair, took off his glasses, and bit the ear piece. He opened his mouth to respond, but instead pointed to Olivia's laptop. "More checking. Less talking."

The room went quiet, except for the clicking of keys, taps on a mouse, and quick scratches from Lauren's pencil.

"I'm hungry," Lauren said. "Do we get a real lunch or a prisoner's one?"

"Food's pretty good," Danny said. "I ate every meal here when I set up the canine program with Ben. Same as the inmates. No special orders."

Olivia sat back in her chair, relieved for other eyes to take over.

"Forget food. Munch on this." Woody, Ryan, and Danny scrambled to stand behind her. "A picture from 1975. Althea and Simon Pennington at the opening of a new wing at the museum. And according to the caption, the third person with them is Tony Corelli."

Ryan gestured to the screen. "Her money . . . his name on the plaque—Pennington Gallery for Emerging Artists."

Woody stooped to Olivia's ear. Even beneath the government-issue soap, she could pick up his scent: the tropical breeze of laundry detergent in his white cotton shirt, and the hint of cedar in his shampoo. He squeezed her shoulder. "Good job, sweetheart." The words radiated tingles over her neck as he straightened. "Each of you tell me what you see. Liv, you first."

"Simon is a handsome man," she said. "Good eye-candy at a formal event. Strong features and great hair, lots of it, and perfectly cut for the longer style of the seventies. He enjoys working a room. Althea is wearing too much makeup, though. I think women who wear that much are trying to cover up something inside." Althea's dark hair had been stacked high on her head, with loose curls cascading on each side like pull chains on a lamp. She reminded Olivia of Elizabeth Taylor in *Butterfield Eight*. "Beautiful woman—arresting blue eyes like yours, Woody, and the same chin and mouth—but there's no emotion on her face, a painted shell. She would've been fifty in 1975, seven years before Simon died. Tony Corelli is watching her. Simon and Tony are on each side of her, like she can't escape."

"Excellent," Woody said. "Lauren?"

Olivia turned her laptop to face her sister.

Lauren squinted. "Kill me now if I had to wear a shiny dress like that, I'd be miserable too. Althea's mouth is tight, like she can't wait to get home and take her shoes off." She paused and went serious. "Tony looks like a liar. You know the type. Tells people what they want to hear, then screws them over. Simon's a bully. All smiles in public, but I'll bet Althea never wore short sleeves. It would show bruises from squeezing her arm too tight."

Woody scratched his chin. "Interesting." He pivoted to his left.

"Danny?"

Olivia shifted her laptop. Ryan moved to stand behind Danny and grasped her shoulders.

"Simon has mean eyes," Danny said. "He could've been abusive. Men get a weird expression when they're on the hunt. Tony doesn't want a meal that isn't Althea. Small bites with a sharp knife."

"An observation only a woman could make," Woody said. "Ryan?"

"Something's going on." Ryan leaned in. "All three of them look guilty to me, but I wouldn't trust Tony Corelli or Althea. When in doubt, focus on the ones who are alive." He bumped Woody's arm. "What do you see?"

"Althea is dead sober and thinking of doing something, either to Simon or Tony. I'd like to know whatever it was she did between 1975 and 1982. Maybe I could've prevented it."

All heads turned when the conference room door opened. Ben stepped inside with a letter-size box and a padded envelope. "Here's your two FedEx packages, Woody."

Chapter 14
The Delivery

At noon on Saturday, a tray of tuna fish sandwiches, several small bags of potato chips, and a bunch of bananas were delivered by a member of the kitchen staff. Lunch didn't draw an eye from the FedEx box, however.

Olivia ripped five sheets of paper from the legal pad and distributed them to each person in the room. She kept one for herself. This was Woody's show, so she didn't speak, but she did watch his face. His expression became guarded as he tore the strip on the top of the box. Della and Asher's letters pulled Woody's own zip strip of internal emotions.

A single bundle of eleven envelopes, tied with cotton kitchen twine, slid from the box and thumped to the table. A folded note and a picture fell out behind it. The photo was of a young girl.

Olivia leaned in and reached for the photo. The girl looked to be about ten years old, with dark hair and crystal-blue eyes. "Who's this?"

"Margie probably stuck that in at the last minute," he said and plucked the photo from her fingers. "A story for another time, but not today."

Olivia thought Margie wasn't the only one in a hurry. Woody

snatched that picture a little too fast. Duly noted and filed for rumination later.

"I have to ask, Woody," Lauren said and reached for a bag of chips. "Why didn't you read these letters when you found them with the books? I wouldn't have been able to stand it."

Olivia grimaced at her sister for changing the subject. There was something about that photo Woody didn't want her to know. He'd shoved Margie's note and the girl's photo into the back pocket of his jeans. A tight hug and a butt pat ought to do the trick.

Woody broke off a banana from the bunch. "I know this might sound odd coming from a lawyer, but I honestly didn't want my mother's story to be true. As long as I didn't read them, the possibility existed that it was all a misunderstanding. Highly unlikely, but a thread of reasonable doubt gave me hope." He peeled the banana from the bottom up to prevent fibery threads. Olivia had learned that trick from him. "Liv and I were going up to Wolfeboro to read these, make it a project while I got caught up with my practice." He glanced at Olivia and smiled. "I didn't want to do it alone. I needed a writer, someone I trust, to interpret the relationship between Della and Asher. There's no one to defend here—and it's too personal."

Trust was exactly the word Olivia would've used at this moment. The photo burned an indelible image in her brain.

Danny reached for Ryan's hand. "Good answer. So romantic."

"Rainey . . . " Ryan hesitated. "Do you have any idea how miserable you're going to make my life?"

Woody started the cascade of laughter. Olivia joined in, but with only a chortle. She'd hoped he wouldn't get maudlin, and he didn't.

Straightening the blank piece of paper, Woody said, "Liv explained to me a way to do this using a writer's technique. We're going to add a legal spin." He took a bite of his banana and swallowed. "There are eleven letters from Asher. Liv's going to read them aloud in date order. Each of us will listen, and then give comments about our impressions." He turned to Olivia. "I love it when you read aloud."

"It's like narrating an audiobook," Olivia said and pointed.

"What's in the other FedEx?"

Plastic bubble packing crinkled when Woody turned the puffy envelope face down. "Nothing. Just some business I'm finishing up."

A second instance of Woody hiding something. Olivia vowed to confront him about them when they were alone.

Danny wrote her name at the top of her paper. "This is like a game show."

"Like *You Bet Your Life*," Lauren said and tore open the bag of chips. "I shouldn't be eating these."

Woody took a seat and tapped his onyx pen end over end. "Depending on what we hear, we'll come up with our next move. The floor's yours, Liv."

Not wanting to break the twine, Olivia struggled to untie the knot. The twists frayed before she pulled the ends away. She lined up the small envelopes of thick cream-colored custom stationery, the size of note cards, in date order of the postmark.

"Your handwriting is quite similar, Woody," she said. "They almost could've been sent by you."

Woody went stone-faced. "I noticed that, too, when I found them. But let's proceed."

Olivia pulled the first folded card from the envelope. "It's very short. Here goes." She took a breath. "August 8th, 1946. 'I had such a wonderful time this summer with you and Ellen. How lucky can a guy get? I'll get you both back in next year's volleyball tournament. You two are ruthless. Have fun at Brewster this year. Congrats on the scholarship, Della. Ellen told me she's going to be a cheerleader. I'll write again when I get settled in my apartment.'"

Pens scratched on paper around the table. Woody broke the fuzzing of ink. "I didn't know she went to Brewster."

Lauren kept writing, and without looking up, she said, "She and Mom were older than what Mom wrote in her book. The character of Becky Haines was only sixteen. Della must've been around nineteen."

"Keep going, Liv," Woody said.

Olivia reassembled the first letter and opened the second one.

"September 4th, 1946. 'Got your note, Della. Let's all meet on the beach on July 7th, on that same one at Indigo Lake. It's the best spot. Nine o'clock. Mark your calendar. Gives me something to look forward to.'"

Danny raised her eyes. "Like Mom's book, and what Della told us."

"Except for one thing," Lauren said. "They were a cozy three-some, not a twosome."

Ryan pointed to the paper. "That's progress right there. Two women competing for one man is a gingerbread trail to a crime of passion."

Woody smirked. "I thought you'd say that July seventh in 1947 was the day aliens crashed in Roswell."

"Right you are. I shoulda caught that."

Olivia set the envelope aside. She opened the next one. "October third. 'Thank you for sending the watercolor. It captures the autumn colors perfectly. I miss being in New Hampshire. The first year of medical school is all academic. I can't wait to be hands-on. I learn so much better that way. Your classes going well?'"

Lauren grimaced. "Doesn't sound like he wanted to have his hands all over Della."

"Della sent an Indigo Lake watercolor to Asher," Woody muttered, thinking out loud. "Now there's four prints that we know of . . . Della, Ellen, me, and Asher. Next."

"November twentieth. 'Happy Thanksgiving, Della. I'll be suffering through parties at the house from now through New Year's. I wish I could come up to see you and Ellen, but Father is using my winter break to show me off. You know, 'my son, the doctor,' and all that nonsense. Will write soon.'"

Everyone around the table remained silent, but Olivia suspected they were all writing the same notes. The door had opened to Asher's family.

Olivia set the note aside and took the next. "December tenth. 'Merry Christmas, Della. Did you get the present I sent? I gave one to

Ellen too. She probably told you she's coming up here. Father invited her to Christmas dinner. Ellen said you were doing well at Brewster. Go Bobcats! My sister is going to introduce us to her boyfriend. We'll see how that goes.'"

"What did he give her?" Ryan said.

Woody let out long whistle that circled the room. His expression alighted with thought. "Think about the one unusual thing that both Della and Ellen had."

"Mom's crystal apple," Olivia said. "They both got Christmas presents from Asher. Mom always said that apple came from our grandfather."

"Holy shamoly," Danny said. "That's where Mom's Steuben apple came from? I'll bet Dad didn't appreciate that."

Lauren narrowed her eyes. "Nor Asher's introduction of Simon to William Woodard."

Olivia plowed forward. "January 4th, 1947. 'Miserable cold. Can't shake it. What a way to spend the rest of the winter break before I hit the books. I wish you could make me some soup. I'm in bed eating crackers and cheese. Why is it that doctors don't like going to the doctor? They know too much, that's why. I'll go if I'm not better in a few days.'"

Ryan shrugged. "I hate going to doctors too. Can't blame him for that."

Olivia opened the next card. "February 12th, 1947. 'Hope this arrives by Valentine's Day. Do you have a date for dinner? I would take you myself, but I'm living on coffee and cigarettes. Can't eat. Classes are wearing me out. Be well.'"

"Asking her if she had a date?" Danny pursed her lips. "*That* doesn't sound romantic."

"Sounds like a half-ass offer for a pity date," Lauren said. "That's worse."

"Shhh . . . Four more," Ryan said.

"March twentieth." Olivia opened the note, stopped, and re-checked the envelope. She raised her eyes. "Woody?"

"What's the matter, honey?"

"It's . . . the card is to Ellen, but Asher addressed this envelope to Della."

The pen in Ryan's hand froze. "The wrong envelope?"

"Mom must've been getting letters from Asher too," Lauren said. "Read it, Liv."

Olivia blew out a breath. "'Althea is dating a horrible man named Simon Pennington. Father is so mad. I'm afraid he'll do something drastic. Althea came to me last week in tears. I tried to talk with him, but he told me to stay out of it. He's given us his blessing. Father loves you, Ellen. I have a surprise for you when you come up in a couple of weeks. I love you more than life itself.'"

"Oh my God," Lauren said. "He was in love with Mom."

Olivia's heart raced. The pieces started to clarify. "Do you think our Dad knew?"

"They hadn't even met yet."

"I didn't find any letters in Mom's things. Did you?"

Lauren shook her head, then Olivia swiveled her chair to Danny.

"I never found any, Liv," Danny said. "She must've destroyed them."

Olivia placed the note away from the others and took a new one from the dwindling stack. "April 14th, 1947. 'I don't know why you're so angry, Della. Did I hurt your feelings? I'm under a lot of pressure, and I'm so tired. I can't deal with your accusations. I'll write later.'"

"Asher didn't know he'd screwed up," Ryan said and crossed his arms like Mr. Clean. "Bad move on his part. Kinda like that auto-populate of the wrong recipient on an email."

"You got that right," Woody said.

"We're down to the last two." Olivia pulled the card from the envelope. "May 17th, 1947. 'Well, she did it. Althea up and married Simon. None of us were invited to the civil ceremony. I think she did it for revenge. Father had a terrible fight with Simon. He found out what Father had done with the will. I'm worried. His heart is worse off than he'll admit. I can see the swelling in his legs and broken capillaries on his face. His blood pressure's too high.'"

"What did he do?" Lauren said.

Woody blew out a breath. "I think . . . it must be what Rizzo said about the inheritance. Althea told Simon she'd been disinherited after they were married, but we don't know when. I'll bet my grandfather changed his will after that letter. Read the last one, Liv. We need to talk about this. It changes everything."

Olivia monitored Woody's expression as she picked up the last envelope. His eyes shifted with spinning thoughts, stringing them into truth. The smell of tuna fish suddenly made her stomach queasy. "June 20th, 1947. 'I can't do this anymore, Della. Your last letter was upsetting. Please stop. When we meet on the beach next month, I'll explain. I need to move forward in my life. Everything will be on my shoulders. I may have to quit school.'"

To let her heart slow, Olivia took her time to slip the last note back into the envelope. She neatened the stack to match up the edges. "Well, there you have it. A few things in these letters are obvious. Others prompt conjecture."

Lauren crushed the empty potato chip bag. "What are the bombshells here?"

"Asher didn't love Della," Danny said. "He loved Mom."

Olivia nodded. "Nothing in these letters is from a man in love with Della. She read into them what she wanted. I wish we had the ones Della wrote back to Asher."

Danny crossed her arms. "He played her. Didn't come clean. I'm sorry, Woody, but that was a rotten thing to do to Della. Asher pit her against Mom. Gave them both glass apples and a watercolor of Indigo Lake."

"Maybe a bombshell for Della," Ryan said, "but something else happened closer to home for Asher. There are two distinct incendiary devices . . . Ellen and Asher, and Althea's marriage to Simon set off a firestorm about money. He sounded frightened in that last letter."

Woody rocked his glasses between his fingers. "Motive. Della found out about the relationship with Ellen in March, when she got my father's misdirected note. My mother must have been filled with rage. Six months of torture. She poisoned Asher in September."

Olivia locked her gaze on Woody. "Plotted like a spider, just like Mom described in *Indigo to Black*. Sounded like Della stalked and harassed him."

A pall settled over the table.

Woody traded his glasses for his onyx pen and rolled it in his fingers. "Ryan? You're the detective here."

Ryan rubbed his face. He snatched a wedge of tuna fish sandwich from the plate and took a bite. "I think Ellen was lucky to stay alive. If Asher was going to marry her, then Ellen would've been queen of the manor, not Althea. Smells like two separate crimes were committed against one man. Love and money. Most crimes involve one of the two. Your father was a dead man . . ." He traced the number *one* with his forefinger. "Only Della got there first."

"We know what happened for love . . . " Woody glanced at Olivia. "Now we follow the money." He reached for his phone and pointed to Olivia's laptop. "We're going to Boston, Liv. We need to book three rooms at a hotel near Beacon Hill for tomorrow night."

"Who are you calling?" she said.

"Casey Carter. He'll come pick us up with the chopper."

Chapter 15

Reinforcements

On Sunday morning, Olivia watched through a window as the helicopter came into view of the rooftop helipad at Allenwood Prison. Woody buttoned his coat and tugged on his gloves.

"Casey's here," he called to the others. "I'll bring him in to meet everyone."

"What about the SUV you rented?"

"Ben's going to turn it in for us. We'll use Casey's Jeep when we get to Boston. My Porsche's been at the Norwood airport since the end of October. I need to pick it up."

Olivia delighted in the way Woody's face beamed in anticipation. He loved his car, and the buddy factor would even the hormonal odds. She turned to Lauren. "Put on some lipstick."

A frantic dig through her purse produced an uncapped tube of lip balm. Lauren picked off the fuzz. "I got this from the dentist when I had my teeth cleaned."

Danny stepped forward and held out a sponge wand of rose-tinted gloss. "Color inside the lines."

"You look fine, Lauren," Woody said and tucked his gray scarf under his coat. "Don't listen to them."

Plumes of snow blew from the perimeter of the heliport. The rotors of the six-seat Airbus Dauphin growled as Casey Carter touched down the chopper. Olivia had been curious about Woody's best friend. From his bad-boy expression, Woody was anxious for Casey to meet Lauren. When the blades slowed, Casey removed his headset, swung open the pilot's door, and slid from the seat. Lauren's eyes widened.

"C'mon," Woody said. "I'll introduce you."

"Go ahead." Olivia narrowed her eyes. "God knows I can't stop you."

Woody pushed through the rooftop door and stepped toward Casey. Lauren shifted in her boots and attempted to calm her flyaway hair. The shaking of hands ended with an embrace, then a verbal introduction. A wind gust rustled Casey's snow-white, shaggy hair as he gave Lauren's shoulders a buddy-squeeze. His mirrored aviator sunglasses flashed in the bright sun, and a broad smile erupted from his close-cut gray beard. In his sixties, Casey could have landed the cover of *Retired Hot Military Dudes*. Lauren appeared unsteady.

Danny tugged on Olivia's sweater. "Have you ever seen a look like that on Lauren's face? When Casey stepped out of the chopper she could've made S'mores in her sweats."

"He's totally her type." Olivia nodded for emphasis.

"She might wear out the seat of her pants from scootin' around on the cement out there."

Olivia burst out laughing and rummaged in her purse. "Should I give her one of my wet wipes to clean her fur?"

Ryan held back his own laugh. "All right . . . All right. Leave Lauren alone." He pulled on Danny's arm.

"But Lauren's eyes are bulging," Danny said, resisting. "She looks like she's trying to swallow an old shoe. Casey's all puffed up like a rooster."

All heads turned to the window. Olivia's elder sibling was nervous from being out of practice. Lauren did indeed exhibit mating behavior, with a touch of her forehead and a scratch of her upper lip. Exuberant laughter clinched the assessment.

"Whole lot a belly-scratchin' going on out there," Ryan said and glanced out the window.

"Casey's probably impressing Lauren with all his missions," Olivia said. "Woody told me he was in Kuwait, Desert Fox in Iraq, and Bosnia. He retired in '99 after the NATO bombings in Kosovo. He runs a high-end executive flight business in Boston. Knows everybody."

Danny leaned into Ryan's side. "Vets and pets, two of Lauren's favorite things, but I doubt she'll let Casey scratch her belly. Claws and paws."

Olivia swished her hands. "Here they come. Act normal."

The comment produced an eye-roll from Ryan. "What the hell's normal?"

When Casey breezed through the door and took off his sunglasses, Olivia nearly gasped at the unusual aqua color of his eyes, like the blue-green water in glacial lakes. Her gaze darted to Lauren, whose expression reflected that she'd just been saved by a man on a mission.

Olivia extended her hand to a strong shake of scratchy skin. Hand cream would've been too foo-foo for Casey. She'd have to work on that.

"So, you're the woman who finally cracked the code on the bank," he said. "Thought it would never dang happen, not that there haven't been many tries."

Woody set his hand on Olivia's shoulders. "Careful, Casey."

A door had opened only once about Woody's two-year relationship with a lawyer in Boston. The conversation had slammed shut in short order. Olivia had left it alone, despite her intermittent thoughts about it. The breakup had been instigated by his mother, Della. Now, she wanted details of what qualities constituted a best friend with Casey . . . and if that young girl's picture was related. Every day held a nugget of new information that shaped the puzzle of Woody.

"How'd you two meet?" Olivia asked Casey.

Casey searched her eyes for how much she knew. "Kayak race, up on Indigo Lake in Vermont in '95."

Olivia warmed inside. She'd worn Woody's T-shirt commemorating that kayak event after sleeping with him for the first time. The night had changed her life, but the next morning had taken an ugly turn with their clash over her dead ex, Adam. His words had left an indelible mark. *What are you so afraid of?* Now, Woody's gaze met hers. He, too, was recalling the moment.

"You okay?" Woody said.

"Yeah," she said.

Lauren turned to Casey. "How long is the flight to Boston?"

"Shy of two hours."

"Have you ever been married?" Danny said as a follow-up, with her usual candor.

Casey laughed. Then his strong features softened. "No. I didn't think it would be fair to be gone so much."

"But he's been home for ten years." Woody raised his brow at Lauren. "He wants a woman who can weather anything and cook. Tough combination to come by."

A blush rose in Lauren's cheeks.

Danny beamed. "Lauren has a gun, and she can make fake spaghetti from zucchini. She makes popcorn too."

Casey scratched his cheek, audible across his beard. "I also eat out."

"Perfect," Olivia said and turned to Woody. "While you're loading our bags, I need a few minutes with Ben. I'll be right back."

"Wait!" he called out behind her. "We're leaving."

"I'll be fast as a flash."

~ · ~ · ~

"Thank you for everything, Ben." Olivia released the warden's hand. "We couldn't do this without your help."

"I'm bending the rules for you, Olivia," Ben said as he turned the lock on Palermo's cell. The barred door slid open. "Make it quick. Your ride's waiting for you."

"I only need a minute."

Olivia stepped into the prison cell. The old don lay on his bed with Willy by his side. The golden retriever lifted his head at the intrusion.

"We're leaving for Boston, Nicky." Olivia leaned over Palermo to scratch Willy's head. "I couldn't leave without having one last talk. Only you and me."

"I like what I heard of the manuscript," he said. "Only on chapter three."

"I'm not here about that, but I'm glad you like it."

"You made me good."

The pause filled with a quiet dance of respective thoughts. Their interview rules dictated that Palermo be the first to break it.

"Women shouldn't dig into a man's past, Olivia." Palermo's strokes of Willy's head didn't slow.

"You wanted me to dig into yours, Palermo, so that's nonsense. The big difference is that Woody and I are discovering our histories together. I think we're close, but all the pieces are scrambled. My family is mixed up in this too."

"Will change nothing. Get my book done."

Olivia inspected the walls, unable to imagine herself spending the rest of her life in this cramped space. He was on display, like a caged animal at the zoo. At least he had a lamp and an oriental carpet. Homey for what it was. "You'll get your book. Rizzo and Tullio will too. We need to solve this, or Woody's father's death will sit between us like a big lump. He needs to know what happened."

"Eloquent image." Palermo bobbed his bony finger. "Wait for Tony Corelli to die. All will be solved."

"What about Althea? She's the only family he has."

"Her situation will end with Tony's death too."

"Unless Althea dies first."

A second pause signaled a change of subject. For speed, she broke the unspoken rules by taking the lead. "I'm damaged goods, Nicky."

Palermo's thin shoulders beneath the orange jumpsuit rose in a rickety shrug. "Who isn't? Problems. Complications. Two of life's ingredients for happiness." He pointed in the general direction of his tape player. A stack of cassettes, mostly Italian operas, sat next to it. Mozart filled in the remainder. "Look to Puccini. There is nothing new. Jealousy. Fear. Misunderstanding." Palermo paused. "Deception, Olivia?"

She set her jaw. "I'm not a coward. You're the one who told me that the true character of a man comes out when he's pushed."

"I did."

"Goes for women too," she said.

"You even more so, Olivia, but you think too much. Push too much. Your voice is heard without the benefit of touch."

"Can't help it. I'm a loudmouth."

Palermo nodded. "*La Bohème*. Rodolfo falls in love with Mimi when her candle blows out. He has an expression from another world. They stumble in the dark until he finds her face bathed in moonlight. Mimi's life is hard. Rodolfo is jealous. He lives in fear that she is sick and he can't help her. In truth, Olivia, both are damaged."

Olivia reached for Palermo's hand. "For a murderer, you're pretty romantic." His fingers were cool, the bones prominent beneath his thin skin. Blue veins snaked through bruises from blood-thinning medication. "Remember when you told me that if you discover what a man loves, you find his weakness?"

Palermo bowed his head. "I do."

"I never forgot that, Nicky. I kept it in the book. Every chapter starts with one of your quotes. You love so much that you kill. That one is chapter six."

"Makes for good opera." Palermo kneaded her fingers and stilled on her gold wedding band. "Our Mister Rainey's weakness. If you were mine, I would cut off your finger."

Olivia pulled her hand away. "I gotta go. Woody's waiting." She stood and buttoned her wool coat. "I agree with you about Puccini, but I'm not here boo-hooing like *La Bohème*. Don't you think *Gianni Schicchi* is more appropriate?"

"'O Mio Babbino Caro?' I am your father now?" Palermo smiled, showing his large yellow teeth in need of a cleaning. "Ah . . . Lauretta . . . You seek my permission to marry Rinuccio?"

The downbeat for playing out an operatic scene with Palermo swelled her heart. One of his games—his weakness—was to interpret life's meaning through arias. This one had a daughter pleading with her father to marry, Palermo's favorite. "I love Rinuccio, Papa, and I already have his ring. If I don't marry him, I'll go to the Ponte Vecchio and throw myself in the Arno River."

"*Pieta. Pieta.* I like it when you beg, Olivia, but it's unbecoming." Palermo waved his hand, as if bothered by an incarcerated fly. "Did he give *you* a ring?"

"A beautiful one, but it didn't fit my finger. Then I lost it. I don't have the heart to tell Woody."

A wiry eyebrow rose. "An insult. Disrespectful."

Olivia closed her eyes. He was right. She didn't know how to fix it. "Let me go now, Nicky, with your blessing. And don't send any goons. Two guns on the team are enough." She leaned over and kissed Palermo's cool, leathery cheek. "You don't need to say it. We'll be careful."

Palermo shook his finger at the stack of tapes. "*Gianni Schicchi.*"

Olivia slipped the cassette from its case and inserted it into the player. With the press of the PLAY button, the overture bloomed to fill the space. "Should I add this talk to the book as our last interview?"

Palermo grunted. "You need drama, Olivia."

"I guess you're right. Love is dramatic. And I'm in love."

She took one last glance at Palermo as Ben squeaked open the cell door. The old don stared straight ahead with watery eyes. To a glissando of violins and the lilting skip of piccolos, Willy rested his head over Palermo's knees.

But the dog's eyes shifted to her.

~ · ~ · ~

Olivia burst through the rooftop door. "I'm coming!"

The whine of the helicopter's rotors erupted as Woody held out his hand, her red briefcase in the other.

"Where have you been?" he shouted over the din. "We're ready to go." He boosted her inside.

Out of breath, Olivia scooted over Beauregard and took a seat on the leather divan. She pulled the safety belt across her chest, struggling to secure the buckle over her coat. The interior held a corporate feel, with its vanilla upholstery and large windows. Seating accommodated four passengers in the cabin and one upfront with the pilot. Lauren sat in the front with Casey. Danny and Ryan sat across from Olivia and Woody in two swivel chairs. The shake of their heads in unison made Olivia feel foolish about her cat-and-mouse discussion with Palermo.

Pogo wagged his tail as Woody slipped off his coat and sat. "I swear, Liv, I'm going to have a GPS chip embedded in your head to know where you are."

"Don't you dare."

"While you're sleeping."

Casey turned in the pilot seat. "Welcome the Bickersons aboard, everyone."

Pogo and Beauregard ears whipped each other's snouts to settle their gazes on Woody and Olivia.

"My first ride in a helicopter," Lauren said. "I might wet my pants. You think I will when the pressure changes?"

"You're fine up here with me, darlin'," Casey said. "Put on that headset, so you can let *me* know when *you* let go." He flipped a switch. "Now here *we* go."

Lauren squealed and covered her eyes.

Chapter 16
The Spark of a Plan

At eleven o'clock on Sunday morning, after Casey's feather-like landing at Boston's Norwood airport, Woody uttered a wish as he inserted the key into the ignition.

"C'mon, baby. Be a good girl and go."

When he'd gone to Portland last October, he'd left his 911 Porsche in Boston for Casey's helicopter ride to Allenwood to pick up Beauregard. The charter flight to Portland for a Halloween doggy delivery had turned into a life-changing sabbatical through Thanksgiving. After four weeks of neglect, and a snowstorm to boot, he turned the key. The cold engine fired to a grumbly purr.

Woody turned to Olivia and grinned like a kid. "My baby." Beauregard's hot breath visibly steamed when the dog jutted his head between the front bucket seats. Woody gave Beau's ears a scrub. "Yes, you're my baby too."

"What about me?" Olivia said and winked. "Sounds like you're already married to your car and the dog."

"I stand corrected. I'm making room for three."

"I haven't been in this car since you dropped me off after we first slept together. I can zoom back to that conversation like yesterday."

"Me too." Woody lingered a moment with the image of Olivia's guilty meltdown over Adam in the early hours of the "morning after." If he could take back his harsh words to her, he would in spades. She had come a long way, but Olivia wasn't completely his yet. And that third entity in their relationship was one he preferred to be Beauregard, not Adam. Well, maybe there'd be a fourth, but he wasn't ready to talk to Olivia about it. He could barely think about it himself.

"Painful," she said.

Reliving the unpleasant discussion held no appeal. Or maybe she meant literally. Five years of abstinence had ended for her that night. Best to leave the comment alone, but he couldn't. "A lot of barriers to entry."

Woody turned to her hoping for a sparring smile, but instead he was met by a serious expression, one he wasn't ready for.

"Who was that young girl in the picture, Woody? What did Margie's note say?"

"The child of a friend. It was left on my desk, so she included it in the envelope."

"How old is she?"

"Eleven. In the photo," he said cryptically. "Nothing to worry about."

"Do you think we can do this?" she said. "I mean . . . solve this with your family?"

"I have to now, after what we found out."

"What do you hope to gain?"

He paused. "You and me, without all the baggage."

"So . . . you're holding our future hostage until we find out what happened between your mother and father?"

"This is about your mother too."

"I know, but life doesn't go on hold because of the past."

"I'm not convinced that what my mother did won't get in the way. How can I commit to you when I don't know the truth about my own family? And I'm not convinced that Adam won't get in the way, either."

There. He said it. The elephant.

Olivia set her finger to her lips and swallowed. In the silence, the engine and Beauregard's panting were the only sounds. "What if this doesn't go the way you want?"

"Then maybe we'll need more time." From Olivia's shocked expression, he immediately regretted the statement.

"You're getting cold feet?"

"Too many unknowns to talk about this." The temperature gauge rose to normal. Woody's own wheels started to turn. With the shift of the car into reverse, he backpedaled. "No, not cold feet. We're a team, right? So, let's go be a team and figure this out."

Beauregard retreated into the cramped back seat with their luggage.

"Do you know how to get to the hotel?" Olivia retrieved her phone and sunglasses from her briefcase. "Since I don't have a GPS embedded in my head, I'll use this to bark directions. Then you'll get mad at me and go the opposite way. We'll be a typical couple."

"Remember, I know Boston. I lived here for four years before going back to New Hampshire. We're taking a side trip before we check in. And I'll wait to get mad at you *after* we're married." Woody exited the airport garage to a flash of brilliant sunshine. He pulled his sunglasses from the visor. Snow crunched under his wheels as another question burned. "What were you doing in the prison before you came out to the chopper?"

Olivia hid her eyes behind her own pair of shades. "Nothing . . . just saying goodbye to Ben."

The way she said it, Woody wasn't so sure that was entirely accurate.

~ · ~ · ~

Olivia used the forty-minute drive from the Norwood airport to Beacon Hill to shake a sense of foreboding. Time to ratchet this up a notch. A commitment of unconditional love now proved to be full of conditions, some of which she could control, most she didn't know how to.

Although the snowstorm had passed, its aftermath had been left to melt from the Beacon Hill neighborhood, the roads too narrow to accommodate a snowplow. Cars had done part of the job. She searched for a sign as Woody eased the car to the curb, lucky to find a tight space on the tight street already tight from ruts.

Olivia gawked at history—homes where people lived *inside* history, nearly all hosting a relative of a founding father or two. Anchored on the corner of Joy Street stood a three-story, red-brick Greek revival townhouse, in pristine condition for nearly two centuries. A perfect symmetry of stacked multipaned windows nestled between shiny black shutters.

Woody shut off the engine and pointed. "Althea's house."

"You're sure this is the right address?" she said.

"Ryan looked it up for me. And the Pennington & Corelli law firm is only a few blocks away. The Massachusetts State House and Suffolk County Superior Court are walkable from their offices."

In an instant, Woody's phantom family became real. Olivia envisioned a line of generations coming home to fancy dinners and luxurious sheets—gloved Woodards in bustles, tipsy flapper Woodards bouncing in beaded dresses, Woodard Daughters of the American Revolution in drab tailored suits, and finally Althea herself, in a smart, matching knit set with a long rope of pearls, still stylish today. Old money at its most in-town refined.

Olivia couldn't shift her gaze from the red-brick townhouse. "The Boston City Jail is close by too."

Woody chuckled. "Is that why you put us up at the Liberty Hotel? Used to be the old Suffolk County Jail in the nineteenth century."

"Of course," she said and waved her hand. "A nod to Palermo and the boys. It's quite spiffy. Plus, they allow dogs." She leaned forward to peer up to the second-story windows. No adorned figure stood watch for a peasant invasion. "You think Althea wears classic Chanel suits?"

"I'll bet she does." Woody paused. "You think she's happy or sad today? That would tell us quite a bit."

"In general, or just today?" Olivia had similar thoughts about elderly people who lived alone, no matter their financial situation, but wealthy ones tended to live with more regrets, witnessed by staff. She figured there weren't many goals left to shoot for except mending fences.

"Today is Althea's ninetieth birthday. It would've been my father's, too, being that he was a twin. The death certificate confirmed it."

Olivia turned to assess Woody's expression. His eyes offered her an invitation. "What do you get for a woman who has everything?"

"Nothing without an appointment."

With her forefinger, she traced small circles on Woody's knee. "My turn to have an idea."

"Here? Not in the car, Liv."

"Hold that thought, but it would've been nicer an hour ago." She gave his hand a quick pat. "Let's make an appointment."

"What? Go knock on the door?"

"No. Better." Olivia reached into her satchel. "We'll leave Althea a copy of Mom's book with a note. Make her come to *us*, Woody. Test the water."

Woody paused and stared at the dashboard. "You're setting a fire—a dangerous fire."

She threw Woody a sideways glance, similar to the kind he gave her. "Let's soap up the grease and see what happens."

"Shoot me now." Woody rubbed his forehead. "Go ahead."

Olivia retrieved a pen and a yellow notepad from her case. They became the tools of a new game with the rip of ruled paper. Her heart pounded like the hooves of a racehorse.

"Use me as bait," she said. "Althea will see my name when she reads the acknowledgments. If it comes from a strange man—especially a lawyer—she'll get spooked. Althea can research me, and she'll think I'm an author who wants to meet her. Which, by the way, is the truth, Counselor."

"Not the whole truth," Woody said. "She might think you're trying to woo a donation out of her for the Pogo Trust. And, by the way, I'm not strange."

Olivia took a sip from Woody's water bottle and composed the words, friendly and not too complicated.

Dear Mrs. Pennington,

Please accept this gift of a good read for your birthday. If you would like to meet, call me at the Liberty Hotel as soon as possible. I'll be in town for only a couple of days.

Sincerely,

Olivia Novak

She handed Woody the paper. He scanned the note and held it out to her. "Add a phone number."

"Right." Olivia poised her pen. "Your cell. That way, Althea's forced to communicate through you." She inked the number under her name and folded the ruled paper into a long strip. It became a bookmark when she tucked the paper between the center pages. "There's a mail slot in her front door."

Woody drained the water bottle. "You're an arsonist." He peered around the seat to Beauregard. The dog shifted as if the pads on his paws were on fire. "You hear that, Beau? Your mother is an arsonist."

Olivia pulled the door handle, letting in a rush of cold air. The bottom edge of the car door scraped an icy ridge of snow.

Woody groaned. "Watch the paint."

Before lowering her sunglasses on her nose, Olivia locked her gaze on his. "I'm the one burning up. I'll be right back. Then we'll go to the hotel for a hose down."

Beauregard whined at the repeat scrape of the door. She pushed it shut with her hip.

Chapter 17
Althea Reads

At four o'clock on Sunday afternoon, Althea Woodard Pennington stood at the fireplace in the living room, watching the low flames snap and pop. Cheery. Lived-in. From December to February one of Freed's tasks at sundown was to light the fire. Sundays were for casual lounging, today in navy wool slacks and a gray cashmere sweater. No jewelry. Of course, makeup and styled hair. Ninety shouldn't look ninety. Althea lit a jarred candle and set it on the mantle, next to the Steuben crystal apple. Today was Asher's birthday too.

This formal room held her best acquisitions of modern art, a pleasing contrast to the details of old-world craftsmanship. The scrolled leaves carved into the fireplace surround calmed the edginess of the Picasso above it; jagged veins in the marble of the hearth met the abstract lines of a Joan Miró sculpture; and curved ceiling molding complemented the liquid layers of sunset colors in a Helen Frankenthaler painting. The moment she had bequeathed the pieces to various museums, Althea became a visitor here.

The Steuben apple, deliciously smooth and clear, was the least expensive piece in the room but her most treasured. Who on earth should she bequeath that piece to? No one could ever appreciate it as much as she did.

Her favorite scents of lavender and oak filled the air. Althea blew out the match and tossed it into the fireplace, its smoky threads trailing like Tony Corelli's hateful voice. Her visit to Tony's office on Friday had grated on her through the weekend. Poisonous words. Threatening words. The words of a thirty-three-year Devil's bargain.

Althea sat in the overstuffed chair of cream-on-cream stripes, defined only by the reverse sheen of reflected light. She slipped on her reading glasses, attached to a thin gold chain, and snapped open the Living section of the Sunday edition of the *Boston Globe*. Her housekeeper pulled back the drapes and switched on the white lights of the ten-foot Frasier fir in the front window. The brush of heavy brocade fabric tinkled the delicate ornaments.

"I can hear you thinking, Posey," Althea said and feigned interest in an article about innovative holiday gift-wrap techniques. "Don't say it. I know I shouldn't have gone to see Tony Corelli."

"I worry," Posey said. "You know I worry. That man upsets you so."

"All too true."

"And today, of all days." The housekeeper brushed away an imaginary speck of something from her dress.

"I relished letting him have it. Hateful old coot." Althea turned the page to Pet of the Week. A spaniel. Her own precious Ducky had loved to sprawl out in front of the fire. Every day of the last three years had been empty without his companionship.

"You can say no." Posey straightened a glass heart that had slid to the end of a branch.

"It's more complicated than that. What are we having for dinner? Cheer me up with something simple."

"Cornish game hen, French green beans. Devil's food cake with two candles."

"Perfect. No blaze of glory requiring a fire extinguisher." A pause drew Althea's gaze from the page. Posey stood behind the couch and smoothed her hand over a chartreuse velvet pillow. "And?"

"Someone left a gift for you. Must have come through the mail slot. I found it on the floor in the entryway."

"What is it?"

"A book and a note. Rather sweet for a stranger to know it's your birthday."

"Who is it?"

"The author, Olivia Novak."

The name sounded vaguely familiar. Maybe in a store window. "Have you read her books?"

"Not this one. This isn't one of Novak's."

"Please don't speak in code, Posey. You're acting like she delivered a bomb with a timer."

Her housekeeper padded to the entryway. Althea folded the newspaper and set it on the glass coffee table, next to a bowl of dried lavender buds. Experience had taught her that people didn't reach out without an attached agenda.

Posey stepped back into the living room with the book. A yellow piece of paper protruded from the top of the pages.

"Did you read the note?" Althea held out her hand.

"For security reasons, ma'am. I didn't see anything amiss."

Without additional comment, Althea unfolded the paper and read it. "Interesting. Staying at the Liberty. Close by." She extended her hand for the book. "*Indigo . . . to Black.*" The title rang a bell, but the cover art and the author name sent a ripple of electricity through her core. Althea gasped at the image of a lake in autumn. Her gaze settled on the author name. "Ellen Dushane?"

"The cover seems familiar." Posey shifted her eyes toward the doorway.

"Bring me the small watercolor in the dining room. It's part of a grouping that came from Asher's apartment."

"Yes, ma'am." Posey retreated.

It couldn't be the same. Coincidence? Most assuredly. Althea flipped to the back flap of the cover jacket for more information about the author:

Ellen Dushane wrote but only one book. After her death in 2013, the manuscript for Indigo to Black *was found in Ellen's safe by her three daughters: Lauren Lyndale, Olivia Novak, and Danielle Dushane. In honor of their mother's memory, a portion of the proceeds from* Indigo to Black *will be donated to the Pogo Charitable Trust, which funds programs for the training and placement of therapy dogs. Animals offer their love with no judgment, and their loyalty knows no limits.*

Althea's chest tightened at the author photo. Even in her eighties, she couldn't mistake the smile beneath a brimmed gardening hat. She fanned the pages for anything else stuck inside the book. Nothing. The front flap of the cover held more information about the premise:

No one stands up sixteen-year-old Becky Haines. On a quiet stretch of beach on Indigo Lake in Vermont, Becky meets the man who steals her heart, a young medical student from Boston. He's handsome, wealthy, and he loves her—or so Becky thinks. A promise to reunite the next summer fuels burning passion as she waits for every agonizing month to pass. Then she waits some more. He doesn't show. Only a delivered note holds two words: I can't. *Oh, but Becky can. And she's going to get her revenge.*

A strange uneasiness rolled in Althea's stomach when Posey held up the small framed watercolor.

"This one, Mrs. Pennington?"

Althea toggled her magnified gaze from the art piece to the book cover on her lap. The same. Almost the same. Slight differences in the movement of the water. The flames of fall colors in contrasting hues. No doubt they were done by the same artist.

"Posey?"

"Ma'am?"

"Save yourself the trouble of dinner. A turkey sandwich will do. Have Freed build a fire in my study." Althea stood and tucked the book under her arm. Her chained reading glasses dropped to her chest.

"Are you sure?"

"I'll take that slice of devil's food cake now. I need to clear my calendar for tomorrow."

"You have a board meeting at the Children's Museum at two."

With determined steps, Althea moved to the foyer. "Cancel it."

~ · ~ · ~

At six o'clock on Sunday evening, Beauregard leaped out of bed for his dinner and a quick walk. A lazy afternoon of a luxurious nap for three had concluded with a mad scramble to get dressed.

Olivia stood in black slacks and fussed with the snag Karen had made in her winter-white sweater. She gave up, draped a paisley scarf over her shoulders, and straightened the bed covers.

At the floor-to-ceiling window, which offered a panoramic view of the Charles River, Woody checked his phone. His brow furrowed.

"Anything?" she said and fluffed the pillows.

"Not yet. Let's go." Woody slipped his tweed blazer over a white shirt and jeans. He held out his hand. "Leave it. We're getting back in that in a few hours."

"It's the principle." Olivia smoothed the spread and grabbed her briefcase. She eyed it to make sure the Tiffany's bag was inside. No way would she leave Woody's wedding band in the room. Suddenly, their afternoon meant everything.

Woody nudged her and Beauregard out the door. Before pulling the door shut, he patted his breast pocket, then the back of his jeans. She saw the lump of his wallet before Woody felt it.

"What did everybody else do today?" she said, corralling Beauregard at the elevator.

"Ryan and Casey snooped around Pennington's law firm. Casey connected Ryan with his contacts at the police precinct." Woody pressed the DOWN button in rapid succession.

"What did my sisters do?"

"They went with them. We have a recon team."

"*We* didn't do anything. A what team?"

"*You* did plenty. Reconnaissance." Woody kissed the top of her head and gripped her shoulders when the doors parted. He guided her inside. "When you gave Althea *Indigo to Black*, this party went into high gear." After pressing the button for the ground floor, Woody checked his phone again.

Olivia went quiet as the elevator descended. The afternoon suddenly felt like a lost weekend while the world swirled forward. She'd been so focused on Woody that the ramifications of her actions dimmed her afterglow.

Beauregard quickened his steps to keep up through the atrium lobby. The three-story red-brick architecture deserved its own conversation. But now was not the time. Granite and iron still carried the pastiche of the Suffolk County Jail's colorful history. The catwalks were once the cell blocks that held Boston's most infamous criminals. A prison theme carried into the Clink restaurant, with private dining nooks defined by bars.

"There they are," Woody said and urged her forward. "I told you we were late."

Beauregard gave a nose-to-nose greeting with Pogo. Ryan and Casey stood. Her sisters enjoyed basking in their superior positions. They knew something she didn't.

"Sorry," Olivia said. Woody held out her chair and waited for her to sit before taking a seat next to her. "Men take so long to get ready."

In unison, the dogs slid to the floor and rested their heads on their paws.

Lauren caught Casey's eye, then she glanced at Olivia. "Especially after *your* afternoon."

"And where were you?" Danny said to Lauren. "I knocked on your door before we came down—and you didn't answer."

Lauren didn't answer. Olivia glanced at Danny when she spotted an iced tea in Lauren's hand. This was seriously getting serious—fast. It was well past wine o'clock.

Casey shifted and shook his scotch. "Lauren wanted to see my house. I ordered you one, Woody."

"I ordered for you, Liv," Danny said.

"I ordered room service," Ryan said. "I watched *The Godfather* on STARZ while I surfed the internet about Pennington and Corelli."

The table erupted with laughter. Lauren cleared her throat for everyone to shut up when the server approached the table with a tray. He distributed a scotch on the rocks and a glass of cabernet.

Woody set his phone on the table and shifted his glance at Olivia. He gave a slight shake of his head. No call.

"We worked hard to give you two the afternoon off," Lauren said when the waiter retreated. Her hand disappeared from the top of the table. Olivia figured Casey's knee was its destination.

Woody held up his scotch. "I've got my car, my woman, my family, and my best friend around me. And once I down this drink, what more do I need?"

"The car got first place in that lineup, my friend," Casey said.

"No particular order intended. The scotch can be rearranged."

Ryan leaned forward and lowered his voice. "Check this out. The four of us went to Corelli's office."

Olivia swallowed a sip of wine, then took a second before a chaser sip, not fully hearing Ryan, still wallowing in the *my woman* part of Woody's toast. That label didn't fit. After their open-hearted conversation in the car, she wanted to be referred to as *a wife*. Her gaze circled the restaurant. Everyone appeared to be deep into their own chatter. Woody gripped her fingers in anticipation of information.

"Casey made my job easy today," Ryan stuck out the thumb of his other hand. "This guy can get past any velvet rope. Danny distracted the security guard in the lobby, and Lauren started an argument. Casey and I got a look at the sign-in register."

"One name popped out, Woody," Casey said. "Althea Pennington signed in for a visit with Corelli on Friday afternoon."

Woody took a healthy sip of his scotch and shook the ice. "They're still connected?"

"Apparently," Ryan said. "Then we went over to the precinct to meet with two detectives Casey knows."

"Served with them in Iraq back in the nineties. Desert Storm," Casey said. "They're all over this, because of Corelli's possible inside connection on the force. They think it might still be happening." He signaled the server that his tumbler needed a refill.

"Little Buddies." Lauren held up her tea.

"We think that's how their clients get a walk."

"Payoffs?" Woody said.

Danny nodded. "I'm telling you. Money comes in, but you can't trace where it goes out. I'll bet it's totally for payoffs. I looked up their non-profit financials."

"You need that call from Althea," Ryan said.

Olivia turned to Woody. "They know what we did with the book?"

"Brilliant move, Liv," Lauren said.

Woody spread his hands. "I called Casey, who told Ryan. He told Danny, who told Lauren while you were taking a shower."

Olivia gawked. "But you were in the shower with me."

"Not the second time."

"Olivia, you don't even need a damn ring to marry this guy," Casey said and turned to locate the server. "Let's order."

Olivia's stomach dropped. Did Casey know that she'd lost Woody's ring? If he did, then Woody knew. Her gaze shot to her sisters. They both shrugged. The table went quiet when a new type of ring sprang forth: the music of Bruce Springsteen's "Local Hero."

Woody scraped back his chair and stood.

"It's Althea Pennington."

Chapter 18

The Call

At ten forty-five on Monday morning, Woody pulled the car in front of Althea Pennington's house. The snow piles had melted with a warm-up, enough to see the curb. His aunt had dictated the time—eleven o'clock—with a voice that lacked any tone to indicate he was family. No chord had been struck, or even a hint that she'd read the book. In a calculated move, Woody had functioned only as Olivia's social secretary. Althea wanted to meet her, not him.

Last night, sleep had eluded them both. Beauregard lay between Olivia and him, attempting to soothe their discussion and silent gaps of thought. Woody needed her fully awake now, her strength becoming his weakness, although he'd never admit that out loud.

He tapped the steering wheel. "The time of this meeting was carefully orchestrated, Liv."

Olivia pulled down the visor to check her lipstick. "How so?"

"Althea gave herself an out, the opportunity to cut off the discussion before lunch. If she's getting what she wants, she'll ask us to stay for a meal. Ever try to get an appointment with a lawyer at eleven o'clock? You won't. Options open."

"I couldn't take a bite if she offered, but emotional chess makes for good fiction."

"This isn't fiction," he said.

"I have to think of it that way, or I'll toss my cookies."

Woody paused, the suggestion triggering his own urge to purge. "Our history's in there. Both yours and mine."

"Maybe." Olivia flipped the visor and turned to him, her lips sufficiently shiny red to match her suit. Her eyes volleyed to meet his. "You're the one who said finding out the truth can be more important than winning."

"Why do you have such a good memory?"

Olivia swallowed the compliment. "If what was in the police report is true, I'm scared to death that we might find out my mother was involved. Scared to death."

"It's strictly informational at this juncture."

"But that's not why we're really here. Is it, Woody?" Olivia turned toward the stately townhome's front entrance. "This is about you. The only family you have left alive is in there right now—waiting to meet you."

"Meet you, not me." Woody turned to the back seat. Beauregard's tail thumped the upholstery upon eye contact. "I hope Althea allows dogs in her house. Better refer to Beauregard as Beau. She might think we're Confederates."

"Not when she hears *your* voice. You're a Yankee all the way."

An itch he couldn't scratch filled his gut. Woody checked the clock on the dash. "Let's go."

Protectiveness urged him to open the door first, but also in case someone was watching, Woody raced around the car to open Olivia's. She grasped his fingers and stuck out her red high-heeled foot like Cinderella. He fought the urge to draw her into his arms.

"My, my, Mr. Woodrow Rainey. You're acting like a blue-blood already." She flipped the seat forward and, with a jingle of his collar, Beauregard glided out.

At the front door, an illuminated button sat next to a speaker box. Woody pressed it. A rather pleasant buzz released from inside.

"Teamwork?" he said.

"Teamwork." Olivia nodded. "If I screw up, I'll buy you a mea culpa with whipped cream."

"May we help you?" The woman's voice sounded stiff with authority.

Woody started to lean toward the speaker, but Olivia wedged herself in front of him. "My name is Olivia Novak. Mr. Rainey and I are here to see Althea Pennington. We have an appointment."

"One moment please." The speaker clicked to silence.

Olivia smirked and shrugged. "The appointment is with me."

"Should we start keeping score? I'm sure I'll owe you a healthy share of mea culpas, too, by the time we leave."

"Or get kicked out." Olivia glanced at her watch. "We're five minutes early. This is good."

"Uh-huh." He tapped her on the shoulder. "Read me. I'll give you a signal if I twist my class ring." Woody held out his right hand. "Then you can be bad."

"I'd rather have you twist a different ring," Olivia said.

"Now you know how I feel."

The latch on the shiny black front door clicked, making them both flinch. Beauregard's tail wagged with anticipation, like a Looky-Lou invited to a private open house.

~ · ~ · ~

The front door opened in silence from well-oiled hinges. From Woody's somber expression, Olivia figured she'd pushed him too far. He carried a air that she couldn't predict. Time for shadow-boxing. An older woman in an unadorned black dress stood at the threshold. Olivia took in every detail to prepare for the impending conversation. Below the hem of the woman's dress, flesh-colored hose met matching black-strapped shoes with thick heels, the straps tight like her gray bun. The woman appeared to be in her seventies. The real keys to the manor were held by her, and without her approval, no dice.

Olivia urged Beauregard inside for the sniff test. With one step into the foyer, Beau stopped and nosed the pine scent. Olivia's breath caught in her throat. The curve of the mahogany banister on the staircase nested a tall Christmas tree, surely lit for their arrival, like the long arm of a protective lover. Wrapped in all-white lights, the tree's branches held an orchestra's worth of silver ornaments, all musical instruments. She pictured a coiffed *Rebecca* descending the stairs in a swirl of reflective silk. The elegant architectural details—the marble floor, carved molding, and varnished pocket doors—whispered their witness to treaties signed, sealed, and celebrated. Old money, indeed, outranked new money of equal quantities.

"I'm Posey, Mrs. Pennington's housekeeper. Do you have a calling card?"

Olivia flinched from her trance when Woody caught her eye and tried not to smile. As she fumbled in her case, Woody whipped out a business card from his breast pocket and handed it to the woman. "Woodrow Rainey. Please call me Woody," And this is my—"

"Olivia Novak," she said to make it easy. At her age, labels other than *wife* proved awkward. *Fiancée* still felt odd. *Partner* sounded too politically correct, maybe even lawyerly. *Girlfriend* came off as adolescent. And *lover*—much too intimate in front of staff. Best to skip the qualifier altogether.

The woman studied the card and paused her gaze on Beauregard. "A service dog? Are there any issues we need to accommodate?"

"Not at all. He's a working therapy dog. One of the mascots of our family's charity."

"Ah . . . very good," Posey said. "May I take your coats?" Olivia slipped off her overcoat, as did Woody his gray cashmere, and handed both to the housekeeper. "Wait here, please."

Posey moved to a hall closet, and then rushed down a ruby-red hall runner. Maybe it had been changed out for the holidays. Olivia checked the lapels of her own ruby-red suit, thinking if she lay down on the carpet she'd disappear. A waft of lemon polish and aged wood swirled in the housekeeper's wake. *What must it be like to live in a house like this?*

"My introduction of you shouldn't be that difficult," Woody said in the quiet.

Olivia shifted, her stomach full of nerves. "Duly noted. We'll stop for whipped cream." A grandfather clock from somewhere in the house struck eleven evenly spaced *bongs*.

On cue, the purposeful steps of an elderly woman, sure-footed and erect for ninety, followed the runner to the foyer with Woody's business card in hand. Althea Woodard Pennington. Eleven o'clock clearly meant eleven o'clock. Olivia had expected Althea to be demure and frail since that picture of her from 1975, but this grande dame had the confident air of Katharine Hepburn with a twist of Anne Bancroft—refined, elegant, and tough. Althea's dark eyebrows contrasted with the sweep of her silver pageboy and still-bright blue eyes. She'd gone white-gray, the kind of gray that made women want to abandon coloring their hair. Her eyes resembled Woody's, more so in person. Same long lashes too. Her features were set off by an unadorned black turtleneck and Black Watch tartan slacks. Diamond studs, the size of Cheerios, flashed like laser lights on her earlobes. Olivia waited for Althea to speak first.

"Althea Pennington," she said and extended her hand.

No doubt she was related to Woody. Olivia picked up the scent of lavender when she offered them each a firm grip. "Olivia Novack," she said. "Thank you for accommodating our tight schedule."

Althea turned to Woody. "Are you Mr. Novak?"

Olivia groaned inside. Woody's hand lingered beyond a normal shake. The first touch of new family carried a sting. He showed no outward offense at the question, but Olivia sensed his male pride shrunk with a blossoming bruise.

"Woodrow Rainey," he said. "Please call me Woody. I'm Mrs. Novak's . . . lawyer."

Olivia widened her eyes. Let the games begin.

The linger of Althea's gaze assessed her and Woody's relationship behind the *Mrs.* title; then she smiled when her eyes shifted to the badge on Beauregard's yellow vest. Without pretense, she stooped and smoothed her hand over the labradoodle's head. "He's a beauty. What's his name?"

"Beau," Woody said. "A gift for Olivia. Her family runs a charitable trust for the training and placement of therapy dogs."

Althea straightened and took aim with her gaze. Olivia was in the scope. "I read that in the notes of the book you so kindly left for me, Mrs. Novak. Let's sit and have a chat." She swept her hand toward the formal living room, its tall pocket doors already open like a tear in a spider's web.

Olivia stepped into a sun-washed room decorated in a neutral palette of cream and gold, with abstract art and sculpture so bold that a museum curator would struggle for breath. Shocks of saturated colors shouted their message to a soft landing in goose down and Italian cotton. A warm wash of forest-fire shades drew her attention to a Frankenthaler painting, which had earned its own wall above the curve of the couch. Olivia summed up the vision as Federal meets Fellini.

Woody normally hid his feelings, but the imminent conversation sparked a strange intensity behind his eyes. *Read me,* it said, but not in a playful way. Their normal sparring had only been a training ground for a high-stakes poker game.

"Sit." Althea gestured to the couch. There it was again, a dog command. Althea took a seat in an overstuffed chair by the fireplace, filled with charred logs but empty of flames. If the woman could've planted herself any further away from Olivia and Woody, the draft from the flue would've goose-bumped her skin.

The order to "sit" struck a nerve in Olivia. Woody had uttered the same command to her after his mother had died. Their conversation had sealed their attraction—with disastrous results the next morning. Out of respect for formal etiquette, Olivia sat on Woody's left side to communicate their unvoiced relationship. Closer to the heart, or possibly to uphold the medieval tradition of freeing his right hand for a chivalrous sword. Beauregard wedged between them and sat on the floor, preferring the protectiveness of both her and Woody's knees. To calm herself, Olivia inhaled in the scent of dried lavender buds in a neon-orange bowl on the coffee table. She appreciated the artful pairing of purple and pumpkin to complement the bold artwork in the room.

"Did you read the book?" Olivia finally said to break the tension.

"I did indeed . . . in one sitting," Althea said and crossed her legs, tight enough for her calves to kiss. "I couldn't put it down. However, I'm not sure why you gave this book to me. Why not one of your own books, Mrs. Novak?"

"My mother told a fictional story that we think is based in truth. In fact, we know it's true."

Althea gazed at Beauregard and held out her hand. The dog trotted to her and set his head over her lap, lured away by the human powerhouse in the room. "All very interesting, but what does this have to do with me?"

"I believe you knew my mother."

"From?"

Olivia grasped Woody's fingers. "As you read, my sisters and I found the manuscript for *Indigo to Black* in my mother's safe after she died two years ago. Her maiden name was Brooks, Ellen Brooks."

Althea's expression didn't waver. "*That's* Ellen Dushane? Ellen . . . Brooks?" Her fingers kneaded Beau's chin a little faster, which prompted a stretch of his muzzle and a headshake. "I haven't heard that name in years."

The buttons on Olivia's white blouse pulsed in rhythm with her heartbeat. The author photo must have triggered Althea's recognition of her mother's identity. The woman wasn't the pro that she thought she was at covering her emotions. Olivia followed Woody's gaze to the mantelpiece. A Steuben apple. He twisted his class ring for her to keep going. "I met Woody because of my mother's book. The main character, Becky Haines, is based on his mother, Della Rainey. Della was my mother's cousin."

Woody leaned forward. "You see, Mrs. Pennington," he said,

"Della—my mother—made a confession before she died. She was in love with your brother, Asher. Did you know about that relationship?"

"I certainly did not." Althea studied Woody's business card, and then narrowed her eyes. "What is this, Mr. Rainey? Why should I be concerned about some past indiscretion of your mother's? One—and only one—woman shared Asher's life."

"Who was that, Mrs. Pennington?" Woody remained focused, but Olivia picked up a hint of resentment in his voice. The collar on Althea's turtleneck appeared to tighten, and Woody took advantage. "Ellen Brooks?"

Olivia held her breath.

"Yes," Althea said, her voice barely a whisper. "They were very much in love." She raised her eyes. "You look like her, Olivia. Do your sisters share the resemblance too?"

"All three of us in different ways." Olivia pictured her mother's face replacing her own in a magic mirror.

"Did Ellen have a happy life?"

"I thought so until I found that manuscript. Now, I'm not sure."

"I should like to meet your sisters." Althea's eyes shifted to Woody. "I sense you want to share something else with me, Mr. Rainey."

Woody studied her. "The young man who was poisoned in the book was based on your twin brother—Asher."

Althea laughed out loud, a bitter laugh to cover her discomfort. "I must give you credit for your creativity. Impossible. Asher was only twenty when he died." The woman steeled her gaze as her fake smile evaporated. "Pure nonsense. I've never heard of a woman named Della Rainey."

"We know how Asher died," Olivia said. "We believe my mother documented the truth, but never meant for it to be published."

Althea froze. She didn't respond, but something else lurked behind her eyes—fear.

"It pains me to say this," Woody said, "but my mother made a death-bed confession when she passed away last year." He leaned forward and tapped the tips of his forefingers together. "My mother told Olivia and I that she had poisoned your brother because she was jealous of his relationship with Ellen. She also told me that I'm the product of relations between your twin brother and my mother. Asher was my father. I'm your nephew."

Althea's eyes shifted with confusion. Her fingers stilled over Beauregard's ears. "You're a liar."

The woman's words jolted through Olivia's body like electricity. "No, he is certainly not. He's the most honorable man you'd ever want to meet."

Woody offered a slight upturn of his mouth. He searched her eyes like a mind reader. Either Woody relished her protectiveness, or he was about to squirt more soap in the oil.

The bowl of lavender blossoms drew Woody's gaze. He dragged his hand through the buds like a fortune in valuable coins. With his palm to his nose, he reclined on the sofa cushion and crossed his legs. "Can you imagine having to live with a crime like that, Althea? I certainly can't. That's why we're here."

"What do you want from me?"

"Della revealed that I had a family I knew nothing about. My mother got pregnant from Asher right before he died. As the product of that encounter, and as a lawyer, I find it not the most comfortable of situations for me. I decided to dig further and found that the murder case didn't close with my father's death. There's more, isn't there?"

Althea's breath became shallow as she examined the pattern on her slacks. "This is absurd."

"But I don't believe that my mother was the only one who wanted to kill Asher."

Olivia had never seen Woody in action, with his every word, every gesture orchestrated to extract information. Did he attach a name to this technique? *Widow Wipe-Out? Dowager Drill-Down?* In a signal for her to remain quiet, Woody set his hand on her arm. Her twist of his class ring turned into a beg for the talking stick.

He gestured to the fireplace, but Woody's gaze remained on

Althea. "That crystal apple on your mantle is a duplicate of the one I found in my mother's possessions, and it's also identical to the one Olivia found in Ellen's after she died. Not a coincidence, Althea. I also have eleven letters from Asher that were sent to my mother. You're welcome to read them, but my father mentioned he'd given both her and Ellen the same gift." Woody pointed to the Christmas tree in the front window. "A Christmas gift, in fact."

Wrinkles formed around Althea's mouth. "Good God. You want money, don't you? This is an attempt at extortion." Althea straightened her spine and brushed her hands over her wool slacks, as if soiled by the conversation. Beauregard licked her fingers, not ready to give up on the petting session. She pulled her hands away.

"I'm not here for money. Far from it." Woody said. "Olivia and I want to protect you from what we believe is a continuing threat. You're my aunt. We're family."

"Family." Althea spat the word and waved it away. "When you're at the end of the line, Mr. Rainey, the sentiment weakens. No one cheers, except for the charities, when you cross to the finish. I guarantee you that someone will be cashing the check and, I assure you, it won't be you."

Woody didn't flinch. "Shall we talk about Simon then? How about his former partner, Tony Corelli? I know about both of them too."

Olivia turned to him, openmouthed. Forget the soap. Woody had lit a match and had thrown it into the gas tank. She could tell this was only a warm-up.

"What happened between you, Simon, and my father?" Woody continued. "Were the three of you little buddies?"

At the last two words, Althea stood. The flicker of her diamond studs betrayed her shaking body.

Beauregard trotted to Olivia's side, overwhelmed by the tension racing around the room. She wrapped her arms around the dog. Nicky Palermo's words filled her head: *The true character of a man comes out when he's pushed.* "Woody . . . What are you doing?"

The question hung unanswered as Woody stood and stepped

toward Althea. "Let's end this. My mother died a tortured woman. Ellen wrote *Indigo to Black* because she was tortured by Asher's death. I think you're tortured too, Althea. Olivia and I will help you, but you'll need to trust us first. You have nothing to lose."

"Get out . . . I want you both out of here." Althea eyes searched the room. "Posey!"

Chapter 19

Left with Truth

The house settled to silence as Posey shut the front door and turned her back to the curtained glass panel. Althea couldn't meet her assessing gaze.

"Mrs. Pennington . . . Are you all right?"

Althea set her hand on her forehead. "I don't really know."

"He's lying," Posey said. "He doesn't know about Simon. He couldn't."

"Agreed. But I don't need to demand a blood test to know our Mr. Rainey is Asher's son. Age can't diminish the similarities. And Olivia Novak might as well have been a mature Ellen at first glance."

"I've never met either one of them. I can't say."

"Trust me. That much is true. Could you make me a cup of mint tea—no, chamomile—and bring it to my room? Then take the afternoon off. I need to be alone."

"I . . . I don't want to leave you."

Althea gripped the banister and started up the staircase. "Please."

"I won't go."

"Suit yourself."

With every step of her climb, Althea recounted the discussion with Woody and Olivia. Woody . . . Woodrow. Olivia . . . No doubt Ellen's daughter. How strange they had found one another. Althea paused in the upstairs hall, along a line of family pictures. Simon never earned a spot on this wall, nor had her father. The frames held only pictures of her and Asher, from infancy to young adult. The last one in the long line was of Ellen and Asher together, a month before Asher died. Althea herself had taken the picture that afternoon at Boston Common, his arms around Ellen while she laughed, but his expression hadn't masked his fear of death. Althea pictured the ring Asher had planned to give Ellen in its leather box, tucked away in her dressing table. The proposal had never happened, and Althea was the only one who knew why. Not Simon. Not her father. Not even Ellen. Convenient to blame Simon, though. But she'd never imagined Asher's death wasn't a suicide. Ellen's book had been a revelation, confirmed by her daughter.

Althea meandered down the hall to her bedroom, a quiet sanctuary once filled with arguments and bruises. Her room had been redecorated after Simon's demise. Taupe walls had been repainted to warm buttercream with drapes of soft sage. The four-poster bed held a thick comforter of matching silk, feminine yet strong. Althea sat on the corner of the bed and wrapped her arm around the post. She shouldn't have ordered Woody and Olivia out of the house. They belonged here, not her. The dog belonged here too. A home should be about loyalty, no matter what, and those three exemplified it.

Two ghosts had sat in her living room. A reincarnated couple. Together at last. Same spark but backed by wisdom that comes with age. Woody had all the same features as Asher's, like her own—his blue eyes, dark brows, strong chin—and if Asher had lived, Althea imagined his hair would have silvered like Woody's, like hers.

Althea pulled Woody's business card from her pocket. She stared at the embossed details of his life and career. Rainey, Bonner & Braden LLC. He'd gone to Yale. The thick ring on his right hand was unmistakable. He had opened a practice in Wolfeboro, New Hampshire. Had his been a happy childhood?

Ellen's family had been in Wolfeboro. She'd married and moved away, never to reach out again. Her daughter had now, too, graced this house. Althea had wanted to take Olivia in her arms and bring her upstairs to see the photos. The resemblance of her features, right down to the mannerisms and determined lilt of her voice, had exuded the truth.

The phone number on the card prompted a burn in her fingertips. The next move sat with her. Fix this egregious error of judgment. Doing so would set off a firestorm, but Woodrow had been right. *You have nothing to lose.*

Althea raised her eyes as Posey's footfalls in the hall were accompanied by a clatter. A teacup against its saucer.

"Your tea, Mrs. Pennington."

"Thank you." Althea extended her hand. "Please set the tray on my dressing table. I need to get my lawyer on the phone."

With slow ceremony, Posey poured a steaming flow of chamomile tea in the cup. "Are you sure that's what you want to do? What about Mr. Corelli?"

"He's not my lawyer. Tony can go to hell. What's he going to do? Kill me?"

Posey secured the lid on the pot but continued to fiddle with it. "It's not beneath him."

Althea set the cup to her lips, sipped, and swallowed. "All I know is that when I took Mr. Rainey's hand, it was a duplicate to Asher's. And Olivia's was Ellen's."

The velvet pillow got a fluff, then Posey swept her hand over the bedspread. "Do you think Mr. Rainey is married to Olivia Novak?"

Althea turned, bewildered by the question. "I . . . I assumed they were married. She wears a wedding band."

"Pardon my contradiction, ma'am, but I don't believe they are. The introduction was awkward at best."

"Then they should be. Couldn't you see it? How they touched each other? Looked at each other? All that silent communication?" Althea suppressed the rise of emotion in her throat. All witnessed gestures she, herself, had wanted, ached for, but never received. She stood and moved to her dressing table. Inside the top drawer sat the small leather box. She hadn't opened it in over thirty years, couldn't bear to. Now, she couldn't bear not to.

Posey stepped forward as Althea opened the latch. The only sound as she cracked open the velvet lid was her housekeeper's intake of breath.

"Beautiful isn't it?" Althea gazed at the four-carat oval solitaire, set in a simple setting so as not to detract from the stone.

"I don't recall you ever having worn that, ma'am."

Althea offered her housekeeper a sad smile. "Heavens no. It doesn't belong to me. This is the ring Asher intended to give to Ellen. I suppose now it should belong to Mr. Rainey to give to Olivia. Yes, her ring." She closed her eyes as Posey squeezed her shoulder.

"Will you accept their help?"

Without answering, Althea snapped the ring box closed and set it back in the drawer. She picked up the teacup and moved to the window. A wash of sunshine hit her earrings as she peered to the street below, creating a shimmery rainbow of reflection over the drapes. "Will they come back, Posey?"

"I don't know. They were upset when they left."

"I'm such a fool." Althea took another sip of tea. "Let's prepare a proper lunch in the event they do. The lion's out of the cage."

Chapter 20

The Conversation

Olivia adjusted her sunglasses—to hide her eyes, if nothing else— as a shield from the tension. Woody drove the car in silence. She didn't even know their destination: she wasn't sure he knew either— he just drove, traversing the narrow streets of Beacon Hill far too fast for conditions of blinding sun on slush. Beauregard stretched across the back seat with his head on his paws, unfazed by the pull of tight turns. Words scrambled in Olivia's head and inched back together. Her voice would unleash the conversation that paced inside a cage.

"You pushed Althea too hard, Woody," she finally said. "You were a different person in there. I almost didn't recognize you."

Woody stared straight ahead. "Take it easy, Liv. Best let things cool off before you start dissecting."

"When she accuses you, she accuses me. How can you be so calm? I wanted to punch her in the face for what she said to you."

"I had to crack her shell. It's not always pretty."

"What did you want to happen? For Althea to open her arms and give you a hug, or just confess and be done with it?"

"I'm not sure," Woody said. "Reactions can be a wild card."

"This isn't a case. This is your family . . . our family."

"Althea was protecting herself. I hit a nerve about Simon." Woody tightened his grip on the steering wheel. "I wanted answers, maybe acceptance of our help."

"You can't whip her and expect her to trust you. Althea's like a shelter dog. You might find her not adoptable."

"Writers and their metaphors." Sunlight flickered off the lenses of Woody's sunglasses. She was reminded of a laser scope with a hunter behind it. Yet another metaphor.

"Is that how all lawyers act?" she said. "Or just you? My lawyer, Ted Beal, doesn't act like that."

"Everyone has two sides when there's a job to be done. You don't think Ryan flips a switch when a gun's being pointed at him? Casey, when he was flying on a combat mission?" He turned to her. Finally. "You have a second side too."

"No, I don't."

"Yes, you do. I read one of your romance books while you were working on Palermo's manuscript."

Olivia braced herself. "Which one?'

"*South of the Borderline.* Your female character, Lola, is fully committed, both feet in. With me, you have one foot in my bed and one foot planted on the floor." Behind his sunglasses, she caught the shift of his eyes in her direction. "And by the way, I thought I was your lawyer."

A flush of heat crept up Olivia's neck with Woody's words. They hurt. It was time. "Pull over. Please stop."

A chunk of melting ice slid down the windshield. Woody switched on the wipers. Olivia interpreted the action as an attempt to swish away her words. Finally, he turned on Mount Vernon Street and slowed the car, their second pass down this road. Woody pulled to a quiet space along a line of red-brick townhouses. Bare trees provided no shade. The engine simmered on slow boil.

Olivia simmered too. "Turn off the car."

The engine silenced. Drips from the trees ticked a random percussive rhythm on the roof. Woody's jaw tightened. "Talk quick. I need to call Ryan to give him an update."

Not exactly a gold-embossed invitation for conversation, but she pushed forward. "Althea has everything and nothing. She's damaged, maybe beyond repair." Olivia set her hands on the heat vent, still warm. "That woman has never known passion."

"I haven't either, until I met you. You're passionate about everything, almost too passionate."

"Yes, I am. I have Adam to thank for that. He loved life—being alive. And he loved books and art."

"And you."

"I hope he did, but secretly I wasn't sure." Olivia unhooked her seat belt and turned to face him. "I'm not going to sit here and pretend I didn't love Adam. We didn't have kids to carry on a legacy, so I immortalized him in my books."

"Never wanted any?"

Olivia couldn't meet his eyes, even from behind her own sunglasses, for fear that Woody would think her a hormone-warped woman. "We were too selfish for that step. His legacy is in me and in my damn books. Not the one we planned for. I didn't want to share the real Adam with the world—that was private—so I made my character Latin in this latest series."

"He's in print. I can't compete with that, Liv."

"I'm not asking you to, but you're better positioned with an inside lane."

"How do you figure?"

"You're alive . . . and you have me. At this very moment, I'm more alive than I've been in the past five years. You did that for me—not control-freak-me—*you.*"

"You certainly are one."

Olivia rolled her eyes. "So are you, but until today you had more class about it." She searched his face with a sense of purpose. "And what about you? Did you ever want kids?"

"Yes."

"And?"

"I always wanted kids, the nuclear family kind. Not the kind of family I had growing up. I didn't get a lot of training how to do it right."

"But somehow you came out fine." Olivia sensed he wanted to tell her something, but the tension in Woody's expression eased with defeat.

"I should just shut up," he said. "Lawyers don't make good fathers."

She tipped back her head. "I don't know how to do this, Woody. You're so different and kinda moody. I can't give you children. I'm too old. It would be a Pope-certified miracle."

"I'm not asking you for kids. God knows I'm too old for that too. Look . . . I've never pried into your and Adam's relationship. Part of me doesn't want to hear it, but I want full disclosure, Liv. I need to know."

A visible breath escaped her lips as she removed her sunglasses and tucked them into her briefcase. "This feels like a deposition."

Woody took off his own sunglasses and tossed them on the dash. "You're not on trial. It's me. Just me. Talk about your marriage."

Olivia swallowed with a tight throat. "In 1979, we fell in love and got married. I was only twenty, the same age as your father when he died. A kid. I didn't know what I was doing then, any more than I know now. We had nothing and didn't care, but we had that thrill of discovery. We settled in and were an inseparable unit for over three decades. He loved rock music, albums, books, and art. We collected turn-of-the-century posters."

"Where are they? I didn't see any in your house when I was there. No pictures of Adam, either."

"I sold the posters at auction. I couldn't bear having them on the wall. The pictures are put away in a box in the garage, along with his personal possessions."

"Is that why you bid on the portfolio of *Maitres* at the auction?"

"Kismet. An unplanned crime of opportunity."

"What did you love about him?"

Olivia pictured herself as a bug under a microscope, with a mag-nified eye looming above her. "Little things. That he loved words and read the dictionary. That he took forever to get through a museum because he had to read every single placard. I had to wait for him in the gift shop. He'd challenge me with facts most people wouldn't care about."

"Like what?"

Olivia shrugged. "Burial rituals of the Vikings, how many inches in a mile, how a hydroelectric dam works. You wouldn't have wanted to play *Trivial Pursuit* with him. He could recite the notes on an album sleeve verbatim. I had no clue how fragile it could be. All those years of reaching, building, and working toward something. We had so much to do. Gone. For three years after the accident, I spent every free minute trying to find that damn white Suburban that killed him. Twisted, dysfunctional passion gone awry, out of control."

"When you told me about the accident, I fell in love with you. I wanted you to be that obsessed with *me* to do such a crazy thing. I was jealous. But it must've been torture for you."

Olivia turned to the back seat. Beau shifted in anticipation of a treat. She dug in her satchel for the resealable bag of kibble and held out a mound of it on her palm. The dog's tongue became courage. "I fell in love the moment I saw you, more in love than I've ever been in my life."

"When you walked into my office, mad as hell with your dukes up, you took my breath away. I'm the one who's getting you in your prime."

For a moment, Olivia tried to think of a self-deprecating quip. Truth welled up instead. "I stepped into your office and fell, Woody, fell hard, fell to my knees inside. I didn't see it coming. My heart's about to burst here. Say something."

"You already know how I feel about you, Liv. I brought you Beauregard to prove my commitment." Woody squeezed the skin between his brows. "Let me rephrase that. I love you, more than you know."

Olivia inhaled his words like aromatherapy. Then she groaned. "But you've never been married. It starts with the bathroom door closed, then it's left open because we won't be self-conscious. The first year, we'll take long showers together until the hot water runs out. After that, you'll say, 'Leave the water running, and I'll hop in after you.' Lingering good-night kisses that steal sleep will turn into hoping I don't wake you up when I drop my book on the floor."

"You're a real romantic. A steel-belted optimist."

"You have no idea what you're in for. I'm like one of those voo-doo doctors who reaches into your chest and pulls out your beating heart. At this stage of life, I just won't settle for anything less. Mediocre is unacceptable."

"I want that from you too, without sharing you with a ghost. I don't want to be continually compared to Adam."

With a grit of her teeth, she decided to pull back the scrim. "If we move forward, you'll have to help me. I've lived through all the stages of marriage. So much doubt. Little things that made me insecure and big things that made me question our commitment to one another. I can't erase thirty-two years." Her forehead started to itch. She rubbed her skin until it stung. "You don't know how it'll be. We'll endure stomach flu, with both ends burning. We'll both have fevers and fight over who's less sick to make soup and wring cold cloths." She counted down on her fingers. "Lovely menopause—night sweats, day sweats, morning sweats. Bursting into tears at breaking a wine glass or losing my keys. I put Adam through the ringer." She turned and wrinkled her nose. "Don't worry, that part's all done. He did you a favor."

"Thank you, Adam," Woody said and dangled his hand on the steering wheel. "Mother Nature is a cruel parent—for men too. Do you honestly think unmarried guys live in a perpetual state of 'first date,' Liv? The past few months with you have been incredible, but it's not a real life. It's not that I can't share. Until now, I've never found anyone I wanted to share it with. I vacuum, do laundry, and sweat to a stink when I kayak. I work on Saturdays and Sundays, sometimes seven days a week, depending on my caseloads. I go to the grocery store and read at night. And men have their own physical issues at our age. At least you women can fake it." Woody hesitated. "And guess who picked me up after my last colonoscopy? Margie, my paralegal. Now *that's* alone without dignity. I love Margie to death, but damn . . . "

Olivia squinted. "Ouch. That's horrible. I don't know what unmarried men do. I grew up with all sisters. Adam was the only man I'd ever been with, besides you."

"Seriously?"

She threw him a sideways glance. "Okay, let's qualify that. A real relationship, not relations I had before Adam. College doesn't count."

Woody nodded. "An important technicality. Keep going. Nothing you've said, so far, spooks me."

"I made a terrible, unforgivable mistake with Adam. The worst kind."

"Did you have an affair?"

"God no. Worse."

"What then?"

The question hovered for a few seconds as Olivia's chest tightened. "I took him for granted. Assumed he'd always be there. We became a pair of old shoes, like the ones you keep around because they were your favorites once. It had become solid-gold boredom. After Adam died, I regretted every wasted day that I didn't touch him, didn't say that I loved him, or didn't whisper a sexy surprise in his ear." She turned and met the endless blue in Woody's eyes. They were glass. "He didn't do any of those things for me, either. I was slowly starving to death, and I didn't know why. I would've thanked the stars if he'd ever come up behind me and nuzzled my neck for no reason, turned off the stove and planted a kiss on me, held me just because, or left me a note as a reminder that he loved me. But he didn't. I was so lonely in his company, and anything I tried ended up making me more frustrated. You won't waste any days, will you?"

"No, Liv, I won't. I'm so sorry."

"You asked for full disclosure, so I'm giving it to you. Little gestures mean everything to keep a long-standing marriage from disintegrating. I love it when your eyes tell me a secret from across a room, one only we know between us. My emotional clock resets when you grab my hand and say, 'Let's go.' The cop and perp stuff we played in New York was amazing. Almost like sex . . . almost." She dabbed the outer corners of her eyes. "I love you whether you do that stuff or not." She glanced at him. "But it would be better if we both promised to make the investment."

Woody pulled her forward to a hungry kiss. He ate her up like in a pie-eating contest, and then pulled away. "I take it back," he said. "You are a romantic, and you're doing a lousy job of trying to talk me out of marriage."

She took his cue to lighten the mood. Deep-dish conversation required small spoons. "Then here's a request for you after we're married . . . "

Woody spread his hands. "Give me all you've got."

"No show-off burping. Guys do that." Olivia tried, without success, to not smirk. "And sports on TV *can't* be an all-day affair."

From the glint in his eyes, the baton had been passed. "We have to watch the Olympics, Liv—nonnegotiable—summer *and* winter. I promise to burp super quietly only every two years."

"Does that mean they're loud the rest of the time?"

"Not around you."

"Adam wasn't handy with fixing things, so I've never had to endure a butt crack squeezing out of a pair of jeans. Not sure I could handle it."

Woody cracked a smile instead. "I'm a lawyer. I write checks."

"No plumbing or electrical?"

He shook his head.

"Damn." Olivia tapped her forefinger on the dash to drum up a compliment. "But you're good at getting spiders. That, right there, rates pretty high, Woody."

"I've proven myself a good spider-getter."

"We could get shingles, you know. I had chicken pox."

"Me too. I got the vaccine. You'll need to get one when you turn sixty."

Olivia nodded, but the thought of turning sixty made her nauseous. "It's not 100 percent, but that's not the point. There could be traumatic medical issues."

"Did you go through any with Adam?"

"I raced him to the emergency room several times. He reacted to insect bites, especially bees, wasps, and fire ants. Every time he got stung was worse. We stored EpiPens in the car, in the kitchen, and in the garage." She nudged her satchel at her feet. "And in here. The last time, though, was a doozy."

"What happened?"

Olivia took in a breath. The details exploded as though an indelible photographic memory. "A wasp. Adam was working in the yard in shorts. He was a stubborn hero flying in the face of the enemy. The sucker got him on the leg. He burst into the kitchen and stared at me with these wild eyes, and said—so quiet—'I've been stung.' Those three words triggered my instinct. Within seconds, he turned the color of a ripe tomato, and his tongue started to swell—right out of his mouth, like something in a case at the meat counter."

"Whoa . . ."

"His breaths were shallow and fast, so I knew he was in serious trouble. I grabbed the injector from the cabinet, threw the safety cap across the floor, and rammed it into his thigh to eject the needle." Olivia reached across the console and mimicked the motion against Woody's leg. He flinched. "I pushed in with every bit of strength I had and counted to ten—one one thousand, two one thousand—slow and even to keep him calm. I held him as he staggered to the car, and then I ran every red light to get him to the emergency room. I was losing him right before my eyes."

"Christ. Didn't you call 9-1-1?"

"No time. I called from the car. A police cruiser intercepted me to clear the way. When I got Adam to the hospital, the doctors were all over him. Anaphylactic shock, a hair's breadth from cardiac arrest." Olivia set her hands over her face to quell the flashes of detail. "They didn't tell Adam how serious it was, but a doctor took me aside to prepare me for the worst." She turned to Woody, his face reflecting the pain she felt inside. "Then it happened . . . in an instant."

Woody set his hand on her knee. "What?"

She grasped his fingers. "The thrill. We zoomed back thirty years when the antihistamines took effect. I held Adam's hand and his face turned back to its normal color. He smiled at me, and I filled with so much light that I didn't know what to say."

"That's all it took? A smile?"

"I'm a cheap love drunk. Doesn't take much to tongue-tie this romance writer." A puff of air escaped her chest. "So I had to come up with a good line for Adam to hide how afraid I'd been."

"This ought to be good. What'd you say?"

"That if I'd known his tongue could get so huge, I would've married him sooner."

Woody burst out laughing and thumped the steering wheel. Her hysterics joined his to steam the windows. She couldn't catch a breath as wave after wave of release ignited Beauregard to erupt with a series of barks. Then Woody quieted and stared at her. All color drained from his face.

"No . . . is it possible?" he said, almost to himself.

Olivia's giggles dissolved. "Is what possible?"

Woody's cell phone rang. He retrieved it from his coat pocket and checked the screen. "Pennington and Corelli."

"Oh my God. Answer it."

Olivia couldn't blink as she studied Woody's face for his brief phone conversation.

"I'll be there, but I won't be alone," Woody said and then disconnected. He handed her his phone. "Put your seat belt on, Liv." His foot jammed down on the clutch as he cranked the ignition. The tires spun and fishtailed over the slush with the push of the gearshift. "Call Ryan. We're going back to Althea Pennington's house. Tell him to meet us there with Casey, your sisters, and Pogo."

Olivia couldn't focus. "Slow down. Who were you talking to? And what did I say before the phone call? Did I give you some kind of clue?" To keep her balance, she gripped the dash. Beauregard barked at the back window as townhouses raced by.

"You want thrills and plenty of hot water?" Woody said. "You're about to get some. Adam may have solved this." He shifted and floored the gas pedal. "And for the record, that was the best sales pitch for marriage I've ever heard."

Chapter 21

Climbing Under Woody's Skin

After shouting his theories on his race back to Beacon Hill, Woody skidded on the ice and pulled to a stop, one block from Althea's house. Olivia turned in the seat and offered him her best wild-eyed stare. Adrenalin pumped in Woody's expression. His eyes darted left and right as the Porsche's exhaust raced past the window.

"They're about five minutes away," Olivia said. "Are you sure you want to see Tony Corelli?"

"I'll have Ryan, Casey, and Beau. This car stays with you." Woody shut off the engine and set the keys in her hand. "Be careful with my baby. You do know how to drive a stick, right?"

Although her stomach dropped, Olivia vowed to be a pillar of strength. "The only way a *real* woman drives—in heels."

Woody leaned over and planted another kiss that tingled her toes. "God, I love you." She inhaled his breath as he ran his forefinger under her chin at the softest part. "You can do this, Liv."

Olivia forced herself to swallow and massaged her neck, like the way she got her Himalayan cat, Freesia, to take a pill. "Okay. Let's review this again. I'll get Althea talking about what pains her most. Guide her with questions of what we already know the answers to, so we can uncover new information. Listen and anticipate her next line. Tell Danny to watch her mouth."

"Right." Woody straightened when Casey pulled his Jeep to the snow bank across the street. Doors slammed.

The inside of the car buzzed with Ryan and Casey's muffled voices. Danny jumped out from the rear door with Pogo, the new sheriff in town. As if reeling out a strip of caution tape, Pogo immediately peed a line of yellow along the sooted snow pile. Lauren checked inside her enormous handbag as Casey whispered in her ear. Her sister smiled and nodded as she showed him, Ethel, her small gun.

It had been a decade since Lauren's face had appeared so relaxed and confident. The tension eased in Olivia's chest. Her sisters and Pogo would be by her side, along with Lauren's gun. As Olivia listened to their discussion, a string of suspicions looped, most of which she couldn't voice. Woody trusted her to get them. And for the first time she felt like his true partner.

Woody's face remained serious, but adventure lit up his eyes. Olivia had never seen him in action in a courtroom, but she suspected this exceeded a calculated pace in front of a jury box. Woody turned, stepped back to the car, and opened the door. He leaned across the driver's seat.

"You call me if you get into trouble," he said. "Get it out of her, Liv. You, Lauren, and Danny can do it. I doubt you guys will need Ethel."

"And Ryan?"

"Yes, he has his gun with him. Casey has one too. We'll be fine."

A panic of second thoughts churned in her stomach. She pointed to Althea's house. "You have more of a legacy in there than me, Woody. What are you expecting me to win?"

Woody bored his blues into hers. "Finding out the truth can be more important than winning."

"I'm actually hearing those words from a lawyer who charges an outrageous hourly rate?"

"I stand by that and always have."

"I'm scared to death about why Tony wants to meet with you."

"Think of me behind glass whispering in your ear. I can't be in two places at once. We're a team, Liv. I'm counting on you. Any last questions?"

She shook her head.

Woody glanced through the side window and rolled his fist at Casey to get going. His gaze shot back to her. "Then give me a good line. I need one."

"You must love me a lot to leave your car in my hands." Olivia tugged off her gloves and squeezed a blop of hand sanitizer in her palm. After a vigorous rub, she held out the travel-size container to Woody. "Want some, Counselor?"

He held out his hand. "Yeah. Gimme a shot. Smells like lavender."

~ · ~ · ~

Olivia's heart knocked as she pressed the speaker button next to Althea's front door. If it had opened, she'd planned to stick her foot through. No messing around.

Danny leaned to the glass side panel, trying to see beyond the sheer, pleated curtain. "Beautiful house."

The zipper on Lauren's coat got a nervous tug. *Zip-zip. Zip-zip.* "She's probably got speakers and cameras all over the place," she said. "I wish I could've seen Althea throw you and Woody out."

Olivia worked her jaw. "Like two cats that took a dump on her furniture. Humiliating. Woody really pissed her off."

"What do we do if she won't answer?"

"I'll pound." Olivia tapped her red-heeled foot. "We're stuck here. I told Woody I can drive a stick."

"Can you?"

"Sorta . . . not."

"Oh, boy . . . " Danny said and elbowed Olivia's arm. "Someone with silver hair is coming down the stairs."

Lauren grimaced. "She must have been upstairs sharpening her teeth."

When the door swung open, Olivia inhaled. It was the house-keeper. "Posey . . . Don't throw us out," she said and leaned to the side. Althea stood behind Posey at the base of the stairs. From her contrite expression, the rage of an hour ago had dissolved. Posey turned for silent instructions. Althea nodded.

"You came back," Althea said and let out a breath. "Come in."

"I thought it best to come with my sisters." Olivia shrugged off her coat and handed it to the housekeeper, who eyed her with uncertainty. "You said you wanted to meet them."

"Where's Woodrow?"

"He felt terrible that he upset you. That's why we're here. We wanted to talk to you alone."

"About our mother," Danny said and held out her hand. "I'm her youngest, Danielle, but call me Danny." Instead of a shake, Althea embraced her. She held out her arms to Lauren.

"And this must be Ellen's eldest."

"Yep. I'm the old lady of the trio, Althea." With wide eyes, Lauren returned the hug and pulled away. "You smell nice, like the fancy soap nobody's supposed to use in the guest bathroom."

Althea chuckled. "Something Ellen would say."

Never one to be left out of a hug distribution, Pogo nosed Althea's slacks. She pulled the poodle to her side. "Magnificent. He's a therapy dog too?"

"The big enchilada," Danny said. "The namesake of the Trust. This is the famous Pogo."

"Where's Beau?"

Olivia tensed. "He's with Woody." An image of Woody putting Beauregard in harm's way at Tony Corelli's office made her mouth dry. With Ryan and Casey in the mix, there was far too much testosterone in one place.

From the about-face of Althea's personality, Olivia could only conclude that Woody's thorny questions had hit several nerves. In an hour of reflection, Althea's makeup had been freshened, but the remnants of sadness couldn't be disguised.

Lauren and Danny followed Althea into the formal living room. Lauren stood in the center of the room and turned a three-sixty. She glanced at Olivia and mouthed, *Wow*.

Danny drank in the room's elegant, soft tones against the boldness of artwork. She had no trouble voicing an opinion. "It's like a beauty shot in *Architectural Digest*."

A fire crackled in the living room fireplace. The decorated Christmas tree, too, had been lit. The ornaments danced with wild abandon in the reflection of warm light. No longer interested in decorative details, Olivia took her former seat on the couch. Lauren and Danny flanked her, forming an age-ordered line of Ellen Dushane's DNA.

For a moment, Althea assessed each of them. Lauren glued her knees together from the scrutiny. Danny fluffed her hair at the attention. Olivia analyzed Althea's face for clues to the source of the woman's agenda.

"All three of you look like her," Althea said and took a seat in her chair by the fireplace. "Beautiful."

Olivia eyed her. "Quite the jolt to find out about our mother's relationship with Asher."

"Life would've been very different," Lauren said and bumped Olivia's thigh. Her eyes shifted to the crystal apple on the mantle. Olivia nodded.

"I'll say," Danny said. Her gaze made another lap of the room.

Althea fingered one of her diamond studs. "Equally so for me to find out about Woodrow's mother and Asher. I honestly didn't know."

The road of *what ifs* would complicate Olivia's mission. She imagined Woody whispering the next words in her ear. "Seems a few people were interested in Asher, not just our mother."

Althea turned away and gazed into the fire. "All these years, so much you don't know. People do despicable, horrible things for money."

"Not Mom," Danny said. "Mom wouldn't have cared about that."

"Like your husband, Simon?" Lauren said.

Olivia's concern for Woody prompted her own offering. "Like Tony Corelli?"

The answer came with Althea's slow nod.

"Woody's offer to help you was genuine," Olivia said. "You're now the only family he has."

Althea expression turned curious, not defensive. "Why did Ellen write that book?"

Lauren collapsed back on the sofa cushion and sighed. "You didn't really know our mother, Althea," she said.

Olivia pictured her sister wanting to put her feet up on the coffee table to settle in for the long haul. "Mom had a lot inside her to get out," she said, "but Mom was protective of family. What Della did put Mom at odds with her instinct. Looking back now, the three of us believe she left the manuscript for *Indigo to Black* for us to find."

"Will you tell us the rest?" Lauren said. "We already know some of it's bad."

"Let's have it," Danny said.

Althea recovered with an inhale. "I made so many mistakes, a few I regret, one I don't. Not that I didn't have a right."

"Like what?" Danny patted Pogo's rump for him to sit.

"I married for what I thought was love. My father saw in Simon what I couldn't . . . or wouldn't. At the time, Simon came with three attractive qualities: he was handsome, powerful, and dangerous." Althea gaze floated to the Christmas tree. "I was dating Tony when Simon wooed me away. Tony never got over it."

"And what did your father do?"

"He was furious. He hated both Simon and Tony, so much so that he disowned me and changed his will to leave everything to Asher. Only Asher existed for him, anyway . . . always had I suppose. But my brother and I were close, bonded. Twins share a relationship that no one can truly understand. To force Simon to show his intent, Asher told me not to say anything to Simon about the inheritance. He said it wouldn't matter in the end."

Olivia glanced at her sisters and leaned forward. "Why? He was going to marry our mother."

"He couldn't, Olivia."

"Why?"

"You see . . . my brother was dying."

Olivia's jaw released. "What?"

"Leukemia, just like our mother, Alice. I had to force him to go to the doctor, but it was too advanced. Back then, treatment was crude, a ticking death sentence. He made me promise to not say a word to anyone, not even our father. His heart wouldn't take it. Asher said the inheritance issue would be fixed after he died." Althea swallowed. "Wait it out."

Olivia's gaze ticked to Lauren, then to Danny. Both of her sisters' eyes widened.

"Did our mother know?" Danny said.

"No. But she came to me, concerned about Asher's erratic behavior and that he didn't look well."

"You knew and didn't tell Ellen?" Olivia said.

"Asher made me promise to keep his condition just between the two of us. I honored his request."

"How did Simon find out about the change in your inheritance?" The question came out from her rehearsed mental list, but the word *leukemia* made her own blood race about Woody's.

"A fight with my father over my dwindling bank account. Even in his weakened state, the great William Woodard delighted in carrying out his scheme as a final retaliation." A bitter burst of breath released from Althea's lips. "He told Simon that he'd left everything to Asher. From that moment on, Simon made my life a living hell."

The fire drew Olivia's gaze. Its snaps and pops recited a repeat rhythm of Althea's words. Woody had no idea about the leukemia. "I'm sorry . . . I—"

Lauren picked up on Olivia's stumble. "Did Simon . . . abuse you?"

"In every way imaginable, and some you can't," Althea said. "I was terrified Simon would kill Asher . . . or me."

Danny squared her shoulders. "As it turned out he tried to, but Woody's mother apparently got there first."

Althea closed her eyes. "All this time. I was convinced that Simon had arranged it, because of the timing of my father's death and Simon finding out about the will. When the police questioned me, I told them it must have been a suicide. Simon would've had me killed me if I'd voiced my suspicions."

"What about our mother?"

"Ellen knew nothing." Althea gave a tired wave of her hand. "She was devastated by Asher's death and left town without a word after talking to the police. She wouldn't attend Asher's funeral, even though I begged her to come. I think she felt betrayed that Asher hadn't been honest with her about his health." Althea's shoulders sunk. "Now I know why she didn't answer. Poor Woodrow. He was only trying to make amends for something he, himself, didn't do."

A sensation of floating swooned in Olivia's head. She recalled her own words to Woody in the car. *There could be traumatic medical issues.*

Althea shifted her gaze to Olivia. "Are you all right, dear?"

"Yes . . . Yes, I'm fine." She pressed her eyebrows. *The letters. The cold Asher couldn't shake. Doctors don't go to the doctor.* "How was Simon after the funeral?"

Althea covered her devastation with a hostess smile. "I ceased to exist."

Pogo nosed the bowl of dried lavender buds on the coffee table. With a sniff and puff, the buds blew into a scattered ring on the glass. Dried kernels dotted his snout with what looked like purple Rice Krispies.

"I'm sorry, Althea," Danny said. "Pogo made a mess." One by one, Danny picked the lavender buds from the dog's wet nose. Olivia held out her hand, and Danny set them in her palm. A succession of canine sneezes sent a spray of saliva across the coffee table. The clear crystal bee now had spots.

A sad smile crossed Althea's face. "Gives Posey something to do."

Olivia rolled the wet buds to release their scent. It allowed her to seize the moment to bring up Woody's theory. "I love lavender, Althea. Don't you?"

Pogo took a few slow steps toward Althea, but he stopped and gazed at Danny.

"Go ahead, Pogo," she said. "It's okay."

Althea held out her hand to the dog. "I love lavender very much."

The crystal bumblebee next to the bowl of lavender drew Olivia's attention. Pogo had given her a much-needed reminder to stay on point. The question she'd asked of Woody after Della's death popped in her mind. *Don't some people who deceive leave a trail to thumb their nose at the world, to prove they're smarter than everyone else?* Woody had given her the ultimate comeback. *Premeditated murder, Olivia, not a deception.*

"My former husband planted lavender in our yard," Olivia said. "We had to remove it when he got stung. He was allergic to bees. Deathly allergic."

"That's right, Liv," Lauren said. "I forgot about that."

Althea raised her eyes and searched Olivia's face. In that moment, she knew her words had hit their mark. She kept her composure, but Althea immediately showed every year of her age in the sag of eyes and the lipstick infused lines on her mouth. The weight of truth revealed her albatross. "I thought you were married to Woodrow, Olivia. Did your first husband die?"

"Woody and I are engaged, but yes, my first husband was killed. Not from a bee sting, but the last time he was stung nearly ended with cardiac arrest. If I hadn't had the auto-injector he would've died."

Danny turned. "When did they invent those Epi-things?"

"The 1970s." Olivia stood and moved in front of the fireplace, tightening the distance between her and Althea. She held out her hands to warm them. "Simon was allergic to bees, wasn't he?"

Althea ran her hand over the back of her neck. "Yes, he—"

Posey entered the living room with a tray and set a plate of shortbread cookies on the coffee table, along with assorted packets of tea and a pot of hot water. She stepped to Althea with a concerned expression. "Don't, Mrs. Pennington. Please, don't."

"This has to stop, Posey," Althea said.

"I'm not going to stand by and allow you to accept blame."

"Blame for what?" Lauren said.

The housekeeper turned, her lips stiff with determination. "I watched that man torture this woman for years," she said and pointed to Althea. "The way he talked to her was a disgrace. He humiliated her in front of his despicable friends. He stole from her. He struck her. I know, because I nursed her injuries."

"Posey. Enough . . . please." Althea set her head in her hands.

The housekeeper held up three fingers. "Mrs. Pennington had the status, the grace, and the breeding. Simon wanted it all, along with her money. And his partner wanted it too."

"Tony came to my defense." Althea's chest heaved. "His solution was my undoing. Tony told me about Simon's bee allergy. Simon never went into the yard. He told me how to do it."

"Tony Corelli?" Olivia said.

Posey nodded and smoothed the waist of her black dress. "She didn't do it. I told Mrs. Pennington that I would. She didn't need to be involved."

"Is this true, Althea?" Olivia said and grasped Althea's shoulder.

Althea placed her hand over Olivia's. "Consider yourself a lucky woman, my dear. Woody loves you. I saw it in his eyes." Althea didn't answer the question but had employed a Woody technique. She'd redirected.

"Mr. Corelli said he'd take care of her," Posey said. "Turns out it was the other way around."

Danny shifted. "So . . . *you* killed Simon?"

"Before I served lunch, I brought a bee into the kitchen on cuttings of lavender sprigs. With a tissue, I picked off the bee and carried it carefully in my hand. I set the vase on the dining table and served the water. I dripped some on the back of Simon's shirt. I apologized and wiped his shoulder with the tissue. The bee crawled onto his collar, and then I left the room."

Althea's expression hardened. "I watched that bee sting him, and I stood over his body to witness his suffering. I wanted him to beg, but he didn't. He called me a foul name before he choked on his tongue. He died staring at my face."

"I waited to make sure that man was dead before I called the authorities," Posey said and stared at the bowl on the coffee table. "I saved that arrangement and dried the buds. They're replaced with new ones every two weeks. Their scent never lets either of us forget that we made things right."

Olivia squeezed Althea's hand. "We'll protect you, both you and Posey. Our mother would've wanted us to."

Lauren stood and stepped to the Christmas tree. She leaned into a branch and plucked off a few needles. She held them to her nose. "Simon's cause of death will remain as cardiac arrest. Are we all agreed on that?" Her gaze circled the room. "This is a chick conference with important bylaws."

"Agreed," Danny said.

"Agreed." Olivia nodded for emphasis. She kicked off her red heels and knelt in front of Althea. "This is what family's all about."

Althea dabbed at the corner of her eye with her polished fingernail. "You're going to tell Woodrow, won't you?"

"Of course, he's family. Believe me—he already knows."

Lauren poked at a mercury-glass angel; its sway gave the appearance of flying to a clarion call. Pogo trotted to Lauren's side and sat, fascinated by the movement. "How much have you handed over to Tony?"

"One hundred thousand per year," Althea said. "On my birthday, every year since Simon died."

Danny stared into space, her eyes shifting with the calculation. "Over three million dollars. That's enough to get the attention of an auditor."

"Woody will stop this, Althea," Olivia said and inspected the woman's elegant hands. Only minor spots, but the veins protruded with blue. "He's protecting you now. Woody's meeting with Tony in his office as we speak."

Althea released Olivia's fingers and rose to her feet. With a slight teeter, she cried out, "No!"

Chapter 22

Heroes

At two o'clock, Woody stopped in front of the glass doors that led to the offices of Pennington & Corelli. Before he gripped the handle, Beauregard gazed up with inquisitive eyes. Woody gave the dog's head a scrub.

"Good boys love the law," he said and thumped Beau's side. With his tail in a vigorous mid-wag, Beau turned his head to Ryan, who leaned over a water fountain pretending to drink.

"I'll be downstairs in the lobby," Ryan said without turning. "The boys just confirmed they heard every word. They're listening in the car out front."

Casey adjusted his own earpiece. "I'll be by the elevator. Say 'cash the 'check' and we'll be in there like a shot."

"C'mon, Beau." Woody glanced at the dog's collar and held open the glass door. Beauregard sauntered in first.

The lobby bore the stamp of high-net-worth billings and generous retainers. No doubt, the spoils were distributed with favors and bribes, which probably included tickets for box seats to the Celtics. Rich wood paneling lined the walls. A blue-blood thug club. Several copies of *The Robb Report* sat on a side table, fanned in a measured arc.

Like most established law firms, the middle-age woman behind the reception desk presented herself with the deportment of a seasoned professional. Paid well from the look of her. Expensive suit.

Veneer. The whole firm appeared to have a thin layer of respectability, but he'd bet that very few clients visited the office. Woody figured the real meetings were held in the back rooms of restaurants or at the jail. A sprawling holiday flower arrangement of evergreen sprigs and white lilies filled one entire corner of the counter. Beauregard's nostrils pulsed, picking up the scent.

"Good afternoon," Woody said and slid his business card toward the woman. "Woodrow Rainey for Anthony Corelli."

"Mr. Corelli doesn't see clients anymore"—she studied the card and raised her eyes—"Mr. Rainey."

Woody held her gaze. Standard answer offered to anyone she didn't recognize. "I'm not a client. In fact, I don't know why I'm here." He offered her his best smile. It appeared to work, because her expression softened. "I have somewhere else I need to be, but Tony requested this meeting. My service dog is due to make his rounds at Mass General. You'd best check. Otherwise, I'll be on my way."

"He doesn't share his calendar with me." The woman's brows knitted. Odd she didn't pick up the phone. Instead, she made quick steps down the paneled hall. A blue-suited associate leaned from his office doorway and retreated. Beauregard took three steps forward.

Woody held out his hand. "Wait here, Beau."

Setting up the wire on Beauregard's collar and talking through a plan with the detectives had eaten some time. With a significant head start, Woody had to believe Olivia and her sisters were making progress with Althea. If Althea and Tony were conspiring, Olivia had intercepted the ability for Althea to give Tony a heads-up. Beau's tail stood straight up as the receptionist came back

down the hall. The closer she got, the faster Beau's tail showed his anticipation.

"Mr. Rainey, please follow me," she said. "Would you like for the dog to remain with me?"

"Thank you, but no."

Associates and administrative staff occupied small offices in a long line. Each glanced up from their keyboards when Woody and Beau passed by. The conference room and larger offices sat empty but were elaborately decorated, with the grandest at the end of the hall. Typical.

Tony Corelli sat behind an expansive desk, hunched in a suit he used to fill. Today he resembled a marionette with a few broken strings. A wheeled walker, with neon-green tennis balls on its front legs, sat parked next to the desk, ready to give Tony clumsy flight. Other than Woody's business card on a leather blotter, no other piece of paper occupied the desk's surface. Instead, a remote control sat inches from Tony's claw-like hand. A flat-screen television in a wall cabinet scrolled stock symbols beneath a muted talking head. Bookcases were dotted with photographs of celebrities, politicians, and policemen, all shaking hands with younger versions of Tony. The most elaborate frames held photos of Althea Pennington, black-and-white glossies to present-day color ones, marking every phase of her long life. A man obsessed. None of the photos bore images of Simon.

"What do you want with Althea?" Tony said, his robust voice coming out as a growl. He wiped his bottom lip with his knuckle. Small talk wasn't on Tony's agenda.

Woody nudged the dog forward. "No introductions?"

"I know who you are. Sit."

At the command, Beauregard sat back on his haunches. Woody took a seat in a substantial leather club chair. At below eye level, the chair's position had been designed to make clients feel ill at ease and inferior, a not-so-subtle message of Tony's control. From the spider veins peppering the end of the man's bulbous nose, Woody half expected to be offered a drink from a hidden bar in the bookcase.

"You were at her house with some dame. Lawyers who drive fast cars are trolling, Mr. Rainey."

Woody crossed his legs. "How did you know I was visiting?"

"Your license plate says New Hampshire. Small practice up there with a couple of partners. Bet you want that operation to grow. The state's slogan is 'Live free or die.' Which do you subscribe to?"

"Is that a threat?" Woody stroked Beauregard's head to keep him facing forward.

"I ask the questions, and I asked you one."

"Can't family members make a friendly visit?"

Tony flicked the corner of Woody's business card. "Althea has no family."

"You're mistaken."

"What do you take me for?" Tony glanced at the scroll of ticker symbols on the flat-screen television. "I'm her family."

"I'm her nephew. Blood family."

Tony clattered the remote. He finally found the OFF button. "Since when?"

"I recently found out that her twin brother, Asher, was my father."

"You're an ambulance chaser, Mr. Rainey. Rich dead people aren't hard to find. Fabricate a connection, move in, then you extort money."

Woody smirked inside, but he kept his expression stern. "Is that an ad hominem description of me or you?"

"You'd better stick to litigating tainted maple syrup, Rainey."

"And you should stop going after Althea's money."

"Donations."

Woody smoothed his hand over the curved arm of the chair. "To a dubious charity that could use a thorough audit."

The bags under Tony's dark eyes lifted. "Our charity is audited every year."

"By someone who benefits from doling out a passing grade? I had to downshift my intellect to figure that out. Too easy."

"Won't find anything."

Time for a bluff. "Little Buddies isn't so little. Althea's agreed to show us a record of every check you cashed. You cashed the checks, but did you provide her a tax-deductible receipt?" Beauregard's collar drew Woody's eye. His words went into the mic and disappeared before he could rephrase. He hadn't meant to use the code phrase. The dog shifted his front paws, releasing a delicate jingle of his ID tags.

"Not tax-deductible. I follow the rules." Tony's expression tensed as he pulled a handkerchief from his pocket. He wiped his mouth and drilled his watery gaze into Woody.

"Your rules," Woody said. In the silence that followed, their eyes locked in unspoken conversation. *Keep Tony talking.* Woody pointed to the bookshelves. "You don't have any pictures of Simon among your collection of memories, even in the ones with Althea. Odd for a firm that still bears the Pennington name."

"Tradition."

"The sign-in log downstairs shows that Althea came to see you on Friday afternoon. What did you two talk about?"

Tony worked over his lip. "Still a good-looking woman."

"She's ninety, Tony. You're more interested in the booty in her bank account."

"Not it."

"Enlighten me."

The leather groaned when Tony leaned back in his chair and rocked. He winced at even that small amount of movement. Beauregard's head nodded with every chair squeak. "Althea . . . What an exquisite creature. She asks" —he spread his hands— "and I do. I make things go away. And I'm damn good at it."

"By making sure she inherited the family money? By getting her away from Simon?"

"Wicked woman. We use each other. Always have."

Woody took a chance. "So you helped? Got rid of her brother who stood in the way of the money? Then got rid of Simon, so you could move in to take his place?"

"I don't know what happened to Asher." Tony raised a wiry brow. "I'll never figure that one out."

Although tempted, Woody held back the details to keep Tony talking. "No, I suppose not. But you know what happened to Simon."

Tony's eyelids hooded. "What the hell are you talking about?"

Woody spread his hands. "Do you believe in ghosts, Tony?"

"No."

"I'm learning that the dead speak loud and clear—in letters, in books, and in the expressions on the faces of those who knew them. The living can't move on until the truth comes out."

"Can't pin Simon on me." Tony tapped his forefinger on the arm of his desk chair. "I'm an idea man."

"Not a pin exactly. More like a sting." Beauregard's gaze shifted from Tony to Woody and back again. "The bee allergy was your idea, wasn't it?" At least Woody hoped so. He had to trust that Olivia was making progress with Althea about the theory.

"Cocktail talk."

"Brilliant, Tony. You could get rid of Simon and free Althea without being implicated."

"Simon was planning to kill her. I had to stop it. Ungrateful, wretched woman."

"When she didn't come running, you turned on her."

The wrinkles around Tony's eyes deepened. "What do you want? How much?"

Woody shook his head. "I don't give a damn about the money. I'm not one of those problems that you can magically make go away. I'm here to protect Althea from you. Let her go."

Tony's hands shook as he slid open his top desk drawer. Expecting for him to retrieve a checkbook, Woody inhaled when Tony pulled out a .38 Special. No doubt it was loaded.

"I can't," Tony said.

A wrinkled note in Woody's office safe held the same two ghostly words. His father had written them to Della, and Olivia's mother had made them indelible on the pages of her novel, *Indigo to Black*. Olivia, herself, had uttered the two words to Woody in her desperate attempt to hold on to Adam's memory. Now, the words could take him away from the one person who held his future. *Olivia*. She wasn't a ghost. Woody didn't want to become one. The ring box in his breast pocket pulsed with the truth of what he stood to lose. A strange sensation crept up Woody's legs as he stared at the gun's barrel. Beauregard started to whine.

"Don't do it, Tony," he said. "I'm getting married."

"Lucky you." The man grasped the gun and pointed it at him with a surprisingly steady hand.

Woody sat frozen, unable to take a full breath when the office door banged open. He didn't turn, but his pulse pounded plenty. For some reason, he thought last moments would feel different.

"Put it down, Tony." Ryan's voice. "I'm a cop. And more are on their way up."

In one smooth leap, Beauregard soared over the desk. Woody lunged for the dog, but only the end of Beau's tail slipped through his fingers. The gun fired with a pop. Tony fell from the chair with Beau on top of him. The gun clanged against the Tony's walker and slid across the carpet. In an instant, Ryan secured Tony's hands behind his back, pinning him to the floor.

Tony groaned. "You're a fraud, Rainey."

"Check Beau, Woody," Ryan said. "Anybody hit?"

Woody called the dog to his side and inspected his fur for blood. "No, he's okay."

Beauregard nosed Woody's tweed suit coat. A strange metallic smell of iron drew both of their attention to a tear in his left breast pocket. He stared at it, more curious than concerned. He patted the square lump. Still there. A sweat broke across his forehead. His white shirt grew damp. A blooming circle of bright red had soaked his shirt and jacket lining, warm and sticky.

"Ryan?" he said. "We have a problem."

As the detectives cuffed Tony, Ryan holstered his Glock and met Woody's gaze. Woody opened his lapel. "Casey . . . Call an ambulance double-quick." In one swift move, Ryan pulled off Woody's jacket.

"Already did, when I heard the gunshot," Casey said and eased Woody into the chair. Words scrambled as Casey burst the buttons on Woody's shirt. The hard press of his hand ignited a searing pain in his chest. "You're gonna be okay, buddy. Look at me."

Woody raised his eyes to his friend. "You've seen worse, right?"

"Much worse."

"Get what they needed, Ryan?" The furniture in the office started to spin.

Ryan nodded. "Plenty. Keep talking."

Woody gripped Casey's arm. "Tell Olivia . . . to cash . . . the check."

"You said the code words fifteen minutes ago. That's why we're in here."

"And make sure . . . she gets my jacket."

Ryan pulled out his phone. "Liv can drive a stick, right?"

Woody forced out a weak smile. "What do *you* think?"

"That maybe Olivia shouldn't cash that check, 'cause your mechanic's gonna need a hefty retainer."

Chapter 23
First Gear

"You're too upset to drive, Liv," Lauren said and slammed the door of the Porsche.

Olivia let out a sob and stared at the grid pattern on the shift knob. "What the hell? Seven gears? I'm not going to the moon here."

Danny jutted her head between the front seats. "The back is designed for a Hobbit. Go, Liv. Pogo and I are getting claustrophobic."

"I can do this. I watched Adam."

"You never drove the Volkswagen?" Lauren said, her mouth agape.

Olivia thrust her high heel on the clutch and fired the ignition. "A Volkswagen is just like a Porsche."

"How so?"

The engine purred. "They're both German. So far so good."

Lauren leaned in and squinted. "First is to the left and up. Go."

A whimper escaped Olivia's lips. "He's okay. He's okay."

Pogo whined and shifted on the back seat, impatient to get going. Danny rubbed the dog's chest. "Ryan and Casey are with him, Liv. Mass General is one of the best."

Olivia pushed the knob forward, but the car didn't move. The engine only revved. "Dammit."

"The parking brake's on," Lauren said and pointed. "See the light on the dash?"

With a yank of the release lever, the fear disengaged in Olivia's chest. "Noooo . . . I can't. I can't go through this again." Her forehead knocked against the steering wheel. Tears rolled over the shield of the car's insignia. She turned to Lauren. "If I screw up Woody's car, he'll kill me."

Lauren opened the passenger door. "Get out. Come around."

Danny slumped against the back seat and stared at the roof lining. "You can't drive a clutch, Lauren."

"I do now. If I have to, I'll put it in neutral and 'yabba-dabba-doo' us to the hospital with my bare feet." Lauren bolted from the car.

Olivia hauled herself from the driver's seat and slid on the slush in her heels. Grasping the hood, she inched herself toward the passenger side. In the exchange of places, she stopped and searched her sister's face. A thousand words and images passed between them as the car's exhaust raced past them in the chilled air. A trade of strength and weakness, yet again. Lauren squeezed Olivia's shoulders, a gesture that said what she couldn't.

Danny smacked the back of the seat. "We could've been there by now." Pogo barked to punctuate the urgency.

Lauren pressed the clutch and grasped the gearshift. She jutted her chin toward Danny's reflection in the rearview mirror. "Was it your bright idea for me to quit smoking?"

"Damn straight," Danny said.

The car lurched backward and bumped the Audi parked behind them. Olivia grabbed the dash. A pulsed alarm started to blare, accompanied by Pogo's barks.

"That was reverse, Lauren," Danny said and dug through her purse.

Lauren gritted her teeth. "Hand to God, Danny. One more word outta you and I'm going to rip out a clump of your hair, roll it, and smoke it."

"The Germans aren't getting along." Danny sighed and flipped through a spiral notepad. "Better leave a note with Olivia's information. She's supposed to be driving."

Panic ejected Olivia from the car to inspect the rear bumper. A slight crease graced Woody's fender, but the other car appeared untouched. "Oh God."

Danny fluttered a piece of paper from the passenger window. Plucking it from her fingers, Olivia wadded the note and shoved it in her coat pocket. She couldn't take in one more scenario.

Olivia gathered the bottom of her coat, sat, and slammed the car door. The seatbelt got a yank and a click. "Now can we go?"

"I think I found first," Lauren said. "It's not that far to the hospital. All downhill. I won't shift."

The grind of metal made Olivia's heart sink. At least they were moving.

~ • ~ • ~

At three o'clock, Lauren lurched the Porsche toward the emergency bay of Mass General. Olivia's ears buzzed from twenty minutes of the engine's scream in first gear, a mirror of the thoughts in her head. The unthinkable had happened before and may happen again. She'd not been able to talk to Adam before he died. So much to say. So much left unsaid from the past. This time had to be different.

"There's Ryan, Casey, and Beau," Danny said and pointed.

"Pull up to the door," Olivia said to Lauren, barely able to get out the words. Pogo stuck his head between the front seats. His cold, wet nose nuzzled her neck.

Olivia released the seat belt's buckle as the car jerked to a stop. She grabbed her briefcase and burst from the passenger side. Woody's wedding ring had to remain near. The door hung open in mid-yawn as she raced to talk with Ryan.

She gripped his jacket. "Where is he?"

Lauren caught up to Olivia's side, breathless. "What's happening?"

Ryan met Olivia's gaze. "Hold here a sec. I want to talk to you before you go tearing in there."

"Help!" Danny shouted from the car. "Pogo and I can't get out of this damned backseat."

"Give me the keys," Casey said. "I'll get 'em out and park Woody's car. Lauren, why don't you come with me."

In her puffy coat, Lauren wrapped Olivia in her arms. "He'll be okay. This isn't like before." She moved with Casey to the car. "I'm coming."

Not like before. Olivia's stomach clenched with the anticipation of Ryan's words.

"Look. I won't lie to you," Ryan said.

"Tell me."

"He's been shot. That's all I know."

"Where? How bad?"

"Chest. We don't know how bad yet. The doctors are with him. Let them do their job." Olivia met his concerned eyes, trained eyes, blue eyes like Woody's. "Nod if you understand me."

Olivia's throat closed in an effort to keep a flow of tears in check, but her head moved up and down. "Take me to him, Ryan."

"Promise me you'll be calm? Gunshot wounds produce a lot of blood. It's normal."

"On a scale from one to ten."

"Maybe a four." Ryan released her and held back Beau. "But Woody's in room three."

The automatic doors of Emergency whooshed open. Olivia's long wool coat billowed behind her. *Room three.*

"Hold on," said a middle-age woman from behind the check-in desk. "Your name?" She held out a sheet of labels marked with the word VISITOR and a Sharpie pen.

Olivia halted, offended by the question. "I'm . . . Mr. Rainey's wife."

From nowhere, Danny rushed forward with Pogo and grabbed the sheet of labels and wrote *VIP* on it. To the woman's shocked expression, Danny peeled off one and stuck it to Olivia's hand like a high-five. "Go with Ryan, Liv. I'll wait here with Beau and Pogo for Lauren and Casey." The dogs appeared confused about which job to do. "Stay here, Pogo. Sit, Beau."

A squeeze from Ryan's hand started Olivia's trek down a hall of examining rooms with sliding glass doors. Each step held something new, yet oddly familiar. *Like before.* A wall dispenser of hand sanitizer drew her gaze, but she kept moving forward.

The door to room three sat open. Interns and nurses moved in and out in their urgent, practiced dance. She grabbed the arm of a young intern from the stream.

"Can I see him?"

"He's awake," the young intern said. "But he won't be for long. He's headed to surgery."

"Surgical one. Stat!" another doctor said into the phone. He ignored her and stepped to a light box that held a skeletal image of Woody's chest. She glanced at the X-ray. An obstruction of solid white had embedded beneath Woody's left shoulder. A nurse changed an IV bag full of blood. Olivia wished it were hers. She had no clue if her blood was compatible with Woody's.

"What's his blood type?" Olivia said and moved to Woody's side.

"O-negative," the nurse said. "Lucky we had some on hand. He's lost quite a bit. O-negs can give to everyone, but he can only receive that type."

Her eyes closed like a curtain to start a new act. "He can have mine. I'm compatible. I'm O-negative."

"Liv . . . " Woody's eyes floated to focus. How many of her did he see? Olivia set her hands on each side of Woody's face and kissed his forehead. Touch. His skin felt cool and clammy. "I'll kill the bastard. I swear I will."

"Just a . . . scrape," Woody said and reached for her face, missing it.

Woody's naked body under the sheet rendered him helpless. She should have been the one to remove his jacket, his shirt, and his slacks. That intimate task should have been hers to perform. Olivia's gaze trailed from Woody's face to the soaked red gauze packed below his left shoulder. *Say something stupid.*

She leaned close to his ear. "It's been way too long time since I've driven a stick."

Woody attempted to throw her a medicated smile. "Since never? Not that hard, honey. In heels I'm sure you're amazing."

Panic rose in her own chest at the tube snaking into Woody's arm. Deja vu held no comfort. The harder she tried to shift her emotions into neutral, for Woody's sake, the more she wanted to grab him, hold on, and wail.

"I can do anything . . . in heels," she said.

Woody struggled to take a breath. "Take 'em off . . . I love your feet. Lemme see your feet." His faint smile flattened to a wince.

Olivia turned to the surgeon. "This is how we normally talk. He's fine, right?" No answer. She gazed at Woody's face, hopefully not for the last time.

A pedal released like the report of a gunshot. The bed started to roll, and Olivia quickened her steps to keep up.

"I won't leave you," she said, but the momentum forced her to let go. "What's happening?"

"There's a bullet in there," the surgeon said and stopped. The bed kept going. "I need to get it out."

Olivia grabbed the lapels of the surgeon's white coat. She glanced at his name embroidered on the pocket. "Dr. Ehrenfeld . . . I want to go in with him. Please . . . he's losing consciousness."

"I gave him a sedative. Preps him for the anesthesia to save time." Dr. Ehrenfeld glanced down at her clenched fingers, his expression only tolerant. "Your husband is probably going to be fine, Mrs. Rainey, but we need to move fast. He's lost a lot of blood. I'm sorry, but you can't go in."

Olivia searched his eyes. Their color disappeared from her

memory in an instant. Some kind of olive. "I'll stay out of the way. I'll gown up, wash up, and shut up. You won't even be able to tell that I'm not Mrs. Rainey yet."

"Wait with your family. From the X-rays and CT scans, nothing major was hit, but I've got to get that bullet. I'll find you when I'm done."

"Can I at least walk with him to surgery? Please?"

Dr. Ehrenfeld attempted to pry her hands from his coat, but Olivia couldn't loosen her grip. "He's already on his way while you've been talking to me. Now, I've got to gown up, wash up, and concentrate."

Olivia fingers eased. She stared at the wrinkled cotton, as if it had been a bad attempt at origami that required a do-over. She smoothed the fabric over his chest, but her desperation had left the evidence from too much starch. "You could have just said 'shut up'. Would have been more effective."

The surgeon's expression softened. "I have more discretion out here, but you certainly don't want to hear me say that in there. What's your blood type?"

Olivia panicked all over again. "I . . . I'm O-negative."

"Good. Mr. Rainey needs yours. If you want to do something for him, go back to Emergency and give them a few liters. It'll make you feel better. I'll find you. I promise." He nodded to Ryan, who was coming toward them. She'd been ceremoniously handed off. *Get her out of the way.* The hem of the surgeon's white coat disappeared around the corner.

Olivia turned. "He needs my blood, Ryan."

"You'd better get moving then," he said.

"What's your blood type?"

Ryan shrugged. "No clue. And don't ask me my Social Security number, either."

"Do you know Danny's blood type?"

Ryan spread his arms. "Same as yours . . . O-negative."

"You mean to tell me that you know mine and Danny's but not

your own?"

"Lauren's too. I made it a point, in case any of you were ever in an accident."

Olivia shook her head. "After thirty-two years with Adam, can you believe I still have no idea what his blood type was?" She stared at Ryan with the realization. "You're the most honorable, unselfish man I've ever known."

A rush of O-negative pounded in her veins, an overflow she had no right to hold inside. Her mother's blood pumped in her veins too. Ellen would be quite shocked at how her daughters' lives had progressed. Danny was lucky to find Ryan again. Olivia, herself, was lucky to find love—twice—and with Della's son no less. Lauren might get lucky again.

"Where's Casey?" she said.

"With Lauren."

"And the dogs?"

"With Danny."

"What about you? Where will you be?"

"Right here if you need me."

Olivia wrapped her arms around Ryan and squeezed with every ounce of neediness inside of her. His warmth obliterated the sounds of the ER—slide of doors, click of computer keys, beeps, and squeaks of wet shoes. He couldn't save her from what she could only do herself. Hell equaled helplessness. She wasn't helpless and would never allow herself to be again.

A young nurse rushed down the long corridor with a white drawstring bag, puffed with contents. The way the woman held out the plastic bag, almost breathless, it might have been laundry that missed the cleaning cart. "Here are Mr. Rainey's clothes. I put his watch in here too. Did he have any other jewelry?"

"No . . . I don't think so," Ryan said and watched the handoff of Woody's effects.

Olivia set her hand on her forehead. "A ring . . . on his right hand. A Yale class ring."

"We left that on," the nurse said. "Couldn't get it off, but it won't be a problem. We're more concerned about swelling on the left side."

A crush rolled over Olivia's chest when the nurse turned and walked away, literally having left her holding the bag. Woody's last words exploded in her head. *Lemme see your feet.*

She turned to Ryan. "I'll meet up with you in the waiting room."

"Are you sure?"

"Two things I have to do . . . by myself."

A burn radiated through her toes. Olivia kicked off her shoes and jammed them into the bag. Quick, light steps escalated into a full run back to Emergency.

Chapter 24
Letting Go

"I need a doctor!" Olivia held up her left arm. She waited for the staff to descend, but they didn't. The white bag of Woody's clothes swung at her side. She might as well have been hailing a taxi with her recycling. "I was just here with Woodrow Rainey. A gunshot. Please help me."

Nurses straightened and stared with instant assessment. Several doctors raised their eyes from computer screens and turned.

Olivia slapped her bare foot on the linoleum. "Don't make me beg."

In the uncomfortable moment of silence, Olivia searched for a familiar face. She spotted the young blond intern who had attended to Woody. He broke from the pack and approached her with his baby-face and blue eyes.

"What's the matter?" he said. "Mr. Rainey's gone to surgery."

"He needs my blood, O-negative." Olivia held out her arm. "Take it. Take as much as you can without killing me."

"I'm sure we have enough."

"It's personal"—she glanced at the badge clipped to his pocket—"Dr. Michaels."

The doctor guided her into Woody's former trauma room, trailed by the attending nurse. He slid the door shut. "Roll up your sleeves."

The room without the bed made Olivia cough to hold back the welling tears. She shed her wool coat and red suit jacket, and the release of each sleeve button of her blouse made her hands shake. The blouse floated to the floor like an exhausted, battle-worn flag. Embarrassment was the least of her worries. She held out both arms.

"Preference?" Dr. Michaels said. "Both have good-looking veins."

"The right. There's something else I need you to do with the left."

The doctor raised his eyes, inquisitive. "Have a seat."

The nurse tapped Olivia's arm. "Just a stick. Want some juice if you feel woozy?"

Olivia shook her head. She didn't even feel the prick of the needle. A ribbon of blood snaked through the tube. She pictured it pumping into Woody. Her gaze ran the length of her arm and stopped at Dr. Michaels, who had been watching her.

"Powerful stuff you got going into that bag," he said. "Worth a pretty penny to people with that type."

"Worth a fortune to Woody, and to me. It's not enough, though. There's something else." Her heart escalated to a pound.

"Calm down, sweetie," the nurse said. "Filling a bit too fast. You'll get faint."

Olivia held out her left hand. The gold band that had once held everyone at bay had become a fragile display for attention.

A pat on her back weakened Olivia's knees. The tears came in silence. She'd learned how to keep them quiet after years of experience. "I can't do it myself . . . I can't."

"Take a breath," the young doctor said. "What is it you want me to do?"

Olivia sniffed and swallowed. She'd reduced herself to a scared child inside. "I want my new ring; the one Woody gave me. This one's choking me. Cut it off."

Glances exchanged between the nurse and the intern. The nurse stepped to the door. Ball bearings scraped when she pulled the curtain over the glass.

Dr. Michaels turned the switch on a swing-arm lamp. After a twist of her ring and a squeeze of her scabbed knuckle, he smirked. "It certainly won't get over that. You've made a valiant attempt."

She nodded. "Is Dr. Ehrenfeld a good surgeon? Please say yes."

"One of the best. Mr. Rainey is in good hands." Dr. Michaels rolled a wheeled cart in front of her and guided her hand to it. She splayed her fingers. The nurse ripped open a package of gauze.

"Not the finger, just the band," Olivia said, recalling Palermo's suggestion for dismemberment.

"Good thing it's quiet right now. In about two hours I wouldn't be able to take the time to do this. Five o'clock is the witching hour."

"Why?"

"Accidents, drunk drivers, distracted moms on their phones in traffic. We don't go anywhere during the evening commute." The doctor chuckled. "I take it that's not Mr. Rainey's ring."

Olivia closed her eyes. She zoomed back to her own witching hour of five thirty when the phone rang. "I'm a widow. My husband was killed in a hit-and-run accident five years ago."

"I'm sorry. I didn't mean—"

"I'm getting a second chance," she said. "Some people don't get even one in a whole lifetime."

Stillness screamed in the room. A drawer opened and closed. A faint moan emanated from the neighboring room, followed by a string of profanity. Olivia turned. Poised in the doctor's hand was an electric surgical saw. Palermo's words resonated. The device could cut off her finger. He set it on the tray in front of her while the nurse changed the IV bag for an empty one. Olivia figured she was about to fill it in an instant.

"You sure you want to do this?" he said.

She met his eyes, so bright with his whole adult life still ahead. "Are you married, Dr. Michaels?"

"No, but I will be this summer." A slight smile signaled he was out of his comfort zone. "We can't agree on the size of the guest list.

The parents are involved."

The nurse rolled her eyes. "Ugh. You're doomed, Dr. Michaels."

For one last indulgence, Olivia's forefinger grazed the gold band. Vows meant forever, but sometimes fate had other ideas. She refused to give up on romance.

"Run away with your bride, just the two of you," Olivia said. "Grab a passerby as a witness." She inhaled to steady her shake. "Say those vows with every ounce of sincerity you have inside you and make love to her until the sun comes up. Then order room service. Be prepared to start all over again. Stamina is your friend, so get some good sleep the night before. You'll never be younger than you are today." She raised her eyes to the intern, waiting for an eye roll. Instead he was staring at her, a bit incredulous. She took advantage of an engaged ear to impart her brand of wisdom. "Oh . . . one more thing. Don't go out with the guys and be all hungover. You'll ruin it, with no second chance to make the day special."

The nurse only smirked as she removed the needle from Olivia's arm. She pressed a cotton ball on the entry point and bent her arm to prevent leakage.

"Works for me," The doctor said and snapped on a pair of nitrile gloves. "Now for phase two."

Olivia barely heard his voice. "Thirty-two years from now, you won't remember who was at the reception. After a few weeks, you won't look at the pictures again. You'll never want to see that out-of-style tux again. She'll never wear the expensive dress again." A veil of something personal crept into the intern's expression. "But you'll remember each other's faces for the rest of your life. If you love her, marry her as soon as you can. More than anyone, you know how life can change in an instant."

"Keep your arm closed, sweetie," the nurse said.

The doctor blinked. "I take it you're not a party planner."

"No. I'm a writer, and I'm desperately in love with a man on an operating table. You're going to wear a ring, right?"

"Oh yeah."

"Good man. After a week, it'll become part of you. You won't be able to imagine your finger without it." Olivia nodded to the saw. "Cut it off."

The medical-grade blade fired up with a high whine. Her finger vibrated with a swath of heat for only a few seconds on each side. The halves fell away to the steel tray with no more than a shiver and two clangs.

Olivia stared at the shape of her empty finger, its indented white strip untouched by the sun since she'd been twenty. It looked like someone else's finger. So weightless. So naked. So vulnerable. The gold had been impervious for decades. Today, it had become liquid. The tears she'd been holding back finally let go and fell to her hand like a christening.

"Easy-peasy," the doctor said and rolled off his blue gloves. He tossed them into the bin.

The nurse squeezed Olivia's shoulder and handed her a tissue. "Not quite, Dr. Michaels. You have a lot to learn about women. Should've taken notes."

After a nod of acknowledgment, the doctor scooted his low chair to a cabinet. He pulled out a small zip-top bag, like the ones that held extra buttons and thread on a new sweater. He dropped in the two razor-edge halves of gold like phantom limbs. Olivia swiped the tissue under her eyes when he zipped the strip. Sealed. The pieces of a marriage had become artifacts, markers of time to be reunited with their artifact mates in her nightstand.

The nurse smoothed a barcode label on the two blood-filled bags. "I'll take these to the lab, and then they'll be off to the OR." A strange wooziness engulfed Olivia as she watched her blood leave the room. Psychological, of course, but real nonetheless.

Dr. Michaels patted her hand and set the plastic bag in front of her. Olivia didn't move to touch it. Instead, she leaned forward and placed her hands on each side of the doctor's face. Beneath the blond stubble, his skin felt soft and young. Many more shaves lay ahead to toughen him up.

"Do you know your bride's blood type, Dr. Michaels?" she said.

The doctor's eyes widened, probably more from her touch than the inability to answer the question. He offered only a slight shake of his head.

"Find out. I'm learning that lesson myself today. Now we're even. I hope my blood will save Woody's life. If he doesn't need it, then I hope it can save someone else's. But I want you to know that I'll owe you for the rest of my mine."

A flush of pink crept up his fair-skinned cheeks. "A little dramatic, don't you think?"

Olivia teetered in her attempt to stand. She pressed her hand on her forehead. "No . . . I don't think so."

Chapter 25
Wake Up Call

A warm, pressing weight rendered Woody's legs immovable. His eyelids fought the effort to open. Faint light slivered through a thin line. Where it came from he didn't know. In stages, he became aware of his body. Sounds crept in with beeps and clicks. He remembered arriving at the hospital in an ambulance, with faceless people taking off his clothes, but not much after that. Had Olivia talked to him? Maybe he'd dreamed saying something about her feet.

Objects in the shadowed room clarified. The window's reflection showed it was dark outside. His gaze roamed, but he couldn't make out the numbers on the wall clock. No watch. The tight binding around his chest restricted his ability to take in a full breath. When he attempted to raise himself, a shot of pain tore through his left collarbone. Beauregard's head and paws were stretched over his knees. Sound asleep. On his right side, Olivia's mahogany hair spread over the white blanket. Her head rested on the mattress, as she, too, lay sound asleep with her hand over his. His heart sank when he spotted that she was still in the same clothes from yesterday.

A strange quiet loomed in the hall, like an empty courtroom resting with anticipation of a new day. A television in the next room erupted with a wave of laugh track from some sitcom. The odor of antiseptic prompted a need to brush his teeth. Water. He needed water. Next to Olivia, the swinging arm of the side table held a plastic cup of the Holy Grail—: melting ice. With shaky fingers Woody reached for it, wincing and gaining clarity as he sipped from the straw.

The open door threw light on a chair that held a white plastic drawstring bag and Olivia's red satchel. On the floor, her ruby shoes lay toppled like wounded soldiers from battle. He closed his eyes. What torture had he put her through for a second time in her life? He drained the cup.

With the crackle of ice, Beau lifted his head and blinked his sleepy eyes. Woody smiled, wanting to reach out, but the pain burned in his chest and left arm when he tried. An urge to shout out for meds bubbled up, but he stifled it. A clear head was mandatory for a conversation when Olivia woke up.

"Shhh . . . I'm fine," he said. "Don't wake Mommy."

Beauregard scooted his hips to move closer, swishing his yellow therapy-dog vest. At that moment, Woody believed the embroidered badge with Pogo's likeness should contain *two* fuzzy faces as mascots of the Pogo Trust. *Hero Access Required.* He vowed to make that a goal. Beau set his head on Woody's stomach. No return touch required.

The tips of Olivia's unpolished fingers twitched with a dream. What images had she obsessed about while he'd been out? He almost didn't want to know—but he did. Woody did a double-take. Something had changed.

Below the scab on her knuckle, a white strip of skin curved in like the waist of a naked young woman, somewhat virginal. The empty finger he'd wished for. He should have been with her when the gold band had come off, but Olivia had needed to be alone for the closure that had come with breakage.

Ryan's off-the-cuff comparison of marriage to coconuts became deep insight. At the time, Woody hadn't fully understood its meaning. Now, he did. He wanted to suck on her knuckles and eat her fingers, and this situation—injured and in a hospital bed—was the shits. He remembered Ryan's words about marriage: *You're going to love it.*

With his IV-tubed right hand, Woody grazed Olivia's ring finger. He'd never see it this way again, sensitive and vulnerable. She stirred at his touch. When she lifted her head, Olivia offered him a smile that filled him with light.

"Hey, you," he said.

"Woody . . . " she said in scratchy voice and licked her lips. "I've been so worried. Does it hurt?"

"Not after you opened your eyes. Is my suit jacket in that bag on the chair?"

"No . . . I hung it up. It's ruined. I doubt it can be repaired."

"I don't care about the jacket. I'm more concerned about what's in the breast pocket."

The chair scraped the linoleum as Olivia stood and switched on the light over the bed. She stepped to the freestanding closet and pulled out his tweed suit coat. Tears welled her eyes as she opened the lapel, its lining stiff with a dark stain. "See? You said it was just a graze, but that bullet could have killed you." She returned to his bedside and sat with the jacket bunched in her arms.

"What did the doctor tell you?" he said.

"That you were lucky, but it took four hours to fix the damage. The bullet deflected and lodged in your chest muscle under your collarbone. It missed your lung, but it nicked a rib. Dr. Ehrenfeld said you had well-developed pecs, which saved your life. You won't be kayaking or rowing for a while."

A breath of relief came easier. "I think what's in the breast pocket saved my life—and Beauregard. He knocked that gun out of Tony Corelli's hand. I swear Tony was going to kill himself and take me with him. Beau gave Ryan time to put Tony in a lock until Casey brought in the cops. A hero through and though."

"Ryan and Casey filled me in. I have a boatload to tell you too. How did you know what Althea did, Woody?"

"By what you said in the car. And that bowl of lavender on Althea's coffee table. I'm sure you saw it too."

"I did."

"And why send only my sisters and me to talk to her?"

"In the way Althea looked at you. She obviously loved Ellen a lot, which meant she'd love you and your sisters too."

"Angry as she was, I thought the same thing when Althea looked at you." Olivia hesitated. "There's something else she told us."

Woody squinted as he pushed the button to raise the bed. She now had his full attention. "What?"

"There's a reason for Asher's death to be labeled a suicide. Althea didn't know what Della did, but Asher was dying. He had leukemia, like his mother . . . your grandmother."

Stunned, Woody searched her eyes. "I . . . never put that together."

"Threw *me* in a panic for a lot of reasons."

"What do you mean?"

"Since you're his son, I worried that—but you have a different blood type. Asher was A-positive. Della's O-negative blood saved your life. And now mine is pumping in your veins. You took both liters I gave you."

The tightness in Woody's chest eased. "You . . . gave me yours?"

"We're the same. I wouldn't stand for you to have a stranger's blood."

If he could love Olivia more than this moment, Woody couldn't imagine what it would take. She coursed through him now, inside, healing him with her platelets and cells. It never occurred to him to ask her blood type. "I should've subpoenaed his medical records. What about Althea?"

"The disease missed her. She was lucky."

"You've been doing your homework."

"You've been out for hours."

"I counted on you to get to the truth, and you did."

Olivia folded his jacket on her lap. "Della's letters gave the clues, Woody—Asher getting sick, living on coffee and cigarettes, unable to eat, and not wanting to go to the doctor. Even without the rat poison, he wouldn't have survived." Olivia blew out a breath. "It would explain his irrational behavior toward Della too. Last gasp of fear and giving her what she wanted. An angry act. Only Althea knew about his condition. She urged the medical examiner to that suicide conclusion to not ignite Simon. She thought Simon poisoned Asher and blamed him for it all these years. She had probable cause, but not in the way she thought."

"Slow down. I caught about a quarter of that." A spasm of pain radiated over his ribcage.

"They were all guilty, even Althea." Olivia rubbed his arm. "Don't blame her, Woody. Seeing you again will mean the world to her. She's a lovely person, someone you'll want to know." Olivia ran her fingers through his hair. "Never enough time."

Woody didn't think it was possible to top the transfusion of her blood, but this did in spades. "I never want to die before you, but I probably will."

"Don't *ever* say that." She fiddled with a button on his jacket. "A word of advice. We womenfolk want to die in the arms of our men. If we believe otherwise, then we have to set things up differently."

"Pull out what's inside my breast pocket."

Olivia reached to the inner lining. Her expression collapsed when she pulled out the turquoise ring box and the folded check. The leather lid bore a tear and a brown scorch mark. She held up Wannamaker's check, which showed a ragged tear through the word *books* on the memo line.

"Deposit that check," he said. "It's still negotiable. The auction house made the wire transfer into my account yesterday."

Olivia gave him a slow nod, but her eyes remained focused on the ring box. The bent hinge caused her some struggle to crack it open. She sucked in a breath.

"My ring . . . "

He basked in her possessive description. "I've been waiting for you to say that."

Olivia slipped the diamond band over the scab on her left knuckle.

"Fits, like it was made for me." Her dark eyes sucked him in with their shine. "I let Adam's go about four hours ago. When you went into surgery, I'm afraid I instigated a little drama with an intern in Emergency. Tough stuff."

The image reduced the word *drama* to an understatement. The handoff of his clothes, alone, had likely set her off. That poor intern might need counseling after getting an earful from Olivia. "Weird to say, but that makes me feel pretty damn good. I'd want you to have an equally hard time letting go if that ring were mine."

"Where'd you find this? I thought I'd lost it." Olivia gave him a sheepish glance, the kind of gesture that loosened all his muscles. "I didn't have the guts to tell you."

"You never lost it, Liv. Before I headed to Karen's office, I took yours to Tiffany's and had it resized."

"But *we* were at Tiffany's."

"I told the salesman to not say anything if you came in. You're such an open book. You proved me right in the bathroom at Karen's office. When we left New York so fast, I had the ring overnighted to me at Allenwood." Woody's legs numbed from Beauregard's weight. When he raised his knees, the dog flipped to his side and let out a groan. "I couldn't believe that salesman's name was Adam."

Olivia rolled her eyes. "Believe me, I had a moment over that little ditty too. But he told me his partner read my romances. He likes hot leading men, not women."

The trill of her giggle was infectious. Woody winced when he couldn't hold in a laugh. Olivia held out her hand to the light. The box hadn't done the ring justice.

"The second package delivered with the letters?" she said.

Woody nodded, but even that small movement caused an ache. "I kept it in my pocket to have you close, kind of a charm really, until you said something."

"And that third thing?"

"What thing?"

"The note and the picture of the little girl."

A whirl of anesthetized thoughts circled his mind. A biggie that was getting bigger every day. It had to be dealt with. "No big deal. Just something I left on my desk. We'll talk about it, but not right now."

"A love of your life that I don't know about?"

"Don't be ridiculous."

"I'm not going to let it go, but you're getting a pass for health reasons." Olivia let out a tired sigh. "You're a beast, Woody. You put me through hell."

"I know. I feel bad now—" he pointed to her empty hand—"but your gold one put *me* through hell, Liv. I needed to know you wanted my ring. Only mine."

"Not the only." Olivia padded to the chair in bare feet. She reached inside her red case and retrieved a crinkled laminated gift bag. She pulled out a black velvet box. "This is the real reason I went to Tiffany's. Lauren and Danny approved."

To cover the emotion welling inside him, he goaded her. "You want me to wear one?"

"Nonnegotiable." Olivia opened the lid and rocked the box.

"I'd wear a washer if it meant I was married to you," he said.

Olivia plucked out the band and stepped around the bed, showing it to Beauregard. "What do *you* think, Big Guy?" The dog's tail thumped against the mattress. "No, it's not a treat."

Pride eclipsed the strangeness of it when Olivia slipped the platinum band on his left ring finger. Public display of a union would take some getting used to.

Olivia squinted. "It's not too big?"

A puff of painful breath escaped his lips instead of words. Olivia's fingertip traced the thin lines of decoration on the band. Simple at first glance, but its meaning became more complex and significant. "It's my turn to give you a good line."

Olivia leaned over him, her face so close he could feel her lips move. "Out with it, Shakespeare."

A swoon reignited the haze. "Find the hospital chaplain and get your sisters in here."

Olivia's face brightened like a Girl Scout making a cookie sale. "Are you sure?"

"You're wasting time."

Her eyes narrowed. "No filing of a protest later that I coerced you under duress? Like Doris Day and Rock Hudson in *Lover Come Back* when they eat all that VIP candy?"

"No, Liv. You got it backward. Doris accuses Rock of coercing *her*. Hurry . . . before I go to sleep. If I do, I want to wake up married."

"Ryan, Casey, and Pogo too?"

"All of them. I want witnesses."

Olivia scrambled for her shoes. She hopped to the doorway and stopped. "Give me back your ring, so I can give it to you again." Quick scrapes of her heels made him chuckle as she rushed back to his side. The trade-off completed when she wiggled the band from his finger and set her diamond one in his hand. She closed his fingers around it.

"Hey, hey. Watch that arm," he said. "Before you go . . . Where's my car?"

"Safe and sound in the hospital parking lot."

"Any problems?"

"Pffttt . . . Easy, peasy," she said and leaned in close. "I love you so much . . . "

The way her lips moved against his became a moment of healing. All pain had disappeared. Olivia *click-clacked* from the room before Woody could get out the floating words. His palm filled with sparkly heat. A cold, wet nose grazed his knuckles. Then a rough, warm tongue probed his fingers.

"I live you . . . love." Woody drifted into weightlessness.

Chapter 26

Hope

Olivia bumped to a stop at the nurses' station. "Where can I find the hospital chaplain?"

"Is everything all right, Mrs. Novak?" the night duty nurse said.

"Fine. Fine. If you tell me where the chaplain is, you can call me Mrs. Rainey in about half an hour."

The nurse's face brightened to a full smile. She pointed. "There's one on every patient floor, two doors down from the main elevators."

"Thanks." Olivia trotted backward, nearly losing her balance. "And don't give Mr. Rainey any more meds." She blew the nurse a kiss. "Make him beg. *Pieta. Pieta.*" She turned and bolted toward the elevators.

Seven rapid pushes of the button didn't speed the car's descent to the lobby. Her pulse slowed, the realization hitting her that this exercise wouldn't be the real thing. They had no marriage license to make it legal. Woody must be still fuzzy from meds to not have thought of that detail. No matter. The sentiment counted more than the technicality.

When the elevator doors parted, Olivia burst into the waiting area to a display of human debris. The scene required serious assessment.

The people critical to her existence lay stretched out on the couches, asleep. The body count gave no clue whom to wake up first. Lauren snored with her head on Casey's lap. Casey's snore was directed to the ceiling. Danny had her arms curled around her knees in a chair. Pogo lay on his back, legs splayed and ears inside out. Ryan had stretched out on the couch with his arm over his face. Olivia zeroed in. She shook Ryan's shoulder.

Instinct sent him bolt upright on full alert. "Everything okay?" He blinked.

"More than okay," she said. "Woody's awake. He wants to get married . . . now."

"Right now?" He glanced at his watch. "It's after ten."

"Can you give me away?"

Ryan rubbed his face. "Yeah. Sure. Why don't you wait until Woody can stand up?" He swung his legs from the couch and set his elbows on his knees. "Woody's as crazy as you are, Liv. Better wake up Casey." Ryan eyed Pogo and shook his head, as if recalling the events of the past six hours. The dog flipped to his feet and released a full body shake. "Where's Beau? He and Pogo probably need a squirt."

"With Woody. He'll let me know when he's gotta go."

The power of suggestion prompted Casey to lift his head from the back cushion. "I gotta wiz like a racehorse."

Olivia poked Lauren. "Wake up. You and Danny need to be my bridesmaids."

"What the hell are you talking about, Liv?" Lauren shifted to face Casey's . . . stomach.

A grin erupted on Casey's face as he stretched his arms on the back of the couch. "Hey, what can I say? It's been a long day." The expression on Casey's face gave Olivia pause. Her sister had been busy. Olivia figured an unlocked hospital supply closet or a trip back to the hotel had been involved. "Lauren has to share you. Woody needs a best man, since Ryan's going to give me away."

Casey tapped his fingers. "Let's do it."

Danny stirred and unfolded her legs. "What's going on? Is Woody okay?"

Ryan stuck his thumb toward Danny. "Your little sister needs an hour to get dolled up."

Waiting wasn't in Olivia's plan. "I'll call Althea and give her an update," she said. "She needs to represent Woody's family. How do I look?"

Ryan grimaced. "A little fuzzy around the edges."

A laugh erupted from Casey. "Like a desperate woman about to marry a man with narcolepsy."

~ · ~ · ~

Althea sensed her eyelids drooping with her body's need for sleep. The dancing fire in her study had died to smoldering embers an hour ago. With the door shut, Freed hadn't been able to keep an eye on the logs. Not even Posey had been allowed access for the discussion with the two Boston police detectives. Before today, they'd been nothing more than suits in the shadows. Althea had anticipated their arrival after the shocking news about Woodrow. The detectives had arrived right on cue.

Her empty tumbler begged for a refill of whiskey and soda, but Althea set it on the side table instead. "So, there you have it, gentlemen. The whole distasteful story. If you think me a menace to society, go ahead and clamp the cuffs on my wrists right now."

"Won't be necessary, Mrs. Pennington," said the older of the two detectives. His clean-shaven face revealed a scar on his chin that appeared to deepen in the glow of embers in the fireplace. "We got what we wanted from Mr. Rainey's recording. Thank you for corroborating the information."

The other detective had been taking notes with a deadpan expression. Finally, he leaned back on the love seat and made eye contact. He gestured to the Christmas tree, its crystal ornaments sparkling for attention. "That's why your tree's full of bees?"

Stripped bare of her secrets, Althea nodded. "No prison sentence could be harsher than the past sixty-eight years since I married Simon. The only bright light in this mess was to discover that I had a nephew, and he's going to marry the daughter of a woman my brother loved. Had I known, it might have changed the course of everything . . . absolutely everything. Any update on Woodrow's condition?"

"He was still in surgery last we checked, but we've been with Tony Corelli, and now you, for the past several hours."

Althea rung her hands. "I must call Olivia. Are we done?"

"For tonight. We have your word that you'll testify when the time comes?"

"If necessary. But let me ask you a question."

"Go ahead."

"How deep did Tony's talons go into your department?"

The older detective leaned forward. "Deep. You and Mr. Rainey have been quite helpful. Your dead husband and Tony Corelli were up to their necks in it. Tony kept the bribes going full steam, even after many of the officers had died of old age. Until we gather all the evidence, we need this to remain confidential. That's why we wanted to meet you here. Quite a few of our officers were on the payroll of their little charity."

A shallow breath was all she could manage. "Little Buddies?"

"Seems so," the younger detective said. "We'll need your help to follow the money—your money—in that charity."

Althea offered a slow nod of acknowledgment. "Whatever you need. I have a record of every check." The diminishing glow of the embers drew her gaze, and with them her fear retreated. She didn't even fear the inevitable scandalous publicity and vicious gossip that was about to descend. "Charity begins at home and such nonsense?"

The older detective chuckled. "Something like that."

Althea stepped to the side table and switched on a lamp. "If you don't mind, may I ask who came to you with this information? The proverbial heads-up, so to speak?"

"Casey Carter, a close friend of Mr. Rainey's. We served together in Iraq. I suspected something like this was going on in the department for a long time, but we couldn't find proof. Mr. Rainey's information about your brother gave us a whole different direction. It's the break we were waiting for."

The younger detective closed his notebook and retracted his pen. "Hard to know who to trust, isn't it?"

Althea let out a bitter laugh. "Oh, my dear, I wouldn't quite know where to start." The anniversary clock on the mantle released one delicate chime. She glanced at the time. Ten thirty. The people who trusted her were waiting. Concern turned to urgency. "Do you think Woodrow's all right?"

"When we talked to Mr. Rainey before his meeting with Tony, he was quite emphatic that you should receive complete immunity."

The telephone released a long ring. The detective hadn't answered her question, but hopefully the outside line was about to. Althea knees weakened. "At my age, gentlemen, a late-night call is never good. It means someone has died."

Three knocks on the door of the study drew Althea to open it.

Posey stood frozen, her expression stiff with concern. "Mrs. Novak is on the line for you, Ma'am."

"I'll take it. Thank you." Althea reached for her housekeeper's hand. Their years of shared history passed between them, well beyond the titles of employer and employee. "All's fine, dear. Don't go any-where."

Althea stepped to the desk and inhaled. She picked up the re-ceiver. "Olivia? Do you have news?"

"He's going to be fine, Althea," Olivia said. "Woody's awake. He wants to see you."

The call she'd wished for. Althea closed her eyes in silent thanks. Although not particularly religious, she though the moment deserved a tithe. "You must be so relieved, as am I."

"Can you come to the hospital? Woody wants to get married tonight. He wants you with us for a thousand reasons. I hate to ask so late at night, but it would mean so much to both of us."

Althea raised her eyes to the plaster medallion of vines on the ceiling. Her throat erupted with an itch. "I wouldn't miss it. Give me half an hour."

"It's not too late?" Olivia said.

"No dear. It's not."

"We'll wait for you."

Althea set the phone in the cradle. A pinch between her brows prevented tears. She turned. "I must cut this short, detectives. I hope you understand. My nephew needs me."

The young detective stood. "All okay?"

"Quite. In fact, Woodrow wants to get married . . . *tonight*. I'll need to represent his family." Althea inspected her outfit of black slacks and cream silk blouse. The statement sounded strange, even to her. "Have you met his bride?"

Both detectives shook their heads. The young one spoke up. "We hear she's a pistol."

"Your loss, gentlemen. Are you going by the hospital?"

"Want us to drop you off?"

"Please. We'll continue our conversation in the car, but I need to change. Can you wait ten minutes?"

"Sure."

Althea turned to Posey, still standing in the doorway. "Have Freed on standby to pick me up from the hospital when I call."

Posey smiled. "Yes, ma'am."

With every step up the stairs, Althea shed the imaginary chains of Jacob Marley. It had been ages since she was wanted. Needed, yes, but truly wanted? She marched along the upstairs hall and stopped at the photograph of Asher and Ellen. She kissed her forefinger and set it on the image of Asher's face, now Woodrow's face.

"We're going to make it right, you and me. Better late than never. You have a legacy."

Althea moved to her bedroom with a new sense of purpose. She plucked the ring box from her dressing table. Ellen's engagement ring now belonged to Woodrow. The line of succession had renewed importance. She tossed the box on the bed and threw open the doors of her closet.

As if magnified, the cream-colored Chanel suit with black piping drew her gaze. Yes, the Chanel.

Chapter 27
Indigestion

The sensation of a presence prompted Woody's eyes to open. Staring over him was a man with a white collar. Was he dying? Then he remembered. His conversation with Olivia wasn't a dream. He glanced at his left hand. He hadn't been married while he'd been asleep.

"Are you sure you're up to this, Mr. Rainey?" the chaplain said. "There's no rush. Maybe you should rest."

"No, no. I'm awake. Give me a minute." He pressed the button on the bed's remote to raise himself up, holding back an urge to cry out from the pain. Beauregard adjusted to the new position and rested his head on Woody's knees. The dog's sleepy gaze shifted to the group gathered in the room. When Olivia stepped to Beau's side and ran her fingers through his fur, her citrus perfume swirled over the bed, an aroma fresh with anticipation. The combination of her scent and a waft of antiseptic served as a reminder that he needed a shower and a clean shave.

Pogo paced the room like the nervous groom. Ryan plopped on the lounge chair and lifted the footrest. Danny had freshened up, but her face held remnants of the worry Woody had put them all through.

Casey wrapped his arm around Lauren's shoulder. The beaded embroidery on Lauren's taupe sweater glinted with the movement of her leaning into his chest. "Get the show on the road, buddy," he said, "or we're going back to the hotel for snooze time."

"We're almost all here," Olivia said in response to his antsy comment. "Althea's on her way."

"Althea?" Woody said.

"She wants to be here. We need to wait for her."

"Have you thought about vows?" the chaplain said, a slight note of irritation in his voice.

Of course, knockout words would flow from Olivia. "I'll make them up as we go," she said. "I tend to think spontaneous is better for some things."

Vows. The fog of sleep had cultivated a thousand words, unchecked and easy. Expectations ran high, though, since Adam had read the dictionary. Olivia's expectations ran high too. Woody's mind made a frantic grab of a few choice phrases. As he did so, he looked around the room. The love of his life, his new family, his best friend, the dogs. Olivia still wore her red suit. She hadn't gone back to the hotel to change.

"We don't have a license," he said.

Now, Olivia's expression softened. She'd come back to him. "The license is a formality we can get later."

"Do you have the rings?" the chaplain asked.

Olivia held up his wedding band like the top prize won from a treasure hunt. "Here's Woody's. He's got mine."

Woody opened his palm. Empty. His heart sunk with a new ache in his chest. "It was here . . . in my hand." New information might come forth when he raised his eyes to Olivia.

Olivia met his confused stare. "My ring? Where's my ring?" She lunged and patted the mattress. Beauregard scrambled to stand. Pogo halted his pace. Lauren whipped back the blanket, exposing Woody's hairy legs below the cotton gown. Danny stooped to check the floor under the bed. Casey shook his head and laughed. Ryan watched the chaos in the reflection of the dark window.

"I had it, Liv," Woody said. "I swear I didn't move. Beau's been right here with me."

The room went silent. All heads turned to Beauregard. His ears caught lift as he pivoted his gaze, seeking mercy.

"He ate it," Casey said. "Betcha a million bucks."

Ryan pulled the lever on the lounge chair. The footrest snapped down. "Yep. I can see it in his eyes. Guilty."

With her fists planted on her hips, Danny let out a sigh. "Well . . . There's only one way to find out," she said. "Hold the ceremony until I get him to give it up. How long has it been since you had the ring in your hand, Woody?"

"I fell asleep. No clue."

Olivia stepped forward. "About half an hour? Maybe forty-five minutes on the outside. I went down to the lobby to round up you guys, called Althea, and then I went to see the chaplain."

Lauren wrinkled her nose. "We have to wait for the ring to be blessed."

At the snap of her fingers, Danny moved toward the door. "Beau, down. C'mon." She pursed her lips. "When did you last feed him, Liv?"

"Maybe four hours ago?" Olivia's turned with a matching nose wrinkle. "After a very productive walk."

The labradoodle jumped from the bed and, with reluctant steps, moved to Danny's side. His tail hung like the handle of an abandoned wagon. The chaplain patted Beau's head.

Danny turned to the chaplain. "Hmmm . . . I'll call you when we have a delivery. Could take a while. This might be a morning wedding."

Like a sail, Lauren billowed the blanket over Woody's legs. "Channel-cut was a good choice, Gorilla Boy. No sharp edges."

Danny pulled open the door. At the threshold stood Althea Pennington.

"I hope I'm not too late," Althea said, not moving into the crowded room.

For a second time, Woody struggled for words. When their eyes met, the void of missed years closed.

Ryan stood with a single clap of his hands. "All right. Everybody out. We're over the limit. Let's all go back to the hotel for a shower and shut-eye . . . in Casey's Jeep." He directed his gaze at Olivia and tipped his head to one side. The gesture fell into the category of an accusation. Woody rendered a guess at what the gesture meant.

Olivia scraped an empty chair to Woody's bedside. "Good idea. I think you two need some time. Brides shouldn't wear red." She leaned over him and whispered, "We'll talk about it *after* we're married."

Woody smirked. "I'll wait for Danny and Beau. Get horizontal, because you're going to need all the rest you can get if something happened to my car."

"You must be feeling better. You're feisty. See you in a few." Olivia turned and waved Althea into the room. They embraced like women do, with a bond of shared secrets. He may never know the full extent of what they discussed, but Woody couldn't mistake the admiration on Olivia's face for Althea's Chanel suit. She'd had his aunt pegged, right down to the black piping and pearls.

Althea grasped Olivia's shoulders. "He's all mine until he's yours, Olivia." The door closed before Althea turned to him. Her presentation smile fell as she sat in the chair, still gracious in her movements. For a moment, they only stared at each other.

"Thank you for coming," he finally said.

"You're just like him, you know," Althea said. "I thought I'd faint when you first came through my front door. Your eyes are unmistakable."

"They're like yours."

"Some features hold their uniqueness at any age."

Woody reached out his hand to her, thankful for the pain of doing so. She grasped his fingers and squeezed. "You should talk to the detectives, Althea. Tell them everything you discussed with Olivia that's relevant. When I get out of here, I'll go with you."

"They came to me. I had quite a long evening at my house after they finished with Tony. This is one noose the bastard won't be able to slip through."

Even mild profanity from Althea surprised him. Woody doubted many people had ever heard it from her. He considered it an acceptance, a position of confidence. "Are you worried about your safety? If you are, we can hire a—"

"No. I'm not afraid anymore. I suspect they'll be keeping watch when this ugliness blows open."

"Do you need a lawyer? I can't represent you, but I'll find someone who can. My old firm is here in Boston."

"I've got one, but not for criminal defense. They don't want to prosecute me, Woodrow, thanks to the recording you made of your conversation with Tony. They're willing to exchange immunity for my cooperation. No, I'm going to see my lawyer this week for a different reason."

"For what?"

Althea gazed at him in an odd way, as though he'd missed the punchline of a perfectly good joke. "Why . . . Woodrow, you're my only heir. I'll be changing my will."

With a wince, he sat upright. "Wait. Wait. You don't even know me."

She patted his hand. "Give it some time. I'm not worried."

For the first time since waking up, words started to flow. "No, Althea. Before you do anything, you need to consult your adviser, your lawyer, your bank."

"Nonsense. Blood inherits. I'm not here to negotiate, my dear."

The words gave him pause. "I don't know what to say to that."

Althea smoothed her silver hair. She glanced at the black slip-knot buttons on her knit jacket. "Just make the right choices. I assure you, you'll make far better ones than I've made."

A few of Beauregard's wavy brown hairs littered the white blanket. An image of the dog pacing downstairs with Danny to produce Olivia's ring signaled a real life—not this, presented to him now. On what should be their wedding night, Olivia would be walking into the hotel room alone. He formulated an answer.

"Ellen would've been your heir, not me," he said, "had Asher married her."

Althea crossed her legs. "Not meant to be. Why did you postpone your little ceremony? It's hardly a shotgun wedding." She chuckled at her own directness.

"The dog ate the ring."

"Sounds like what we used to say about homework."

"We're waiting for the Tiffany's specimen to . . . *emerge*."

Althea sniffed. "Love doesn't just *emerge*, dear. You could have used a twist-tie to get married, if necessary." She fingered the pearls on her necklace. The movement of her manicured fingers spoke of sadness.

"A long story for another time," he said. "I should've been there to protect you from Simon."

"An exercise in futility. You love Olivia, don't you? The way you look at her says you do."

"More than anything. I can't explain it."

"Ahh . . . That's the key, isn't it? A highly unconcise answer."

"How about that she challenges me like no other woman I've known. When I'm with her, I'm living inside a novel. Every day is a plot twist. No one's ever gotten into my head like her. I'm not sure how to interpret it."

"Writers do that, Woodrow. I'm sure she thinks the same about you. Lawyers do that too, but it's usually a one-way relationship at arm's length to hide their passion."

Woody contemplated the comment before admitting to himself that she was right. Redirect. "She's been asked to write a screenplay of *Indigo to Black*. With everything we learned over the past few days, I'm not sure how to feel about it. Could be an invasion of your privacy— and mine."

Althea shrugged. "Part of the story is already out in the world. Mine is about to be, whether I like it or not. Olivia owes it to Ellen."

Breath came easier now, and with it a banishment of the pain. A new life had begun for him with Ellen's book, and with his help its legacy could grow beyond anything Olivia and her sisters would imagine. He owed it to Beauregard. The dog was still working on his behalf.

"If you and I are in this for the long haul, Althea, there are a couple of things you'll need to agree to."

His aunt tilted her head with a mischievous glint in her eye. "Out with it. I'm quite tired."

"First, call me Woody. Second, if you want me to be the steward of your estate, then do me a favor."

"Anything."

"Allow me to go with you to the meeting with your lawyer. I'm sure I'll be released tomorrow. I don't want to complicate my new life before it's even started. Let's come up with a different plan."

"This will add to your new life . . . Woody." She uttered his nickname with a sense of wonder.

"Yes, but I don't want love to be complicated by money. The two need to be mutually exclusive."

"Very well then." Althea unsnapped the black-leather clutch in her lap, not large enough to hold even a wallet. Althea didn't need one. Someone else held keys to her car and front door, and she charged on account for whatever she desired. A ring box took Woody off guard.

"If that ring you gave Olivia doesn't *emerge*," she said, "then give her this. Asher was going to give it to Ellen. I, too, want to be a good steward of his legacy."

Althea set the gold-embossed box in his hand. He didn't dare open it, sure that it was more than Olivia would want.

Chapter 28
New Eyes

At eight o'clock on Tuesday morning, Olivia tapped on the door of Woody's hospital room. This wasn't how she wanted their union to go. Expecting him to be resting, she found him sitting on the bed, showered and fully dressed in his slacks and wrinkled white shirt. His left arm rested in a sling. He faced the window, his back to her. Althea lay in the lounge chair in front of him with her feet up, sound asleep.

"Woody?" Olivia said and moved toward him. She pointed at Althea and threw Woody a questioning look.

Woody turned and set a finger to his lips. He nodded to the spot next to him. "C'mere."

"What are you doing?" Olivia sensed a very different mood since leaving Woody's side at midnight.

"Watching her sleep."

Olivia sat next to him and rubbed his back. "You smell good."

"Hospital soap. So do you."

"Hotel soap . . . what Danny didn't steal." Olivia assessed her choice of the sky-blue silk blouse and winter-white wool slacks. No time to buy something new for the occasion. Yesterday's advice to the

ER doctor about spontaneity went out the window with Woody's odd expression.

"She doesn't look ninety when she's sleeping, does she?" he said and nodded to Althea. "My guess is that she hasn't slept like this ever."

"She doesn't look ninety when she's awake, either." Olivia drank in Althea's relaxed face, much different from yesterday. Must be a pleasant dream. A slight smile crossed her lips. The buttons on her Chanel jacket rose and fell in a steady rhythm, highlighting the sheen of her pearls. Her polished toes glinted through sheer black hose. Black patent-leather pumps sat askance next to the lounge chair. "Althea became your aunt last night, didn't she?"

"We talked until two."

A shadow descended behind Woody's whispered words. Something new had passed between Althea and him, which he was still disseminating. She wanted to ask, but whatever it was must be too raw, too fresh. "You think I'll look that good at ninety?"

"If I'm not blind. I'll be ninety-five."

"You all right?"

"Fine. Doc says to watch for infection, but I'm cleared to leave with a serious case of 'be careful what you wish for.'"

"Need a painkiller?"

"No. I'm going to need every wit in my crystal-clear head."

An uneasiness crawled up her throat. Olivia's imagination took off, not in a good direction. "Any news from Danny on the Beauregard front?"

"Not yet, but Althea did produce this last night." Woody handed her a gold-embossed ring box. "Sunglasses required."

She didn't want to open it, but curiosity compelled her to unhinge the brass hook. From his phrasing, Woody had only made an offer to show, not an offer to accept. Her throat went dry when she opened the lid. A desperate grab for the orange juice on Woody's breakfast tray quelled the parch.

The enormous oval solitaire released a show of fireworks in the morning sunshine. This was the ring that symbolized Asher's love for her mother, and the one Woody's mother had attempted to kill for. This heirloom had more family history than facets.

Olivia re-secured the lid and set the box in Woody's hand. "Keep it safe. I'm holding out for something better."

"You don't want that monster, Liv?"

Olivia smirked and stuck her nose in the air. "It's too big."

Woody didn't laugh. Fatigue had dimmed his spicy sense of humor. Something even bigger than the ring lurked. She slipped Woody's wedding band over her forefinger. The metal had warmed from holding it so tight.

Althea stirred and opened her eyes. She offered a sleepy smile. "Good morning, dear."

"Thank you for watching over Woody," Olivia said to her and turned to him as she added, "He might've fled the scene if you weren't here."

Woody squeezed Olivia's fingers in silent communication. "Althea, Goldilocks is holding out for a twist tie."

Lowering the footrest, Althea slipped her feet into her low-heeled pumps. "Twist tie it is. Call your sisters, Olivia. After Woody's discharged, we'll move the event to the house. Then we'll have a family dinner. Leave all the arrangements to me."

Woody rubbed his clean-shaven chin, avoiding Olivia's gaze. "I appreciate your enthusiasm, Althea," he said, "but I think Olivia and I need to talk. We might have to alter our plans."

A queasy tension rolled in Olivia's stomach, a split second before the hospital room door burst open. She whipped her head toward the intrusion. Beauregard bounded into the room and took an airborne leap on the bed. He turned in a circle and licked Woody's face.

Nearly slipping as she rounded the doorjamb, Danny raised her fist in triumph.

"We got it!"

~ · ~ · ~

Olivia shooed Danny and Althea from the room. She closed the door and paused with her forehead resting against the wood. A new urgency alarm rang in her head. She braced herself and turned. Woody remained sitting on the bed, her diamond band tight in his fist. His expression held back a thousand thoughts. She half expected him to pop her ring in his mouth and swallow it.

"What's wrong?" she said, moving to stand in front of him. "Something's happened."

"Yes, it has, and not only for me. It affects both of us, and your sisters too."

She held both sides of Woody's face and searched his eyes. "Tell me, please."

Woody's gaze drifted to the window for a few seconds and returned to her. "You know what this whole ring debacle taught me?"

What had, or hadn't, she done? What expectations had she failed? Olivia settled on the obvious, the one revenant entity that invaded her and Woody's relationship. "That I made this so hard because of Adam?"

"Yes, and no . . . But what you said about your relationship with Adam made it obvious."

"What?" Olivia spun through her selfish, off-the-cuff ramblings in the car, most of which she couldn't remember. She wanted to gobble back all the words like spilled popcorn.

"The real value of something isn't appreciated until there's a threat of loss. I was so irresponsible to not have my affairs in order before I took such a crazy risk with Tony. We hadn't even started our life together yet. I stared down the barrel of that gun and understood everything I'd lose if he'd pulled the trigger. And then he did. But only thanks to Beau, he missed. A fluke."

Olivia's shoulders slumped. She started to respond, but he stopped her.

"I could've lost you." He took her left hand and floated his wedding band from her forefinger, the caretaker finger, and exchanged it for her diamond one, now sparkling clean. He slipped his platinum band over his empty left ring finger and admired it. "There. That's better. We'll do this for a while."

Olivia couldn't speak. *A while? What did that mean?*

Woody raised his eyes to her. "Beauregard swallowing your ring was well-timed."

"How so?"

"I need a couple of weeks."

Olivia bit her bottom lip to keep it from quivering. "Okay . . . "

"Althea wants my help to get through Tony's arraignment and do a formal deposition with the detectives. We need to have a serious family meeting."

"Why?"

"Althea wants to make me her heir."

"What?"

The walls of the room closed around her. Disruption. Plans were changing that affected her life, discussed without her input. Life had become one big curve ball.

Althea's world was one Olivia didn't want or need. The money had wrapped the woman in betrayal and misery. That kind of wealth got in the way by changing people. It might change Woody. At this moment, Olivia didn't believe she could cut it in the blue-blood world, or even begin to meet the expectations of what living that way required. Better to find out now. Put the genie back in the bottle and walk away. The past few months were only a tease, a temporary distraction from grief. Brick by brick, she'd have to rebuild her life. What kind of device could sew the pieces of her heart back together?

"But I told her no," Woody said. "Althea's money doesn't belong to me. I'll work with her for an alternate plan, but I need to flesh out what that means."

"Holy shhh—"

"Shhh . . . " Woody set his finger to her lips. "Don't say it. Not in front of Beau. He's been through enough trying to take one." The way he held her gaze, Olivia believed the dog might still be wearing a wire. A smile bloomed on Woody's face. "And I have to fix whatever the hell you did to my car."

A breath might've come in handy. Oxygen deprivation made her blurt out something stupid. "Woody . . . Who needs seven gears to drive?"

He chuckled. "The car needs to recover, and so do I. I'll drive it out to Portland, and I promise to beat the moving van before Christmas day. In the meantime, start that screenplay before you work on Rizzo's and Tullio's books. I'll stay out of it with Karen, but I want approval rights. It'll be my story too."

"I don't know the ending."

"I do."

Those two words she'd waited for sent her into a renewed spin. "Let's bust you out of this joint. I'll show you the dent in the bumper."

Woody eyes widened. "How big?"

"With the new clutch, you won't have any trouble meeting your deductible."

He groaned. "Full disclosure, Liv."

Olivia wrinkled her nose. "How long can you drive downhill in first gear?"

"Not long."

"Lauren did it."

Chapter 29
Home with No Woody

At three o'clock on Thursday afternoon, after the five-hour flight from Boston to Portland, Olivia climbed the wet steps to her front door. An earlier cold rain had glued dead leaves to her dormant perennials. The Japanese maple sat empty, its delicate branches reaching out to mourn their loss. A few leaves stuck to Beauregard's paws as he danced to get inside, so she brushed them off before she turned the key.

Home with a ring and no Woody. The fallout of learning their family truth, the truth behind *Indigo to Black*, should have forced her to remain at his side. She understood Woody's need to sort through his affairs alone, a rationalization of the tasks at hand, but the reality stung when the rest of the family dispersed to resume normal life.

The house sat silent, like it had every time she'd returned to it for the past five years. Beau, her protector, rushed inside and trotted through the downstairs rooms to check things out. He ended with a nose-to-nose chilly Himalayan greeting with Freesia, who had been waiting on the upstairs landing. The spot was her cat's favorite lookout post to assess space invaders. Olivia got an overhead feline scowl.

Olivia set her suitcase, computer, and satchel by the stairs. She kicked off her shoes and padded through the living room, dining room, and kitchen. Everything appeared to be in its place. From the fresh-napped *V*s on the carpet, the house-sitter had vacuumed. All looked the same but vastly different with a new perspective. Where might Woody's possessions fit into her carefully organized, clean world? Some things may have to go. But not today or tomorrow. She'd shut herself away to write while the details were fresh. The Christmas tree would need to be downsized for the first time since the year of Adam's death. Karen had emailed edits of Palermo's manuscript, which Olivia had ignored through Woody's ordeal.

Palermo. She needed to talk with him. Video was her only option. An exhaustive list of discussion items had to be addressed, but the top item was to thank him for his help.

The freezer held the usual suspects for dinner. She pulled out a package of chicken breasts, too much for one, and set it in the sink to thaw. Frozen green beans would have to do. She picked up the phone and dialed.

"Want to come over?" she said to Lauren.

Between hiccups and gasps, Lauren finally eked out a response. "Yeah."

"What's the matter?" Olivia's mind raced through the possible list, but tears led to Lauren's heart. Anything else would bubble up as defiance.

"Casey just called to make sure I got home all right. Do you know how long it's been since someone cared enough to do that?"

"I call you, Lauren. I care."

"That's different. When Woody comes out, you'll have him there."

"But I don't have him right now. And he might change his mind and not show up at all. I'm bracing myself. Pull yourself together and get your butt over here with your wine box."

"I'm done with that. I can't live like this. I've lost three pounds in a week."

"We'll make hot tea and a plan instead. You can help me with the screenplay. This time it's not all about Mom; it's about us."

"Are you going to make your Cornflake chicken?"

"Yep."

Olivia hung up and smiled. After all they'd been through, life had come full circle. Their ordeal had started with making Cornflake chicken that had led to breaking into Ardy Griffin's house—now Lauren's house—to rescue Pogo. An innocent offer to dog-sit had set her and her sisters' course in motion with the mob. At the height of their grief over their mother's death, Pogo had saved them with a sense of purpose. Then they'd published Ellen's manuscript *Indigo to Black*. None of them could ever have predicted how all the pieces had come together.

Now, two years later, a new story would start with Cornflake chicken. At this moment, Olivia knew exactly the screenplay she wanted to write. She'd deliver to Karen a crowning achievement of loss, discovery, and family, with all three of them finding love again to pull them forward. The ending might only be a wish, a wish for what she'd want to happen. *Fix it all in fiction* had, and always would be, her mantra. Yet again, she would surprise Karen with something new. Maybe not the story in *Indigo to Black* . . . but *Indigo Legacy*, a suitable ending for how her mother's book had changed so many lives.

A quick knock and a squeak of the front door shook Olivia from her thoughts. As her sister stepped into the kitchen, Lauren wiped her eyes on her sleeve and held up a wine box of white zinfandel.

"I changed my mind," she said. "One more time, with feeling."

Olivia smiled. "Let's call Danny."

~ · ~ · ~

After a too-heavy dinner in Althea's dining room, Woody unpacked his suitcase for a week's stay in one of three guestrooms, grander than any five-star hotel. Althea wouldn't hear of him keeping a room at the Liberty Hotel. The parting with Olivia, her sisters, Ryan, and the dogs at Logan Airport had emptied his capacity for small talk with Althea over brisket and roasted potatoes. He didn't have the heart to tell her that red meat wasn't his first choice of protein. Olivia had a distaste for it too. With not much in his stomach, he'd trudged upstairs to unpack, fighting the urge to take a pain pill to ward off the ache in his chest.

Woody gazed at the details of the guestroom, its antique four-poster bed offering what promised to be a fitful night's sleep. Posey had stacked extra blankets on the divan under the window draped in thick fabric of black and gold stripes. He gave a cursory chuckle at another not-so-subtle tribute to the infamous bee.

A scotch over ice waited for him downstairs in Althea's study. His aunt wanted to have a chat before turning in. Woody closed the door to the guestroom and strolled down the line of photographs in the hall, ones he'd walked by earlier but hadn't taken the time to absorb. All of Asher and Althea, except for the last one: Asher with his arms around Ellen Dushane. He could have been staring at a younger version of himself and Olivia. In a way, he had blood from them both pumping in his veins. Olivia hadn't fully understood the meaning of what she'd done with the transfer of only two liters.

Woody grasped the mahogany banister and descended the staircase to the main floor. A strange sense of peace settled over him with the glow at the end of the back hall. Althea's private study. The door stood open.

He knocked twice on the doorframe and pointed. "Is that empty chair and scotch for me?" he said.

Althea swirled her Manhattan and took a sip. "Certainly is. I trust you didn't take any pain pills?"

"No. I'm toughing it out." Woody sat and reached for the crystal tumbler on the side table. He took a swallow and enjoyed the initial burn as a distraction from the ache. "An interesting choice of decoration in the guestroom."

Althea smirked. "You caught that, did you? I figured you would."

"Really, Auntie. Your sense of humor is wicked."

"The decorator did question my choice of palette." Althea

plucked the cherry from her drink and popped it in her mouth.

Woody chuckled. Something Olivia would say. He went quiet and stared at the wedding band on his finger, only a placeholder without vows. "Never thought my life would take this turn."

"Enjoy it while you can," Althea said.

"What do you think she's doing now?"

"Wondering if you're going to show up. To her, you might as well have left her at the altar, Woody."

"But this is important. Sitting here with you. I wasn't going to leave you with Tony's arraignment tomorrow."

Althea sighed. "I've been alone a long time."

"And that's why. You need me."

"So does Olivia."

"What do you want me to do? What are your wishes?"

"We'll go to my lawyer's office in the morning. The arraignment's not until two. We have a ten o'clock appointment to make you my executor."

"I understand, but that's not what I'm asking." Woody took a deep swallow of his scotch. "What are your wishes for the money?"

"That you do something meaningful with what I'm handing you." Althea shrugged and stared into the fire. "Me? Scatter me where you will. A place where I can belong to an unpopulated landscape would be nice. It's more important that you and Olivia create a better legacy than what I could've done by myself. Two are better than one."

"I can make that happen."

"I trust that you will."

"Where did you scatter my father's ashes?"

"I didn't." Althea stood and drained the rest of her Manhattan. She stepped to the fireplace and stared at the lazy flames. With near ceremony, she reached for a hand-carved box on the mantle. She held it as though it were the most precious possession in her grand house. "Take them with you, Woody. A mountain would be nice for Asher to rest. Maybe you can make sure I join him when the time comes."

Althea handed him the wooden box. Smooth cherrywood met his

fingertips, a box made by a master craftsman to hold something personal and special. A father had been waiting for his son all these years. He didn't dare open the lid for fear of what the gesture might release. Olivia could come up with eloquent words for a moment like this, but Woody could only stare at his aunt's face. An alive female version of the man in his hands. He set the box next to his scotch and stood in front of her.

Althea ran her hand over the bandage beneath his shirt. "I'm so sorry, Woody. I did this to you."

He pulled his aunt to his aching chest. Her bones were thin, but he held on. Silence crackled with the fire.

Althea took a step back and grasped his hands. "And when we're done tomorrow you'll go to her," she said. "Promise?"

"I need to go up to Wolfeboro. Deal with my practice and talk to my partners."

"Always the lawyer. That's bull, Woody. Go to Portland as fast as you can."

Chapter 30
Full Circle

"That's bull, Liv," Danny said. "Of course, he'll show up."

"I'm not so sure," Olivia said and turned the browning chicken in the pan. "His world's been turned upside down."

"You tend to do that to people," Lauren said. "And do that to yourself too."

Olivia eyed her sisters, both inspecting her for a response. She pivoted to the sink and washed her hands. Pogo and Beauregard flanked her, wagging their tails for an answer.

"Even if he doesn't show up," she said. "I'm in a better place than I was two years ago."

"Mom was alive two years ago," Danny said. "Look at all that's happened: drama, drama, drama."

"I haven't thanked you both for coming to New York to rescue me. I never dreamed we'd find out the truth about Mom, and that Woody would find his family. I feel bad for Dad that Mom had the love for someone else her whole married life. I can't imagine what burned inside her for decades. I had no clue."

"She married, but not married her true love. But Dad was Dad and I loved him."

"Me too." Olivia took a breath. "But now I almost feel like I had two dads."

"Helluva screenplay, Liv," Lauren said. "Your fingers will fly tomorrow."

"You've got that right. If Woody does show up, I'll have an ending." Olivia folded a hand towel and hung it on the handle of the oven door. "Is Ryan okay about you coming over, Danny?"

"He's still processing what happened. When I left with Pogo, he was staring at *Sharknado* on SyFy."

"Cool," Lauren said.

"What do you think would've happened if Mom had married Woody's father?" Danny popped out the question that lurked beneath Olivia's skin, the question that she dared not ask.

"None of us would've been born," Olivia said. "Mom would've been a rich widow, rattling around that house on Beacon Hill. Maybe Mom and Althea would be living there like two old biddies."

"But that didn't happen," Lauren said. "And here we are, three menopausal biddies waiting for two men to show up, and a third on a couch watching *Sharknado*."

Olivia started with a chuckle. Lauren and Danny escalated to laughter until the three of them were wheezing. The pain of love and loss. Lauren quieted first, then Danny. Olivia poked the chicken as she took stock. She had lost Adam and found Woody. Lauren had lost her husband, Mark, and found Casey. Danny had nearly lost Ryan, but it had been Pogo that brought them together again. The source for their healing had been their mother, Ellen Dushane.

Lauren took a deep pull on her iced wine. "Do you still have that old message Mom left you on your answering machine before she died?"

"Sure do," Olivia said. "I'll never erase it."

"Play it. I need to hear her voice."

"The chicken's ready. You sure you want to hear it again?"

Lauren offered a slow nod, but her lip started to quiver with uncertainty.

Olivia turned off the stove and stepped to the phone. She scrolled through the saved messages, several of them from Karen and the treasured ones from Woody. The caller ID from the one from her mother still indicated their father's name: William Dushane. She pressed the speakerphone button on the handset and set it on the kitchen island.

"Hi, honey. It's Mom. I'm sitting here in the car at Walgreens, the one on Arlington and McLoughlin. Danny went inside to pick up my prescription. I have to talk fast. A white Suburban just pulled in. Here's the license number: 226-EEK. Just like a monkey. 'Eek Eek.' Got it? Love you."

An encore of the series of beeps in musical tones ended the call. At the prompt of the mechanical instruction Olivia hit SAVE. Saved for another round of ninety days, an exercise she had performed for the past two years.

Danny reached for a napkin from the holder and squished it over her eyes, just as she'd done the first time Olivia had played the message.

"Mom never figured out how to hang up a call on her Jitterbug." Danny even repeated the same words of her initial response verbatim.

Lauren inhaled to stop her own flow of tears. She scooted back the counter chair and stood. "I'll set the table."

The phone weighed heavy in Olivia's hand. She stared at it, picturing her mother stored in the cache of voice mail and waiting to be retrieved. If she could only make a return call to talk with her, cry and laugh with her about all the trauma of wedding rings: receiving one after Woody's proposal in the women's bathroom, Beauregard swallowing her ring, wearing Woody's without a commitment, cutting off Adam's, Lauren receiving the ring intended for Ellen and Asher's union that didn't happen, and everything else. Absolutely everything else. Mom would've loved the drama of it all.

The phone shivered with a ring. Olivia jumped and pressed the button.

"Mom?"

~ · ~ · ~

"Olivia?" Woody kicked off the thick comforter. "Are you okay?" Naked, he stepped to the window in the dark.

"I'm sorry," she said. "I thought you were someone else."

"Your voice sounds different. What's the matter?"

"We just listened to an ages-old message from Mom. Hearing her voice, Woody . . . it was strange. Her voice. I'm so relieved to hear yours."

"I've been wanting to hear you voice too. In an even stranger way, I heard my father's voice tonight. Althea gave me Asher's ashes."

"No . . . "

"Yes." Woody rubbed his forehead. A car eased down the narrow street, its headlights mapping a path. The snow piles at the curb had dwindled to ragged brown ridges, like a mountain range on an elaborate train set.

"We have to scatter them with Della's," Olivia said.

"Wasn't exactly a happy union, Liv."

"But a union that resulted in you, Woody. Maybe ours can change the course, turn it around."

Woody closed his eyes, her words a soothing analgesic. *Did he deserve her?* Responsibility had always taken first place. Love had taken a back seat. He'd need to rearrange his thinking. He pictured Althea giving him a poke and a nudge.

"Have you started writing yet?" he said.

"I'll start writing tomorrow morning. I won't come up for air until you call me after the arraignment tomorrow."

The clang of silverware downstairs prompted Woody's stomach to grumble. "Have you eaten?"

"About to. Lauren and Danny are here. I couldn't face an empty house tonight."

"Never again, Liv. When I get there, you'll never be alone again."

"I've needed to hear that. And you won't either. Get some sleep. You must be exhausted."

"I will, and I am."

Woody hung up and plugged his phone into the charger on the nightstand. The house rested quiet and dark. The time had come to raid the refrigerator. He tugged on his jeans and carefully pulled a white T-shirt over his head, igniting a sharp pain in his shoulder. He padded down the stairs in bare feet. The sudden squeak on the landing quickened his steps of his lifeline to the kitchen.

The Sub Zero held leftover brisket, potatoes, and rutabagas, along with a roasted Cornish hen under plastic wrap. He reached for the hen. The stream of light from the refrigerator shadowed the granite island of the kitchen designed to accommodate a crew of caterers. A plate. Where the hell was a plate and the microwave? Woody opened cabinets to glints of gold-rimmed coffee cups, crystal glasses, and wine goblets. He whipped around when the kitchen sprung to life with overhead light. Busted.

"I thought I heard someone in the kitchen," Posey said and tightened the belt on her fuzzy robe. She patted her pinned hair under a sheer scarf that knotted above her forehead. She had been practiced in her monitoring of every sound in the house. Her face without makeup made her appear younger. "What can I get you, Mr. Rainey?"

He let out a breath. "I didn't mean to disturb you, but I'm famished."

"You didn't eat much at dinner. I'll make you something."

"Anything would be fine, but I'm happy to do it myself. Please, don't put yourself out for me. I just need to know where everything is."

"No trouble. Scrambled eggs and toast?"

"Sounds like heaven."

With practiced efficiency, Posey pulled a small fry pan from a lower cabinet and set it on the stove. A puff of flame licked the stainless steel. A square of butter raced around it and bubbled. One-handed, she cracked three eggs on the rim of a mixing bowl. After a splash of milk, she churned them to a froth. A sizzle erupted from the pan when she poured in the mixture. Woody watched her process with fascination and eyed the salt and pepper. Posey picked up the signal, smiled, and sprinkled.

"Were you ever married?" he said.

"Briefly before I took this position," Posey said. "For two years. My husband left me for another woman. I was in a bad way when the employment agency sent me to the interview with Mrs. Pennington. She was in bad shape too. We had a meeting of the minds, so to speak. Our bond goes back a long way, Mr. Rainey. Decades."

"Explains a lot. Don't you want to retire?"

"And do what? Second guess the decisions I've made in my life?"

"Do you regret your actions?"

"I'm not saying what we did to Simon was right, but we did it for the right reasons. He was going to kill her. I knew it, and so did she."

"Kills *me* to think you both had to live with that for so long."

"A long, long time."

"Can I ask you another question?" he said.

Posey didn't answer, but her straightened posture did.

Woody pulled out the counter chair and sat. He studied the pattern in the granite countertop. He found a perfect likeness of a hummingbird. "Did you ever have children?"

"Yes. A daughter."

"Do you see her? Are you close?"

Posey sighed. "We lost touch years ago. I keep tabs on her, but her father took her from me when he remarried. I had too much responsibility to look after Althea."

"Your job over family. Believe me, I know the choice you had to make." Woody traced his finger over an abstract pattern of what appeared to be a flow of lava. "What's she doing now?"

"Oddly enough, she's a parole officer right here in Boston."

"You should at least have dinner with her."

"Perhaps."

"Can I ask you a third question?" Woody said. *The power of three yields the truth.* He also figured the power of three tested patience.

The spatula slowed its trek around the pan. Posey tapped the rim and turned down the heat on the burner. "You're a lawyer through and through."

When their eyes met, Woody sensed he'd get an answer. "Am I right to say that you weren't the one who released that bee on Simon?"

The housekeeper held his gaze in silence, possibly assessing the consequences of a response. "It's more complicated than that."

"Your loyalty knows no bounds."

"Mrs. Pennington has been very good to me, Mr. Rainey. I would've done anything to protect her, and I did on many occasions. I still do, and I always will."

"A collaborative effort."

"After all these years, ours is a partnership. I'll be loyal to her until the day she dies." Posey turned. Two pieces of bread descended when she pressed the lever on the toaster. She pulled a china plate from the cabinet and a fork from a drawer. She set them both in front of him with a black linen napkin. Of course black, so as not to shed lint. "You swear nothing will happen to Althea if she testifies against Mr. Corelli?"

"Nothing will happen to either of you. It serves no purpose. The detectives are focused on cleaning up the fraud in their department."

Scrambled eggs toppled on the plate in front of him. Posey retrieved the toast and scraped butter all the way to the edges to ensure every bite would taste the same. A growl released from his stomach at the savory aroma. He picked up the fork and dove in. With his mouth full, he raised his eyes.

"You do know, Posey, that I'll make sure you're taken care of for the rest of your life."

"I appreciate that, Mr. Rainey, but I ask for nothing."

"Not the point. Loyalty should be rewarded." Woody nodded to emphasize the point. "Can I ask you one more question?"

"You will, no matter what I say."

"How do I not be torn between Olivia and Althea?"

"Leave all this behind. Neither of us is hurting a soul, other than ourselves. I'll take care of Althea. Go live your life and make Olivia happy. You won't regret it. She's a lucky woman."

Woody swallowed with a thick throat. His gaze circled the designer kitchen. "I'm the lucky one, Posey."

Chapter 31

Truth

At ten o'clock on Friday morning, the week before Christmas, Olivia sat at her computer in the den. She hit SAVE on a long diagram of scenes and plot points. Rays of sun streamed through the French doors. In front of them Beauregard lay stretched out to enjoy the warmth. Freesia had curled up on the club chair, snuggled in the afghan. A bright sunny day had finally arrived. The outline for the screenplay of *Indigo Legacy* was taking shape.

Olivia needed a break from reducing her mother's story to flashbacks, cuts, and transitions to distill it down to a fast-paced two-hour drama. Her fingers had banged out scenes of the book auction, Tiffany's, Allenwood Prison, Althea's house, Mass General . . . and her and Woody talking in the car about Adam. Every day had yielded a new discovery, as though she were living the story in real time. Woody had received his father's ashes only last night. Tony's arraignment would take place today. What else would possibly happen?

She'd been writing since five in the morning, with her brain firing on all pistons. The last cup of coffee burned in her stomach. Olivia clicked off the desk lamp and stood to stretch.

"Who wants to go for a walk?"

Beauregard scrambled to his feet. His toenails clicked over the hardwoods to retrieve his leash from a hook in the mudroom. Olivia followed and shrugged on her jacket. A few wadded plastic bags were already stuffed in the pocket. Lauren would be up reading the paper, but Olivia needed solitude, space to think.

"Beau, let's go."

Details of the houses in the neighborhood clarified with her heightened awareness. When had the Tudor across the street received a fresh coat of paint? The bare maple tree in the yard next door could use a trim. The Christmas lights around the door of another house had been left on in the bright sunshine. She should at least get a wreath for her own door. Beauregard slowed his gait to match hers. He stopped and sniffed a fresh spot on a lawn to make a deposit. Olivia waved the plastic bag to acknowledge a neighbor tending to piles dead leaves. Every pull of the rake revealed a strip of bright green.

"You doin' okay, Olivia?" her neighbor called out.

"Fine. Fine. All ready for Christmas?"

"The kids are getting spoiled." Another swipe. More exposure of green grass. "My wife finally read your mom's book. She loved it. Did all that really happen?"

"Yeah. It did," she said and stooped to clean up after Beau.

"Will you sign it?"

The dog gazed up at her and wagged his tail. "Sure. But I'll never live up to my mom. I'll come by soon. Enjoy this lovely day, Gotta keep moving."

Every step forward around the block pushed Olivia's thoughts to the file box stored on a shelf in her garage. She and Woody had given closure to her mother's past, and one last task was required for the final closure of another life. For five years, the most personal of possessions waited, all shut away in a box of denial. She'd glanced at the box every time she pulled the car in or out of the garage, hurried past it to retrieve a tool, or balanced her hand on the lid to fetch a suitcase. Before Woody arrived on Christmas Day, she had to be ready with a whole heart—and a piece of it still beat inside that box. With a new sense of urgency, Olivia turned and led Beau back to the house.

A strange stillness loomed inside the garage. Every sound and smell intensified after the door rolled shut. The tick of the water heater punctuated the earthy odor of damp cement. Olivia knew right where to go. Like human ashes, the file box had lost its weight with the passing of years. When she'd originally stored the box away, her weak arms had been barely able to lift it to the shelf. She blew the dust from the top of it and stepped into the house. A backward shove of her foot closed the mudroom door behind her.

Olivia set the box on the kitchen island. She pulled off the lid on thirty-two years. Inside sat her and Adam's wedding album, with a cool-headed man making vows to a hot-headed woman. She had burned for life at twenty. He had burned for grounded security at twenty-eight. He would've been sixty-five now and dependent on her dreams and wishes. Passion came somewhere in between. Passion hadn't shown up in that last decade. She'd nearly starved to death, but when her romance books had finally taken off, Adam had celebrated the royalties. Before then, he'd poked and prodded about her needing to seek a different profession. He hadn't believed in her.

The wedding photos in a coffee table album held so much promise but hadn't delivered. Olivia set it aside. The boutonniere, brown and dried, that had sat in the refrigerator behind the butter dish for so many years, had crumbled to dust in a baggie. She pulled out Adam's dead cell phone and plugged it into the charger. She'd never stopped paying the joint cell phone bill. One of those dysfunctional secrets she'd kept private, even from her mother. Adam's leather wallet, the one she'd given to him years ago, had suffered around the edges from use. The leather was shiny and smooth. She opened it and stared at his driver's license. The photo had been taken before the gray had crept over his temples. So handsome. The man who had triggered her obsessive quest for justice. She'd invaded his wallet only once in thirty-two years, to retrieve his Social Security and insurance card after the accident. At the time, those two items forced the invasion, but the rest had been unimportant. Her head hadn't been clear back then.

Today, she wanted to inspect everything with new eyes.

A wad of paper money still sat in the billfold. Three pennies spun on the counter when she pulled out the bills, like a magic trick. Stuck between two twenties and a five were a receipt and a folded note. The final grocery receipt showed an amount of ninety-seven cents for three lemons. Why not three for a dollar?

Curious, Olivia unfolded the white paper. The top edge was ragged, a result of its hasty rip from a memo pad. She didn't recognize the upright swirls of the handwriting. Not hers. Hers leaned to the right. Not Adam's, either, since his writing had leaned to the left. The lettering stood perfectly upright.

I love you, sweetheart. When you tell your wife tonight, you'll be all mine.

Olivia stared at the note, dumbfounded. On the fifth pass, the words triggered a wave of nausea that tightened the muscles in her stomach. The room started to spin. She lunged to the kitchen sink and retched.

~ · ~ · ~

Two car doors slammed outside. Olivia widened her eyes at Lauren. Another needy phone call had prompted a new family emergency, but this one called for a full complement of emotional resources.

Lauren raced to the peephole. "They're here," she said. "Thank God." Her sister opened the door and stood on the stoop to shepherd Danny and Ryan inside.

The contents of the file box lay strewn across the kitchen floor. Olivia had shoved it from the counter in a fit of rage before calling her sisters. Beau held court on the fan of papers, as if preventing any contamination of a crime scene. The offending note of betrayal lay on the kitchen island as evidence that she'd not misinterpreted its meaning.

Danny stepped into the kitchen with her arms outstretched.

"C'mere," she said. A fresh wave of tears erupted when Olivia wrapped her arms around her younger sister.

In full uniform, Ryan stepped past her and Danny with a mission. He'd abandoned his duties, yet again, to come to her rescue.

"Lemme see the note," he said.

Olivia swiped her forefingers under both eyes and pointed to the kitchen island.

Pogo raced inside and nosed the papers on the floor. He picked out one and clenched it in his mouth, an invitation for Beauregard to spill the full details. A certified copy of Adam's death certificate now had teeth marks.

A cast of disappointment dulled the brightness in Ryan's eyes when he read the note. "No mistaking the meaning of that, Liv." He tossed the paper on the counter like the last draw of a playing card, the final acknowledgment of a bad hand. "I'm so sorry." He reached for the cell phone. Enough juice had pumped into it to ignite the screen. "Have you looked at this? Checked the voice mail?"

Olivia's throat tightened. "I didn't dare. I never did anything back then, either, except to see if there were any photos of the white Suburban. There weren't, so I put it in the box."

Ryan glanced up at her from the screen. "Don't."

"Want me to check it?" Danny said to Ryan. "Maybe it should be a private sister thing."

He held up is hand. "No. I'll do it."

Lauren's eyebrows disappeared beneath her bangs. She took off her glasses and rubbed her eyes. An accusation was about to launch, and Olivia didn't think she could handle it.

"You mean to tell me you never checked his phone or took Adam off your phone contract?" Lauren said. "What the hell were you thinking, Liv? You've been paying for it for five years?"

"Have I ever," Olivia said.

"Unfinished business," Danny said. "Like Adam was giving you the business."

A vocal response wouldn't come out. A thread of hazy memories of denial clarified and twisted into an ugly string of acceptance.

As she thought about it now, it had been irresponsible. The signs were there, but she'd refused to consider a betrayal. Over the past hour, she'd paced around the house, racking her brain to remember the clues. That last year with Adam produced a confusing change in his personality. He had withdrawn from her, been less open and communicative, and avoided her gaze. No eye contact. What should have been Saturday morning errands had extended into the late afternoon with no explanation. Out of nowhere, old files had been shredded. Her files. It had been odd that Adam had been so enthusiastic to run to the store for the lemon that fateful night. Now, she believed the quick trip had been an excuse to get away from her for a private conversation, out of earshot. Ryan was about to listen to the proof of her suspicions.

With the charging cord still snaking from the outlet, Ryan scowled and set the phone to his ear. He squinted and closed his eyes. A garbled woman's voice discharged from the receiver, unmistakable even from across the kitchen island. Young. Light. Musical. A tone of affection. Olivia caught the words *your wife* and *but I'm selfish*. She pictured herself a hawk with a mouse on her radar. Saliva filled her mouth.

"Who is she?" she said. "What's her name?"

Ryan sighed and yanked the cord from the socket. He wound it around the phone in a tight coil. "I don't know. She didn't say."

"Trace the number. Map it on GPS."

Lauren threw a warning glance. Their eyes met and locked. "Olivia . . . don't get obsessed again. I know you. This leads to no good."

Her sister was right. It had ended with Adam's death. Olivia's heart squeezed in its attempt to pump away the hurt, a hurt that could never be reconciled. What would be gained? What could be fixed by going back down that ugly, unproductive rabbit hole? All those wasted hours—days, weeks, years—of hunting an automobile to honor her loyalty to Adam. She pictured herself as a sorry-ass Elmer Fudd hunting wabbits. Adam had been going to pull the trigger on the *wabbit* called his wife, but he'd been killed first.

Danny stepped to Olivia's side and rubbed a circle on her back.

"You have Woody now, Liv. Focus on him, not all this crap. You'll be much better off."

Olivia pushed her hair from her forehead. *Woody loves me, respects me. He would never hurt me like this. Focus.*

"Ryan?" Lauren said. "Do you still have Liv's journal of dysfunction that I gave you a couple of years ago, the one with all those of license plate numbers of white Suburbans?"

"No," he said. "I had it shredded. The case is long closed." Ryan held up the outdated flip-style cell phone. "This goes with me to be destroyed too."

"Tell Woody about this, Liv," Danny said. "You have to. His ring is on your finger."

Olivia stared at her diamond band. Without the seal of vows attached to it, the missing promise of loyalty, respect, and honor left her on shaky ground. In response, she started to shake uncontrollably. Her anger over Adam's betrayal had nowhere to go.

I had so much trust," she said. "I never dreamed he had betrayed me. I feel like such a fool. I should write a note to the police force for all the hell I put them through. And you too, Ryan."

Paper crinkled on the floor. Pogo pushed on his front paws to scrunch the documents, a lure for Beauregard to become a coconspirator. To avoid a reprimand, Beauregard bounded toward the French doors. The wadded paper stuffed in Pogo's mouth resembled Popeye's spinach. Olivia pulled the slimy police report from his muzzle and opened the patio door to let the dogs out.

Chapter 32
The Arraignment

At two o'clock on Friday afternoon, Woody held open the heavy glass door of the downtown Boston office building. He tucked the thick binder from Althea's lawyer under his arm and guided his aunt toward the waiting black Rolls Royce Phantom. Freed took over the care duties as Althea slipped into the expansive back seat with practiced grace. The meeting with her lawyer had yielded the desired result. Knowledgeable and decent, his aunt's attorney had been enthusiastic about drawing up the papers.

Woody checked his phone. A voice mail awaited from Olivia. He needed her voice now, no doubt offering lyrical words of support for Althea and him to face Tony in the courtroom. He had news to share with her too. The phone warmed as he held it to his ear.

"I'm in a bad space, Woody. Adam betrayed me before his death, even after death. Our marriage was a sham. He had someone else. I found the evidence in his wallet." The sound of tears erupted from the receiver. "Adam loved someone else. I'm so stupid. Please call me."

Woody inspected the roof lining of the car, stunned. *She doesn't love Adam. She doesn't love him.* A burn of unity, of oneness, pulsed in his own chest. He should be in Portland to hold her. An overwhelming sense of guilt for his selfishness made him want to ship his car, skip the arraignment, put off going to Wolfeboro, and head straight to the airport. He turned to Althea. Concern shrouded her eyes.

"Everything all right, dear?" Althea said.

"As soon as we get to the courthouse, I need a moment to call Olivia. Something's wrong. Terribly wrong."

"What on earth happened?"

"I'm not completely sure, but she found out something about her dead husband. And it wasn't good."

"You should go to her, Woody. I'll be fine. I don't even need to be at Tony's arraignment." Althea tapped the headrest of the front seat. "Freed? Take me home. Woody has an emergency."

"No, Althea," Woody said. "We're already headed to the courthouse. I'll call her when we get there to find out what's going on." He tried to stay calm, but his insides twisted. "Can you get us there faster, Freed?"

The driver glanced in the rearview mirror. "Not in this traffic, Mr. Rainey. Construction."

A flagger forced the car to stop to allow the oncoming traffic through. Woody leaned back in the seat to calm himself, but his leg kept going. Althea set her hand on his kneecap to still it. "We're almost there," she said. "She's strong. She'll be fine. She has you."

And she doesn't love Adam anymore, Woody thought. This had become an emergency as the reality of the physical distance widened between him and Olivia, literally spanning the continent. The faster he closed the gap, the less time for the beast of obsession to get its claws into Olivia.

"Let us off, Freed," Woody said. He opened the car door and grabbed Althea's hand.

As Woody shepherded Althea up each step to the courthouse, he reminded himself to be patient, not to push. He parked his aunt on an upholstered bench in the lobby and took in the scene. A stream of thugs and police entered the courtroom, the latter on the take, no doubt. Their turn was coming. Now that this situation had become personal, he thought even innocent observers were guilty. Spectators and reporters queued to empty their pockets, ready to catch a glimpse of the infamous Tony Corelli. Keys clattered in trays before streaming through the metal detector.

Woody leaned toward Althea and pointed to the courtroom doors. "Go ahead through security and take a seat, any seat. And save a place for me. I have to call Olivia."

Althea offered him a slow nod. "Don't be too long."

"You can do this. I'll be right by your side. I just need a few minutes." He patted Althea's hand and helped her to stand. She held her head high. Such a strong woman, steel-encased gel, just like Olivia.

In a near panic, Woody dialed Olivia's number as he moved to a window to get a clear signal.

"I'm here, Liv," he said when she answered.

"I need you. It's terrible," she said. "Worse than when Adam was killed."

"I'm on my way after I get through the arraignment. I'll get on a plane and put my car on a transport."

"What about your partners?"

"I'll tell them over the phone. I won't go up to Wolfeboro."

"You have to." Her voice jittered.

Woody ran his hand through his hair. "No. Margie will help me."

"Once you're here, I won't want you to go."

"I want to be with you. You need to give me the details. I can't believe what Adam did, and I don't want you to be alone."

A few seconds of silence lingered. "It's like he died twice."

"Althea's waiting for me in the courtroom. The arraignment's about to start."

"Go. I just needed to hear your voice. Call me when it's over."

"I will. I love you, Liv."

Woody disconnected and searched the empty lobby. He dashed to the security area and tossed his wallet and keys into the tray, stepped through the scanner, and snatched them up on the other side. He rushed to the double doors.

Nearly every space in the courtroom was occupied: cops in uniform, executives in off-the-rack suits, thugs in custom ones, and the usual fodder who get a charge out of seeing the accused in the flesh. Tony Corelli had commanded a crowd after his mug shot had been splashed on the front page of the *Boston Globe*. A quick assessment yielded what Woody guessed to be an equal balance of those who wanted Tony to fry and those who wished him free to continue supplementing their income. He caught the flash of Althea's earrings, just as she turned and raised her hand. He moved toward the front of the courtroom. After a quick nod to the state prosecutor and the two detectives, Woody scooted into the row to the saved space next to his aunt.

Althea's nervous fingers worked the chain on her black patent-leather purse. The back of Tony's head ignited Woody's anger. He waited for Tony to turn around, but he didn't.

The court reporter poised her hands over the keyboard and gazed around the room. The judge breezed through the side door. The bailiff squared his shoulders. "All rise."

The chatter in the courtroom quieted. Woody held Althea's arm to guide her to her feet. He steadied her when her knees buckled.

A *pop* caught his attention. Woody turned, not knowing from which direction the sound came. Someone must've dropped something. The door at the back of the courtroom closed in slow motion. His gaze circled the courtroom and stopped—Tony Corelli listed to the left and fell to the floor. A gunshot. All heads turned to find the source, but only gasps and screeches released like hungry bats at sunset. Woody turned to Althea, her eyes a mirror of the shock he, too, felt. A spray of bright red blood and brain matter stuck to Althea's soft-pink wool suit. Woody stared in disbelief.

"My God," he said.

Althea's face went slack at the pool of blood trailing across the hardwood floor in front of them.

A few seconds of silence loomed before panic erupted in the courtroom. The benches emptied as attendees fled for the doors.

A hit. Someone didn't want Tony to talk. Someone who had been allowed to bypass security.

Althea collapsed in his arms.

~ · ~ · ~

So fragile, Woody thought as he helped Althea up the stairs to her bedroom. If not for the incessant ache in his shoulder, he would have carried her. Posey had raced ahead to prepare the linens. Odd that Althea hadn't shed a tear in the car as she gazed out the window. Her pillar of strength had crumbled when Woody had grasped her hand to help her into the house.

"Get this suit off me," Althea said as Woody guided her to the bed. Until now, he'd not entered her private space. "Throw it in the garbage. I'll never wear it again."

"It's all over," he whispered. "All over." His gaze met Posey's in a silent agreement to take over.

Althea lay back on the pillows and shook her head from side to side, her eyes shut tight. "Strip me bare. I need a bath. That abominable man is all over me."

Button by button, Posey released the bloodstained closures. "Woody, start the tub," she said. "Please hurry."

He raced to the bathroom next to Althea's dressing room and turned on the faucets full blast. Not too cool. Not too hot. Tony's drying blood bled up the cuffs of his white shirt. He let the water run over them until they faded to rims of peach. A white spa towel hung over a warming rack. He whipped it from the rail in anticipation of helping Althea to the tub. To save her dignity, he'd wrap her in it. Tony Corelli had reduced her to this. Now, the two most important women in his life had been damaged in one day. *Hold on, Liv. I only have one strong arm.*

The edges of the sink steadied Woody. He steeled his gaze at the mirror. The towel hung over his shoulder as if he'd completed a workout at the gym. Flecks of dried blood in his hair shook his thoughts back to reality. There were two possibilities for who was responsible: a crooked cop or someone who had acted on orders from Palermo. The don was twisted enough to think he was doing them a favor.

Olivia would know what to do. Olivia could find out who had done this.

Olivia had grit.

Chapter 33

Palermo

At four o'clock on Friday afternoon, Olivia hung up the kitchen phone in a trance. The hand towel slid to the floor when she attempted to hang it over the handle on the oven door. The dryness in her mouth made her tongue rough as sandpaper. The urgency in Woody's voice filled her with a sense of dread. Tony was dead. The mental image of what Woody and Althea had witnessed could never be erased. Her personal crisis paled in comparison, a mere emotional blip. This she could do something about. A clear head lifted her cloud of guilt.

Beauregard nosed her hand for a treat. Too early for his dinner, but she dug in the kibble bin and gave him a handful to soothe his need for attention. She stroked his long nose and gazed into his alert brown eyes, soulful and finely tuned to her emotions. So loyal. So committed. She'd do well to follow the dog's example.

"Come in the den with Mommy," she said. "Wanna see Uncle Palermo?" Beau wagged his tail and led the way.

Anger made her heart pound. She'd call Ben first to add a layer of perspective. Palermo would be in his prison cell, listening to opera, and probably basking in the success of his latest triumph. Yet another trust had been violated. How could she have been so blind to the twisted motivations of others? She didn't want to be distrustful or guarded, but Palermo had taken advantage of her benevolence and focus to publish his memoir. A litany of changes to Palermo's manuscript rolled through her mind, not the least of which would be to switch the dedication to R. D. Griffin. He had been the purest mobster of all, the one relationship she didn't regret.

Olivia dialed Ben's direct number. He'd have it forwarded to his cell phone if he wasn't at his desk.

"Olivia?" Ben said when he answered.

"I need to talk with Palermo," she said. "It's mission critical."

"Are you all right?"

"No, Ben. Tony Corelli was shot at his arraignment in Boston today. Put the pieces together and see to who they point to."

Imaginary crickets chirped in the moment of silence that hung. Then: "What do you want to do?"

"I need Palermo on video. I want to see his face." Olivia's jaw stiffened. "Please, Ben."

"Be at your computer in twenty minutes. We'll call you."

Olivia hung up and turned to Beau. The dog sat at attention next to her. She took a cleansing breath. "We'll have to wait. Play ball?"

Beau gazed up at her, delighted at the surprise. He trotted to the French doors. A rush of cool air circled the room when she opened them. Olivia snatched the squishy ball from its bowl on the bookshelf and squeezed it like her own form of hand-muscle therapy.

Every throw-and-retrieve prompted Olivia to check her watch. Fifteen minutes remained to release Beau's pent-up stress. With every toss, she got out the ugly words she wanted to say to Palermo. *Stay calm to extract the truth. Turn the tables.* Breathe. Throw. Breathe. Throw.

Beauregard slowed to a trot and lifted his leg on her hydrangea, which needed a trim in the spring. Worn out, he returned to her with a flapping tongue.

"It's time, Big Boy. Let's go in."

Two minutes to spare. From a window view, Freesia had been

watching the play session with a scowly puss. Olivia couldn't make everyone happy, least of all herself.

A chime woke the computer screen from its sleep. She scrambled to the desk chair and rolled forward. A click of the camera icon made the video image appear. Palermo sat in a chair, shifting to cross his legs with self-satisfaction. His body language screamed superiority and control, especially in the way his bony hands dangled over the arms of his chair. Olivia blurted out the words that had been stuck on her tongue for the past fifteen minutes.

"You did it, didn't you?" she said. "Why?"

Palermo worked over his lips like he'd eaten a tasty rodent. "Olivia . . . where are your manners?"

"Manners? You killed Tony Corelli in open court."

As he spread his hands, Palermo's long, deadly fingers extended beyond the edge of the screen. "How could I do that? I'm in this five-star hotel."

"You had it done."

Palermo's milky eyes stared at something off camera. He turned back toward her voice. "He was a problem . . . for you, for your future husband—for us."

Olivia's throat swelled for the onset of tears, but she held them back. "What kind of problem?"

"Tony . . . he never lets go, Olivia. It would have been unfortunate for you to not have a chance at happiness."

"He was going to have Woody killed?"

"Your Rudolfo is free." Palermo swished his hand, like an annoyance had been resolved. "We're family, you and me. We take care of each other. Tony was about to talk. He has nothing to lose. Happens at his age."

"You're just as old, Nicky. What about you? Did you talk?"

"To *you*. I talked to you."

"Are you going to kill *me* now?" Olivia's hand shook on the mouse as she clicked *mute*. Her string of profanity caught Beauregard's attention. Freesia raced from the den.

Palermo worked that lip of his again. "Your heart is one I could only hope for, Olivia. No . . . I get redemption through your naivety. Absolves me."

She clicked the microphone icon again. "You didn't answer the question." Olivia pictured all positive energy flowing from her body. The void filled with toxicity. She wanted a shower to wash away the cheapness of life in Palermo's world. "You took advantage of me."

"I love you like a daughter, and I will protect you."

He'd twisted it. Everything. She'd been so stupid, just like with Adam. He'd taken advantage of her too, with his moral ambiguity—the money, the books, her loyalty, her trust. The image of the other woman's note filled her thoughts:

I love you sweetheart. When you tell your wife tonight, you'll be all mine.

"We're done, Palermo," she said. "You're fundamentally different than me and wired in a whole other way."

"You'll do whatever you need to achieve what you desire." The old man bobbed his chin. "I have no doubt."

"That's not true."

"Yes, Olivia, it is true. I like that about you."

"The book will be published, but this is the last time you'll ever talk with me. I wanted to be by your side when you died, but now you . . ."

"Go live your life. I've lived mine."

With that comment, Olivia ended the session and shut down the computer. Palermo didn't get it. He didn't care about her, only his ego, his superiority. She snatched up the phone and punched in Ben's mobile number. On the third ring, he picked up.

"Call me when he dies, Ben," she said. "There'll be no more memoirs after Palermo's. I don't have the stomach for this. Danny will keep the therapy-dog program going. We'll fund it another way, some-how. I promise."

"Olivia . . . hold on."

Olivia hung up the phone and set her head in her hands. Two levels of betrayal. Maybe she'd been all wrong about Woody's commitment too. Trust used to come so easily. Now, she trusted nothing. She had to call Karen. Her agent needed to know about the change in plans.

~ · ~ · ~

At nine o'clock on Saturday night, Woody pulled the car in front of his Colonial that doubled as his law office and home. The drive to Wolfeboro, New Hampshire, had been fraught with guilt, but at least the weather had cooperated to shave off half an hour from the trip. Woody hadn't wanted to leave Olivia alone in Portland. He hadn't wanted to leave Althea in Boston, either, but he'd only done so at Posey's insistence. He stared at the wooden sign by the front door—*Rainey, Bonner & Braden, LLC.* A former life had given birth to a new one.

He turned the key to silence the hot engine. If he was to make it to Olivia's by Christmas Day, a long to-do list of tasks had to be tackled before heading across the country. The weekend would be for packing. Monday morning would start with a partner meeting while the movers loaded a van. Then he'd be off for the four-day drive. The clutch had miraculously checked out fine.

The green-shaded lamp on his desk glowed in the front window, just as he'd left it when he'd gone to Portland three months ago. *Thank you, Margie, for keeping the home fires burning,* he thought as he opened the car door. He hauled his leather duffle bag from the back seat and trudged up the front walkway. Most of the office furniture on the first floor would be left behind in the sale of his share of the partnership, but his private apartment upstairs needed to be emptied.

When Woody stepped through the shiny oak front door, his welcome came from the comforting hums of office equipment. He set down his duffel bag and slid back the pocket doors, arms outstretched, and assessed his office. The pain in his shoulder reduced to only a twinge from the movement. A combined scent of lemon Pledge and Windex lingered as he stepped inside. The fireplace sat dark. The tankards on the mantle gleamed. Margie had dusted the side tables, lamps, and the framed credentials too. Surely Olivia would have given a thumbs-up assessment.

The screen of his console phone on his Federal-style desk glowed with a fat zero. No messages. Margie had retrieved and distributed them all to his partners. A few notes still graced his blotter in his own handwriting. Those notes didn't mean anything to him now. He moved to the mantle and retrieved the pewter crematory urn that anchored the middle spot. His mother. Della had sparked this new course, as if she'd planned it with that fateful, desperate call to sue Olivia and her sisters. He'd not given Della enough credit.

Woody set the urn on the desk and sat in his heavy wooden banker's chair, an antique one his mother had found at a liquidation sale when the bank in Center Tuftenboro went under. As he swiveled, he yearned to hear another sales pitch for marriage before signing on the dotted line. She'd be making dinner, no doubt fussing to get it just right for Lauren, who'd be kibitzing across the kitchen island. He reached for the receiver.

"What are you making tonight?" he said when Olivia answered.

"Homemade trail mix," Olivia said, "so it's in the pantry when you get here."

"Only raisins, no other dried fruit?"

"Right. Not too sweet."

"Almonds, cashews, and pumpkin seeds?"

"A trifecta of protein."

"You do love me, don't you?"

"More than anything." He sensed a pause. "I've had too much time to think."

"About what?" Woody fanned a pad of sticky notes.

"I need to show, not tell. I'm going to show you the moon. Every little thing I'm feeling. I won't save it for my books. How's your shoulder?"

"Much better. I'm regaining my strength. Adam's specter has been between us, Liv. I didn't want him there." Woody wanted to grip her face, her cheeks, and look into her endless eyes. "I'm in my office trying to figure out what to take."

"He won't be between us anymore. I can't go back and fix what I didn't even know happened. I'm ready to move forward, beyond him. Put sticky notes on things and assess your choices tomorrow."

"No shadows?" Woody gazed around the room. Shadows loomed everywhere.

"No shadows. I know that now. I never had what I thought I did. Nothing like you. You'll have to get me through the hurt, but there's no going back. Ever."

"Music," he said. "Your words are music."

"What do you want me to play when you get here?"

"Me, Liv. Play with me. I'll be there in four days."

"I'll have Dean Martin's Christmas album on the stereo. The tree's decorated. Fresh, by the way. It's Oregon."

"We'll be married by New Year's."

"The best present ever. Go stick notes to your stuff and get here in one piece."

Woody hung up with a new sense of purpose. He wrote the word *take* on several Post-It notes and peeled them off one by one. The first one was stuck to his mother's urn.

Chapter 34

The Books

At two o'clock on Friday afternoon, four days since leaving New Hampshire, Woody pulled the car in front of an impressive three-story Victorian house. He let the Porsche idle to calm from its trek up the steep hills to the upscale Ravenna neighborhood that overlooked downtown Seattle. To stay on schedule, he'd timed this side trip for a dinnertime arrival in Portland. Knowing Olivia, she'd be buzzing around the house with clean sheets, futzing to make more room in the closets, and defuzzing the furniture of Freesia's and Beauregard's hair. The air in the house might still hold a hint of fresh evergreen, maybe Pine-Sol after the Fantastik and 409. Olivia had a lot of cleaners that she considered her favorites. He'd only shaken his head when she said Fantastik made plastic shine the best.

Woody dialed Casey's number. His friend picked up on the first ring, as if he'd been waiting for the call.

"Are you there yet?" Casey said.

"Five or so hours away," Woody said. "Can you fly out to Portland?"

"Like I have no plans?"

"I know you've been talking with Lauren every night. Olivia told me. Want to see her?"

"How can I resist a woman with soft lips, hard talk, and a gun. She's under my skin."

"Want an adventure?"

His friend provided an answer with an exhale of breath.

"Good choice. I've made mine. And I need a best man."

"I'll be on my way," Casey said. "I'm in Kansas City. I'll keep going to Portland Airport. Pick me up there."

Woody ended the call and gazed at the Victorian across the street. The pieces were coming together, and hopefully culminating inside this house.

In clearer weather, Barry Wannamaker's home enjoyed a panoramic view, punctured by the landmark of the Space Needle. Today, a thick mist swallowed everything but the Christmas lights around the front door of the house next door, another impressive gingerbread Victorian. The decorations glowed like haloed Rudolph noses through the fog.

Wannamaker's house sat in a shroud of mist. Details oozed through as Woody stared at it. The multicolor paint job of marine blue, black trim, and subtle maroon insets accentuated the details of the wraparound porch. He thought of what Olivia might say: *New money trying to be old.*

Depending on the outcome of this meeting, Woody hoped this trip to see Wannamaker wouldn't be his last. Seattle was only a three-hour trek from Portland. He pulled the parking brake and retrieved his briefcase from the passenger seat.

The fresh scent of evergreen and *eau du marina* emerged from the thick fog. West Coast air had its own unique quality, complex and alive, with the combination of forest and water. The colors of the house became more robust as Woody moved up the walkway to the porch stairs, his legs stiff. A workout at Olivia's gym might be in the plan.

Barry Wannamaker opened the oak and etched-glass front door before Woody reached the top step. Casual in jeans and a thick cable-knit sweater, Barry offered a stiff smile with a slight air of caution.

"I was surprised to hear from you, Mr. Rainey," Wannamaker said and removed his wire-rimmed glasses. "Come in."

"I'm sure you were." Woody extended his hand. "I wanted to see you before heading down to Portland. I trust my mother's collection found a good custodian?"

"Indeed." Wannamaker's face had taken on a yellowish cast since their meeting at the auction in New York. Dark circles rimmed his eyes. "I'll show you."

One step into the entryway gave Woody a newfound respect for the man. An expansive round stained-glass window of reds, purples, and greens warmed the gray light above the landing on the staircase. It ushered the home's lucky inhabitants to the second floor. But the house was dead quiet.

Woody followed Wannamaker to one of two sets of ten-foot pocket doors flanking the entry hall. Barry slid back one pair with a smooth roll.

"Incredible," Woody said and took in the glass-fronted mahogany bookcases that lined the library. A warm fire snapped and popped, filling the room with an aroma of oak. In the center of the impressive room were four oversize leather chairs with side tables, arranged in pairs and separated by a low coffee table. A bay window sat behind Wannamaker's antique desk. A stained-glass lamp, its glass shade hand-painted with colorful pheasants, shined a light over the most important of the man's personal business. Over the fireplace sat a veined-marble clock, topped with an iron black panther in mid-hunt of two antelope. Carved-wood elephant heads supported the mantle with their trunks. But Woody's gaze pulled to one bookcase of the dozen or so that lined the room. He stepped to the shelves and stared through the rippled glass.

"You kept the collection intact," Woody said and turned.

"Oh yes," Wannamaker said. "A travesty to split it up."

"Olivia was right."

"How so?"

"I made a mistake, Barry. I shouldn't have sold them. I'll pay you double—no, triple, to have them back."

Wannamaker raised his brows, and then gestured for Woody to take a seat.

Woody sunk into one of the leather chairs and set his briefcase on the oriental carpet. He smoothed his hands over the rounded arms of the club chair. Wannamaker took a seat across from him and stared into the fireplace. The man appeared to be exhausted from the effort. For nearly a minute, only the crackle of burning wood had a voice.

"Mr. Rainey, they're not for sale at any price," Wannamaker finally said.

"I thought it was worth a try," Woody said. "You see, a lot has happened since we did our deal in New York. But I understand your reluctance to part with them."

"No . . . I don't think you do."

Woody tipped his head, curious. "Educate me."

"I'm reading them, Mr. Rainey. Every single one before I die, which in my case will require more speed than time."

"Why? If you don't mind my asking."

"Ironic, but this hematologist is dying of a blood disease—acute lymphoblastic leukemia. Cancer of the bone marrow and blood. Doctors don't make good patients. We're quite good at focusing on other people's ailments but deny our own. I waited too long for a bone marrow transplant."

"I'm so sorry, Barry. Really I am." Woody paused. "How long? I mean, until . . . ?"

"A few months. I've got six months, tops. Years ago, a diagnosis meant days. Now, if I'd had it treated sooner, my survival chances would have been upwards of eighty percent to live a normal life."

Woody rubbed his chin. A new sense of urgency peeled back the protocol to ask for a favor. He'd had too much time to think on the road trip. "Can I ask you a professional question?"

"Of course."

"If I show you an autopsy report from 1947, can you tell me if you see anything suspicious in the blood analysis?"

"I can try," Wannamaker said. "Is the body able to be exhumed for proof?"

Woody winced as he lifted his briefcase to his lap. "Unfortunately, not. Cremated." He pulled out his father's death documents and handed them over the coffee table.

Wannamaker took the pages and held them under the lamplight. The glow of ripe fruit came to life on the shade and set off a rumble in Woody's stomach. His thoughts shifted to the image of Olivia making trail mix with raisins. In the long silence, he picked up the scents of aged wood and vintage paper.

"A relative?" Wannamaker said and adjusted his glasses.

Woody plucked a piece of invisible lint from his wool slacks. "My father."

Wannamaker nodded and flipped over a stapled page and raised his eyes. "Are you worried that you might have inherited a disease?"

"No, actually. I just had surgery. My doctor went over my bloodwork before I was released. All normal, but my grandmother died from leukemia when she was in her forties. My father had a twin sister. She's ninety now. She didn't inherit the disease."

"By the age of ninety, the disease would've been apparent. What is it you want to know? There's quite the list of components in your father's blood analysis."

"The toxins you'll see on page three were from rat poison. I've learned that it can take up to two weeks, at lethal doses, to kill someone—even a rat. My father died within hours. I want to know, in your opinion, if the leukemia killed him before the rat poison did. Sounds like splitting hairs, I know, but for personal reasons it's an important distinction."

Wannamaker eyed him, and then studied the papers. "Give me a minute."

Woody's gaze circled the library. Even Althea's home paled in comparison. Unable to sit still, he stood and strolled back to his mother's book collection. The spines lined up like literary soldiers behind the glass. He had an urge to read the titles aloud, but Olivia's voice whispered them in his head. Thoughts of her ignited an itch in his core that he desperately needed to scratch. His pulse escalated the longer Wannamaker studied the pages.

The glass door of the bookcase released a squeak when Woody reached for Daphne du Maurier's *Rebecca*. The platinum wedding band on his finger still drew his fascination. He'd underestimated the power of a piece of metal. The attachment of vows really would make a difference when they finally happened. "Do you mind if I look at this one?"

Wannamaker didn't raise his eyes from the documents. "No. Go ahead."

With a thick throat, Woody pulled *Rebecca* from the shelf, taking care to not disturb the binding, and smoothed his fingers over the cover. He could easily get another edition, but not this one, the only copy Olivia wanted.

Without uttering a word, Wannamaker stood and stepped to a different bookcase next to his desk. He pulled out a thick volume and flipped the pages. With intense focus, the man took the open tome to his desk and set it down with a dull *thud*. When he sat, the hematologist-turned-patient had become a hematologist again, not dying from bad blood but alive with a purpose.

Woody leaned against the bookcase and started to read. Periodic glances at Wannamaker revealed nothing from the man's expression, but the extended silence shouted complications. Woody had nearly finished the third chapter when Wannamaker's voice startled him into closing the book.

"You're right about the poisons, Mr. Rainey." Wannamaker pushed his glasses to his forehead. He could have been a scholarly fly. "Your father certainly did have an advanced blood disease and serious toxins in his system. But in your father's case, they set off a firestorm of his already weakened immune system. He had no defense. Any anticoagulants would've flooded his system with internal bleeding in under an hour."

Woody closed his eyes. *Della didn't know.* "Would my father have survived those poisons if he were healthy?"

"Most likely. In fact, they're regularly given in stronger amounts to patients with clots to thin the blood. They can *save* the lives of people who need them. In his case, though, disastrous."

"Tipped him over the edge?"

"That's why the time to death became so compressed. The chemicals would've caused his system to go haywire. We've come so far, medically speaking, but in 1947 the doctors didn't have treatments for the disease if it was snowballing unchecked. I didn't even see any prescription drugs in his system."

Woody contemplated the man as if he were an expert witness. "So you're saying that the rat poison didn't kill him?"

Wannamaker lowered his glasses to his nose. "You're a lawyer, Mr. Rainey, who is trying to shepherd me toward the conclusion you want. A medical diagnosis doesn't eclipse intent. The rat poison only sped up an advancing disease."

Woody nodded, mulling over the statement. He himself had escaped the disease, saved by his mother's blood. A shred of comfort eased his mind about his mother's crime. Della hadn't known about Asher's disease. If she had, would she have gone down the poison road at all? Did she only intend to make him sick, not kill? A compelling argument could be made. "Understood. Thank you, Barry." He held up *Rebecca*. "Have you read this yet?"

"Years ago. Amazing story. It deserves a reread, especially that first edition. As I recall, though, the ending is better in the Alfred Hitchcock movie."

"It's personal for both Olivia and me, not just the story but this very book."

"What happened?"

"Ghost of her dead husband got between us. Long story, but it took me getting shot to break her bond with him. Then she learned a truth that brought us closer together." Woody pointed to his chest below his left shoulder. "I put Olivia at risk too. You of all people would appreciate the connection to the story, but this particular copy made her bid against you at the auction. I survived that . . . and this too."

"Take it. She's a spitfire."

"That she is. I'll get you another copy." Woody stared at the ghostly graphic on the cover. A similar ending mirrored his own quest for the truth of two ghosts—his father's and Olivia's former husband. Asher had died from the betrayal of his own body, not from the mob or Woody's own vengeful mother. And Adam had been killed while betraying Olivia. No fairness lay with these truths, but they would affect his and Olivia's future course.

The indelible memory of Olivia's blood-red shoes under the stall door in the women's restroom erupted a smile that eclipsed Woody's thoughts. At this moment, the book auction seemed like a lifetime ago. He raised his eyes to Wannamaker.

"We all have a legacy, Barry," Woody said. "My future wife and her sisters have a family Trust that supplies therapy dogs to ailing inmates in prison. They do good work. I'm going to expand it once Olivia and I are married."

Wannamaker paused, then nodded with his own brand of under-standing. He studied the room like a visitor in his own home. "When I die, I want to leave all these books as part of my wife's legacy. My wife was an avid reader, but she died in 1990 after an auto accident. It's not about the money."

"Same thing happened to Olivia—her first husband was killed in a hit-and-run car accident. She knows what you've been through."

"My wife loved books. I'd like to honor her memory. After I read them, do you want the collection back?"

Woody took a breath at Wannamaker's unexpected offer. "More than you could ever know."

"I'll put it in writing, Mr. Rainey. You've given me a mission to live long enough to finish them. I'm at Raymond Chandler, moving alphabetical by author."

"Trust me, when you get to Dickens, you'll linger," Woody said. "I must admit that I held back a few, including *The Big Sleep*. You'd probably want to read *The Maltese Falcon*, *Little Women*, *A Study in Scarlet*, and *Five Weeks in a Balloon* too."

"I need to read all of those."

"I'm sure Olivia will be happy to send them on loan. But if I can take *Rebecca* with me to Portland, I'll be a happy man."

Wannamaker stepped from behind the desk and handed Woody back the autopsy documents. "Legacies are tough to create without kids."

"I'm figuring that part out. Olivia has one more member of the family to meet."

"Who's that?"

"My daughter."

"I see." Barry's gaze lingered for a few seconds. "Some things happen for a reason. Does Olivia know about your daughter?"

"Not yet, but she will." After tucking the book and the papers into his briefcase, Woody took his time to close the zipper, a sound Olivia appreciated. He offered Wannamaker his hand. "You're a good man, Barry."

"Get on the road, Mr. Rainey. I imagine your fiancée is already checking her watch. We'll be in touch."

"I have two more stops to make. Then I'll be on my way."

Chapter 35
The Arrival

At six thirty on Friday evening, Olivia glanced at her watch. Lauren tapped the keys on her laptop, playing a computer game of "find the hidden object."

"Did you talk to Casey today?" Olivia said and stepped to the small Christmas tree in the breakfast room. All-white lights cast a soft glow into the kitchen. The picture-frame ornament of Beauregard needed an adjustment. Freesia's photo above it signaled the cat's superior status. Lauren had been watching with her ears.

"Will you quit puttering?" Lauren said. "And yes, I talked with Casey. He seemed in a hurry to end the conversation when I called him at noon. I don't know if this is going anywhere, but it's fun."

"What kind of fun?" Olivia moved Beauregard's picture up one branch.

"He sexted me the other night."

"Did you at least close the drapes?"

"I did. Then I danced around in the living room to Twisted Sister."

Olivia moved back into the kitchen and grabbed a dish towel from the oven handle. She swept it over the glass top on the stove. "You need management. Danny should be here."

Lauren shifted her eyes from the screen to the digital clock on the microwave. "They're at that Christmas party with all the cops. Holiday heroes."

Olivia tapped her fingernails on the counter. "Great. Everybody's a designated driver. Does Ryan have to blow into a breathalyzer at the door?"

"Party game." Lauren took off her glasses and squinted. "Help me find a blue telescope."

"I need the Hubble to pinpoint where Woody is. It doesn't take five hours to drive from Seattle. He's not coming."

Lauren shrugged. "Where's he gonna go? It's a helluva side trip to Puyallup. They chew, spit, and brush that one tooth after they clean their gun."

"I'm chewing and spitting. Give me your gun." Olivia stared at her sister.

"Why?"

"What day is coming?"

Lauren rubbed her forehead. "Oh, crap. I forgot. Your anniversary."

"How am I going to get through that day if Woody's not here?"

Lauren grimaced. "Does Woody know?"

"I never mentioned it."

Both of their gazes shifted to Lauren's glass of wine when a rumble of a low hum rippled the surface.

"A car engine," Olivia said, almost breathless.

"I'll check." Lauren scooted back the chair and raced to the peephole in the front door.

Olivia darted to the cabinet under the sink for her new savior in a bottle—: Fantastik. The kitchen island got several squirts and a blurred wipe with the hand towel. The lights of the Christmas tree in the breakfast room radiated a twinkle show in the shine.

"Uh-oh." Lauren turned, her eyes accusing before her words. "Do you have on a thong or Lollipop cottons?"

Olivia smoothed her hand over her backside. "No panty lines."

"Good woman. Your man just pulled in."

~ · ~ · ~

Woody let the oil in the engine settle before he switched off the ignition. "Whatcha think? Is she cleaning or racing to the bathroom?" he said to Casey. The motion light on the garage illuminated and cast a golden stream over the hood of the car.

Casey glanced at the quaint Tudor and settled his gaze on Olivia's front door. A red ribbon fluttered from the evergreen wreath. "Is Lauren in there with her?"

"No doubt."

"Those two are so opposite. How's that work?"

"Like heads and tails of the same coin," Woody said.

"Flip?" Casey said and laughed.

"Naaah. I've got the head case. You explore a fairy tale." Woody turned to his friend. "You wouldn't have just flown from Kansas in your own plane if Lauren wasn't the perfect start of the rest of your life." He reached into the breast pocket of his jacket and set the ring box in Casey's hand. "Should've been her mother's. Olivia has the ring she wants. Danny has her mother's official ring. This one remains unfinished with the last sister."

Casey stared at the box. "Not sure she'd say yes."

"Life's short, bud. You're not getting younger."

Casey cracked open the leather box. In the glow of the driveway spotlight, the fire of the diamond radiated over the windshield. "Are you kidding me?" he said. "I could've navigated without instruments with this."

"Your future." Woody pointed to Olivia's front door. "Trust me. Lauren's in there."

Casey rocked the ring in the light, mesmerized by its aura. "You're a friend."

Woody grasped the door handle. "I'm a friend who wants you to be as happy as I am. Wait here."

~ · ~ · ~

He showed up. Her life might be complete. At the eruption of the doorbell, Olivia tossed the toothbrush in the metal cup and checked her teeth. Downstairs, Beauregard let out three urgent barks. She held her palm in front of her mouth and puffed for the blowback, then fluffed her hair.

A quick spritz of citrus cologne preceded a smooth of the comforter on the bed and a straightening of the throw pillows. She pulled open the double doors of the closet and swept her clothes to one side in a squashed clump. Woody needed some elbow room.

"Olivia?" Lauren called out—altogether too fake. "Woody's here."

Olivia raced back to her bathroom and freshened her lipstick with gloss. Men liked shiny. With slowed steps, she moved to the landing and grabbed the banister. To accommodate the thump in her chest, her ribs expanded.

"You did come," she said to Woody standing below in the entryway. "I had my doubts."

Instead of a response, Woody spread his hands in surrender, then stooped to corral the dog. Beauregard turned a whining circle at Woody's knees, powered by a wagging tail.

With every step down the stairs, Olivia summoned her best Norma Desmond from *Sunset Boulevard*. The descent deserved to be savored. Woody's sudden scent of cedarwood soap triggered a fire of every nerve. When her lips finally touched Woody's, she believed she was the one who had come home.

Lauren stepped into the entryway with her fists on her hips. "Gimme a break already. Come in the kitchen and buy me a drink."

~ · ~ · ~

"The moving van is on the way," Woody said. "I don't have much.

What I really need is right here and in the car." He turned to Lauren. "You might want to grab my duffel bag in the car."

"I'm not a porter." Lauren said.

"I know this, but you'll want to get my bag."

Lauren grimaced and sighed. China rattled in the dining room when she closed the front door.

Olivia's quizzical expression earned him a win with his surprise. He squeezed her shoulder. "I think we'll be alone for the rest of the night. Please tell me you have a fresh toothbrush and a razor?"

"Of course," she said. "I have a glass vase in my bathroom labeled with your name, but you're in for a girly shave. It's not the best razor, but it'll make your knuckles smooth."

A sadness had crept into Olivia's voice. Her attempt at humor couldn't disguise it. He pulled her toward the kitchen. "C'mon. We have a lot to discuss."

A crystal tumbler of ice filled with two fingers of whiskey. Woody pulled out a counter chair and sat. He studied Olivia as she uncorked a bottle of cabernet and filled her wineglass. Something else lurked under her skin, and it wasn't him.

A few moments of silence settled over the kitchen island. Her sip of wine killed some time. Then, he couldn't endure the suspense.

"Out with it, Liv." Woody shook the ice and squinted with the swallow. A warm rush filled his chest.

"It's just that . . ."

"What?" The muscles in his abdomen squeezed.

"My former anniversary is on Saturday," she said. "After everything I found out, I don't know what to do. Maybe I should be alone on that day."

Woody studied the empty tumbler and reached for the bottle. What he was about to say deserved a refresh. He tipped a splash, stopping shy of the amount he really wanted. "Then we'll get married on Friday. Gives us both a fresh anniversary."

The words hit home. Olivia's mouth popped open.

"Really?" she said and set her wineglass on the counter with a *clang*.

"Really."

Olivia moved around the barrier of the counter to perch his knee. Her eyes met his. "What about my sisters? They're expecting a big to-do."

Woody grabbed words not previously thought out. He didn't know where they came from. "A little to-do then. I'll whisk you to Mount Hood. We'll spend a few days on the mountain at Timberline Lodge."

"We'll need chains."

Woody grasped her hands and twisted the diamond band he'd given her. "Snow me in, Liv. This needs vows attached to it. Otherwise, it's nothing more than jewelry."

Olivia's face descended on his. He devoured her.

~ · ~ · ~

On Monday morning, a ten o'clock appointment and a scratchy shadow of stubble urged Woody from the warmth of the covers. Beauregard groaned and yawned with a whine. Olivia turned and wrapped her arms around a pillow, unaware of the meeting he'd set with her lawyer. This meeting wasn't just about Olivia; it was about him and the rest of his life.

Woody rummaged through the clear-glass vase on the bathroom shelf. A label with his name in scrolled handwriting signaled forethought and planning: cinnamon-flavored toothpaste, floss, travel-size shampoo and conditioner, and muscle-relief gel. He plucked out a razor and shave cream. Did Olivia know how much he loved her? In a blink, her form appeared behind him in the mirror, her arms easing around his waist. He watched her in the reflection, knowing her arms were real because of her soft skin.

"We'll never get anything done today if you keep doing that," he said.

Olivia's cheek grazed his back. "I want to watch you shave. Each man has his own technique. Like making love. I want to know yours."

He turned and grasped her shoulders, smooth and unblemished. An urge to kiss her neck paled the urgency of the appointment. "That's it. Call your sister. She's holding my bag hostage."

Olivia leaned into him. "I think Casey's holding her *and* your bag hostage. Want me to make scrambled eggs?"

"No, I have something I need to do for a couple of hours. I'll be back by lunch."

The expression on Olivia's face fell. "But . . . that's not fair. You just got here. What do you have to do that's more important?"

"I need to make sure Ted Beal is okay with me marrying you."

"Don't be ridiculous. I don't answer to him."

"I have to ask someone for your hand, and I don't think your sisters will qualify. Besides, it'll take you two hours to pick out something to wear up to Timberline Lodge. But you could wear jeans and fleece for all I care. That's what I'm wearing if you don't get my duffel from Lauren. Go roust her and Casey out of bed."

"I don't own a pair of jeans."

"You'd better go buy some. If you're going to be married to me, then you'll need a rugged pair."

~ · ~ · ~

After Woody breezed out the door in the same clothes he'd arrived in, Olivia made a new list over coffee. Woody's bag remained a hostage when Lauren didn't answer her home phone or mobile.

The litany of tasks over the next three days would start with a pair of jeans—the kind, the cut, and the fit. Boots or loafers? Fancy sweater or casual? Justice of the peace or a priest? The advice she'd given to the emergency room doctor now became real: *Run away with your bride, just the two of you. Grab a passerby as a witness.* All she needed was Woody's vow, but it wouldn't be legal. A piece of paper would ink a different reality.

The identity crisis erupted with a fresh page. Her author name, which had always been her married one, would become a pen name for her books. At the time, so many years ago, it had been a point of pride to have taken Adam's name. Now, she wanted to shed it to erase its meaning of betrayal. Olivia Dushane Novak would become someone new: Olivia Dushane Rainey. She filled every square inch of the paper with the name in all its forms, just as she had when she was twenty. Who was this man she trusted enough to take his name?

The *R* became a struggle. The swirl pulled back to the ergonomic comfort of an *N*, and with it a pang of insecurity crept up her spine. What was Woody meeting about with Ted? Two lawyers duking it out over a prenup? The thought reduced her to a deal point, like a mail order bride with a dowry of assets and addendums. All she wanted was something simple: the wrap of Woody's arms when she fell asleep, and those same arms holding her when awoke in the morning. The discovery of Adam's betrayal, however, gave her cause to question her judgment.

Chapter 36
Lawyer Talk

The offices of Delaney and Beal held a solidity and warmth that was unusual for a law firm. It must've been the abundance of cushy furniture and comfortable chairs. A nice touch to have clients want to linger on the billable clock. Woody shifted and crossed his legs to stay on point, but one side of his throat ached when he swallowed.

Under Ted Beal's scrutinizing stare, Woody became overly aware of his pinpoint Oxford shirt being a bit ripe, never mind the creases. Even though he'd showered, his jeans and white shirt could use a wash. The crummy taste in his mouth intensified a dull headache and malaise.

A manila folder labeled *Novak* sat open on Ted's desk. "You know, Woody," Ted said. "You've worn one pair of underwear longer than you've known Olivia."

Woody's chest muscles tightened with the release of a chuckle and a cough. "You might be right."

Ted's tanned face turned serious. "I've known Olivia since she was in college. She's more than a client. I have a responsibility to protect her . . . assets."

"Our goals are aligned, then," Woody said and cleared his thickening throat. "I want to take care of her."

"Sounds like Olivia needs to take care of you."

"I'll be all right." Denial didn't make Woody feel any better, now that he was hyperaware of the symptoms. Getting horizontal sounded pretty good. Soup. He needed Olivia's homemade chicken soup, not canned.

"She's pretty independent. All her assets are in a revocable trust. What are your intentions?"

"That's where they'll remain," Woody said. "I want you to draft a prenup to reassure her of that fact. And I want to set up a new trust going forward, one that covers both of us with my assets."

"Noble of you."

"Not really. I owe her that." Woody leaned back and draped his arm on the empty guest chair for support. His thoughts fuzzed. "I received a windfall because of Olivia. I consider half of it to be hers. And there's something else."

"I'm listening." Ted closed the file folder.

"Olivia told me that you want to retire."

Ted turned to the wall of windows, where his gaze met a view of evergreen treetops. A squirrel raced up the trunk of one of them and settled on a sturdy branch. Its tail flicked at the reflection of itself. "Hell. I've been wanting to retire for five years," he said. "I've prepared Olivia for that fact. I'm seventy-two, but I'm not sure what I'd do, except play golf. Some men waste away without a sense of purpose. I've always lived for my next client."

Woody studied Ted's expression, a wash of lost time hung in the sag of his eyelids, a future void of arguments, briefs, and rebuttals. That realization had aged Ted ten years beyond his birthdate. The man had worked for work's sake, with nothing personal and passionate to show for it. Woody would have had a similar fate had he not met Olivia.

"What if I made you a proposition, Ted?"

Ted shifted his gaze to Woody. The squirrel outside the widow appeared to be interested too. "What'd you have in mind?"

"Off-load your other clients to a colleague but let me take over the management of the Pogo Trust. I can expand it to do more—more dogs, more prison programs, more books—but I'll need your help. Be a consultant between golf games. I have another resource, too, who can help us. It would only be part-time."

A wash of possibilities crossed Ted's expression, a reveal that Woody believed wasn't often shown to clients sitting in his guest chair. The press of Ted's lips gave away the most, and then a glance at the thick folder. It held the evidence that his work had made a difference.

"Too bad you didn't know Ellen Dushane," Ted finally said. "Olivia's mother was quite a woman."

"Tell me." If he could keep Ted talking, then the pressure to be articulate lessened. His thoughts became heavier by the minute. Had he gotten a flu shot? He couldn't remember.

"Tough cookie to put up with the girls' father." Ted shook his head. "Ellen never got enough credit for being a full-time mom. She's still very much alive in her daughters, all three of them. Their dad, the successful one, ended up being the disappointment."

"Funny thing, fate," Woody said and rubbed his neck. Clammy. His headache had escalated to downright pain. "I feel I know her."

"Yeah. Funny, isn't it?"

"Olivia is a pretty damn good version. And in two days, she'll be my wife."

Ted's eyes widened. "Not one for planning, are you? And from the looks of you, you'll be getting married in bed."

"I almost was, but I've been a planner all my life." Behind Ted's shoulder through the glass window, the squirrel's jaws worked a nut like it was listening. "But I haven't lived what I planned. Never realized I needed a partner to make it happen."

"Who, me?"

Woody released a weak laugh and sighed. "No, Ted. I'm taken. I'm marrying Olivia."

Ted turned red.

~ · ~ · ~

The holiday-red sweater wouldn't do for a wedding—too prosaic. The cream one would be trying too hard to be festive. And not the thin white one; it showed every lump and bump. Olivia had worked herself into a state. Thick sweaters and cotton turtlenecks littered the bedroom floor like a pileup of fresh roadkill. The only items she'd thrown into her leather case with certainty were perfume, a razor, and a fresh tube of toothpaste.

Olivia picked up a black cable-knit sweater from the foot of the bed. She squished the yarn and held it to her face. She'd worn it last night. Woody's aroma had permeated the fibers from close hugs. Was she really a grown woman, already shot past menopause? Today, she was a girl with a long history, full of adolescent insecurities and half-baked wisdom from her mistakes.

"Who am I?" she said aloud. "I'm going to be a wife, on top of a lover, a writer, a daughter, and a sister. Thank God I'm not a mother." The identity crisis had taken hold. Its talons dug deep into her skin. She had an urge to drop everything to work on the screenplay, a place of safety from life, and the one activity that had put her at odds with Adam. She had an identity as a writer that he hadn't appreciated. And each identity held the requirement of a different wardrobe. Jeans. She needed jeans.

The ring of the phone jolted Olivia from her thoughts. The extension in the bedroom lit with Woody's mobile number. She threw the black sweater on the floor.

"Where are you?" she said. The edge in her voice surprised even her.

"I'm on my way home," Woody said. "Good talk with Ted. I'll tell you about it tonight over a glass of wine, fine wine." An uncomfortable pause. "Are you okay?"

Like a curtain, Olivia lowered her eyelids. *Trust.* "So, you had a good meeting?" She wanted to kiss his forehead, take in his scent.

"I did. I love you. I'm tired. I need a serious nap."

"Take one. I'll join you after I go buy a pair of jeans."

"Knowing you, that might take all afternoon, but I want to see you in them."

In her way, Olivia took the high road, the road with a hint of sarcasm attached to cover her real emotion. "How hard can it be?" she said. "Two legs and a zipper arranged in a way that'll make my butt look good. I gotta go. I'll be back here in an hour to work on the screenplay."

"Then you'd better get moving. I want to read what you've written so far."

Music to hear ears. She knew he really did want to read what she'd written. A new and exciting partnership erupted in her lonely world of words. Adam never wanted to read her work, but he certainly had wanted to see the monetary result. Woody wanted to know what she had to say.

Olivia hung up and raced down the stairs. She grabbed her purse and keys, and then stopped short in the entryway. She raced back up the stairs. No way could she leave the clothes on the floor in her bedroom—their bedroom. Even thoughts required a self-edit.

Chapter 37

Lightning Bolt

Olivia pulled her car out of the garage and spotted Casey sitting on Lauren's front steps. Steam from his coffee cup chased a current of chilly air. Olivia pushed the car into park and shut off the engine. A pair of jeans had become suddenly unimportant. This was her sister's future at stake, not her own priorities. One booted foot, then the other, exited the car.

"Hey," she said and crossed Lauren's driveway. "You okay?"

"Yeah, I'm fine," Casey said and looked away.

"What's wrong?" His tone set off alarms. "Tell me."

"I want to marry her, Olivia. I need her, and she needs me."

"Don't you think it's a little fast? You hardly know each other."

"I know enough."

"Okay." Olivia searched to the left and right of her street. She drew in a breath and zeroed in. "Then what's her blood type?"

Casey smiled without missing a beat. "O-positive. I'm a rescue guy, remember?"

"She got that type from my father. Actually, I'm surprised Lauren knew her own blood type." Her sister had layers she didn't know about. "Unless you took some and tested it."

"Yeah, she told me."

Olivia met his ocean-blue eyes. She watched him rake his fingers through his full head of white hair. Her sister deserved this man, to be happy and partnered. "So . . . you want to get married," she said. "Do you have a ring?"

Casey threw her an embarrassed smile. He reached into the pocket of his down jacket. The rescue battalion crest on his lapel shifted when he pulled out an antique ring box. *The box.* The box that Althea had given to Woody. Her face must have become a landscape to be inspected when he handed it to her, because Casey surveyed every one of her features.

"It was supposed to be your mother's," he said.

"I know." Olivia's chest tightened with a memory flash. She'd never forget the look of desperation on Lauren's face when Danny broke the news of their mother's death. The moment was still so fresh that she'd swear she could pick up the aroma of Lauren's cigarette smoke. Her eyes drew back to Casey's. "How did you get this?"

"Woody thought it should go to Lauren," he said. "Might make everything right, right?"

Olivia shook herself back into the moment and inhaled. "Yes. The right thing to do—for a lot of reasons—but make this ring about your relationship with each other, not about our mother." She handed him back the box. The mood needed a refresh. "Have you farted in front of each other, yet?"

He chuckled and took the bait. "Not audibly, but we will."

"Then you're not in love. That's what Lauren says. Total honesty, remember?"

"Maybe by tonight." His face went somewhat serious. "How about you and Woody? Total honesty? You know everything?"

"I'm pretty sure. We're totally open with each other."

"He told you then. I'm glad."

"Told me what?"

"About his daughter."

Olivia threw her keys on the kitchen counter. "Well, add another damn title to the list," she said. Freesia trotted to her with wide eyes. "Mommy's okay, Baby Girl. Just not great."

She'd tried to hide her shock in front of Casey by pretending she'd been informed, but his three words set off a riot of questions and life-canceling insecurities. She should have trusted her instincts that an untruth had wedged itself between her and Woody. How old was this daughter? Hadn't she made it clear that he could tell her anything?

Freesia rubbed a circle around Olivia's calves. She picked up the cat and cradled her in her arms like a baby. Freesia blinked with doughy eyes. She set the cat in front of the food dish and piled it with fresh kibble. Freesia gobbled everything down.

What other surprises lurked inside Woody? Now that she thought about it, all the talking came from her, not Woody. *Lawyers*. He was an expert at extracting information without revealing anything. Olivia turned on the hot water and stuffed a packet of cleaner into the sink disposal. She flipped the switch.

To the whirring grind and a bloom of blue foam, it dawned on her. A mother? She didn't know how to be a mother, nor had she signed up for that loss of individual freedom. As the foam retreated, she softened with the responsibility of being a role model. Holidays might be filled with a bigger family, more than just her sisters and Ryan and Woody. Casey was in the picture now. And a daughter.

"What the hell am I supposed to do with all this?" she said as she rinsed the sink.

Panic filled her chest at the hum of the garage door going up. Olivia made a desperate grab for words.

Chapter 38
A Moment of Weakness

"Tell me about your meeting with my lawyer. What made it so great?" Olivia said as Woody stepped into the kitchen. Anger percolated to the surface. A cleansing breath reminded her to keep it in check.

"It was all right, but I'm not," Woody said and tossed his keys on the counter with hers. "I'm coming down with something."

"You were fine when you left this morning."

"It hit me all at once in Ted's office."

Woody did look sick. A glassy, lethargic cast shaded his formerly bright blue eyes. As in book plots, the timing of serious conversations required judgment.

"Get yourself under the covers. I'll make you some vegetable soup."

"Sounds like heaven. And are you going to do some laundry? What I'm wearing needs a wash."

Olivia pulled out a saucepan as her gaze trailed Woody toward the stairs. She made extra noise with the bang of a serving spoon. A can of chicken broth got two hard *V*s with the opener. He'd get soup all right, and she'd bet Woody's clothes would be in a pile on the bedroom floor. A *whoosh* of water from the shower streamed through the pipes. And there was now a 100 percent chance she'd get sick too. But that man had captured her heart and held it in his hands. Move forward and work this out or cut ties and return to a life of solitude, devastated all over again. She slammed the freezer drawer and cut the top from a package of frozen mixed vegetables.

She'd forgotten how differently men and women dealt with being sick. Women were caregivers, through thick and thin, but women longed to be held when they came down with a cold. Men wanted to go away and not be touched, but they sure wanted to be taken care of in the process. Women weren't allowed to be sick. Men were.

Olivia grabbed a napkin and a soup spoon. With a package of Saltines snugged under her arm, she steadied the bowl. Eating in bed would get negotiated, a being-sick exception. She anticipated cracker crumbs stuck to her back by tomorrow morning.

When she entered the bedroom, Woody's clothes were, indeed, piled on the floor next to the bed.

~ · ~ · ~

Woody stirred from a congested haze when Olivia's form dipped the edge of the mattress. The jostle made his head hurt. He sensed a life conversation coming on, but he didn't have the strength. He had so much to tell her. Organized thought escaped him when he couldn't breathe through his nose.

"You think we should postpone?" Olivia said. "You might not be well enough on Saturday."

"Baybe," he said, unable to breathe. Even with his fuzzy head, he picked up something else in her voice. He turned to her and attempted to focus. "Did you get jeans?"

Olivia avoided his gaze and blew into the bowl of soup. "Noooo . . . but I did have an interesting conversation with Casey that changed my shopping plans."

Maybe my life plans, Woody was tempted to add. Now Olivia had his attention. Woody eased himself upright and propped the pillows. He swallowed the draining congestion that irritated his throat. "Continue."

"You lied to me."

"About what?"

"Having a daughter."

Oh, boy. He should've had a talk with Casey in the car and with Olivia before now. "I didn't lie to you. I didn't say anything, because I didn't know how."

"Semantics. It's still a deception. That's a big deal, Woody, especially for someone like me who's never had children. Tell me everything. I won't get mad, but I want full disclosure. Isn't that your line?"

Full disclosure. Those words Woody understood and appreciated. A cleansing breath started the story. It had become normal to keep Emily private. His shoulders relaxed as he emptied his mind of the details he'd held close for too long.

"I was so young when she was born." Woody rubbed his forehead. "I was only eighteen. It was a mistake."

"A mistake. Huh . . . " The extra comment came out of her with a puff of air. "Were you married?"

"No. I had law school ahead of me. I was in no position to raise a family. Besides, we were only friends who went too far in a moment after happy hour."

Olivia studied him, but he could see her mind working through the course of questioning. Maybe she should have gone to law school. She was sure drilling him like a lawyer.

"Does she happen to be a waitress at Wolfe's Tavern in Wolfeboro?"

"How did you know that?" *Damn. Was she clairvoyant?*

"I remember how that waitress made comments about you when we stayed at the Inn. You should have seen the look on her face when you walked in to meet us for dinner. I remember her name was Nan. I remember that, clear as day."

"We've been friends since grade school. That's all it is and ever was, Liv. Hormones got involved."

"What's your daughter's name?"

"Emily."

"When was the last time you saw her?"

"Just before I got here. I detoured on my way to Portland before I picked up Casey at the airport. She works in Chehalis, Washington. I hadn't seen her in person since she graduated college in 1995, but we've talked on the phone."

"No wonder you were so willing to leave Wolfeboro and move out to Portland. It wasn't for me."

"You have it all wrong, Liv. I wanted to move to Portland for you. Emily being out here sealed the deal that it was meant to be."

Olivia remained quiet, which amounted to an invitation to continue. He did.

"I had to sneak out of town when Emily went to law school at Lewis and Clark in Portland, and also for her graduation because Della never knew I had a daughter. I supplemented her scholarship, which her mother appreciated. She was Phi Beta Kappa. Liv, and will be a huge a resource for us. She works for a law firm for non-profit entities."

Olivia took a spoonful of soup and stuck it in her mouth. "Look, Woody. Nobody enters a relationship at our age without baggage. I've had plenty. I'm not upset at the fact you have a daughter, but I am disillusioned that you didn't trust me enough to tell me."

"I didn't mean to keep it from you." He sighed. The response sounded cliché. He waited for Olivia to mention the literary *faux pas*, but it sailed past her unnoticed. "Well, maybe I did. We've been so focused on our mothers and my new family."

"I could've been getting to know her." Olivia tapped the spoon on the bowl. "You know . . . I'll bet your daughter has your blood type. If I hadn't happened to be the same as you, your daughter might've saved your life." She turned to him with an expression that amounted to a directive. "*We* should know her. Together. I will have a daughter, too, when we get married."

"I . . . was hoping you'd feel that way. but I— " Woody thoughts blurred. "I mean . . . "

"What *do* you mean, Woody? You either willing to share her, or you're not. Tell me."

"I talked with her about our pending marriage. She's nervous about meeting you. I told her that she'd love you."

Olivia stood and stared a hole into his soul. "You two figure it out and let me know." She held out the bowl. "Eat your soup before it gets cold."

The bedroom door closed with barely a sound, but he heard the slam nonetheless. Woody took a tepid sip of broth and set the near-empty bowl on the nightstand. Olivia had eaten the best stuff from the soup. The pillows *whooshed* as he sunk into them. His aching muscles twitched in a battle between psyche and flu germs. Beauregard released a long groan and laid his head over Woody's knee. The dog's gaze shifted toward his cell phone on the nightstand. Woody reached for it.

Chapter 39
The Wedding

The drive to Timberline Lodge on Saturday wouldn't hold that special moment, the one Olivia had spent months longing for. At least the arrangements she'd made wouldn't go to waste. They could go there for Lauren and Casey if Woody ditched her at the last minute. More time for her and Woody was in the cards. Maybe spring held their union.

Woody held out his hand for yet another tissue. Everyone needed attention, including the dog. Beauregard's wet nose nudged Olivia's shoulder. The gesture left a dark spot on her ivory turtleneck sweater. When the metal tire chains caught patches of dry asphalt, the friction made a racket inside the car. Their jingle and thump forewarned of the arduous trek ahead.

Side glances caught Woody wiping his nose and working over his bottom lip. She'd bet her bank account that Woody hadn't made that phone call. The air in the car tensed.

"Didn't you ever want children?" Woody said, breaking the tense silence. Instead of glancing at Olivia, he checked the rearview mirror. His voice came out too loud, but Olivia attributed the volume to the question's importance. Beauregard whipped his gaze from the back window. For a moment, Olivia connected to the dog as if he had human understanding.

"At one time, I did," she said, "but Adam talked me off the ledge when I was thirty-eight. That age holds a desperation about it for women. For me, it was a do-or-die moment against the body clock."

"Adam didn't want children?"

"No. And I truly believed that if I'd pushed, he would've left me."

"Seems kind of selfish."

"He was selfish, and so was I. There was so much we both yearned for. We just weren't in sync about what we wanted out of life."

But Adam had never done any of the things he said he wanted to do. He hadn't had the self-confidence. Instead, he'd waited for her to do the achieving. A scroll of her accomplishments—all lined up on the bookshelves in the den—ran through her head as book cover images. Each one held her dreams, fantasies, and wishes, all nicely tucked away in their pages. Safe. Today, those novels felt like failures.

No guidebook in the world could map Olivia's way forward. The late, great Ellen Dushane had been full of advice for healing relationships that went off course, especially in her own family. Olivia hadn't appreciated how tough it must have been to raise three daughters to do the right thing. Mom's trick was that she had been an expert at forgiveness.

Now, the man sitting next to her could make her whole, an equal partner, if only she had the guts to forgive Woody for the deception, forgive Adam's betrayal, and ultimately forgive her mother for dying.

Chapter 40
Ashes

Last night's dusting in the Willamette Valley required plows on Mount Hood. Only the tops of the first-floor windows of Timberline Lodge peeked above an undulating line of bright white. "They made it. There's Lauren's car," Olivia said and pointed to her sister's red Honda. The car sat in the near-empty parking lot like an overripe strawberry nestled in drifts of whipped cream. Next to it sat Ryan's police cruiser. The family assemblage was complete.

The engine ticked a countdown after Woody shut off the ignition. For once in her life, Olivia couldn't pluck any words—never mind the right ones—from the thick air in the car. She swallowed instead. Woody turned in the seat and reached his hand across the short console's distance between them. He might as well have been a mile away when his hand took hers. *Here it comes.*

"Liv . . . " Woody fingered her knuckles like a picket fence.

"Out with it," she said, her voice no more than a whisper. *Woody's going to let you down hard. He didn't even phrase your nickname as a question.*

"We should like who we are so much that we can afford to give some of ourselves away." Even beyond the lingering flu symptoms, something in his eyes appeared joyous, not regretful or even nervous.

His expression got her attention. A pang of jealousy rippled through her gut that she, herself, hadn't come up with that line.

"I absolutely agree," she said and squared her shoulders. "I love me."

"And I love you too." Woody released her hand and pulled the keys from the ignition. "And it's a good thing, Lauren and Casey are here for you and me today. They're witnesses. Ryan and Danny came up last night with Pogo."

"But . . . " Woody put his forefinger to her lips, but her voice found a way around it. "I had a different outfit for this moment . . . and shoes. Incredible shoes. I thought you didn't want to do this now, and that we were here for—I don't know—some sort of getaway weekend."

"Don't worry about it," he said and sniffed. "You could wear flip-flops and I wouldn't give a damn."

"It's the middle of winter." Although impossible to stay mad, she gave it the old college try. "Just remember, Woodrow Rainey, even wives like the pursuit of courtship, especially older ones. We like romantic surprises. That shouldn't stop when we're married. What about that phone call you were going to make?"

"I made it." Woody tossed the keys in the air and caught them with his other hand. His free one squeezed her knee, to the point where she nearly ejected through the closed sunroof.

"Emily's here?"

"Yes. She's about to become your daughter too."

~ · ~ · ~

Olivia detoured at the front entrance, a hard right to the ladies' room. She stared at herself in the mirror to assess what Emily would see when they met. Her gaze circled the sink to make sure it had been cleaned. It had. *Daughter? What did that mean?*

Thoughts whirled with images of school clothes, puberty, sex talk, and how the hell she would keep her house clean. What if one of her treasures got broken? *Wife, writer, mother.* Her mother had been all three. A newfound respect bloomed in her chest that Ellen Brooks Dushane had accomplished it all. In retrospect, a fancy career seemed unimportant in the line-up.

The heavy wooden door of the restroom squeaked open behind her. In the mirror's reflection, Woody appeared and leaned against the doorjamb and studied her. His crossed arms signaled that this was going to be a one-way conversation, a two-way one only if she could keep her mouth shut.

"Emily's all grown up, Liv," Woody said. "I can see on your face that you're raising her." He ducked to check the stalls for occupants.

"Just us," she said.

"From here on out, are we going to work out all of our problems in the women's restroom? How 'bout you talk to me instead of to yourself in that mirror?"

If Woody could've have stripped her of a witty comeback, it would've been at this moment. Olivia's pretense caved. "Can I have a do-over to get used to the idea? I think I can be a good mom, Woody. Really, I can, but I need time to process this."

"You'll be fine," Woody stepped to her and took her fingers with a touch of empathy. "She's all grown up."

Olivia's throat grew thick and itchy. His meltdown smile served as an immediate reminder of why she was marrying him—and with a touch of dimple no less.

"She's forty-four. Her degree in business law will help us, Liv."

Olivia immediately believed she'd been gypped out of motherhood. She had gone from delivery room straight to a girlfriend talk over slow-roasted coffee and pastry. Emily couldn't be bossed, consoled, or influenced by Olivia's values. This wasn't the way bridedom was supposed to go.

"C'mon, you need to meet her," Woody said. "I think you'll be pleasantly surprised."

~ · ~ · ~

With precision radar, Olivia spotted Emily standing at the enormous fireplace that graced Timberline's lobby. No mistaking the silky dark hair, with just the first wisps of gray, and bright blue eyes. Her carriage relayed an elegance that plucked at Olivia's insecurity. Emily wore the deportment of having gone to a prestigious school and earning impressive scholarships. Olivia guessed that Emily had never been without a date on Friday night, either. She homed in on Emily's left hand. No ring. *Hmmm* . . . The young girl in that schoolgirl photo held only a hint of the beauty of the woman who walked up to Olivia now.

"I love your books," Emily said. "I've read everything of yours since Woody told me you two were going to be married."

"Then you've been busy," Olivia said. "You've had some time to get to know my work. I would've liked the opportunity to get to know yours too. I have some catching up to do." Not quite like the doctor handing over the babe-in-arms—but close. A whir of images from birth to adulthood sped behind her eyes, accompanied by xylophone and screeching-brake sound effects that came to an abrupt halt. Most of the milestones of Emily's life had already happened. What was left for her? A mother-daughter talk about hot flashes and estrogen on slow drip?

"I'm a fast reader," Emily said. Her wide smile was the spitting image of Woody's. Uncanny, that miracle of DNA.

Olivia shifted in her suede pumps. Yet again, her toes were wet from melting snow. They would dry into a map of the Old World. "I'll give you the Cliff's notes. When it comes to plot, I can name that tune in five minutes. My earlier books are romance."

"From what I read, there are more layers to your stories, than the average romance. Don't sell yourself short. But I'm most interested in your mafia series. I'm a non-profit legal consultant. I want to help you with the work of the Pogo Charitable Trust. I think all of us together can take that outstanding cause to a higher place."

"My not-so-little foray into memoir—truth—but I've always been honest in every book I've written . . . at the time I wrote it."

"I'm sure they were completely genuine." Emily's persuasive lawyerly expression softened to a smirk. "I did have an idea I wanted to run by you."

"Shoot away. I'm full of advice for everyone but me."

Emily leaned close and set her hand on Olivia's forearm. "What if we rebrand the Little Buddies scam charity in Boston and turned it into a prominent puppy training program as an offshoot of the Pogo Trust prison program? We'll need to do some serious PR work, but we could undo the damage of those mob ties. And then we tie in your sister Lauren's new children's book series into the campaign. A percentage of every book sale can go to puppy training. I'll bet we can partner with the Boston police department, because they'll certainly need help cleaning up their reputation."

Olivia burst out laughing. "If you only knew what we've been through to get to this point. Brilliant. I should introduce you to 'the boys' in prison. Palermo might actually crack a smile."

"It wasn't that hard. You and your sisters—my aunts, I guess— did everything. I just connected all the loose wires together. Should I call you my stepmom?"

Olivia stopped short at the last sentence. An urge to peer over her shoulder to see who Emily was talking to bubbled up from inside, but she knew in her heart the word was meant for her, to make her feel good. She teetered in her heels. The air in Timberline Lodge suddenly filled with the aroma of her mother's baking bread, her White Shoulders perfume, and her citrusy hand lotion. How lucky her mother had been to have three daughters who thought about her every day, for whom the silliest things were the most precious and indelible. Words couldn't escape Olivia's lips, but they shouted from inside: *I love you . . . Mom.*

"Just call me Olivia. That's fine," she said and turned with a sense of being watched. Seated in a leather club chair, Woody had been studying her. He must have known what she'd been thinking.

"C'mon, you," he said and stood. "We're burning daylight, and I can't wait one more minute to be married to you."

The way Woody walked toward her, as if she was the only one in the room, shortened her breath. "You don't *really* want to marry me, do you?" she said.

"And break the news to your sisters? They'd give me a wicked smack, and so would Ryan and Casey. Emily too." Woody's Peck's-bad-boy smile became ultra-serious. "Yes, Liv, I do want to marry you."

"I want to marry you too."

"Then let's do it."

"You've got the ashes, right?"

Woody hesitated before he said, "Della's and my father's ashes are in the car. My wife can take me to the family spot after our ceremony and lunch."

Olivia took a deep breath. *My wife.*

Today her new life would begin, and with it the gift of closure. Olivia raised her gaze to the timbered ceiling. The chandelier above her wasn't made of the fragile crystal prisms that had started this journey; it was a hand-forged collar of heavy iron and racks of deer antlers. Surely its soft light called for a celebration of the circle of life and its fragility.

From here forward, Woody would be by her side. And after their wedding lunch, her mother would finally be united with Woody's father for eternity.

Epilogue
Two Years Later

Olivia ran her fingers through her damp hair and crawled into bed—on the right side. She slipped her reading glasses over her nose and pulled the bookmark from chapter twenty of her third reread of *Rebecca*. She glanced at Woody's nude body in the bathroom as he raked a razor along his jawline.

"Are you sure you want to move away from writing romance?" Woody said. "You have a big following."

"Writing the screenplay for *Indigo to Black* and those mob memoirs got my creative juices going for adventure," she said. "If I win best screenplay from the Writer's Guild, that could be huge.

"It could lead to an Academy Award."

Olivia lined up multi-colored sticky tabs for an evening of plotting the next book, a thriller about a clairvoyant sleuth. She turned. "We have to win for Della, Althea, my sisters, and Mom. Althea's coming. She deserves an entourage."

"It's an honor just to be nominated. Isn't that what they say in the biz?" Woody adjusted the towel around his waist. "You sent it to

Palermo to read. What did he say?"

Olivia contemplated the comment. "Don't care. Doesn't matter."

"You obviously care, or you wouldn't have let him read it." Woody removed the towel altogether and scrubbed his damp hair with it. "If all's meant to be, it will happen. I think you'll change your mind on Palermo."

Olivia never wanted to speak of Palermo again. Her shoulders relaxed as she admired Woody's still-fit body. The raised tear on his chest had healed, but the evidence served as a talisman of their journey together. Every time she grazed her fingers over the ragged scar, the size of a quarter, she was reminded of how unpredictable life could be. As much as she knew it her core, the visual evidence held a tactile reminder.

How different her and her sisters' lives would've been if her mother hadn't left a piece of her life in the safe. The boost from *Indigo Legacy*, the movie, had created a resurgence of interest in the book. A whole new audience now appreciated her mother.

Like a kid, Woody took aim at the laundry basket in the closet and made the rim shot. He turned and threw her a thrill-grin. The magic of small triumphs.

Olivia pulled back the covers and patted the empty mattress on the left side, being careful not to disturb Freesia. With a scoot of the cat's rump, Woody crawled under the covers, prompting a sour-puss mew of interrupted slumber. Beauregard lifted his head, annoyed at the disturbance, and flopped his muzzle over Woody's leg. The dog's long limbs shivered in a deep stretch that settled with a long groan.

Jules Verne's *Five Weeks in a Balloon* sat on the nightstand. Woody reached for it and balanced his tortoiseshell reading glasses on his nose. "You know we live in *their* house," he said and pointed to the animals on the bed.

"Speaking of that, you do know that Emily's arranged for an awesome new design of the Pogo Trust badge for the official vests—" Olivia glanced at Beauregard—"for Pogo and this free-loader."

"An important step for the new branding campaign when

Lauren's next Pogo book launches next month." Woody lowered the book and glanced at her. "Fun shower, huh?"

Olivia leaned in for a deep kiss. She was amazed every day that this man was her husband. "The best."

"That new tankless water heater is a godsend." His finger dragged over her cheek. "The hot water will never run out, Liv."

Olivia sunk into the pillows. She marveled at how twenty minutes of hot water, body wash, and touch could change how the words read on the page.

"I hope it has a lifetime warranty," she said.

Woody offered a nod. "Forever. I promise.

Author's Note

As an East Coast native, I included many locales of my youth in this trilogy. This book featured New York, Boston, and Beacon Hill. The Liberty Hotel really is the historic jailhouse. So fun.

We baby boomers are still kids at heart, especially when in the company of our siblings. The Dushane sisters allowed me to bask in so many treasured moments—and painful ones too. Yes, the story is fictional, but the sentiment and bond I have with my family is not. I incorporated many personality traits of my real-life sisters into the characters. Making them authentic wasn't too much of a stretch.

My mother is alive and well at eighty-four. She's strong and independent for the first time in her life after having been through the ringer on several fronts. The Dushane sisters' story is an ode to her and a thumbs-up that she did a great job raising her three daughters. I dread the day she will no longer be physically in my life, but she has a permanent home in my heart. The story became a practice session of sorts for what life might be like without her. Writing this series also became a promise to Mom that her daughters will always do the right thing, albeit with our own style.

I've always been fascinated by mobsters. I created the character of Nicky Palermo—and all the colorful thugs—to be both despicable and sympathetic. Their twisted sense of ethics personified that blurry line of doing the wrong thing for the right reasons. I made it a recurring theme that drove the story.

And lastly, thank you to all my dedicated readers. I hit nerves with this trilogy: growing older and acting young, sibling bonds, losing parents, and getting whacked with the unexpected in life.

A completely new book is in the works. This one will take place in Montana, our new home when my husband and I finally retire. Stay tuned.

About the Author

Courtney Pierce lives in Oregon with her husband and stepdaughter. By day, she is an executive in the entertainment industry for Arts and Theatre. By night, characters come alive for her after observing audiences in a theater seat, studying travelers snaking through airport security, or watching commuters when she's stuck in traffic.

Courtney's first three books became a trilogy of literary magical realism, *Stitches, Brushes,* and *Riffs*. Her latest trilogy, *The Executrix, Indigo Lake,* and *Indigo Legacy*, follow the middle-age antics of the Dushane sisters. Courtney has also published two short stories: *1313 Huidekoper Place*, for the 2013 NIWA Short Story Anthology *Thirteen Tales of Speculative Fiction*, and *The Nest*, for the Windtree Press anthology *The Gift of Christmas*. As a monthly contributor to *Romancing the Genres*, her blog articles showcase life as a baby boomer.

As a champion of independent publishing, Courtney is a board member of the Northwest Independent Writers Association and an Advisory Council member for the Independent Publishing Resource Center. She is a member of Willamette Writers, Pacific Northwest Writers Association, and She Writes. Her books are published under the imprint of Windtree Press, an indie author collective.

Follow Courtney's books at her website: **courtney-pierce.com**

Facebook: https://www.facebook.com/courtney.pierce.7505
Twitter: @CourtneyPDX
Windtreepress.com

Also by Courtney Pierce

Fiction

Indigo Legacy
Indigo Lake
The Executrix
(The Dushane Sisters Trilogy)

~

Riffs
Brushes
Stitches
(The Stitches Trilogy)

~

Short Stories

1313 Huidekoper Place
(2013 NIWA Anthology of Speculative Fiction)

~

The Nest
(The Gift of Christmas Anthology–Windtree Press*)*

Made in the USA
Middletown, DE
31 January 2022

60143950R00182